Ali McNamara attributes her over-active imagination to one thing – being an only child. Time spent dreaming up adventures when she was young has left her with a head constantly bursting with stories waiting to be told. When stories she wrote for fun on Ronan Keating's website became so popular they were sold as a fundraising project for his cancer awareness charity, Ali realised that not only was writing something she enjoyed doing, but something others enjoyed reading too. Ali lives in Cambridgeshire with her husband and two children, and when she isn't writing, she enjoys watching too much reality TV, eating too much chocolate, and counteracting the results of the previous activities with plenty of exercise!

Keep in touch with Ali via her website at
www.alimcnamara.co.uk or on Twitter: @AliMcNamara

Praise for Ali McNamara:

'An endearing, romantic and fun read for chick-lit (and rom com!) fans'
Closer

'Utterly enjoyable'
Stylist

Also by Ali McNamara

From Notting Hill with Love ... Actually

Breakfast at Darcy's

Ali McNamara

sphere

SPHERE

First published as a paperback original in Great Britain in 2011 by Sphere
Reprinted 2011

A CIP catalogue record for this book
is available from the British Library.

ISBN 978-0-7515-4740-5

Typeset in Caslon by M Rules
Printed and bound in Great Britain by
Clays Ltd, St Ives plc

Papers used by Sphere are from well-managed forests
and other responsible sources.

MIX
Paper from
responsible sources
FSC® C104740

Sphere
An imprint of
Little, Brown Book Group
100 Victoria Embankment
London EC4Y 0DY

An Hachette UK Company
www.hachette.co.uk

www.littlebrown.co.uk

For those that believe. And those that one day will.

Acknowledgements

Thank you to all the wonderful team at Sphere and Little, Brown for all your help and support throughout the last year, and to my fantastic agent, Hannah, who just 'gets' me and my writing ☺.

Thank you to the incredibly beautiful Great Blasket Island in Co. Kerry, Ireland for inspiring this story, and to my own family for yet again putting up with all the ups and downs of living with a writer!

And special thanks must go to the fount of all Dermot's tremendous technical knowledge in this story – my husband Jim. I simply couldn't have written this book without you. x

One

I've always liked funerals.

There's a reassuring certainty to the whole thing.

Not like weddings. Lovely though they are, filled with all that hope and optimism for the future, I tend to have a slight niggling doubt about whether the happy couple will still be together in a few years' time. Or whether they might be filing for divorce, and paying exorbitant solicitor's fees to argue over one of the gorgeous but expensive wedding gifts still patiently waiting to be unwrapped.

Christenings and baptisms are much the same for me, too. I often find myself wondering, Will this child really be able to keep the faith when he or she is eighteen years old, and being tempted by the sins of the flesh? Especially when you notice that one godparent at the font is updating his Twitter status, and the other's checking her reflection in the holy water.

But then that's me all over; I like to know what's going to happen next. Be prepared – that's what the Boy Scouts say. So

I always like to be. Although I'm not too sure your average Akela would advise taking six changes of outfit with me on a weekend away, when – maybe – only three would be sufficient.

The funeral I'm at right now is my aunt Emmeline's, or Aunt Molly as I used to call her when I was a child. Considering how close we were when I was growing up, I'm extremely ashamed to admit that I haven't actually seen my aunt Molly for more years than I care to remember. I kept meaning to pop over here to visit again, but weeks kept turning into months, and then months into years, and you know how quickly time seems to fly by these days.

When *did* that start to happen? Is it another of those EU regulations, like measuring everything in kilograms and litres? Was time officially speeded up in Brussels one day, and I missed the big government announcement?

The 'over here' I mention is Ireland. Dublin, to be precise. At the moment I'm just outside of the fair city in the village my aunt lived in for the last few years of her life. I don't remember her in this small cottage the wake is now being held in. The house I remember her living in was a huge, sprawling mansion by the sea in County Kerry. As a child, I used to travel over from England to spend my holidays with her while my mother was working. I can remember happy days spent mostly out-doors in the bright sunshine. Even in winter, when we were well wrapped up against the biting sea wind that would sweep across the coast, the sun always seemed to be shining in my memories of Molly.

Why does the sun always seem to shine more in your child-hood memories? Is that something to do with the EU, too?

As I ponder this thought, a lady with tight white curls

breaks into my thoughts. 'Now, another cup of tea, dear?' She's wearing a flowery apron, and is standing next to me waving a pot of tea in my direction.

'Oh, no, thank you, I've already had two,' I say, placing my hand over the top of the cup.

'Cake, then?' She gestures towards a table groaning under the sheer weight of food upon it.

'No, really, I'm fine, thank you.'

'Not from round here, are you?' She peers closely at me through a pair of silver spectacles.

'No, I've come over from London for the funeral.'

'Sure now, how would you be knowing Emmeline?' she asks suspiciously, eyeing me up and down.

'I'm her niece, actually.'

The woman's expression immediately changes to one of pleasant surprise. 'Oh, you must be Darcy, so y'are! Why didn't you say so before, child?'

'Yes, that's right.' I smile at her. 'But how did you know?'

'I'm Maeve. Molly was my next-door neighbour.' Sadness fills her blue eyes as she remembers her friend. But they begin to brighten again as she talks with fondness about her. 'Molly was always talking about you, so she was. About when you used to come and visit her as a child – when she had the big house across in Kerry. Shame you didn't come lately, though ... ' She gives me a reproachful look.

'It's just ... I've been a bit busy with my job and everything.' Once again I feel the wave of guilt that has been flowing back and forth all day wash over me.

'What is it you do again, now? A newspaper reporter, isn't that what Molly said?'

'Kind of ... I'm a features editor on a women's health and beauty magazine.'

'Health and beauty, you say?' Maeve considers this. 'Ah, what's there to write about that? A good scrub down with a bar of carbolic soap and some cold water, that's what's kept me going for over eighty years.'

I look with surprise at Maeve. She certainly doesn't look over eighty. I would have guessed somewhere in her mid- to late sixties at a push, and her skin doesn't look anywhere near that.

'Yes, that surprised you, didn't it?' She smooths out the ruffles in her apron proudly. 'None of your expensive potions and creams for me! You don't need them.' She leans in towards me. 'You take a piece of advice from me, child. Stop wearing all that slap on your face. It'll fair ruin your skin in the long run. Good clean air and clean living is all you need to keep yourself looking young.'

My hand goes subconsciously to the incredibly small Mulberry bag I'm carrying. It's crammed with lipsticks, powders, brushes and compacts – my make-up bag alone would normally be bigger than this tiny effort. But today I've chosen to carry this one because the colour perfectly matches my new pewter-grey Louboutin shoes. I wanted to look my best for my aunt Molly's funeral, even if she wouldn't be there to see me.

'So now,' Maeve says cheerily, suddenly seeming to forget all about her grave warning. 'That's grand someone from Molly's English family has been able to make it over to see her off.'

'Yes, there aren't too many of us left now,' I begin, but

4

Maeve has been distracted by a large man deliberating over a plate of fruit cake.

'Now, can I cut you a slice of that cake, dear?' she asks him, glad to be of service to someone in the food department at last.

As Maeve deftly cuts the man a large wedge of cake, I look around at the motley gathering of people now squashed into the kitchen of the small stone cottage that had belonged to my aunt. I guess by their ages they must be mainly Molly's friends and acquaintances. I'd thought something similar in the church, that it was odd how everyone was so much older than me. Normally at funerals there's a slight variation in the age of the mourners, but everyone at Molly's funeral is around my aunt's age. I'm assuming they must be her friends and acquaintances because I know for sure she had no brothers or sisters other than my mother, and since she passed away when I was twenty, some seven years ago now, I'm the only one left on that side of the family. I try desperately to remember some of the stories Molly told me when I was younger, about her time as a child in Ireland, but as hard as I try nothing is immediately forthcoming. I find it frustrating that memories I want to recall remain buried with those I would rather forget.

Sighing impatiently, I drain the last of my milky tea from my cup. How can I have let this happen? Aunt Molly meant so much to me when I was younger; how can I have just let her drift out of my life like this? I should have tried harder to keep in touch ... I should have made the effort to come over here and visit her. It wasn't like we'd ever fallen out, or anything. We'd just drifted apart. No, that wasn't fair; *I'd* allowed us to drift apart.

'Excuse me?'

I turn to see a slim, smartly dressed young man wearing a suit and tie standing by my side. 'Am I addressing Miss McCall?'

'Yes, you are.'

'Miss Darcy McCall?'

'Yes.'

He looks relieved. 'Oh, good. Then allow me to introduce myself.' He holds out his hand. 'Niall Kearney at your service, Miss McCall.'

'Pleased to meet you, Mr Kearney.' Hesitantly I return his handshake.

He nods.

I smile, hoping it will prompt him into continuing.

'I'm so sorry, of course you wouldn't recognise the name, would you?' He reaches into his jacket pocket and pulls out a business card. 'Here's my card. My father, Patrick Kearney, was your aunt's solicitor and friend for many years. He sends his deepest regrets that he's not here himself today, but unfortunately he's not too well at the moment, so I represent the company on his behalf.' As he proudly informs me of this, he squares his narrow shoulders underneath his slightly oversized jacket.

'I see.' I glance down at the card for a moment. 'But what do you want with me, Mr Kearney?'

The young man furtively glances to either side of him before leaning in towards me. 'First of all, Miss McCall,' he whispers, 'I must insist you call me Niall. I may be a solicitor, but I much prefer the more *personal* approach.' He looks about him again in a clandestine manner. 'And perhaps we could go somewhere a little bit more private to continue our conversation?'

'I'm not too sure . . . ' I hesitate; this guy seems a bit odd.

'It's just,' he looks about him again, gesturing for me to do the same. And indeed, although the others in the room are trying to look like they're sipping at their tea and deeply in conversation with their partners, pairs of eyes are swiftly darting in our direction, then just as swiftly darting away again. Ears are definitely being tilted towards us and hearing aids adjusted, as Niall and I stand awkwardly together on the other side of Molly's kitchen. 'What I have to tell you is of a somewhat delicate nature. I really don't think it needs broadcasting around the room and across the whole of the village in ten minutes flat.'

'Perhaps we could go somewhere a bit quieter, then.' I glance around me. 'How about we step outside?' I suggest seeing my aunt's garden through the kitchen window. 'I doubt there's anyone out there today, it's too cold.'

I slip on my charcoal-grey military coat, which I'm secretly quite pleased to be wearing again. I've only recently acquired this Vivienne Westwood gem online – a steal at seventy-five per cent off. I'd hummed and ha'ed at the time whether to buy it, but on this freezing-cold January day it's been well worth its price tag.

We escape out into the back garden one at a time, so as not to arouse any more suspicion. There is a definite chill to the air as I step outside, and a strong wind immediately begins to gust around me, lifting my long hair up from my shoulders and twisting it in knots around my face.

Damn wind. Of all weathers, I hate it with a passion. It always attacks me, usually when I've just done my hair – in my case, this means my long blonde hair, smoothed and straightened to within an inch of its life. Then, just as I step outside, a strong wind will be lying in wait for me in the sky above, like one of those cartoons of weather you see in children's books. It grins down wickedly at me before beginning its assault on my newly created coiffure. At least with rain you can try to put up some sort of fight with an umbrella. But wind prevents even the use of that form of protection, so making it much the more powerful of the two evils.

The great outdoors and I aren't generally the best of friends, in January, full stop. But after the stuffiness of the overflowing house, even I'm glad to feel the cold, fresh air encircling my face and filling my lungs as I begin to talk to Niall.

'So what's the big secret, then?' I ask politely, as I try and tuck my hair under the collar of my coat. This is all very clandestine, meeting like this in Molly's garden. It's a shame Niall isn't better looking, then this furtive outdoor meeting with a stranger might be quite exciting.

I check myself. I must get out of this habit I've got into since I started working on *Goddess* magazine, of immediately judging everyone on their appearance. I know that's what everyone does – forms their opinion of someone in the first so many seconds of meeting them. But working in the beauty industry as I do, where your appearance counts for everything, it makes this habit so much worse.

Besides, it isn't Niall's fault he's, well, how can I put it kindly . . . let's just say he's no oil painting. The suit he's wearing consists of a plain grey single-breasted jacket and trousers, and he's teamed it with a white shirt and a plain burgundy tie – hardly the most exciting of combinations. He's about five foot seven tall, slight of frame – OK, he's skinny. He wears plain-rimmed silver spectacles. And he has wavy, mousy-coloured hair cut into a neat a short back and sides – all very appropriate for a young up-and-coming Dublin solicitor. He isn't really ugly, I decide upon further inspection, but then he isn't really attractive – he's just … plain-looking.

'No big secret, Miss McCall,' Niall says, interrupting my thoughts. 'I just need to arrange a meeting with you, that's all.'

'Why?'

'To go through your aunt's will.'

At the moment, I'm slightly distracted trying to prevent my Louboutin heels from sinking into the soft muddy grass. Just because I bought them brand new off eBay from a woman who was selling them to pay for her daughter's wedding, doesn't mean I want to dig the garden with them. 'Molly left a will?'

'Yes, and a very thorough one, if I may say so. She knew exactly what she wanted to happen with her estate when she passed on.'

'Her estate?' My ears prick up: solicitors only usually use the word 'estate' if there's a fair bit of money involved. 'So she had some money tucked away under her mattress, did she, my Aunt Molly?' I joke, smiling at Niall.

'Please, Miss McCall,' he says, looking at me sombrely over his spectacles. 'The reading of a deceased's will is never a matter to be taken lightly.'

'No, of course not, Mr Kearney, I … I mean, Niall.' I attempt to look serious and businesslike. 'So when is the reading?'

'That depends on you, Miss McCall.' Niall scouts around

9

him in that same stealthy manner he had earlier, back in the house. Then, as he tilts his head towards me, his pale blue eyes dart around him one more time. 'Because,' he says in a tone so hushed I have to strain to hear him properly, 'I'm pleased to inform you, Miss Darcy McCall, that *you* are the sole beneficiary of Miss Emmeline Ava Aisling McCall's entire estate.'

Two

'I'm *what*?' I exclaim so loudly that a robin perching on a nearby holly bush in search of winter sustenance is forced to take shelter on some guttering. It eyes us carefully, trying to decide whether the two interlopers to its garden are a threat to its winter foraging.

Niall waves his hands at me in a shushing fashion. 'Miss McCall,' he hisses. 'Please, we don't want to draw attention to ourselves.'

'Why?' I demand, trying to push my hair – which has escaped from my collar and is still billowing around my head again – back off my face. 'What's the problem?'

Frantically Niall looks about him again to check no one else has appeared in the garden with us. But only the robin watches from his perch on the rooftop, his head cocked to one side in amusement.

'Because I don't want any of the others in there' – he nods in the direction of the house – 'hearing what we're talking about out here. There's a few people in your aunt's house that might have expected to have been included in her will, and they might not be too happy when they find out they're not.'

'Oh,' I say, turning my gaze away from the house and back to Niall again. '*Now* I get it.'

'*Good*,' Niall pushes his glasses back up his nose. 'I'm glad we've got that established at last. So now you understand what's going on, when can we meet to go through all the formalities?'

'Formalities?'

'The reading of the will.'

'Right, of course. Well, when would you like to?'

'How about tomorrow at my office?'

'But I fly home tomorrow – to the UK.'

'I see ... What time?'

'My flight is at eight-thirty in the morning.'

Niall pulls a face. 'Ah. That makes it somewhat tricky, then.'

'Can't you just tell me now?' I suggest, thinking maybe he could then simply pop a cheque in the post to me, or something. After all, if I was the only beneficiary – which I still find difficult to believe – it's not exactly going to be complicated, is it?

'Miss McCall, the reading of a deceased's last will and testament is a matter that has to be dealt with in the proper manner, with the proper procedures. We simply can't perform a significant and meaningful act such as this between the two of us in the deceased's back garden!'

I manage to keep a straight face as Niall recites all this to me. He doesn't appear to see the funny side of what he's just said at all – his face remains serious and solemn throughout. But as the corners of my mouth twitch a little, he realises that the words he has chosen to demonstrate his point could be misconstrued, and his cheeks begin to flush a shade to rival that of our friendly onlooking robin's breast.

'I ... I'm so sorry, Miss McCall,' he stutters. 'I didn't mean ... Of course it would never cross my mind ... and at a funeral! Not that you're not a very attractive woman ... Oh goodness.'

'Niall,' I say calmly, resting my hand gently on his arm. 'Please, its fine, honestly. I understood what you meant. Look, can I make a suggestion that may solve our problem?'

Niall nods hurriedly as his colour dulls to a salmon pink.

'It may not be the usual, *correct* place where *proper* procedures like this normally happen, but I believe it's where lots of procedures and decisions get made in Ireland. So how about we meet down at the local pub, later on?'

Niall looks unsure.

'I don't see that we've got a lot of choice,' I say, having to let go of Niall so I can gather my hair back in my hands, the wind has got so strong. 'The wake will probably continue now until teatime-ish, and then I leave first thing tomorrow. Or you could always come to my hotel?' I raise my eyebrows, and he blushes again. 'But I don't know what the local gossips would say about that.'

'No,' Niall replies in a voice which, up until a few minutes ago, he's been trying to lace with an air of authority, but is now reduced to a mere squeak. 'No, Mulligan's down the road here will be just fine, Miss McCall. Say I meet you there about sevenish?'

I nod. 'Seven's fine, Niall. Can I ask you to do one more thing for me, though?'

'Yes, Miss McCall,' he replies, looking apprehensive again.

'Can you just call me, Darcy, please?'

Three

Mulligan's pub has comfortable fixtures and fittings, serves good, wholesome Irish food and, among many other alcoholic beverages, the all-important pint of Guinness to its large and ever-changing clientele. It's a traditional Irish pub; but not in the way many an Irish-themed bar would try to have you believe, with shamrocks festooned every which way you turn, and tricolour flags hanging from the optics. Neither is it the opposite: so traditional that there are wood shavings on the floor, and old men propping up the bar like a couple of the pubs I remember my aunt slipping me into as a child, when she wanted to indulge herself in a couple of bottles of beer on a Friday night. I don't remember minding too much, though; I'd be treated to a glass bottle of Coca-Cola complete with straw, and a packet of salt and vinegar Tayto crisps – both of which would keep me amused for a good while in those days. I smile now at that memory, and the feeling of doing something naughty, hiding out in that pub, knowing full well that if my mother had had any notion of where my aunt was taking me, my regular holidays in Ireland would have been quickly curtailed.

I'm pleased I'm allowing some childhood memories to filter back into my brain; too many of them are filed away in my inner box marked 'Do not disturb'. My parents divorced when I was seven, and most of my early memories consist of listening to shouting matches from my bedroom upstairs, or doors banging when my father would storm out of the house after an argument. The worst one was when the door banged and he never came back. My mother was never quite the same after that. I do remember some things about my time with Aunt Molly, though; those were happier times. I really must start working on that internal filter, so that my memories of Molly don't get padlocked away with all the other stuff. Aunt Molly was one of the good things about my childhood, and sitting in that church today listening to the priest talk about her life, it's hit me now, when it's too late to do anything about it, that I've allowed her to get locked inside that box, when where she should have been was close by my side.

I take a swift gulp from my glass and find I'm having to swallow down more than just the rich black liquid of a mouthful of Guinness. Taking another gulp, I place the glass on the mat and take a few deep breaths.

No, a pub is not the place for tears, I tell myself sternly. *If you were going to cry, why didn't you do it in the church?*

I'd wanted to cry in the church, really. As I sat at the back of the church and watched the hunched shoulders in front of me sobbing and dabbing at their eyes, I felt the deepest sorrow. Sorrow at the loss of my aunt's life, sorrow for the grief of the people sitting around me and sorrow that I hadn't made more effort to keep in touch with this woman who had meant so much to me when I was a child. But for some reason, the tears just didn't appear.

But now as I'm sitting in a pub of all places, I can feel tears desperately wanting to fall from my eyes. And as hard as I try not to let them, I can also hear my mother's shrill voice ringing in my ears: 'We do not show our emotions in a public place, Darcy.' I really don't want to be seen sitting in the corner of the local bar sobbing and looking like the village drunk, so I cast my eyes around the room in an attempt to distract my emotions and am relieved to see Niall appearing through Mulligan's big wooden door. He stands just inside the doorway and looks nervously around the room.

'Niall, over here,' I wave, beckoning him towards my table by the fire.

As he hurriedly makes his way over to me, I notice he hasn't changed out of his formal funeral attire, as I have. I'm now wearing a pair of gorgeous faded black Diesel jeans, a baby-pink French Connection soft wool jumper and a pair of black leather Jimmy Choo boots, with heels so high you need to take flying lessons to wear them (thank heaven for sales and credit cards!). Shame – I was quite looking forward to seeing what he'd choose as a casual option. But I also notice he's now carrying a large leather briefcase to complete his solicitor look, which is suddenly a much more interesting prospect.

'Miss McCall,' he inclines his head towards me.

I raise my eyebrows.

'Oh, my apologies – Darcy, I completely forgot.'

'Much better.' Smiling, I gesture for him to take a seat at my table. 'Can I get you a drink before we begin, Niall?'

'Oh no, I *never* drink on duty – so to speak.' Niall pulls out a chair and rests his briefcase on it.

'But I bet you never perform your duties in a pub, do you? So there's a first time for everything. You should really have a drink – a Guinness, maybe?'

Niall looks at my half-empty pint glass in horror. 'Maybe a small gin and tonic then, just to be polite. No, no, I shall get these,' he insists, holding up his hand as I attempt to stand up. 'Can I get you another one, Darcy? Or maybe you'd like something else?'

'Another of these will be great, thanks, Niall.'

Niall nervously puts his order in with Michael at the bar. Then he stands and fidgets with a beer mat while he waits impatiently for the Guinness to settle and separate into its two distinctive colours, before Michael will part with it and allow Niall to carry it back over to me at the table.

'There,' he says, sitting down opposite me, eyeing up the rich black liquid suspiciously. 'Never really been my cup of tea, Guinness.'

'Nor mine, when I'm in England,' I admit. 'It tastes completely different over there. But on the rare occasion I venture over to Ireland I always have to have a pint – it's like a tradition.'

The truth of the matter is I wouldn't be seen dead drinking a pint of anything back in London. It's usually an elegant-looking glass I'm to be found clutching, more often than not containing a trendy cocktail.

'Indeed,' Niall takes a sip of his G&T. 'So: on to business, then.' He reaches down for his briefcase, snaps it open and pulls out some important-looking documents. Then he looks around him, just like he'd been doing in the house and garden earlier.

'We're quite safe here, Niall. I really don't think many of the people that were at Aunt Molly's funeral frequent this pub.'

Niall smiles. 'Probably not. Although the barman did ask me if I wanted a cherry on a stick with my gin and tonic, so maybe they do have the more discerning clientele in here occasionally.'

I pinch myself under the table in an attempt to stop myself laughing. I decide pointing out to Niall that the only cherries Michael ever saw in here were likely to be the ones on the fruit machine, and he was in fact making a joke at Niall's expense, was not only going to be a waste of time but probably a little cruel too. The sort of places Niall probably goes to drink are trendy Dublin wine bars – all chrome seats and blue lighting. Just the kinds of place I end up in on nights out in London with my colleagues from the magazine. Perhaps I'd do well to keep my thoughts to myself.

'So,' Niall continues, 'how did the rest of the wake go? I'm sorry I had to leave but I had some other business to attend to, and on finding out who I worked for, some of the other guests were beginning to ask some very awkward and rather probing questions.'

'It went as well as a wake ever goes, I suppose.' I pause, hoping he'll continue. 'So . . . ' I look at him encouragingly.

'So.' Niall looks at me blankly. 'Right, yes, of course, you'll be wanting to know about the will.' He rearranges the papers in front of him, picks one up as if he's about to begin reading, then he pauses, looks at me and puts it back down again. 'Before I begin, Darcy, may I first tell you how we in the office all wish to say how much your aunt is to be congratulated on her very thorough tying-up of all her affairs. It's made both the organising of her funeral, and the arranging of this slightly *unusual* bequest, both easy, and, if I may say so, an actual pleasure on our behalf.'

I try to look gratified by his comments about my aunt, but all the time my mind is racing. *What does he mean, 'unusual' bequest? Surely my being the only beneficiary makes this whole process quite simple?* I haven't really had much time this afternoon to think about my aunt's will, and nor have I wanted to, really. After all, we've only just spent the day saying goodbye to her. But now I'm here with Niall, I'm curious to know. Maybe her estate is the little cottage we were in today, but why would that be unusual? It doesn't make sense.

'So I'll just start by reading, if I may.' Niall holds up the document again and adjusts his glasses before beginning. 'I, Emmeline Ava Aisling McCall, being of sound mind ...' he begins in a solemn voice.

'Niall,' I interrupt. 'I won't mind if you don't put on your solicitor hat tonight. After all, it doesn't really seem appropriate here,' I gesture to our surroundings.

Niall stares at me for a moment, then glances at the other people enjoying themselves in Mulligan's bar tonight.

'Maybe you could just read the important bits, if it's easier, and cut out all the legal stuff?' I place my hand over his on the table. 'Put it to me in layman's terms.' I think about fluttering my eyelashes at him, but decide that would be taking it a bit too far.

19

Niall hesitates, then he looks down at my hand and nods. 'All right then, I guess it wouldn't hurt just this once.'

'Fantastic, thank you!' I snap my hand away. 'Go for it.'

For a moment, Niall eyes me suspiciously from behind his glasses. 'It seems, Darcy, your aunt was a very wealthy woman.'

'Was she?' *This is news to me*. 'How wealthy?'

'Very. The frugal life she appeared to be living here in the little cottage we were in today, masked a large fortune built up over many years of good investment.'

'Investment – investment in what?'

'Property, mainly. She used to own quite a large estate over in Kerry, I believe.' Niall looks for a particular document on the table.

'Yes, I used to stay there with her, as a child. But that was just the one big house. She bought it when my uncle died.'

Niall, having found the relevant document and now back in his comfortable solicitor's role, again takes charge. 'Oh no, she owned quite a lot of land around the area, too – some arable, some with planning permission to build a large number of houses. So when she had to move back over to Dublin about five years ago,' he consults his papers again. 'She needed specialist medical treatment, I believe?' he pauses to look up at me.

I'm nodding, but I'm ashamed that I don't really know what he's talking about. *I really should have made more of an effort ...* I think again for the hundredth time today.

'She sold most of her land to facilitate the move and the cost of her treatment,' Niall continues, 'and then wisely invested the rest of the money.'

I am utterly amazed now. I had no idea Molly had been

some sort of financial wizard. I just remember her as my slightly eccentric aunt.

'Her financial advisor briefed her very wisely indeed.' Niall picks up another sheaf of papers, and this time I notice they're covered with figures.

'So then,' I ask, taking a sip from my glass, 'just how much money are we talking here, Niall?' I hope I look calm and unflustered by the information Niall is feeding me, when really I need this drink to steady my nerves. I hope he doesn't see my hand shaking as I lift my glass to my lips.

'I'm not actually at liberty to tell you the exact amount just at the moment.' Niall fidgets nervously in his seat. 'But what I can tell you is the entire estate amounts to,' he glances around him in the same way he had in the garden earlier, and then leans across the table, lowering his voice, 'a good seven-figure sum.'

How I hated maths at school – in fact I hate numbers of any kind, even now. What are seven figures? I try to figure this out quickly in my head while I calmly sip at my drink. *There are six figures in £100,000, so what is the most you can get in thousands? That would be £999,999, and the next step up from that would be …*

'Oh my God, that's a million pounds or more!' I hiss, shooting a cream-coloured spray across the table at Niall. A little lands on his white shirt, but the majority soaks his burgundy silk tie forming a large, abstract pattern of Guinness.

'Niall, I'm so sorry!' I leap to my feet and hurriedly grab a beer towel from the bar. I grasp at his tie and desperately begin dabbing it with the towel. 'I'm pretty sure it won't stain, though if we get it off quickly.'

Niall's head has been pulled into a temporary noose caused

by my dangling on one end of his tie. So while I manically dab at the taught burgundy bridge between us, he's incapable of doing anything other than casting his eyes downwards and watching me in horror. Then I'm aware of his eyes slowly lifting again. 'Stop!' he gasps, his voice barely audible. He holds up his hand. 'Just stop, Darcy, please.'

I cease wiping at the fabric and look at him.

The tie is more like a loose rope bridge between us now, as Niall calmly removes it from my hand. Then, equally calmly he removes the beer towel from my other hand and places it back on the bar, smoothing it out before he turns around to face me. He shows no sign of emotion as he blinks at me through his beer-speckled glasses. 'I suppose I've got an excuse to take the damn thing off now,' he says, suddenly grinning.

Thankful he's seen the funny side, I breathe a huge sigh of relief. 'Just as well it wasn't a good one,' I blurt out without thinking, and immediately wish I hadn't. 'I . . . I mean, it's not like it's designer.' I can feel my face flaming as red as the fire burning brightly next to us.

Niall raises his eyebrows, but doesn't appear to take offence. 'No, I don't really do designer ties.' As he grins even more at my embarrassment, I quickly return to my chair before I drop myself in it any deeper.

While Niall carefully removes his tie and cleans the rest of the Guinness from the lenses of his glasses with his handkerchief, I just want to sit happily hugging myself. *I don't have to worry about my overdraft any more!* I secretly shout inside my head as a warm, secure feeling begins to spread right through my body. *Thank you, Aunt Molly. Thank you!* But I try to remain cool and calm while I wait for him to continue with the reading.

'So, where were we?' Niall asks, replacing his glasses once more. 'Ah yes, now, as I was saying, your aunt has left a very large estate tied up within the terms of her will, and as long as these terms are met, then yes, you, Darcy, could end up a very wealthy woman indeed.'

I lean back in my seat and smile contentedly – my maxed-out credit-card bills can be paid off at long last, and I won't have to worry about scraping enough money together for the next rent payment either: I'll be able to buy myself a nice little flat now and I won't have to share any more. Although I wouldn't want to be too far away from my flatmate, Roxi – maybe I can buy her a flat next to mine! And there'll definitely be no more scraping around on the sale rails for bargains. No, from now on it will be straight into the designer showrooms, with fawning assistants desperate to wait on me hand and foot, and pander to my every—

'Wait,' I sit forward again in my chair. 'What do you mean by *terms*?'

'Ah.' Niall slides his glasses back up onto the bridge of his nose. 'You see, this is where the really interesting part comes in.' He smiles nervously at me, and begins apprehensively tapping the ends of his fingers together.

While I start to get a very bad feeling in the pit of my stomach.

'Go on, Niall.'

'When your aunt sold most of her property in County Kerry, it seems she held onto one quite large area – apparently it held some sentimental value for her, and she refused to part with it.' Niall pauses to check if I'm taking all this in. Happy that I am, he continues. 'So as part of her last will and testament she requests that you, Darcy, go and live there, before you inherit any of her money. I believe she wants you to' – he picks up some of the paperwork again, still strewn all over the table, and thumbs through the pages before he reads directly from a sheet – '"experience what I as a child knew growing up, and perhaps to recreate some of the magic we both shared together in the house in County Kerry, and even some new magic of your very own".'

I'm touched, hearing my aunt's words read to me by Niall. I hadn't realised our time together had meant so much to her. But I suppose, for her to have left everything to me like this, it must have, and again that sense of guilt and sorrow over-whelms me for a moment. But something still wasn't adding up.

'So I'm to go and live in her old house for a long summer holiday or something, is that it?' That's actually quite a sweet idea, and it's the least I can do to make up for all the time in her life I've missed out on. An extended holiday in Ireland could be fun. There're some big cities over here, so it won't be all country living. I can cope with that. Dublin and Cork are very cosmopolitan, for a start.

'Er, no, not quite. It's a bit longer than a summer holiday.'

'How long then?'

I see Niall's eyes flash towards my glass, which to his relief is safely placed on the table this time. 'A year,' he says softly.

'A *year*!' I gasp. 'How can I possibly take a year out of my life to come and live in a house over here? What about my life back in London – my friends, my job, my flat? I can't just leave all that!'

'I'm afraid a year is the specified amount of time stated in the will, Darcy, and it's not exactly a house, either.' Niall pulls at where his tie would normally be as if to loosen it. But all he finds is a top button, so he undoes that instead.

'So where am I going to live for a year then, if not in her old house?' I ask hotly.

Niall shuffles his papers around.

'Niall?'

'An island,' he murmurs in a voice so low I can barely hear him.

'Yes, I know in *Ireland*, but whereabouts?'

'No,' he says, looking directly at me now. 'An actual *island*, just off the west coast.'

I sit back in my chair, shaking my head slowly. 'I'm sorry, but I thought I heard you say you wanted me to go and live on an island for a year just then, Niall?'

Nodding, Niall holds up a new piece of paper. 'Yes, I'm afraid it's all here, Darcy.' He taps the sheet of paper to indicate the relevant paragraph. 'Apparently your aunt grew up on the island, as part of a small community. Then as the community gradually faded away and people moved off the island to greener pastures, your aunt's family, as many others did, moved back to mainland Ireland. But your aunt never lost her love for the island, so when it came up for sale in the mid-nineteen-eighties she purchased it and moved back to the area. And she's owned it ever since.'

'I think she might have taken me over there to visit once or twice.' Some vague memories of boat trips across to an island come floating into my mind, and just as quickly drift away again. 'But I can't just go and live there on my own for a year, like some sort of recluse.'

'Oh no, she doesn't want you to go and live there alone,' Niall hurriedly explains as I drain the rest of my drink and desperately look around for another. 'She wants you to set up a whole new community of people to live there with you.'

'What! Whoah, just wait one minute.' This was all becoming a bit much to take in. 'Niall, let me run this by you again, just so I've understood it all properly.'

'Sure, I can imagine this has all come as a bit of a shock.'

That's the understatement of the year. 'You're telling me my aunt Molly has left me and me alone in her will a very large estate?' I repeat slowly.

Niall nods. 'Yes. Very, very large.'

My eyes open wide, but I continue. 'And to inherit any of this I have to go and live on an island for a year with a bunch of strangers?'

'You have to set up and run a small community to thrive and prosper over one year. But yes, that's basically it.'

'And if I do all this, then what happens at the end of the year?'

'According to the terms of the will, as long as you've lived for twelve months on the island with a community of no fewer than fifteen people at any given time, then you will inherit all of your aunt's estate.'

'And I can do what I like with it after that – the island, and any money?'

'Yes, I believe so. The will stipulates a clause only for the first year.'

'And if I choose not to go through with all this ... if I refuse to go and live on the island?'

'Then, Darcy, I'm afraid you will get nothing. The island

will be given to Heritage Ireland, and the rest of your aunt's money to the charity of her choice.'

I sit back in my chair again, stunned, to think.

'I don't wish to influence your decision in any way, Darcy,' I hear Niall say in a gentle voice, while I'm desperately running through all the various options in my head. 'But for your aunt to have put this much thought into her will, it really must have been what she wanted. We rarely see anything like this in the office. In fact, it would have been my father that helped your aunt put this together in the first place, so I sort of feel responsible that it's carried out properly.'

I break from my own thoughts and turn my attention back to Niall.

'I know, and thank you, Niall, you have carried out everything very thoroughly and properly indeed. I couldn't have asked for a better solicitor to explain this crazy situation to me.'

Niall smiles proudly.

'I promise you I'll keep that in mind while I make my decision on what I'm going to do.'

Niall's right. As images of big houses, flashy cars, designer labels and zero credit-card bills race across my mind, the one thought that keeps returning as it grows ever stronger in my mind – is Molly.

Four

'For next month's issue, we need people to cover the following features,' my editor announces from the comfort of her desk, as we all stand crowded into her office at the end of our weekly editorial meeting. 'The top ten haircuts for spring – *Top of the Crops*. The latest beauty parlour, where you can take your designer pooch in for a pampering alongside you – *WAGS to Bitches*. And our regular feature comparing budget and designer products – next month it's fake tans – *Sun-kissed or Just-missed.*'

'I thought we were calling that "sun-kissed or just pissed",' my colleague Sophie whispers to me as we stand listening to Jemima preach the gospel of *Goddess* magazine.

I grin at her.

'Have you got something to share, Sophie?' Jemima enquires, regarding us over her large tortoiseshell glasses.

'No, Jemima,' Sophie calls innocently from the back of the room.

'Then you, Sophie, shall take the top ten haircuts for spring,' Jemima narrows her eyes. 'You look like you could do with some help with that mop of yours.'

'I paid ninety quid for this cut,' Sophie mutters to me, smoothing her hand over her hair. 'Yes, thank you, Jemima, I'll make a start on it today,' she calls, smiling sweetly across the room.

'Lucy, you will take the fake tan feature. A bit of colour to that whiter-than-white skin of yours will do you the world of good. Pale is not interesting, darling, its dullsville.'

I turn to Sophie again, who raises her eyebrows at me in astonishment. Surely Jemima has forgotten that Lucy just returned to work a few days ago after time away recuperating from donating a kidney to her sister?

'And you, Samantha.' Jemima turns her attention now to the person our magazine might have been named after, as she stands, all five feet ten of her, looking resplendent behind us. Samantha is immaculately presented today, as always, and her cool, poised demeanour surrounds her like a cloud of exquisite perfume. She could almost be hovering above the ground in her own angelic glow of perfection were it not for the fact that I know she's wearing the most fantastic pair of red and black Miu Miu shoes today. I'd secretly admired them as she glided past me on the way to the water cooler earlier, and I'd immediately gone on Net-a-Porter to see if I could find out where they were from. Well, I wasn't going to ask her.

'You, Samantha,' Jemima continues, 'shall take the feature on the celebrity beauty salons. You'll fit in there without too much of a problem.'

An enigmatic smile forms beneath Samantha's perfectly

applied MAC lipstick as she acknowledges Jemima's statement to be correct.

Great, I think, while Jemima assigns all the other less important jobs for next month. Looks like I've been over-looked altogether this time. I mean, I never expected in a million years to get the beauty salon gig. Samantha always gets the best jobs – one of the *many* perks of being a niece of one of owners of the multinational that prints *Goddess* – but I'd have expected fake tans at the very least. It's so unfair.

I realise while I'm stewing in my own misery that Jemima is trying to speak to me. 'Darcy, are you with us?' she asks in that super-sweet yet steely-eyed way of hers.

I nod hurriedly.

'Good, I was beginning to wonder. Now, Darcy, I've saved something extra special for you.' Jemima smiles, giving us a brief flash of her new and very expensive set of perfect white teeth.

Now the thing is, when Jemima smiles it isn't necessarily a good thing. I try to guess by looking at the angle on the curve of her mouth whether this smile means good news for me or bad.

Jemima pushes back her ergonomically designed chair and stands up.

Definitely bad.

'I'd like to start a new monthly feature on the magazine,' her eyes glint dangerously behind her spectacles. 'An area we've never ventured into before, but something that's becoming more and more popular with the masses.' She pauses for dramatic effect, while I hold my breath in anticipation of whatever crackpot, anti-ageing, get yourself super-slim in three days scheme she's found now. I can guarantee that if she wants me to experience something it won't be a week in a Champneys health resort.

'Holistic healing,' she announces with a dramatic swish of her hand.

We all stand and stare at her.

'Holistic healing,' she repeats, as though we're hard of hearing. 'I thought we could start with some of the more well-known therapies such as reiki, acupuncture and homeopathy, and then move on to things like crystal therapy, and do some real-life features on people who get spiritual, and even angel healing if we can find some willing volunteers to speak to us.'

I turn to Sophie, my eyes wide.

She grimaces at me in sympathy.

'So what do you think, Darcy?' Jemima asks, putting me on the spot.

I can feel my colleagues' eyes around the room boring into me as they too await my answer. Samantha's lipstick is a lot less enigmatic now and a lot more smug as she surveys me from underneath eyelashes that have definitely been enhanced in post-production, while most of the others simply wince at my discomfort, glad they're not in my shoes.

'It's certainly different, Jemima.' I'm diplomatic. 'But do you think it will work at *Goddess*?' The usual content of our articles about whether a lipstick can actually last all day without being reapplied, or if you really do burn more calories by eating a stick of celery than there are in the celery itself, are hardly considered thought-provoking. 'I mean, is it the kind of thing our readers want to know about?'

'Darcy.' Jemima removes her glasses, which always means business. 'Holistic healing is the next big thing; it's everywhere right now. Just the other day there was a huge mind, body and spirit event here in London at Earls Court, and they're happening all around the country every weekend. One of our sister magazines, *Soul Sister* has a huge, ever-growing readership, and I think it's about time we incorporated these ideas into the mainstream.'

'She's right, you know,' Maggie, Jemima's secretary, who is usually silent while she takes shorthand at these meetings pipes up. 'I was in Selfridges the other day, and they've got psychics in there now. Right in the middle of the shop, not hidden away or anything.'

Jemima nods at Maggie. 'Yes, thank you, Maggie. Now—'

'All the celebs are into cosmic ordering these days, too,' Daisy, one of our interns dares to add. She hasn't been here long enough to realise that you never interrupt Jemima when's she's in full flow. 'I read about it in one of my magazines the other day. Tom Cruise, John Travolta, even Noel Edmonds, he reckons he got back into TV because of it.'

'And is that supposed to be a *good* thing?' Sophie whispers to me.

'Yes, thank you all for your input,' Jemima interrupts, holding up her hand before anyone else tries to join in. She turns to me. 'So you see, Darcy, holistic healing really is the *in thing* right now. It's everywhere,' her eyes flicker briefly to Sophie. 'It's even reached daytime TV, it seems, and we must be the first mainstream magazine to jump on the bandwagon before anyone else does. So I've arranged for you to have a session of acupuncture next week, Darcy, to begin your series of articles with.'

'Great, thank you Jemima,' I grimace at the thought. I don't know what's more painful to me right now – the thought of having needles stuck all over my body, or the months ahead having to listen to spiritual gurus in beads, cheesecloth dresses and sandals chanting and preaching at me to release my inner emotions and breathe in the light. 'I'm sure that will be an ... enlightening experience.'

After the meeting, Jemima asks me to wait while everyone else files out of her office, so she can give me the names of some contacts she thinks will help me with my articles. I'm impressed when the names are produced from Jemima's little black book – she must be taking this new departure for *Goddess* seriously, I think to myself as I return to my desk clutching the precious information. Before I can sit down, I have to remove an old copy of the magazine I find propped up on my chair. The bikini-clad model on the front cover has been decorated all over with coloured drawing pins, and a speech bubble has been drawn in black marker coming out of her mouth, exclaiming 'Ouch!'

I glance around the room, hoping to spot the guilty party sniggering behind a filing cabinet somewhere. But unsurprisingly, everyone is suddenly very busy, their eyes glued to their computer screens. *Hmm ... this practical joke thing always seems funny when it's at someone else's expense.*

Casting the magazine aside, I flop down at my desk. As my hand catches against my mouse, the screensaver of my current favourite Mulberry bag disappears and I stare at yet another photo of this Irish island I've been searching for on Google

Images. *Acupuncture, spiritual healing?* Spending a year on this island is starting to look almost pleasant by comparison.

What has got into Jemima? Our readers aren't interested in learning about how to heal yourself from the inside – external beauty is what's important to a reader of *Goddess* magazine. I'm doomed before I even begin with this one.

This is not what I'd hoped for at all when I got offered the job here. I'd been so excited finally to get a chance to write for a proper women's magazine, after years spent writing articles for a trade magazine about DIY tools. It had been so mind-numbingly boring that I'd actually fallen asleep at my desk one day – just how many words can you write about a screwdriver? Then I'd subsequently landed a job on a teen girl magazine, and it had been fun until they'd decided I was too old to write for them any more. Too old! Being informed you're too old to do anything other than join the Girl Guides at twenty-six takes some getting over. But then I got my job on *Goddess* almost a year ago now, and I thought all my Christmases had come at once. At last, a route into the exhilarating world of fashion I so longed for. So what if *Goddess* was more about beauty and health than fashion? I'd done my research, and I knew they had other big glossy magazines in their family that I might get promoted onto. Then one day, maybe, I'd get a chance to visit a big catwalk show and report on the latest designer collections. The freebies you got working on a fashion magazine were more likely to be shoes and handbags. Beauty freebies are a fantastic perk of my job – when they're actually something we women might use. If companies insist on trying to sell bright green lipstick, it doesn't take a genius to work out their market is going to be a coven of witches on a hen night rather than your average mum picking her kids up from school. They shouldn't need feedback from a beauty magazine to tell them that.

As I stare at the image of the island on my computer screen, my mobile phone rings in my bag that's hanging on the back of my chair.

'Darcy McCall,' I say vaguely, having fished it out.

'Darcy?' An Irish accent comes wafting back down the line. 'Is that you?'

I take a quick glance at the screen – *Niall.*

'Hello, Niall. What can I do for you?'

'I'm guessing, since I've not heard from you, Darcy, that you've still not made up your mind?'

'No, not yet.'

'Have you given it much thought?'

Have I given it much thought? I haven't *stopped* thinking about it. In fact, I've spent so much time on my laptop at home trying to find out information on living on islands over the past few days that if you read my internet history you'd probably think I was *Lost*'s number-one super-fan.

'Of course I have, Niall, but it's a big decision you're asking me to make.'

'I quite understand that, Darcy. The thing is, a package was delivered to the office today. I say it's a package, maybe you'd call it more of a box ... '

'Niall, I'm at work,' I lower my voice as one of the junior feature writers approaches my desk, sees I'm on the phone and gestures she'll pop back in a bit.

'Sorry. You see, the thing is it's your aunt's ashes.'

'My what?' I whisper into the phone.

'As part of the will, your aunt requests you're to be the person that scatters her ashes in her final resting place.'

'Me?' I ask in surprise. 'So where ... No, wait, you don't need to tell me.' I rest my elbow on the desk and drop my head into my hand, 'The island – yes?'

'You guess correctly. But it would be a wonderful opportunity for you to visit the island, Darcy. To see for yourself what it's like before you make your decision. The weather is incredibly mild over here for late January; I'm sure the boat would get across safely.'

I sigh and brush my hand against my computer, causing my coveted Mulberry bag to disappear once more, and the photo of the island reappear on the monitor in front of me. You can only tell so much from a digital image. How can I consider spending a year somewhere I can barely remember having visited before?

'All right; I suppose it wouldn't do any harm just to have a little visit.'

'Fantastic, how about this weekend?' Niall replies a bit too quickly.

'Why this weekend?' I'm somewhat taken aback by Niall's keenness. 'What's the rush?'

'For one, we don't really want your aunt sitting around in our office for too long. Some of the girls are finding her presence a little ... off-putting, shall we say? And two ...' he hesitates.

'And two?' I prompt.

'It's just, I'm not sure how much thinking you've done about your decision, Darcy. And what thought you've given to where you'd live on the island once you got over there. If, of course, that's what you choose to do,' Niall adds hurriedly. 'Only—'

'Only what, Niall?' I'm sensing something else is going on here.

'My parents have been getting some renovation work done on their house recently – quite a lot of renovation work, actually, and it's just been completed. I happened to be talking to the chappie in charge about your dilemma – I mean, I didn't mention the will, of course, just that you were thinking of investing in an island, and how you might go about putting that kind of project together. Darcy, you wouldn't believe all the practical stuff you've got to think about if you go through with this, such as housing, fuel, water supplies . . .'

If I go through with all this, I think, while Niall is still reeling off the island's shopping list. I haven't even made up my mind yet. It should be easy. I go to this island and live there for a year, in the process fulfilling my aunt Molly's last wish and making it up to her for all the years we spent apart. And then if that wasn't enough, at the end of my year I get a bonus prize for all my efforts – simple. But it isn't that simple. I don't want to go and live on some cold, windy island with a bunch of strangers. I want to stay here in London in my warm and cosy flat with Roxi. With all the things we're used to, like shops and TV and the internet and . . . well, after Roxi it's the shops I'll miss most, if I'm honest.

'And the thing is,' Niall continues, while I'm still trying to come to terms with the sudden thought of not shopping for a year, 'if you do come over this weekend, I know that Dermot can come to the island with us to visit – he's already told me he's free. He'd be able to advise you just what would be involved in setting it all up. I'm sure it would help you in making your decision. The will did stipulate that you only have the one month to decide, remember?'

How could I forget? Niall had kindly gone through all the terms and conditions with me, after my initial shock had died down that evening in the pub.

'So, Darcy, what do you say?' Niall prods from the other end of the line.

I roll my eyes. Across the sea Niall might be, but he may as well be here in person dressed as a pirate, poking me on with a sword, towards the end of a gangplank.

Sophie approaches my desk, carrying some hairstyle magazines. Perching herself on the corner, she picks the old magazine up off the floor and shakes her head as she looks at the pin-encrusted front cover.

'Can you just hold on a moment, Niall,' I pull the phone away from my ear. 'What's up?' I ask her.

'I just wanted to know if you were coming out for a drink tonight. We're all going to that new wine bar that's opened up down the road. Apparently they're doing two cocktails for the price of one before seven – bargain. You've got to dress up, though; Samantha's got us on a guest list for a private party that's happening later on, something to do with someone in her family.'

Ooh, I wonder if it's her uncle, the one that co-owns *Goddess*? I never need an excuse to dress up, but I can do without having Samantha to thank for it. 'Sure, sounds good,' I nod. 'We meeting there?'

'Yep.' Sophie drops the magazine on my desk. 'Very funny, I don't think.' She rolls her eyes. 'Can't they think of anything better than that?'

'Obviously not,' I gesture at the phone in my hand.

Sophie nods and gathers her hair magazines into her arms again. 'I see *someone*'s finding it amusing that you're going to have hundreds of needles stuck into you in the name of journalism. I'll leave you to your phone call; I've got to go find me a decent haircut!' She hops down off my desk and wanders back across the office.

'So sorry about that, Niall,' I say speaking into the phone again while I make sure I drop the voodooed magazine into my waste-paper bin this time. 'One of my colleagues had an issue that just couldn't wait.'

'Not a problem,' Niall replies. 'Look, you'll at least come and scatter the ashes this weekend, won't you, Darcy? It's what your aunt wanted. Then you can take a look around the island while you're here. What harm can it do?'

He's right; I'll just be scattering some ashes. I at least owe that to Aunt Molly, don't I? It doesn't mean I'm committing myself to anything.

'All right then,' I sigh into the phone, 'you win, Niall, I'll come over this weekend. You'll arrange everything with this building chap?'

'Dermot – sure I will. You won't regret this, Darcy, I just know you won't.'

Maybe, I think as Niall excitedly begins filling me in on all the details I'll need on how to get there. But really, is visiting a remote Irish island in mid-January going to sway my decision towards wanting to live there? The only way this trip is going to persuade me is if it's able to jog my brain into releasing some of those lost memories of my aunt that are still insisting on remaining hidden away in that locked box I keep inside my head.

Five

When I get back to my flat that night and pick up the post, scattered all over our doormat, I can tell immediately what most of the envelopes are without even opening them – bills. I toss them back on the table by the door with all the others that are starting to form quite a nice little white and brown pile, and head into the flat to see if Roxi's home. But the silence that hits me on entering should be the first clue that tells me she isn't – that, and the fact that the flat is still looking reasonably tidy, just as I'd left it this morning. If Roxi was here, the latest copy of *OK!* or *Heat* would have been abandoned on the settee, and MTV would have been blaring out from the television. Satellite TV was a luxury I could live without; I'd rather spend my hard-earned wages on new shoes or a bag, but Roxi had had this boyfriend for a while who had somehow rigged us up a system where we got it free, and I'd probably thought it best at the time not to ask too many questions. That's the thing with my flatmate, she meets so many people in the pub where she works I never quite know just who she's bringing back here to hang out. But I never have to worry about Roxi; she always manages to fall on her feet. She's like that.

So in blissful silence for a change, I begin getting ready to go out, and as I remove from my wardrobe my brand-new Stella McCartney dress sheathed in its own protective jacket, I savour the anticipation of finally wrapping myself in this gorgeous creation. Since I saw it in Selfridges just before Christmas, I've been absolutely desperate to have a chance to wear it. It's a short cream and oyster-pink shift dress covered from top to bottom in the most amazing sequin detailing. My first casual glance at the price tag had almost resulted in me passing out. But to my credit, I'd stood in the fitting room for at least a minute after I'd tried it on thinking about whether I should perhaps wait and see if it would be reduced in the post-Christmas sales. But what if they'd sold it before then? What if this was the only one? I couldn't possibly let something as perfect as this slip through my fingers. I just had to have it.

I'm turning to and fro in front of our only full-length mirror (we had to block out half a window so we could squeeze it into the bedroom, but who needs real daylight anyway?) and as I see my reflection I know my credit card and I made the right decision. I think I look pretty good this evening.

And yes, perhaps I hadn't really needed the matching shoes at the time, but when the very helpful assistant brought them over and said it was the last pair they had in my size, I knew this outfit was just meant to be.

The Atlantis bar (it seems I can't get away from islands for a second, these days) has been decorated with an underwater theme. Its deep midnight-blue walls are covered in a fine layer of Perspex that actually has running water cascading down behind it. The constant sound of running water is quite relaxing – until you start to need a pee. Then it just becomes torture, and I find myself visiting the ladies far more frequently than I'm used to on a night out. What little seating there is is again made of Perspex, but this time, instead of water trickling down inside each seat base, there's a variety of underwater objects like coral, seaweed and rocks. They remind me of those dodgy toilet seats you can buy with things like barbed wire and sea shells embedded in them.

But the best thing about the bar is that it's filled with lots of people who work in the same industry I do, and that always pleases me. You never know who you might meet somewhere like this, and more importantly, you never know what they might let slip about a job opportunity somewhere a little bit more interesting than *Goddess*.

'So when do we get into this private party, Soph?' I ask, gulping down the last inch of another two-for-one cocktail.

'When Samantha gets here, I guess.' Sophie sips on a long green straw in the shape of an octopus.

'Where is she? Happy hour is nearly over now.' I glance at my watch. *Has it stopped working? That isn't the right time, is it?* I give my wrist a shake.

'There's good news and bad news on that front,' Sophie looks across the crowded bar as the bouncers stand aside to let a small group of people in through the door.

'What do you mean, good news and bad news?' I'm still

concerned about my watch. Stupid eBay, the seller had a hundred per cent good feedback, too. Why do I always get the dodgy designer goods?

'Good news in that Samantha's just arrived. And bad in that ...' Sophie pauses long enough for me to look up to see what's causing her hesitation.

'She's wearing my dress!' I gasp.

As Samantha saunters towards us, her minions in tow, she is indeed wearing the exact same dress, and even worse, the same shoes as me.

And looking a hundred times more fabulous in them than I do, I growl to myself.

'Oh dear, Darcy,' she laughs, an image of perfection looking down at me from her marble pedestal. 'We should have had a little tête-à-tête before we left the office tonight. This will never do.'

I can feel my face flaming, even though I'm desperately trying to remain cool. 'They say great minds think alike, Samantha. Perhaps the same can be said for great style icons too?'

Samantha's mouth does its best to impersonate someone that's smiling. 'Indeed. Did you get yours in the sale?' she enquires, her eyes panning up and down my body like she's X-raying me for a discount tag. 'I'm told it was heavily reduced after Christmas.'

My mouth does something similar. On the outside it looks as if I'm smiling, but internally I'm baring my teeth at her like a rabid dog defending its territory. 'No, actually, I bought it full price in December. I just haven't had the occasion to wear it yet.'

Samantha opens her mouth to reply, but she is distracted by a man waving a clipboard and making his way over towards her.

'Samantha, darling,' he says, kissing her on both cheeks as he reaches us. 'Is this your little gang? We need to get them all through to the other room as soon as.'

'Certainly, Henry.' Samantha takes a quick glance around her. 'Yes, we're all here, I think. Shall we go, then?'

Like tourists following their guide who's holding up an umbrella, we trail after Henry as he makes his way across the room, his clipboard held aloft. When we get safely across the bar to the room where the party is being held, Samantha stands next to Henry by the door and helps him check each one of us off before we're allowed in.

Peeking through the doorway while I wait my turn, I can see an enormous ice sculpture of a mermaid standing elegantly in the middle of the room. Next to her is a long table covered in a white cloth with tall glass vases full of purple orchids and green foliage. Elegant, important-looking people mill about holding flutes of champagne, and waiters are moving busily to and fro carrying more glasses of bubbly and trays of delicious-looking canapés. *Now this is more like where I should be hanging out,* I think as I move closer to the door. *No plastic toilet seats in there.*

At last, it's my turn to enter the gates to heaven.

'No, not you, Darcy,' I hear, as I'm already halfway through the entrance.

'What?'

'I said, not you.'

I turn and stare at Samantha. *Is she being serious?* 'But why?'

'I simply can't have you in there wearing the same outfit as me. There are people in that room I want to impress tonight, and if they see you in there in the same dress it just won't have the same effect. You're welcome to go home and change . . .' a cat-like smile spreads across her pale glossy lips ' . . . and when you return, just give a little tap on the door here and I'll make sure Brian lets you straight in.'

A burly-looking bouncer with a bald head gives a me a brief nod.

I take another longing look into the room again before turning to see Samantha's smug, arrogant face waiting for my reaction. I desperately try and think of a sharp retort, but as usual I can't find the right words to say at the right moment. So, not wanting to cause a scene, I swivel around on my oyster-coloured heels and stride away without saying a word. Marching back into the bar, I hoist myself up onto one of the barstools covered in seaweed.

How can Samantha have the barefaced cheek just to stand there and say that to me? Who *does* she think she is? And, more to the point, how could I have just let her? I should have said something. I should have . . . But as usual I hadn't.

That is just me all over. I never have been very good at confrontation; not for as long as I can remember. I think it's because of my parent's divorce; arguments, shouting matches, big shows of emotion of any kind aren't my scene. Better to steer clear of them than cause a fuss. Don't rock the boat under any circumstances.

Aargh, I think, as I wait for the barman to notice me so I can finally get some service. Roxi wouldn't have let her get away with it; she'd have shown her who was boss. Roxi never let anyone put her down. What would she do if she were here?

*

45

But on waking the next morning, I wonder if I might have taken the boat metaphor a bit *too* far, because as I lay in my bed I feel like I'm actually in a boat that's rocking gently up and down on the waves of the sea. I open one eye at a time and yes, as I recognise the familiar surroundings of my bedroom I know I'm at least in my own flat. But why are the walls wobbling, and the ceiling spinning gently above me?

I close my eyes for a moment again and then, instead of the gentle waves that have been buffeting my bed up and down, a huge tidal wave comes crashing over me, reminding me just what did happen last night.

After I'd decided to deal with the situation in the same way Roxi would, I'd sat on the seaweed-covered stool and proceeded to get extremely drunk for the rest of the evening. So far, so good. I do vaguely remember Sophie and one or two of the others coming away from the party from time to time to see if I was OK, but I have a vague recollection now, as another wave brings more information with it, of me shooing them away and telling them I didn't need any of them because my new friends in the bar were keeping me company. I think I must have meant the colourful cocktails I was drinking at such a pace, because I don't remember talking to anyone in particular that night apart from one of the bar staff. He was very attentive to me all night, mainly I guess because I was spending so much money with him, and possibly because I was drinking alone. He was also incredibly patient, too, listening to my ramblings all evening in between serving his other customers, and I vaguely remember him being especially good when I fell off the barstool. But even he's a bit of a daze now.

I try and sit up in my bed and the room spins even more.

Rolling over towards my bedside table, I pray there's some water in the glass I usually fill before bedtime. But since I can't actually remember getting home last night, let alone getting into bed, I'm not surprised when I find there isn't.

It's no good, Darcy, you're going to have to get yourself to the kitchen, even if you have to crawl.

Somehow I manage to stagger, like a fairground bumper car bouncing off furniture and doorframes on the way, to my kitchen. I'm glad for once that I only live in a tiny flat and not some huge mansion where the kitchen is a half-mile walk and two floors away. As I'm about to open a cupboard to reach for a glass, I hear a noise behind me.

'You made it through the night, then?' Roxi says, standing in the door of the kitchen wearing only a Beyoncé tour t-shirt and kitten-heeled fluffy pink slippers. Her leopard-print sleep mask is pushed up on top of her jet-black hair. 'Only, by the look of you last night when you came in, baby doll, I did wonder.'

'Was I *that* bad?'

'Darce, you were shaking moves around this house that even I would have been proud of. No,' she holds up her hand and pulls her t-shirt away from her ample chest. 'Forget me, even the Queen B herself couldn't have worked it like that.'

'Oh my God, Rox, I was dancing? I don't remember.'

'The fact that you don't recall last night's events is a mystery that I don't think we need to call a professional in to investigate.' Roxi shuffles across the kitchen and picks up the kettle. 'I think we both know what caused that. However, if it was a certain Mr Will Smith dressed in black doing the investigating,' she says, allowing herself to daydream for a moment. 'Then I

47

might be forced into losing my memory too ... Tea?' she enquires, wafting the kettle in my direction.

'Thanks, Roxi, but no ... I think I need to rehydrate myself quicker than that. Quite a lot quicker, in fact.' I lift a glass down from the cupboard and go over to the sink. Turning on the tap to rinse it out in my hung-over state, I forget that our kitchen taps are temperamental, and you have to turn the cold tap on gently at first before you can let it run fully. A huge spurt of water shoots up, soaking the front of my pyjamas.

'Darcy, what *are* you doing?' Roxi shouts, as I stand motionless in front of the sink with the water still shooting up in the air. She rushes over to take control of the errant tap.

As I turn to her, the freezing-cold water soaking through my pyjama top and onto my skin, another memory from last night begins to seep fully into my aching brain ...

'Roxi, I don't think we'll be needing Will Smith, after all.'

'What do you mean?' she asks, looking puzzled.

'I've just remembered everything that happened last night, and it's not good. It's not good at all.'

Six

I tell Roxi everything that happened with Samantha and the bouncer. And as I predicted, Roxi's reaction is somewhat stronger than mine was.

'If only I'd been there,' she says, her dark-chocolate eyes narrowing in my defence. 'I'd have wiped that smile right off her face.'

'Yes I know *you* would!' I can't help but grin at the thought of Roxi in all her Primark and New Look glory battling it out against Samantha in her Gucci and Jimmy Choos. I know who I'd have bet on to come out victorious. 'But you know what I'm like, Rox. Anyway, it was you I was thinking of when this next idea suddenly washed over me. And I say *wash* ...'

Roxi looks at me suspiciously. 'Darcy, you're worrying me now. What have you done?' She takes a bite of her bacon sandwich. 'Are you sure I can't make you anything, honey? It will do your hangover the world of good.'

I shake my head and shift uncomfortably on the sofa in the dressing gown I've now changed into. 'No, really, Rox, you know I can't stomach breakfast at the best of times, and eating something this morning isn't going to make dealing with this memory any easier.'

'I could break into my chocolate stash I keep hidden away in my room, if you like?'

'No, I don't think even chocolate would help me today.'

Roxi almost drops her sandwich in shock. 'Oh my, now I know something ain't right, when you don't want chocolate. You better tell Auntie Roxi, and fast!'

I sigh heavily as I have to take myself back to last night again. 'Well, I'm in the ladies' toilet, and Samantha comes in while I'm washing my hands ...' I begin.

'Enjoying your evening?' Samantha enquires, looking at my reflection in the mirror.

Her face is still unbearably smug as she stares back at me waiting for my reply, and suddenly I feel a wave of intense emotion like nothing I've ever felt before. 'It's about to get a whole lot better,' I reply, leaping away from the sink. The cold tap I've been rinsing my hands under shoots water from its spout at full bore, splashing up out of the basin and on to whatever is in its path.

'Aaah!' Samantha cries as water sprays all over her cream and oyster dress. 'What the hell are you *doing*?'

'Sorry, I must have turned the tap the wrong way there. Silly thing.'

'But look at my dress, it's soaked, it ... it's virtually seethrough now!' Samantha looks desperately at her reflection in the mirror. Frantically she pulls the sheer fabric away from her chest.

Tilting my head to one side, I pretend to examine the situation in the mirror. 'Maybe you could just pop home and change?' I suggest. 'I'm sure Brian will let you back in, if you give a little tap on the door when you get back, that is. Ooops, sorry – did I say *tap*?'

And now, as I finish telling Roxi the whole sorry tale, I cover my face with my hands in shame. 'Oh God, Rox, I can't believe I did that. I don't know what came over me.'

'Is that it?' Roxi smiles in amusement. 'I thought you'd flushed her head down the toilet or something. Blimey, us girls did a lot worse to each other at the school I went to. Where did you go to school, Darcy, Miss Prim and Proper's Academy for delightful young gals?' she grins. But when she fails to raise a smile from me, she continues: 'You're right, though, it doesn't sound like you. Maybe you're just under a lot of pressure right now, with this whole island thing?'

I nod. 'But it's still no excuse. My aunt Molly always used to say if you do something bad, something bad will happen to you, and vice-versa – doing good will bring equal good. Karma, it's called. Samantha will make my life hell now at work, after that little stunt. Maybe I should just go and live on the island after all.'

Roxi picks up her mug of tea. 'What's stopping you from going, anyway? If that was me, I'd be over there like a shot.'

'No you wouldn't. You'd be having the same dilemma I am. How am I going to cope over there for a year without all this?' I gesture round at the flat. 'And how will I cope without you?'

'Darce, you'll be just fine. You don't need me to hold your hand any more. I think I might have been doing that a little bit too long now, anyway. Maybe it's time you stepped out on your own. You can do this, you know it's what you really want inside here,' and she points an electric-blue fingernail towards my heart.

'I suppose ...'

'No "suppose" about it. You go to this island and make it up to your aunt, then after the year is up you can live the dream, do what you want with your life. I'll be fine here, watching over our little pad, until that day comes. I know she must have meant a lot to you, Darce, from what you've been telling me just lately.'

'Yes, yes ... she did.'

'There you go, then.' Roxi places her mug purposefully back down on the table and tries to tuck her ebony legs underneath what little fabric her dressing gown is made of. Roxi wears just about everything in miniature. 'Just go ahead and do it, as Mr Nike says.'

'You know, Roxi, I don't think there is a Mr Nike. Nike was the Greek goddess of victory. I think that's where the name comes from.'

'See, I told you you went to a better class of school than me,' Roxi says, grinning. 'I know nothing about history, completely bored the pants off me at school. Now, I'm going back to bed. I work evenings in that pit of a pub so I can snooze in my bed all morning, not be up playing agony aunt to you at some ungodly hour.'

'You work in that pub because you like getting chatted up by all the blokes,' I remind her. 'The lie-ins are just an added bonus.'

Roxi pretends to consider this while she yawns and stretches. 'There is that,' she admits, climbing up from the sofa. 'I'm not immune to the male of the species in its finer forms.'

'In any form, in my experience,' I mock.

'Darcy McCall, I shall take that as a slight on my good Gospel upbringing, and take immediately to my bed. Even if it probably is true,' she says, winking as she exits the room.

I watch Roxi saunter off in her pink fluffy slippers, and I think again how much I'll miss her if I go to live on the island. Roxi has been my best friend since getting my first magazine job, and leaving all my other friends behind in the small town in Kent where I grew up. We too had met in a pub, when I'd nearly got into a fight, accidentally knocking a girl's vodka and coke all over her. The girl was part of a biker gang who were in the pub that night, but luckily for me Roxi knew the leader and managed to calm the situation. She came to my rescue that night, and we've been friends ever since. But she's right, maybe now's the time to move on with my life, to put right some wrongs, balance the karma out. Or is that the other thing, yin and yang? The system where, when something bad happens, something good has to come along to balance it out?

I pick up Roxi's mug and my glass to take them through to the kitchen, but in the early-morning silence I hear a drip, drip, dripping sound.

'What the . . .?' I ask, looking around me.

Drip drip drip. There it is again. But where is it coming from?

I follow the sound out into the tiny hall and immediately spy a huge grey damp patch bulging through the plaster above. From it every now and then tiny droplets of water are plopping down onto the table beside the front door. The unopened envelopes containing my credit-card bills are doing a great job of soaking up all the water. *At least you're good for something*, I think as I watch the ink becoming more and more smudged the wetter they get.

I move underneath the grey bulge so I can take a better look. It's as if our ceiling has filled itself, for its own amusement, like a huge grey water balloon. But as tiny bits of plaster begin to join the droplets still dripping from above, I realise that our ceiling has chosen me as its first target, because suddenly the balloon above me pops and gallons of lukewarm water begin to cascade down over my head in a strange cocktail of plaster, paint and bubble bath.

'Roxi!' I scream at the top of my voice. 'Get in here, quick!'

And as I stand there, soaking wet, looking up at the new water feature our ceiling has suddenly provided us with, I hear Roxi's voice next to me exclaim: 'Wowie, Darce, you were right about that karma stuff . . . it doesn't waste much time, does it?'

Seven

'You want me to get in *that*?' I peer hesitantly at the little red motorboat bobbing about below me as it patiently awaits its final passenger.

'Sure, Darcy, it'll be fine.' Niall is already sitting down inside the boat wearing a red cagoule and a bright orange life jacket that completely swamps him.

The other passenger on the boat stares up at me, a bored expression on his face. 'Look, is she getting in or not?' he asks, turning to Niall.

'Of course she is. Come on, Darcy,' Niall says encouragingly, beckoning to me. 'This is the only way of getting across to the island right now.'

'It's just that I remember the boat being bigger when I was a child.' I hug my life jacket tightly to my chest. 'This one seems so tiny. Are you sure it's safe to take it across there today? Those waves look awfully big.'

The skipper of the boat, who is patiently waiting to untie it from the harbour, smiles at me kindly. 'I've ferried many a boat across to that island in my time, and this one's quite safe. Plus,' he says looking up at the sky, 'this'll be a calm day on the water – especially for January.'

I smile at him, grateful for his words of encouragement. He seems awfully young, though; usually the skippers of these boats are gnarly old men with brown, wrinkled skin and gappy teeth. Maybe we should have got someone with a bit more experience to take us across. This guy, while cute-looking with his sandy blond hair and bright blue eyes, looks like he'd know more about handling a modelling contract than a motorboat. Now that I've finally agreed to sail across to this island today, I at least want to be in a boat with someone who looks as if they know what they're doing.

Yes: fate, karma, or whatever you want to call it has taken a hand in helping to make my visit to the island today a lot easier to achieve. The new water feature in our flat turned out to be the result of our upstairs neighbour leaving his bath running while going back to bed and nodding off to sleep again. So while our landlord is arguing with the workmen over quotes and prices to get everything patched up, Roxi and I have decided that temporarily vacating our flat is preferable to trying to avoid glancing upwards and spotting parts of Mr Jenkinson that we really don't want to see as he wanders about his flat in just his dressing gown. Roxi is staying in a room over the pub, and I'm kipping on Sophie's rather uncomfortable sofa. So my pre-planned weekend spent in a proper bed in an Irish hotel has come as quite a welcome bonus.

'Right, I'm getting out if she's not getting in,' Niall's boating companion says, standing up inside the boat so that it rocks enough for Niall to need to hold on to the side.

'No, don't do that! I'm coming, really. I just need to change my shoes.'

Reaching down, I pull off my favourite pair of flat pumps and take a pair of UGG boots from my rucksack.

'Why is she putting on slippers?' I hear him ask Niall as he sits back down in the boat again.

'They're not slippers,' I call to him. 'They're UGG boots, actually. And they'll keep my feet nice and warm while we're over there.'

'They might keep you warm, but I doubt they'll keep you dry,' the passenger mutters, shaking his head. 'Have you any idea of the terrain over on that island?'

'Look ... Miss?' the boatman interrupts us.

'Darcy. Just call me Darcy, please.'

'Conor,' he says by way of introduction, as a set of perfect white teeth now appear, matching the rest of his faultless façade. 'Look, Darcy, why don't the two gentlemen do what they're supposed to do and actually act like gentlemen by helping you down into the boat, and then we can be on our way? We need to catch the tide. You don't want to get stranded over on the island if the weather takes a turn for the worse, now do you?'

That's the last thing I want to happen. Gingerly, I take a step down into the boat and my two fellow passengers help steady me while I get my sea legs.

As I pull on my life jacket (which you'd think they'd do in at least one other colour than bright orange), Conor expertly unties the boat, hops aboard and we set sail for the island.

Nervously, I sit opposite Niall and the other chap he has brought with him on the hard wooden benches that line the sides of the boat. When I'd been introduced to him earlier, Dermot O'Connell – Niall's builder friend – had informed me in no uncertain terms that he'd rather be referred to as a 'project manager'. Surreptitiously I eye him, sitting huddled beneath his waterproof coat and life jacket that he can barely get done up. Not because he's overweight, far from it: Dermot's more what you would call *solid*. Muscle probably accrued from years of working on building sites, if what Niall's told me is anything to go by. At first glance I'd assumed he was fairly old, too – well, middle-aged, at least. But now, on closer inspection, I decide he's probably somewhere in his mid-thirties. It's his general demeanour that prematurely ages him, I decide; that and his jet-black hair that's just starting to go grey around the edges.

'Niall here tells me you might be the new owner of the island, Darcy,' Conor calls from the front of the boat as he expertly steers it out to sea.

I glare at Niall. 'Possibly,' I call back up the boat. 'Nothing's really been decide yet.'

'She's a beautiful island. Do you know what you might want to do with her?'

'Not really, no ... like I said, nothing's definite yet. That's kind of why I'm going over there today, to take a look.'

'Ah, well, she's not in her prime in January,' Conor continues as he steers the boat in the direction of the island. 'Now, if you were here in the springtime when the snowdrops first bloom across the valley, or in summer, when the sun sets beyond the hills in deep, blood-crimson red. Or even in autumn, when the leaves on the trees turn more shades of brown than—'

'But she's not, is she?' Dermot interrupts. 'She's here today, so she's got to look at the island as it is now, not in some sort of poet's dreamland.'

'So you'd be a practical man?' Conor asks, turning back briefly to look at Dermot. 'And an English one, too.'

'I am a practical man, yes.' From under the peak of his baseball cap Dermot's dark brown eyes watch Conor without expression. 'And proud of it. But I don't see that being English has anything to do with it. And for your information I'm half Irish, actually, on my father's side.'

I stare at Dermot. That explains his name, but lack of accent.

'Practical men don't see the colours, the landscape, the poetry of the land,' Conor continues unperturbed. 'They see buildings and cables and ways to improve.'

'And what's wrong with—'

'Look, guys,' I interrupt before this goes any further. I'd much rather Conor just concentrated on his driving. *Do you drive a boat? Or is it steer, or some other nautical term I don't know?* 'I'm simply going over today to scatter my aunt Molly's ashes and to take a look at the island she lived on as a child. Any other decisions I have to make about the island's future, or my own, will be made after I've done that, OK?'

'Fine by me,' Dermot shrugs, pulling the peak of his baseball cap further down over his eyes. He folds his arms and returns to his study of the sea.

Conor turns around to wink at me. 'Fair play, Darcy, you obviously know your own mind. I'll just do my job and get you safely across to see Tara.'

'Tara? Who's Tara?' I ask in confusion. 'Niall, I thought you said the island was uninhabited?'

Niall shrugs and holds out his hands.

'That it is,' Conor calls from the helm of the boat again. 'Tara is what us locals call her. Glentara is the island's proper name, and Tara is like a nickname.'

'Oh, right, so no one actually lives there?'

'No one but old Eamon.'

'Eamon?'

'He's been on the island for years; he's like part of the landscape, is Eamon – you'll never get him off.'

'I believe he's a sort of caretaker,' Niall explains. 'I think your aunt paid him to look after the island.'

Conor laughs. 'I'd like to have seen her try and get him away from it.'

We're getting closer to land now, so I lean back against the sides of the boat to get a better view of the approaching island. As always, the wind has been playing havoc with my hair since before we left the shore. I'd been sensible enough to tie it back in a band before leaving the harbour, but even so I still have stray bits flying all around my face as I try to take a closer look at the place I'm expected to call home for the next year.

At first sight, it's much larger than I thought it would be – the internet said 1,100 acres – though I'm not really sure how big an acre actually is. And as we sail still closer, I have to admit the island does look quite pretty, silently watching us approach in our little red boat. I can see crumbling buildings dotted up on the side of one of the hills, and as we near land and I can begin to appreciate all the varied colours of the island's landscape, I'm suddenly reminded of an Irish country song, 'Forty Shades of Green' my aunt used to play on the old record player in her house.

As we pull into a makeshift harbour, and I watch Conor leap effortlessly off the boat clutching a rope, something weird stirs inside me. It's almost like another memory, but I don't know what it is I'm trying to remember.

'So how long will you be wanting on the island?' Conor asks, tying the rope securely to a rickety-looking wooden platform.

I'm about to say that half an hour will give me time enough to scatter Molly's ashes, when I hear Niall say two hours. *Two whole hours!* The trip over in the boat was cold enough, but at least I'd had the life jacket on to keep me a bit warmer. Now as I unzip that and leave it behind in the boat, the wind that is blowing in off the sea is biting right into me. I could do with a nice caramel macchiato to warm me up. But I doubt they'd have much call for a Starbucks around here.

'You'll be a bit warmer once you get away from the water,' Conor says, reading my mind. 'That wind's coming in right off the sea just now. The sun will be out in about fifteen minutes – she'll soon warm you up.'

I look up at the sky, but I can see only dense grey cloud. No hopeful breaks appear in it at all to suggest that there might be some sunshine up there to warm us up at any time today, let alone in the next quarter of an hour.

I zip my Nike puffa jacket all the way to the top, wishing now I'd worn my Burberry earmuffs, or even that fake-fur hat I can never find an occasion to wear.

Conor appears to be the only one of the boat party not

feeling the cold. As he unzips his life jacket he remains in his jeans, boots and thick Aran sweater. 'I'll meet you back here at about one o'clock, then?' he says, glancing at his watch.

'Cheers, Conor,' Niall replies. 'That'll be grand.'

'So this is it?' Dermot slowly turns around as I watch Conor disappear over a hill, a fishing rod slung over his shoulder. 'Where do you want to start, Darcy?'

'I'm not sure . . . what about this way?' It all looks the same to me at the moment. After I'd talked myself into visiting the island, I'd got my hopes up that once I arrived I'd completely fall in love with the place, know exactly why Molly wanted me to come here and never want to leave. But now I'm here, it's just all a bit green, cold and kind of lonely-looking. I point vaguely in the opposite direction to the one in which Conor has departed, and we set off along a rocky path together looking a bit like Dorothy, the Scarecrow and the Tin Man as we wind our way along Glentara's own equivalent to the Yellow Brick Road.

I certainly feel as conspicuous as Dorothy, with short, mousy-haired Niall on one side of me, and six-foot, dark-haired Dermot on the other. Talk about chalk and cheese: you couldn't get two more different men. And as we follow the paths around the island, it's not unlike being in a fairy tale, with wild animals jumping out at us whichever way we turn. Huge, dark birds appear out of the sky as if from nowhere. They're not like the little sparrows and the occasional robin I come across when I put out breadcrumbs on our window ledge in London, that flutter away in fright at the mere sight of a human. Oh, no – these are huge great noisy things that swoop down on us from the cliffs, not seeming to care in the least that we're guests on their island.

'What on earth was *that*?' I ask, jumping in fright when something shoots across our path into the undergrowth.

'I think it was a rabbit.' Niall peers into the bush where the creature has just disappeared.

'Living out here?' I exclaim, immediately thinking of the cute, fluffy little bunnies you see in pet shops. 'Poor things.'

Dermot snorts. 'Actually they *can* manage to look after themselves outside of a hutch! That's unless a fox decides it wants rabbit stew for dinner. Anyway I don't think that was a rabbit, it was too big and too fast; it was probably a hare.'

I eye Dermot for a moment, but decide not to respond. I need him on side right now, because for all his brusqueness he's turning out to be worth his weight in gold for practical information as we walk around the island.

'Right then,' Dermot demands, as we stop at some derelict buildings that Niall informs us were once islanders' cottages. 'Where do you think you'll live while you're here, Darcy?'

'Er . . .'

'If you intend on rebuilding one of these cottages, it won't be that hard to set you up a power and water supply for one person. In fact, it's quite simple. You—'

'Wait.' I stop him. I look at Niall. 'Niall wasn't quite telling you the truth when he told you that I need to equip the island for only me to come and live here.'

I turn back to Dermot.

He raises an eyebrow. 'He wasn't?'

'No, but he wasn't exactly lying, either,' I add hurriedly when Dermot glares at Niall. Dermot is such a huge chap, and

I hope he isn't a violent one too. 'And you really have been so helpful this morning, Dermot, that it seems only fair I tell you the *real* reason we're all here today.'

Dermot glances nervously around him, as though half a dozen cameras are suddenly going to spring up out of the undergrowth. Happy for the moment that Ant and Dec aren't about to leap from behind a rock clasping microphones and informing him he's going out live on ITV1, he turns his full attention to me while I try to explain to him as quickly as I can the truth about why I'm really here.

When I'm finished, Dermot eyes me suspiciously.

'She's telling the truth, Dermot,' Niall says, hurrying forward to back me up. 'I'm her solicitor.'

I smile at Niall. So he's *my* solicitor as well, now?

Dermot, happy for the time being that he's not the butt of some national practical joke, eyes the two of us warily. 'That makes a bit more sense to me now. You don't look like the type of woman that chooses to come and live somewhere like this of her own accord.'

I'm not sure whether to be pleased or offended by his comment.

'What makes you say that?'

Dermot stares pointedly at my UGG boots, which I have to say after our walk around the island are now looking quite the worse for wear. Even though we'd stuck mainly to the paths, it had been a lot muddier than I'd anticipated and now, instead of the lovely caramel colour they started out this morning, they resemble more of a dirty chocolate with extra grass stain detailing that doesn't usually come as standard on UGGs.

Thank goodness I hadn't worn one of my best pairs!

'Yes, well, perhaps I did underestimate how wet it might be underfoot, but that doesn't affect whether I go ahead and eventually come and live here.'

So just what sort of shoes do *you wear here, then, if UGGs aren't any good? Oh – I saw some nice designer wellies on Net-a-Porter the other day. But I couldn't wear them every day for a whole year …*

'So why *have* you brought me here today?' Dermot asks, interrupting my shoe dilemma. He's beginning to look irritated now, and is standing with his arms folded across his incredibly wide chest.

Quickly I debate whether to try a technique I've seen Roxi put to good use many a time with men. It had worked on Niall in the pub, but Niall is a bit different to Dermot.

'Niall suggested your many skills and vast knowledge of the building trade would mean you are just the right person to help me make a final decision on whether I definitely want to come here or not.' I smile up at him in what I hope is a coy manner. 'With all your technical expertise, you're obviously a man of many talents, Dermot.' Again, just like with Niall I stop at fluttering my eyelashes. Roxi seems able to get away with it, but she's Roxi.

A pair of astute dark eyes watch me for a few seconds before their owner decides to reply. 'Flattery, Miss McCall, will get you precisely nowhere with me. However, you have correctly recognised that yes, I do have a certain amount of expertise in this field. Now I suggest you start by telling me *exactly* what it is you propose to do here on this island, *if* you choose to stay, and then I can begin to get a better idea of the project as a whole, and start to advise you appropriately.'

Dermot and I discuss my aunt's requests. He wants to know things like how I'd like to run water and power supplies to the island, and how I'd like to house people once they're over here. And he asks the all-important question: just how much money I've got to spend on the project.

Isn't that what you're here for, to help me answer all these sorts of things? I think as I try to give intelligent-sounding responses to his questions. It soon becomes apparent to Dermot that he's pretty much wasting his time when he's in the middle of explaining to Niall and me in great detail how simple the process of getting water to any future dwellings on the island would be. His mistake is in beginning his explanation by using the word 'physics', which like maths is a no-go area for me, and my mind quickly begins to wander.

'...So it all works by gravity,' Dermot explains. 'Rainwater collects up in a lake in the mountains over there, then runs down off the side through in-cuts that the original islanders would have made. 'Can you see it, Darcy?'

I look up to where he's pointing, and in the distance see a thin trickle of water twisting and turning down the hill. 'Oh, yes.'

'So what you would do is simply intercept the water at the lake before it runs down the hill using pipes of reducing sizes to aid the gravity flow, and make the pressure of the water strong enough for everyday use.'

I think I'm supposed to be impressed by Dermot's explanation.

'We can actually have things like running water and heat, then, if we rebuild these old cottages that were here before?'

Dermot stares at me for a moment, then addresses his next

remark to Niall. 'Haven't I just stood here and explained all that to the two of you?'

'Yes, yes you have, Dermot, and if I may say so, very thoroughly and in *great* detail.' Niall gives me a little nudge with his elbow.

'Sorry, Dermot,' I apologise. 'I don't think I'm really cut out for the technical side of things, as you so rightly pointed out a few minutes ago.'

Dermot nods in agreement. 'Yes, indeed. Look, perhaps you'd best just go and pay your last respects before it's time to head back.' He gestures to the backpack on my shoulders, which contains the urn. 'Will you be all right on your own, or do you want one of us to come with you?'

'That's kind of you, but I'll be fine, thanks. You stay here with Niall; he'll be much better at answering your questions than me.'

Because of the weather, we've stayed mostly inland on our walking tour of the island, but now as I leave Niall and Dermot and walk further out towards the headland I see that, inexplicably, Conor was right. The sun has now escaped from its cloudy prison and shines brightly down onto the grass and rocks around me, warming not only the colours of the landscape, but my feelings towards it too. Breathing in the fresh sea air, which I have to admit does make quite a nice change from the heavy pollution of the city, I pick up a narrow coastal path that weaves its way along the edge of Glentara Island.

Now what was it Conor had said the locals called it? Ah yes, just Tara.

After a while, I pause briefly to take a look out over the clear unobscured view that the sun is now allowing me. From this side of the island I can no longer see the mainland, or any other land for that matter. Only a vast, never-ending sea constantly rolling its huge waves in towards Tara's giant craggy rock faces, which then in turn buffet them right back out to sea again, like a rhythmical game of wet tennis. The crowd is made up of a flock of noisy gulls who hover above, waiting for a stray ball, or more likely fish, to be thrown up out of the waves.

I turn around to take another look at the island behind me. We've managed to explore enough of it this morning even for me to recognise that although the island may seem lonely and abandoned at first sight, it's exceptionally beautiful too. But to live here for a whole year ... now that is another thing entirely. I know from what Niall's explained to me that Molly's provided a generous budget to set the island up with decent housing and basic amenities; I haven't exactly got to camp in a tent and cook over an open fire while I'm here, and even if I don't last a whole year on the island I'm not obliged to pay any of that initial money back to the estate. But I'm so used to living in a city where there are people and mobile phones and the internet. In London, everything is right on your doorstep when you want it. What will I do when I want to pop out for a manicure, or a Krispy Kreme doughnut?

I shake my head. No, this is not the time for that now. I've got more important things to attend to. Turning back to face out to sea again, I shrug my Nike rucksack loose from my shoulders and carefully unzip the main compartment. Then gently I remove the little wooden casket that I have been carrying with me since we left the mainland.

When Niall said he had my aunt's ashes in his office with him, I'd imagined a huge black urn sitting on his desk like you see in the movies. But when he'd presented it to me today, it was just a plain wooden box. Apparently it was my aunt's request; she wanted something that would simply biodegrade back into the natural habitat, and the wood that was used to make the box had to be from a sustainable forest.

'You certainly knew just what you wanted, Aunt Molly,' I say out loud, the words barely out of my mouth before they're whisked away by the wind and immediately carried out to sea. 'And not just about this, either.'

'That she certainly did,' I hear a voice reply. The shock of which almost makes me follow my words down the cliff and into the sea below.

'Whoa, steady there,' the voice says again, and I feel a strong hand on my arm pulling me away from the cliff edge.

Spinning around, I see a pair of cornflower-blue eyes, set deep within a weather-beaten face, gazing back steadily into my own wide eyes.

'Thanks,' I free myself from his grip and stand back to face him properly. 'So, you knew my aunt?'

Now the man has moved a little further away from me, I notice that unlike me he is dressed in faded neutral clothes that blend well with the colours of the land. This is in complete contrast with my attempt at island chic – True Religion skinny jeans, a white DKNY hoody, silver Nike puffa jacket and my now mud-stained UGG boots.

'Yes, I knew her. A fine lady, so she was. I had no idea what had happened until I got her letter the other day.'

'Letter?' I'm intrigued by this. 'What letter?'

The man rummages inside the pocket of his tweedy jacket and pulls out two crumpled sheets of paper. 'A Mr Niall

Kearney sent it to me.' He squints at the top of the first page. 'No glasses on me,' he explains. 'It says she requested I be sent this letter when she passed on.' He pauses to cross himself. 'Unfortunately I didn't receive it until I got all my other mail and provisions last week. I get everything late over here, see? Otherwise I'd have made the effort to come across to pay my last respects.'

'Of course,' I nod, wondering what else my aunt had said in the letter. She seemed to have been very organised before she died.

'I'm guessing you must be Darcy.'

'Yes, that's right, and you must be Eamon.' I feel a bit awkward standing there as he appears to inspect me. Maybe the silver jacket was a bit much. But it hadn't seemed like it in the shop. I'd bought it to go skiing – well, technically I wasn't actually going skiing this year, but you never know: I might get offered the chance.

'That's me, Eamon Murphy.' He moves his battered old walking stick to his left hand and holds out his right for me to shake. 'I look after Tara. Your aunt said in her letter you'd probably be over for a visit.'

'Did she?' I ask, shaking his rough, bony hand.

My aunt seemed to have been able to predict an awful lot. I wonder how much Eamon knows about everything else, though? Niall mentioned she'd employed this Eamon for a number of years to take care of the island, but it seems now they may have been more like friends.

'Is that what I think it is?' Eamon asks, nodding at the wooden box still clasped tightly in my hands.

'It is, yes.'

'Do you mind if I stay? Pay my last respects to Molly now, since I wasn't at the funeral?'

'Of course, Eamon, please do.'

Eamon steps back a few paces, removes his cap and smooths down his white hair.

Rather clumsily, I turn and look back out to sea. I hold out the box in front of me, trying desperately to think of what to say. But I've never done anything like this before, and having Eamon looking over my shoulder really isn't helping much either.

I turn back to him. 'Do you have anything you'd like to say, Eamon? It's just I'm not really very good at this sort of thing.'

'Neither am I,' he says, shuffling back closer to the cliff edge.

'Don't you know some sort of Irish send-off, perhaps – like a blessing?'

Eamon thinks for a moment. 'I know some traditional toasts, but you really need a bottle of the "little green man" for those to work.'

'Little green man?'

'That'd be a bottle of Jameson's whiskey to you. You know, they're drinking toasts.'

'Oh, I see. Are any of them appropriate?'

He thinks for a moment. 'Not really.' But then a fond smile breaks out across his tanned face. 'You know something, Darcy, I might just have the perfect one.'

'Are you sure?'

He nods. 'Now, are you ready with the box?'

'Yes.' I hold it up again and take a deep breath. This is so difficult; there's so much I want to say, but I just don't know where to begin. I wish that the box I keep buried deep within myself could be opened up just as easily as the one I'm holding in front of me right now. 'Goodbye, Aunt Molly, I know this is what you wanted – to spend the rest of your days here on this island, on Tara – and I hope you find peace and happiness at being back here once again.'

I open up the box and shake my aunt free again into the wind. And just like my words, she is immediately swept up and cast away into the clear blue sky, soaring around the island for ever more, like one of the gulls that hover over the sea below us.

As I perform her request, I hear Eamon begin to speak:

May the Irish hills caress you.
May her lakes and rivers bless you.
May the luck of the Irish enfold you.
May the blessings of Saint Patrick behold you.

We both watch in silence for a moment, each of us caught up in our own personal memories of one Emmeline Ava Aisling McCall.

I turn to Eamon.

'That was absolutely perfect. Thank you.'

'So was she, Darcy,' he says, his voice trembling. And as I look into Eamon's eyes, I'm surprised to see they're swimming with tears. 'So was she.'

Eight

Later that evening we're back on the mainland again, sitting in the bar of the local pub we're all staying in. Dermot and I have pints of Guinness in front of us, and Niall is nursing a medicinal brandy after he found the return crossing in the boat a little choppy for his stomach.

'So then, Darcy,' Dermot asks, coming straight to the point as always. 'Have you come to a decision?'

After Eamon and I had cast my aunt's ashes adrift into the strong sea surrounding Tara, we'd headed back down to the rickety little jetty to meet up again with the others. While we'd been walking back to the boat together, Eamon had informed me that he'd lived on Tara virtually all his life, but for the past few years or so much of that had been spent alone. His only contact with the outside world had been his occasional visits to the mainland for necessities such as medical appointments and to pick up essential supplies.

Eamon and Dermot hadn't exactly hit it off when they'd

been introduced; especially when Dermot started telling Eamon how it would be easy to improve the water and power supplies on the island. I didn't want Eamon to start worrying that his peaceful life on Tara might be ruined for ever if I went to live there, so I'd quickly herded my party back down into the little red boat again. There was no point in upsetting anyone just yet, not until everything had been properly discussed and I'd finally decided what I was going to do.

I take a large gulp of my Guinness before answering Dermot's question. Have I come to a decision?

This should be easy: how can I turn down the chance to grant my aunt's last wishes and inherit much-needed money just because I have to suffer a bit of hardship for a year? I'd be mad to – wouldn't I? But now, after visiting Tara today, it has truly hit home how rural the island is. It's just so remote and removed from my usual life back in London. How will I survive living there day in, day out for a whole year?

Then after meeting Eamon, and learning just how much Tara meant to my aunt, my thoughts have been thrown into turmoil once again. I owe Molly for all those years of her life I missed out on. Those lost years, when I should have been there for her. For my aunt to have given me this chance – this huge responsibility – I must have meant more to her than I ever realised.

My mobile phone rings in my bag, breaking the tension around the table.

'Excuse me a moment,' I apologise to Niall and Dermot, grabbing my phone and heading for the door.

It's Roxi.

'*How* long?' I exclaim into the phone, as she informs me that the builders have found rot in the timber joists around our flat while they've been pricing up, and that now, instead of a few days of disruption, ours and Mr Jenkinson's flat above are going to have to be completely ripped apart and it will be weeks, possibly months before the flat is habitable again. Apparently this isn't the first time Mr Jenkinson's bath has overflowed.

'But hasn't Mohamed got another flat we can move into?'

'Apparently he's full right now. He says his brother's got a one-bedroom place out in Hackney you can have temporarily if that's any help, to save you kippin' on your mate's sofa. I'm all right in the room above the pub for now, but it seems our days of sharing are over for the time being, Darce.'

I sigh. I really don't like living alone, let alone in Hackney. Roxi and I have been so happy together in our little two-bedroom flat out in Wanstead; I should have known it wouldn't last for ever.

'Tell him thanks but no thanks, Rox. I think I've finally made up my mind about where I'm going to be living for the next year.'

'You're going for it, then! That's my girl!'

'Yes, but I'm so going to miss you.'

'I'll miss you too, honey, but perhaps this is fate's way of giving you that little push in the right direction.'

'Yes, I have made my decision,' I say with assurance, sitting back down at the table in front of Niall and Dermot when I've finished my call with Roxi. I look confidently between the two men, even though my insides are telling a different tale.

Niall leans forward, eagerly awaiting the next words to leave my lips. Wearing jeans, a white shirt and navy-blue v-neck jumper, he's looks much more casual today than the last time we sat in a pub together. He rests his elbows on the table in front of him. Dermot lounges back in his seat, not appearing at all bothered about what I might be going to say.

'And,' I announce in dramatic fashion, even though on the inside I'm a lot less confident. 'I'm going to do it. I'm going to go and live on the island of Tara for a whole year.'

'*Yes*!' I hear Niall shriek. Blushing, he lowers his raised fist back to the table again. He hurriedly looks about him in case anyone in the pub has seen.

'Are you sure?' Dermot asks, after he's finished rolling his eyes at Niall. 'There's a lot more to this than meets the eye.'

'What would *you* do in my position, then?' This is all I need, someone throwing doubt balls to knock me back again when I've just made up my mind.

'I'd do it, of course. But then I'm not you.'

'What's that supposed to mean?

'Just look at you, for one thing.' Dermot casts his eyes over me with disdain.

I give him a look of equal contempt. 'I hope you're not suggesting that it's because I'm a woman that I might have a problem in taking on this challenge? Because I may have labelled you many things since we met earlier, Dermot, but a chauvinist certainly wasn't one of them.'

Dermot doesn't seem particularly offended by my comment. 'No, I'm not suggesting that at all. It's not the fact that you *are* a woman, Darcy, it's the *type* of woman you are. Just look at you, with your false nails and your designer labels! You won't last five minutes out there on that island without a beauty parlour, tanning salon or fashion boutique within a five-mile radius.'

I straighten the sleeves of my Whistles jacket I'd changed into when we got back from the island earlier. He has the cheek to comment on the way I look, sitting there looking like an advert for Lumberjacks R Us in his baggy jeans, brown boots and checked cotton shirt. I eye Dermot for a moment before I reply.

'First,' and I hold out my hand for him to inspect, 'my nails aren't fake, they're real. Second, I hardly think what I'm wearing today constitutes designer labels – for your information it was all bought on the high street. And third and most important, how could you possibly know the type of person I am? We've only just met today.'

'Oh, I know,' he says with a smug smile, not bothering to look at my outstretched hand.

I close my hand into a fist, and resisting the crazy urge to use it, slowly I bring it back towards my body. 'I see.'

'I mean,' Dermot continues, 'it's been quite obvious from today that you wouldn't have the first idea about how to set up even the most basic of supplies for a community of people to survive out there on that island.'

'No, I have to agree with you there,' I say, nodding my head slowly. 'You're quite right. I don't have any idea about those sorts of things.'

Dermot smiles contentedly to himself while he sips happily on his pint.

'But you do. Which is why, Dermot, I'd like you to be my project manager for the island. And not only that,' I continue to speak while I watch Dermot's face change from satisfaction to surprise, 'I'm really going to need someone on site to help me manage this project for the whole year I'm there. After all, as you've so rightly pointed out, what am I going to know about maintaining technical things like water and power supplies, and what to do if they go wrong? Which is why I'd like you to be one of the community of people living on the island with me. What do you say, Dermot? Are you up for the challenge, or are you worried you might break a nail?'

I hear Niall giggle from the other side of the table, but I don't let my eyes waver from Dermot's.

Dermot, recovering his composure, simply sits back in his chair again.

'I'm up for a challenge,' he says coolly, picking up his pint again. '*If* the price is right.'

I'm surprised at how quickly Dermot agrees. After the amount of time it's taken me to decide whether I'm going to go and live there, he's hardly had a chance to think about it. 'Money is not an issue. Is it, Niall?' I say, quickly glancing across at him for back-up.

Niall shakes his head.

'Good. Then it looks like you've just hired yourself a project manager, Miss McCall.' Dermot holds out his hand and we shake on it. 'I just hope you know what you're doing.'

'I'm sure I won't regret hiring you, Dermot,' I say, deliberately ignoring his jibe. 'I'm sure you'll do just fine.'

Over a few more rounds of drinks we begin to thrash out some of the technical difficulties Dermot can foresee in setting up an island as a habitable place for a community to live on for one year. It's hard not to drift off when he starts talking about things like bunded tanks for fuel storage. But when he starts comparing things like the costs involved in installing wind turbines and individual generators, my ears begin to take a bit more interest.

'*How* much?' I ask, aghast, already beginning to see my entire budget slipping away before I've even spent my first night on the island.

'On paper, the generator would appear to be the cheaper of the two in the short term,' Dermot explains. 'But environmentally your wind turbine is going to be the greener option in the long run.'

'I've got to make my island budget last a whole year, so we'd better go for the generators.'

Dermot shrugs. 'You're the boss. Obviously at the moment this is all just guesswork on my part. I'll have to draw you up a proper plan with all the individual costings and projections for you to agree on, before any work is begun for real over there.'

'How long do you think it will take before the island is habitable?' Niall asks.

I look over at him. He's been strangely silent up until now.

Dermot makes the tradesman's favourite noise – a sharp intake of breath. 'Ooh, now that's a difficult thing to pin down. It's an unusual project, this …'

'A ball-park figure, Dermot. I mean, how will Darcy be able to advertise for people to come and live on Tara if she can't give them a rough idea of when they can move into their new homes?'

I've not even thought about that. How on earth am I going to persuade fifteen people to come and live on this island? I'm not exactly brimming with enthusiasm at the thought of it myself, so how am I going to persuade others it's a great idea?

'A few months, maybe, if I'm allowed enough manpower to complete all the work, and of course if the weather is kind to us.'

'So April, then?' Niall suggests hopefully.

Dermot nods. 'Mmm, maybe, for the project to be complete – but like I said, it depends on many things. There should be some proper accommodation up and running well before then, though, if you should want to come across earlier to oversee things, Darcy?' He grins.

'I'll bear that in mind, thanks, Dermot.' I smile tightly. But springtime sounds like a much more pleasant season in which to begin this experience than winter, so I doubt I'll be taking up his offer.

Eventually we finish up our discussions for the evening and head off to bed.

Dermot's bedroom is the first door we come to along the corridor, so Niall and I bid him goodnight and continue down the hallway towards our own rooms.

As we arrive at my room, I pause outside the door.

'Are you OK, Niall?' I ask, my hand poised over the door handle. 'It's just that you've been a bit quiet since we came back from the island.'

Niall manages a half-smile. 'It's kind of you to notice, Darcy, but I'm just fine.' He thinks for a moment. 'You know, I'm so pleased you've decided to respect your aunt's wishes in this way.'

'Come on, Niall,' I encourage, suspecting this to be a

deliberate attempt to change the subject. 'I know there's something bothering you.'

Niall looks up from where he's been inspecting the pattern on the hotel carpet for the last few seconds. 'You really want to know?'

'Of course I do, or I wouldn't have asked.'

Niall's blue-grey eyes blink steadily back into mine. 'I'm jealous.'

'You're *jealous*? Jealous of what?'

'Of you. Of Dermot.'

'But why?'

'Because I'd love to get the chance to go and live on the island too, Darcy. That's why I was so keen for you to take up the opportunity. It was just so beautiful on Tara today,' Niall's whole face lights up as he remembers. 'I've only ever lived in towns and cities all my life, but I've always longed to breathe in the fresh clean air every day, to get my hands dirty in God's earth, to do something more physical than push a pen across a piece of paper.'

'But what about being a solicitor?' I'm astonished by Niall's revelation. 'It's your family business.'

'Yes, I know,' Niall hangs his head, 'and that's what makes it worse. But I never really wanted to do this; it's just what was expected of me, to take up the family trade. So that's what I did, without even questioning it.'

'But if you're not happy, Niall . . . '

'But who is these days, Darcy? I mean, who is truly happy when you ask them?'

I've a feeling there may be times when I'll struggle occasionally over the next year . . .

'But you, Darcy, you've been given this fantastic opportunity to break free. You're so lucky. And now even Dermot gets to tag along too – lucky bas— I mean, so-and-so.' Niall blushes.

Niall's right, I'm being so ungrateful about this whole experience. I've been looking on it as an imposition rather than as a wonderful opportunity to do something new with my life. 'Well, why don't you, then?' I ask, without giving it a second thought.

'Why don't I what?'

'Tag along with us too. To the island. If that's what you really want.'

I probably should have given as much thought to my question as Niall gives to his answer.

'It's very kind of you to offer, Darcy,' he says, smiling. 'But I can't.'

'Why ever not?'

'For one, what would I tell my father? He'd be devastated if I just gave up on my career – the business is everything to him. And second, what do I have to offer you? It's obvious what Dermot's got to offer – you only have to look at him. But look at little old me, what use would I be on a remote island in the middle of nowhere?'

It's true; if Niall's thin body got too close to the edge of one of those cliffs, he might easily be blown over by even the smallest gust of wind. But he's been so good to me over the last few weeks, and I've been so tied up in making my own decisions, that I haven't appreciated his help at all. So if this is what he truly wants . . .

'Why not tell your father you're just taking a year out – like a gap year from university?' I suggest in a flash of inspiration.

'I bet you never had one of those. I bet you went straight from school to college to university to working in a solicitor's office.'

Niall nods. 'Yes, but—'

'No buts. If you really want to do this, Niall, then what's stopping you? You said yourself that your father's nearly recovered from his illness now. He owes you a break if you've been virtually running the business single-handed.' I waggle my finger sternly at him as he begins to interrupt again. 'And you can forget about your other excuse. How much use do you think *I'm* going to be out there on that island? We can learn together what it's all about, living that kind of life – I'm sure I'm going to make loads of mistakes along the way. And you can still help me manage all the financial side of things while you're over there, can't you? Probably better than if you were in Dublin.'

Niall considers this.

'Plus, I'm going to need someone on side to back me up when I have a clash of opinions with Dermot. Which, I'm afraid to say, might happen quite often if today's been anything to go by.'

Niall smiles at the last part of my little speech, and then returns to being serious again. 'I just don't know, Darcy,' he says, shaking his head.

'Please, Niall. I could do with a friend out there with me. Otherwise the only person I'm going to know will be Dermot.'

'Don't forget Eamon,' Niall is grinning now.

I roll my eyes. 'Thanks for that. A year on an island with Bob the Builder on growth hormones and Ireland's answer to Robinson Crusoe – that's going to be fun.'

Niall laughs now. 'You do make me smile, Darcy. Oh, go on

then, I'll do it. On one condition, though – that I can square it with my father.'

I throw my arms around him and give him a huge hug. Somehow the thought of having Niall there with me makes it all seem a lot less daunting.

'So now we are three,' I say, releasing him from my embrace. 'Only another twelve more to find . . .'

Nine

'Are you sure you need all this stuff?' Niall asks, eyeing up the back of the people-carrier once more as we drive along the narrow road down towards the harbour. 'I know we're going across there for a year, but will you actually wear it all?'

'It's not *all* clothes,' I keep my eyes firmly in front of me as I drive. These Irish roads are full of twists and turns, and I don't want to crash into a stray sheep wandering across the road. 'There's make-up, and beauty products in there too, and provisions.'

'What sort of provisions? We will be able to get food, you know, there'll be a regular boat going over to the mainland every week.'

Niall and I are travelling together on the final stage of our journey before we leave civilisation and go and live on the island for the year, and my stomach feels as if I'm about to get on one of those huge fairground rides that throw your insides all over the place and charge you for the pleasure.

In the few months that have whizzed by since I visited Tara with Dermot and Niall, so much has happened that I've barely been able to keep track of everything.

I returned to England, and the next morning promptly handed in my notice at *Goddess* magazine. I just dived straight in there before I had a chance to change my mind, and before Samantha had a chance to try and stir up trouble as a result of the water incident. I didn't tell any of the staff, including Jemima, what I was going to do – just that I had other plans for my future. And after the initial shock that I was leaving had died down, it didn't take everyone long to start discussing who might be promoted into my job. Not that I expected any more from them, but it was quite disappointing to think that my boss and her staff who I'd worked with for so long cared so little about the fact that I would no longer be a part of the *Goddess* team. Sophie was the only person I told the real reason, after I had to ask to stay at her flat a little longer, now that the old one was being pulled apart. There seemed little point in trying to rent a new one for a few weeks, and she, like Roxi, thought I was mad. Mad for even considering *not* doing it.

Dermot, after organising all the necessary equipment and manpower to be ferried over to the island, was now living there with the other men who were to work alongside him in one of the few houses that were fit for human habitation. On his return to the UK, he'd set to work immediately on a full-scale plan of action, and had been very thorough about keeping me up to date on everything by email, and occasionally with the odd phone call, before he left. But mostly I'd just OK'd everything, and left it all to him. I was quite happy that he knew what he was doing. I was more concerned about how I was going to pack enough clothes for a year. A lot of my stuff had gone into storage already, because Sophie didn't have enough room in her flat, so after many lists, shopping trips and nights surfing the internet, I'd finally settled on a wardrobe I felt would be appropriate for a year spent in remote, rural Ireland.

Of the three of us it was Niall who had the most trouble cutting the strings, especially with his father. But after several sessions of 'words', as Niall described them – rather than *arguments*, he proudly announced one day over the phone that he had been given a year's sabbatical from the solicitor's, and would be joining Dermot and me on the island in April. Niall then set about placing advertisements in all the national Irish newspapers – and some of the UK ones too – looking for people to come and help set up a new island community.

Do you long to live the GOOD LIFE?
Get away from it all and do something different?
Why not come and be a part of a new island community on the Isle of Glentara, off Ireland's beautiful west coast?
Interviews to be held in Dublin.
For an application form or for further details, please contact Darcy McCall or Niall Kearney

We decided not to mention the one-year legacy in all this. The only people who would know about that would be Dermot, Niall and me. After all, there was no reason why, if it all worked out, the others couldn't stay on after my year was over, if they so desired. I would make sure that whoever I sold the island to bought it as a going concern. It would be only me who would have a time scale built into my stay on Tara.

My part in all this preparation had been to surf the internet; more specifically, the social networking sites. I already had my own Facebook and Twitter pages, and so apart from setting up new pages to advertise both the island and my project, I'd been socialising like mad on them both, trying to find like-minded people who might be keen to try out island living for a year.

I wondered at first if we'd get any responses at all. I certainly didn't anticipate the enormous amount of messages and emails that poured in from willing volunteers, all desperate to be chosen to come and live on Tara. To be fair, a high percentage of them were from slightly odd types, who I wasn't sure about spending two minutes in a lift with, let alone a year living on an island. But Niall and I managed to sift through the cranks and loonies, and filter it down to the people we felt might be worth seeing.

The three of us held interviews in Dublin for all the lucky candidates, where we met people who were perfect for the island, and some who were not quite so perfect. Although who I considered the ideal person to spend a year on an island with was not Dermot's idea of ideal, and vice-versa. As usual, Niall chose to remain impartial throughout.

After the interviews, it seemed quite obvious to me who we should choose to come and share this experience with us. But, as always, Dermot had to make it difficult.

*

'But *why*?' I ask him over and over again as we sit around a table discussing our choices in the lounge of the hotel we've been holding our interviews in. 'What's wrong with them this time?' I glance at the application form Dermot is brandishing in his hand; attached is a photo of a cheerful-looking man with chubby cheeks.

'Just why is The Little Chef coming to Tara?' he asks, waving the form at me. 'Darcy, you need people over there who can work for a year to make this island as self-sufficient as possible, not eat all the profits before we've made any.'

I'm trying to remain calm, but this has been a long day, and it's fast turning into a very long and tortuous night. *Have I done the right thing in asking Dermot to come with us?* He seems to be causing a lot of trouble already, and this is before we've even got there. 'Dermot, we are not simply trying to pick people on a "who can work the hardest" basis, like they're some sort of human pack horse. We do have to live with these people for a whole year; we have to be able to get on with each other.'

Dermot stares at me for a few seconds, then shakes his head. 'I wondered how long it would take you to revert to type,' he says, dropping the pile of applications back down on the table. 'You've already forgotten all about the practical side of living out there on that island, in favour of this becoming some sort of Irish soap opera where we're all popping in and out of each other's houses for cups of tea and coffee every morning.'

'No I haven't!' I've lost my grip on the calmness now. 'I know exactly what we're trying to do here; I've got complete control over the situation. And don't you dare say I'm of a type. You have *no idea* what type of person I am, you … you barely *know* me!'

'Actually,' Dermot smirks, 'you're backing up my point pretty well right now.'

I glare at him, and swipe my drink up off the table.

Niall, using his best United Nations negotiation techniques, finally managed to reopen discussions again a few minutes later. But when the debate continued into the early hours of the next morning and we were still not getting anywhere, I felt I had to put my foot down.

'Dermot,' I'm trying to remain diplomatic. 'I've listened to your point of view, and yes, with a few of these people I can see that you have got a valid point. But,' I add, as that same triumphant expression begins to cross his face, 'with more than a few here, I can't see what your problem is. What, for instance, is your issue with Conor?'

The last person to enter the interview room that day had been Conor, the cute guy who had taken us across to the island in the motorboat on my first visit. He wasn't on our shortlist, but as Niall pointed out while we hastily got him to fill out an application form, someone local would know the island better than most, so we had decided to give him an interview.

'Thanks for giving me a shot,' Conor grins as he sits down in front of us. He looks very different to how I remember him from the boat, so much so that I almost mistake him for someone else. I'm not sure who, but for a split second I feel like I've met him before. Today Conor is clean-shaven, and is wearing a tight white t-shirt, clean jeans and brown Caterpillar boots. His wavy blond hair that was unruly and dishevelled before, today is kept under strict control by a dash of hair gel, and his short-sleeved shirt now allows a rather pleasant view of a pair of taught, tanned biceps that his Aran sweater, on our first visit back in January, had sadly kept a well-guarded secret. 'It was grand out there, waiting with everyone else who's wanting to come and live with us all on Tara.'

'You're a bit confident that you're going to be chosen,' Dermot says, raising an eyebrow. 'This *is* only an interview.'

'Of course, I'm sorry. I'm getting a bit ahead of myself. Ah, but if you don't have confidence in yourself, who else is going to?' Conor winks at me, and I look away as I feel myself begin to blush.

'Indeed,' Dermot continues. 'So then, Conor, what makes you think you're a suitable candidate to be chosen to come and live on the island?'

Conor's face becomes serious. 'I was born and raised with a view of Tara constantly in my sights for the first eighteen years of my life. And in that time I spent many a happy hour on the island walking, fishing, even courting on occasion, as my old grandfather used to call it.' His blue eyes flash towards mine for a split second. 'I'd be confident in saying there's only a couple of other people that know Tara better than me.'

'And who would they be?' Niall asks, picking up his pen. 'Just for the record.'

'Eamon for one, since he's lived there most of his life. No one knows Tara better than Eamon, that's for sure.' Conor turns his eyes to me again. 'And your aunt would be the other one, Darcy. I remember her coming over to visit; it was clear to see she loved that island.'

Conor's last comment compels my eyes to remain gazing back into his longer than they probably should. Momentarily

I'm reminded of the waves that crash against the rocks around Tara – so many shades of blue in one place, yet clear and inviting. Hurriedly I avert my gaze when I realise it's lingered there a bit too long, and pretend to study something on Conor's application form.

'You said you had the island constantly in your sights until you were eighteen, Conor,' I hear Dermot say while I try to regain my composure. 'What happened then?'

'What happens to so many of us when we're young – the call of foreign shores, I'm afraid Dermot. Is it all right for me to call you Dermot?'

Dermot nods.

'I wanted to see the world. So much to Mam's upset, I packed a bag and went travelling.'

'How long for?' Niall asks.

'The next ten years.'

'Ten years? What did you do for ten years?' I'm amazed that someone can just up and abandon their life like that. I think what I'm doing is bad enough, and I'm only moving across the water to Ireland.

'Oh, all sorts,' Conor smiles. 'Take me too long to tell you now. I've been many things to many people me.'

I look down at his application form. That would explain the vagueness of the career section, then.

'Why the desire to come back home now?' Niall asks. 'If you've been travelling for so long?'

Conor's expression changes so suddenly it's like he's swapped it with one of those theatrical masks that has both a tragic and a comic face. 'Me mam passed away, just this last January,' he says, his head bent. 'But she had a good life, and we saw her last Christmas out together before she passed peacefully on New Year's Day, not long before you folk came across to visit Tara for the first time.' A pair of blue eyes now filled with sorrow look up at us. 'I'm an only child, so it was up to me to sort everything out – in fact, all my family's gone now since Mam's passed on, so I've kind of hung around for a bit, to catch up with the past, you know?' He looks with meaning at me.

I find myself nodding involuntarily.

Appearing unmoved by Conor's heartfelt explanation, Dermot continues with his questions. 'What exactly could you bring to us in terms of your skills – aside from your extensive knowledge of the island, of course?'

I stare at him incredulously. Does he not have an ounce of compassion?

Conor doesn't seem particularly bothered by Dermot's lack of empathy. 'Let me see ...' His brow furrows as he thinks about the question. 'When I lived in Australia I worked on a sheep farm for a few months, and then there was the time I was on the fishing boats just off the coast of Alaska. Then I lived on a farm in Africa for a while, and I also worked at one of the Sea Life Centres in Florida when I was over in the States. I learned to scuba-dive that year, too.'

Turning towards Niall, I grin while Conor continues to reel off a list of the very suitable jobs he's had around the globe. Niall gives me a thumbs-up under the table.

'Thank you, Conor,' Dermot holds up his hand. 'It seems you've had some quite varied experience in many fields.'

'I've done my fair share, you could say that.' Conor seems to be back to his usual self again now. 'So when will you be deciding on the lucky candidates?' he asks, those eyes looking directly into mine again.

'We'll be letting the successful applicants know over the next couple of days,' I reply in my formal interview voice, desperately wanting to tell him there and then that if he wants to come and live on Tara with us then I'm certainly not going to stop him. 'Is there anything you'd like to ask *us*, Conor?'

Conor thinks for a moment, then he grins. 'Nope, I think I'm quite happy with everything. If you are, that is?'

I just manage to prevent myself looking like a lovesick nodding dog.

'I think that's all we need to know for now, Conor, thank you,' Dermot says, standing up. He reaches out over the table to shake Conor's hand. 'We'll be in touch.'

Conor shakes Dermot's hand, and then Niall's and then mine. I notice his hand lingers a bit longer in mine than the others, and how smooth it seems in comparisons to Dermot's, which have always struck me as being quite rough when we've shaken hands before.

'Be seeing you soon then, I hope,' he says as a parting comment.

If I've got anything to do with it, you definitely will, I think to myself as he disappears through the door. There's no 'hope' about it. Suddenly a year spent on Tara is looking like a much more interesting prospect.

'I just don't trust him,' Dermot had said that same evening as he knocked back the last of the whiskey that we'd moved on to as the evening progressed, and dropped his glass back down on the hotel coffee table. 'There something about him that doesn't add up.'

I find myself sighing heavily, and not for the first time that evening, as I massage the back of my neck. 'That's not a good enough reason. Conor has lots of talents in so many areas that would make him perfect for the island, as far as I can see.'

'Yep, that'd be right,' Dermot raises his eyebrows and mutters so quietly I can hardly hear him. 'I bet that's not all you see, either.'

'What did you say?'

Dermot ignores me. 'Look, Darcy, at the end of the day it's your island. You're the boss, you make the final decisions. I'm only here to advise – that's what you're paying me for.'

'Yes. Yes, you're right, I am in charge, aren't I?' Dermot can be so overpowering at times that I've almost forgotten I'm paying him to do a job for me. 'Well I say Conor is in, so that's one for definite.'

I look down at the other application forms we've got strewn across the table. We'd had so many applicants we'd decided to accept far more people on to Tara than I actually required; an insurance policy against the odd one or two not liking it and wanting to leave. 'Right, Dermot, I'll let you have your say with him, him, her, her and him.' I pick up some forms and place them to one side. 'And we're already in agreement about all these ... So I'm going to add Caitlin, Ryan and Siobhan to that pile, too.' I look at Dermot. 'They were OK with you, weren't they?'

He nods.

'All right with you, Niall?'

'Yep, you know I liked them,' Niall grins at my assertiveness.

'And I'm going to go with Daniel and Orla, and Aiden and Kathleen too.'

Dermot screws up his face.

'Dermot, doctors and bakers on the island, how can that be a bad thing?'

'If they wanted to be doctors and bakers they would stay in the city. They want to play at being farmers and fishermen, not do what *you* want them to.'

'Let's just give them a go, shall we?' I say, trying to remain patient. 'I liked them.'

Dermot shrugs. 'It's your island.'

'Yes, it is,' I remember saying firmly that night, putting an end to any more argument. 'It's my island. My Tara.'

And now as we pull around the bay that leads down into the harbour, there it is again – my island, in all her shades of grey-covered glory.

For our inaugural trip over to the island, Mother Nature has not chosen to present Tara in her best light. In fact, so much of the island is shrouded in cloud that if we didn't know there *was* an island hiding in there somewhere, we might have thought it was simply a huge grey wad of candyfloss floating out in the middle of the ocean.

Is this what I've given up my life back in London for? I think as I look out over the sea. It had been awful saying goodbye to Roxi a few days ago; we'd cried and laughed and got extremely drunk on tequila and cocktails reminiscing about all the good times we'd had together in our little flat. Then the next morning there'd been more tears as finally I'd set off for the airport, squeezed inside a taxi cab with my many cases beside me.

Driving down the narrow path towards the harbour, with Niall sitting excitedly next to me like a child about to start his summer holiday, we find Dermot already waiting for us. According to Dermot, the Irish weather couldn't have been kinder in the last few weeks, so all the necessary work on the island has been completed slightly ahead of schedule. Although some of the accommodation still needs a few tweaks here and there, it is now ready to be inhabited. So Niall and I are arriving on Tara somewhat ahead of schedule, with our fellow islanders due to join us in a few days' time.

'Nice morning you've picked for it,' Dermot calls, loading some boxes down to the waiting boat as we pull up next to him. Niall and I climb out of the vehicle, me proudly zipping up my new North Face waterproof coat as we walk towards him.

Dermot stares at me as we approach.

'What?' It's unnerving, him looking at me like that. 'Is something wrong?' It can't be my jacket – the internet said it was recommended for all weathers and all mountain terrains. So I *must* be wearing the right thing, surely?

'You've changed something about yourself since the last time I saw you.' Dermot's eyes narrow in deep concentration. 'What is it?'

'Oh, right,' I'm relieved it's not my outfit. I smooth my hand over the top of my head where my hair is pulled back into a long, loose pony tail. 'Yes, I have, it's my hair. I'm a brunette now. I didn't think being blonde would be very practical over there for a year, you know, what with needing to touch my roots up every five or six weeks. So I went to the hairdresser's and had it dyed back to my natural colour.'

Dermot nods knowingly. Although looking at his short black

hair, which is just starting to become peppered with the odd strand of grey at the edges, I doubt the need for hair dye is something that's ever worried him much.

'It suits you,' he says gruffly. 'The dark hair, I mean. It's better than the bottle-blonde look.'

'Thanks,' I smile deliberately at him. I've decided I'm not going to allow Dermot's barbed comments to wind me up any more. 'See, I told you I could be practical when I wanted to be.'

Dermot nods. 'I see you've kept the nails on, though.'

I look down at my newly manicured nails. 'I told you before, they're real.'

'Real they may well be, but they won't last five minutes over there.'

'We'll see about that,' I say with determination.

'So is everything ready for us, Dermot?' Niall interrupts. He sounds like an eager schoolboy about to go on an outing, and has talked about nothing but the island since we left Dublin this morning.

'Uh-huh,' Dermot nods. 'Like I said last week, though, it's not perfect but it's liveable, and there's plenty to be getting on with before the others arrive. So do you two need a hand with your stuff?'

'I'll be grand with mine,' Niall grins. 'But Darcy could probably do with some help to lift her trunks.'

'Trunks?' Dermot turns to me with a questioning expression. 'Don't tell me you've brought so much stuff you needed to pack it all in trunks.'

'No,' I say with a little laugh. 'That's just Niall's idea of a joke. But please bear in mind that this isn't just a holiday, I am coming here for a year, there is a certain amount of things I need.'

I hear a snort of laughter from the back of the people-carrier as Niall unloads his own cases.

Dermot frowns. 'Just how much *stuff* do you have in there, exactly?' he says, heading purposefully around to the back of the vehicle.

Quickly I follow in his footsteps, and find him staring in disbelief at the cases and bags still waiting to be loaded onto the boat.

'It's no wonder you wanted a bigger boat this time,' Dermot says, shaking his head. He turns to me. 'I thought you said a minute ago you could be practical. You're going across to an island. You're hardly going to be parading up and down in the latest fashions every day.'

'It's not just clothes,' I say crossly. 'There are things for my house in there, too. I assume I *have* got a house. I'm not going to get across there and find some fancy wigwams, am I?'

'Yes, you've got a house. You've got the best house, actually, since it's your island. The biggest one, anyway.'

I find myself smiling at that thought. 'Have I? Ooh, what's it like?'

Dermot smiles now too. 'You'll see it soon enough. Look, there's no point in us standing here arguing. You've brought all this stuff with you, so I suppose it's going to have to go over there now. We'd best get it loaded onto the boat.'

'Want a hand?' A soft Irish lilt comes floating down the path we've just driven down.

We both turn towards the voice to see Conor strolling down the hill. He's wearing a large rucksack strapped to his back, and carrying a holdall in his hand.

'Conor, hi,' I call, smiling up at him as he arrives next to us, 'you're just in time. Dermot thinks I've brought too much luggage with me. So we may need a hand getting it all onto the boat.'

'Sure, no problem,' he says casually. 'Let me just load my own bags here onto the boat first, then I'll be across to help.'

I watch while he walks down to the harbour and drops his own meagre belongings onto the deck of the boat. 'I didn't know Conor was coming with us today,' I whisper quickly to Dermot as he tugs at the first of my many cases.

'Didn't I mention it?' Dermot's muffled voice replies from inside the people-carrier. 'I bumped into him in the village and said you and Niall were coming over early. Because you requested a bigger boat this time, I've had to hire another skipper and his boat to take us over to the island today, so we didn't need Conor. But he offered to come early as well, since he's been staying locally in a B and B now that his mother's house is sold. So there didn't seem much point in refusing.'

'Right then,' Conor arrives back by my side. 'What's first?' he pulls his sweater over his head to reveal another tight white t-shirt underneath.

'It's all going over, sorry,' I apologise, trying to avert my eyes from his torso. 'I don't really travel light.'

Conor grins. 'I wouldn't expect you to. Ladies as finely turned out as yourself rarely do.'

I feel myself begin to blush. But I don't think Conor notices, as he's now swung himself into the boot next to Dermot. He immediately grabs two of my heavier suitcases and, with his biceps bulging under the sleeves of his t-shirt, jumps with ease from the boot of the car.

'Back in a tick,' he winks, as he sets off towards Niall still dragging his own cases along.

'What the hell have you got in this, Darcy?' I hear Dermot call from inside the carrier.

I forcefully tear my gaze away from Conor effortlessly handling my cases to see Dermot tugging at a large holdall. 'Er, that would be my accessories bag.'

'Accessories? It weighs a bloody ton. Accessories for what – committing murder?'

'No,' I glare at Dermot. Conor wasn't creating a fuss, so why was he? 'Shoes, belts, bags, that kind of thing. And be careful with that bag, it's designer.'

Actually it's a fake Louis Vuitton holdall, but is Dermot going to know the difference?

Dermot tries to stand up in the people-carrier, but the ceiling is too low and he bangs his head. Trying not to look too annoyed, he climbs out. 'I repeat: Darcy, you are going to a remote island to live for a year. The seals and rabbits don't really care whether your shoes and bag match your outfit.'

'No, but I do. And I won't let my standards slip just because I'm going to be living there.' I point out to sea in the direction of the island, and I'm surprised to see that in the space of a few minutes the cloud has begun to lift, and already I can make out the westerly tip of the island as the sun's warming rays slowly begin to peel away its grey wrapping.

'You tell him, Darce!' I hear a familiar voice call behind me. 'There'll be no green wellies and Barbour jackets for my girl!'

I spin round to see that a taxi has pulled up a few feet away, and just climbing out of it looking amazing in a shocking-pink minidress is Roxi.

101

'Rox!' I call, running over and hugging her. 'What on earth are you doing here?'

'You didn't think I was going to let you to go through this experience all alone?'

I stand back to question her. 'The truth, Rox?'

'I lost my job at the pub, along with the flat.'

'Why, what happened?'

'Let's just say it involved a rather fit guy, a miscommunication about whether he was single and a little fight breaking out, involving several packets of dry-roasted peanuts and a bottle of WKD. Terrible mess, but yours truly came off the victor, naturally. However, sadly it's now left me jobless and homeless.'

I shake my head. 'Oh, Roxi, will you never learn? Well, maybe you're my silver lining now that these clouds have cleared.'

Roxi's eyelashes – which I happen to know are the Cheryl Cole ones from the Girls Aloud range – start to bat when she suddenly spies Dermot. 'Or maybe he's *my* silver lining.' She saunters towards him. 'Well, hello,' she says. 'Who are you?'

'Dermot,' Dermot says gruffly, 'and you are?'

'Roxanne,' Roxi holds out the back of her hand to Dermot. Dermot just stares at it.

'Well you don't look much like a *Dermot*!' she snaps, lowering her bright pink fingernails to her hips as I catch up with them. 'You look more like a *Simon* with that attitude.'

Dermot looks even more confused now.

'Roxi and I are big *X-Factor* fans,' I explain. 'I think she means you don't look much like Dermot O'Leary and more like …' I try not to smirk as I say it '… Simon Cowell.'

'Really,' Dermot says, looking disdainfully at Roxi.

'We've another lovely lady joining us on Tara, I see?' Conor says, joining the group with Niall.

Roxi looks as if she might pass out on the spot when she sees Conor. She looks upwards, presses the palms of her hands together and mouths the words *Thank you*.

'I am Roxanne Whitney Reynolds,' she says, holding out her hand to Conor. 'But you can call me Roxi.'

Conor takes her hand and gallantly kisses the back of it. 'Enchanted to meet you, Miss Roxanne Whitney Reynolds. And I shall be *delighted* to call you Roxi.'

'Oh,' Roxi gasps, 'I love an Irish accent on a man!'

Conor grins, 'Then I'm sure we'll get on just fine, Miss Roxi.'

'And this is Niall, Rox, you remember me telling you all about him?'

Roxi manages to drag her eyes away from Conor for a moment to be introduced to Niall. 'Hey, Niall,' she says, smiling across at him. 'How are you?'

Niall visibly breathes a sigh of relief. 'I'm grand, thank you very much, Roxi.'

'So, she's coming with us?' Dermot asks, looking down at Roxi's high heels, which I'm quite impressed are the exact same shade of pink as her dress. 'Like that?'

'Yes, Dermot, I'm very pleased to announce that Roxi is going to be coming across to join us on Tara, she won't be needing an interview, she's my best friend.' I smile happily at Roxi. 'And,' I lean across to Dermot, lowering my voice, 'If you think I'm OTT with clothes, just wait until you see Roxi in action!'

Ten

So this is the house that I'm to call home for the next year.

When Dermot kept mentioning there were still a few minor things that needed tweaking over on the island, I did wonder whether we were going to arrive to find that 'tweak' meant 'build', and that there would still be walls needing to be erected and roofs waiting to be put on.

But what I'm standing in front of now appears, from the outside anyway, to be a perfect little whitewashed stone cottage. It's very plain, with two four-panelled windows on either side of a solid wooden front door. The roof is covered in very basic grey slate tiles, and an aroma of fresh paint wafts towards me as I stand there staring at it.

'Well, what are you waiting for?' Dermot asks, as he lumps another of my cases onto the rapidly growing pile behind me. 'Go on; go inside, it's not locked. There's no need when there's only us here.'

Hesitantly I walk towards the little wooden door, turn the handle and gently push it open.

'The door still needs a lick of paint,' Dermot says, following me. 'But we haven't really had time for all the niceties – only the basics.'

Inside, I find a small hallway with a flagstone floor, and off that an empty room with a large fireplace. I walk across the hall and again, opposite there's another bare room with another open hearth. Further down the hall there's a kitchen – it's basic, but there's an open fireplace, a range-type cooker, and, I'm pleased to see, a small fridge. By the looks of the fresh, unpainted wood, Dermot has knocked me up a few cupboards too.

'I thought you might use this as your living area,' Dermot suggests. 'The view of the bay is quite impressive from the window.'

I go over to the large window that runs nearly the full length of the room and glance through it. He's right; from here I can see the large sandy bay where Eamon and I scattered my aunt's ashes on my first proper visit to the island.

'And I thought you might like to use one of the rooms at the front as a sort of site office. You know, a headquarters for people to come to when they need something.'

I haven't even thought about that. I guess people will be coming to me for help and assistance to begin with, if they have any problems. After all, this is my island; I'm supposed to be in charge.

'That's why I chose this house for you. We've pretty much managed to adapt most of the cottages to suit, even those that are going to have several people sharing them. All the others are a bit smaller than this one, but I assumed you'd need plenty of space. What I hadn't reckoned on, though, was that it would need to store your vast quantities of luggage.'

I decide to let Dermot's jibe pass just this once, since he's made such a good job on my house. *Wait*, I think, looking around me again, *there is a bathroom, isn't there?* I haven't seen one yet. Oh, my God, I don't have to bathe in some waterfall somewhere, and go to the loo in a hole in the ground?

'Your bathroom is just through there,' Dermot says, as though reading my mind. He points to a small door off the hall. 'Are you all right, Darcy? You're awfully quiet.'

'Hmm? Oh, yes, I'm fine. It's just a bit overwhelming, that's all.'

'What do you think, then – of what we've done? I did most of the work on this one myself,' Dermot adds proudly, looking around at the little cottage.

'It's great,' and realising I sound a bit ungrateful, I add, 'I mean, obviously you've all done really well, considering what these cottages were like the last time I was here. They were virtually derelict then. I wasn't expecting you to turn them into palaces.'

Dermot eyes me for a moment. 'Thanks. I think.'

'So,' I look around at the bare rooms. 'When does the furniture arrive?'

'I don't know,' Dermot shrugs. 'You tell me.'

'No, Dermot, *you* tell *me*. I left everything up to you, remember?'

'No, Darcy. I was quite clear in one of my emails that I would take care of all the structural work on the properties, and I expected you to take care of the furniture and soft furnishings.'

I stare blankly at Dermot as the cold reality of what he's saying slowly begins to dawn on me.

'Let me get this straight, Dermot. Are you telling me that we have twenty people about to arrive on this island to join us in the next few days, and we haven't even provided them with a bed to sleep in?'

'Correction, Darcy, it seems that *you* haven't provided them with a bed, or any other furniture, for that matter.'

I glare at Dermot. How dare he lay all the blame for this on me? I don't remember any email about furniture. Although to be fair, after a while I had been skimming through a lot of Dermot's progress-report emails – they did make pretty boring reading. There was only so much interest I could take in cement, guttering and roofing tiles. Maybe I had missed this one.

'We've still got a few days,' I try to think quickly. 'We'll just have to get some ordered.' *I'll show Dermot I can deal with this little setback.*

'And just how are you going to do that?' A questioning expression crosses Dermot's face at the same time as he folds his arms across his chest.

'Over the internet, of course.' I'm already debating in my head which of my favourite furniture stores might do us the quickest international delivery rates.

Dermot's eyes crinkle with amusement before his mouth lets forth the most almighty snort of laughter.

'What?' I ask indignantly.

'Darcy,' Dermot says, still trying to control his mirth. 'There's no internet access here. We're on an island in the middle of the sea!'

I feel my cheeks flush. Damn it, of course I've forgotten. At home, the internet solved all my problems quickly and with such ease. That's one of the things I'm going to miss most while I'm here. The World Wide Web gave me instant access to any information I wanted at super-fast speed. I used it to shop, to book holidays, to bank – how am I going to live without it for a year?

'Right then,' I try to sound blasé and in control. 'I'd forgotten that small fact. I assume it's the same for mobile phones, too?'

Dermot nods slowly, as if he's addressing a small child.

'So what *are* we going to do, then? We can't have everyone else arriving to no furniture in their houses.'

And, more to the point, with no beds on the island where on earth are *we* all going to sleep tonight? There's no way I'm sleeping on some dusty floor.

Dermot's look of mirth is replaced with a furrowed brow. 'It's a problem all right, Darcy. But it's the first of many you're going to face while you're here. I just didn't think it would be on quite such a large scale to begin with.'

There's a banging on the door.

'Anyone home?'

'Come in, Roxi,' I call, pleased to hear a friendly voice.

Roxi comes swaying through the door, still in her pink heels; how she's managing to walk around the island in them I have no idea. Conor tilts his head as he enters through the low door, followed by Niall, who doesn't need to bend at all.

'So, this is it?' Roxi says, looking around her. 'Hmm, we've got our work cut out if we're to make it into chez Darce and Rox, like the old place. I've watched all those home-improvement shows, I've seen the designers talk about minimalist, but this is taking it to a whole new level.'

'They are a bit on the sparse side, aren't they?' Conor

agrees. 'We've just taken a quick tour of all the cottages; you've done a grand job by the way, Dermot ... '

Dermot acknowledges Conor but doesn't return his smile.

' ... but none of the houses seem to have any furniture in them.'

I bury my face in my hands. '*Oh, God.*'

'What's wrong, Darcy?' Niall asks, coming over to me.

'Darcy forgot to order the furniture,' Dermot says, matter-of-factly.

'No, I didn't forget,' I snap, lifting my face again. 'I didn't know I was supposed to be ordering any!'

'We have no furniture?' Roxi gasps, her mouth hanging open in horror to add to the effect.

'No,' I say miserably. 'And no curtains, or anything like that. People *are* bringing their own sheets and towels and basic equipment, aren't they, Niall? We did ask them to bring that sort of thing?'

Niall nods. 'Yes, but we're supposed to be providing habitable living quarters on their arrival. And really that suggests houses with at least a bed as the bare minimum.'

Dejectedly I nod my head. 'What on earth are we going to do? We can't just ring up Ikea and expect them to deliver to a dozen houses in the middle of the Atlantic Ocean. Can we?' I ask again, looking hopefully between the four of them.

Niall shakes his head.

'They'll just have to rough it for a few days until we can get something sorted,' Dermot suggests straightforwardly. 'They're hardly coming over here expecting five-star accommodation. They're coming to experience getting back to basics, so that's what we'll be giving them – a real taste of basic living to begin with. Me and the other boys have been all right kipping on the floor for the past few weeks. It didn't do us any harm, and they've gone home happy enough.'

I shake my head. 'No, Dermot, it's not good enough. I'm sure you and the other builders have had great fun playing Boy Scouts, but I've told these people what they're to expect when they arrive here, and I can't let them down by not even having the decency to provide them with a bed on their first night here. There has to be another way. There *has* to.'

Roxi puts her arm around my shoulders to comfort me.

'I might have an idea,' Conor says quietly. 'It's a bit of a long shot, to be honest.'

I turn hopefully towards him. 'What is it? Anything's worth a try at the moment.'

Conor smiles at me. 'Well, I was talking to the owner of the B and B I was staying in over breakfast this morning. There was only me staying, and I think she was glad of the company. Anyway, she was telling me that her bookings are down a bit for this year but her sister, who has a hotel up in one of the towns, is doing even worse, and is thinking of selling her hotel because she just can't make a go of it any more.'

We all stand staring at Conor for a moment, allowing what he's suggesting to register in our own minds.

'That, Conor, could be just the answer to Darcy's problems,' Niall says excitedly. 'What do you reckon, Darcy?'

How come they're all suddenly *my* problems, when something goes wrong?

'I'm not too sure about second-hand beds.' I wrinkle my nose up at the thought and look at Roxi. She does the same, but shrugs and holds out her hands.

Dermot rolls his eyes. 'I'd say you don't have much choice.'

'OK, OK, you're both right,' I sigh. 'I'm sorry, Conor, it's a great idea. I suppose we'd better go back over to the mainland and find this hotel, then. That's all right, isn't it, Niall? The budget will stretch to that, won't it, if we can persuade this lady to sell?'

'It won't stretch to you buying a hotel, Darcy, no. But if you can talk the owner into selling you her fixtures and fittings, it might.'

'How quickly can you have the boat ready, Conor?' Dermot asks. 'There's no time like the present.'

'Give me five minutes,' Conor says with a small salute.

'Five minutes!' I exclaim. I can't possibly be ready in five minutes. 'I need to change.'

'Why?' Dermot demands.

'Just look at me.' I gesture at my jeans and waterproof coat. 'I can't possibly go over to try and negotiate buying stuff from a hotel dressed like this. I need to look at least like I can afford it. Roxi, tell them.'

'She's right, she needs to look the part or she can't play the part. It's not rocket science.'

Conor grins at the two of us.

Dermot does his usual eye-rolling. 'Darcy, I'm sure the owner of this hotel won't give a monkey's what you look like, just as long as your wallet's big enough.'

'I don't care, I'm changing and that's that.'

'Looks like it's … *fifteen* minutes, then?' Conor asks hesitantly.

I shake my head.

'Twenty?'

I nod. 'That will be great, thanks, Conor. I'll meet you down at the harbour in twenty minutes.'

'I bet it's more like thirty,' I hear Dermot murmur to Niall.

I ignore Dermot and continue talking directly to Conor. 'Conor, will you come with me once we get over there, and help get me out of this mess?'

'It would be my pleasure to help a damsel in distress,' he says smiling. 'Just you and me going, is it?'

'Yes,' I say without hesitation. 'I'm sure Dermot has lots of structural work to be getting on with. Soft furnishings aren't his department, are they, Dermot?'

Dermot narrows his eyes but doesn't bother to reply.

'Is that OK with you two?' I ask Roxi and Niall. 'You don't want to come back over with us now you're here, do you?'

'No, Darce,' Roxi says, looking with interest between Conor and me. 'You go off on your little shopping expedition.' She links her arm through Dermot's. 'I'm sure Mr Cowell here will protect me while you're gone.'

Dermot looks unenthusiastically down at Roxi's arm that's wrapped around his, and then up at Roxi. But her eyes simply twinkle with amusement as she blinks back at him.

Niall, who's been standing grinning while this whole interlude has been taking place, shakes his head. 'No, I'm grand, but you'll be needing these.' He reaches into his pocket and pulls out a chequebook and a bank card. 'Don't go mad,' he says, passing them to me. 'I know we desperately need this stuff, but haggle with the woman, Darcy. This is *not* a shopping expedition.'

'Niall, I'm an expert at grabbing a bargain. I'll be good, I promise.'

'Conor?' he looks imploringly at him.

'Sure, Niall, I'll keep an eye on her.'

And I find the thought of Conor keeping an eye on me a very comforting one indeed.

Eleven

'You were only supposed to be going for furniture!' Dermot exclaims as Conor and I pull up in the harbour later that day in the little red boat. 'Darcy, how have you managed to acquire three dogs, half a pet shop and an extra person in one afternoon?'

It had been a very successful trip over to the mainland; we'd managed to buy not only the bedroom furniture but a number of fixtures and other fittings from a tourist hotel that, as Conor had predicted, had sadly seen its heyday some years before. The owner, Mary, was a lovely woman and had taken to Conor straight away, so with a little bit of charm – mostly Conor's – and some wheeling and dealing on my part, we'd managed to persuade her into selling us what we needed, even though Mary's furniture wasn't exactly what I had in mind. But since I hadn't got much option, I'd put my own tastes aside for once, and had tried to be content with the fact that at least we now had some furniture coming over in the next couple of days.

Plus, we were also sailing back with some added bonuses for the island.

It had all started on the trip over there in the boat. Conor was steering the craft expertly across the sea as always, while I sat quietly in the back (or is that the stern?) in my newly chosen outfit, a Karen Millen white jacket with navy piping, straight-legged navy trousers and a navy and white striped top. I'd thought the nautical theme might be a cheerful twist as we journeyed across the sea, but with the added extra of my bright orange life jacket now spoiling the effect, my seaworthy outfit was somewhat ruined. So as I sat in the back trying to control my hair from gusting about my head, I began to wonder just what sort of hotel it was we were going to try and buy the insides of . . .

Conor looks back at me, as I sit lost in thought. 'Euro for them?' he enquires.

'What?'

'A euro for your thoughts. I didn't think we were allowed to say "penny" now, with the EU and all.'

I smile now, too. Getting up, I carefully make my way to join him at the helm, steadying myself on the sides of the boat as I go. *The red heeled sandals weren't one of Roxi's better ideas. But she was right; red went so well with navy and white, it seemed such a shame not to wear them.*

'They're not worth a euro, or a penny, really.'

'Everyone's thoughts are worth something, especially to the person thinking them.'

I turn to look at Conor, but he continues to face forward while he speaks, concentrating on the task of getting us across safely to the mainland. His profile is still every bit as handsome.

'No, honestly, they're not,' I insist.

Conor briefly turns his head towards me. 'You're just like your name.'

'What do you mean?'

'Your name, Darcy – it's from the French word for fortress.'

'Is it?'

Conor nods, looking out to sea again.

'Unless of course your name is of Celtic origin,' he continues suddenly, while I'm still considering his first statement. 'And then it would mean dark-haired, which, if I might add, I think suits you much better now with those beautiful chocolate-brown eyes of yours.'

'Th-thank you,' I stutter, not used to compliments quite like this. In fact, of the few boyfriends I had when I was in London, none of them was exactly lavish with his compliments, and if he did choose to shower me with praise, it was more likely to be about the cup of tea I'd just made him, or the fact that I knew the latest football score. 'I think I like the second meaning better than the first, though. I'm hardly a fortress.'

Conor shrugs. 'I only say what I see.'

So I'm not that great at letting my emotions out. But how does Conor know? I've only known him five minutes.

'So what does "Conor" mean, then?' I ask, hoping to change the subject away from me.

'Lover of hounds,' he says without hesitation.

'And have you,' I ask, trying to keep a straight face, 'loved many hounds in your life?'

Conor smirks, but keeps looking ahead. 'That would be

telling.' He turns to me again, his bright blue eyes searching mine. 'But if you want the serious answer to that question – I adore dogs, actually. People, Darcy, they'll always let you down. A dog will never do that; they'll always love you, whatever you say or do.'

'Yes, I know, my aunt used to keep dogs.' A vision of Molly's big old mongrel dogs Bran and Piper suddenly comes flooding back to me. 'They were lovely, dopey old things.'

Gosh, I haven't thought about them in ages. I used to play for hours with those two when I came over to stay with Molly. I was heartbroken when Bran had to be put down. I think Piper eventually died of natural causes some years later, but that was when my contact with my aunt became sporadic. I feel a stirring inside me as too many memories are released from the box at once, and it's immediately snapped shut.

So when, during our negotiations at the hotel, we discovered that the hotel's golden Labrador, Bella had just had puppies, I simply couldn't resist taking a quick peek at them …

Mary takes us along to her kitchen, where we find six of the cutest puppies I think I've ever seen in my life being watched over by their mother, and a young man with jet-black curly hair in his early twenties, whom Mary introduces us to as Patrick.

'I prefers Paddy,' he informs us as Mary fusses about him almost as much as he's fussing over the dogs. Apparently Paddy has been working with Mary in the hotel since she gave him a chance of a job some years ago when nobody else would. 'A bit of a tearaway,' is how Mary describes him to us, and looking at him crouched down in his jeans, Doc Marten boots and a t-shirt that says *Irish Boys Do it Better*, I can quite believe it.

Mary explains that because the puppies aren't pedigrees, she is having trouble selling them. The fact that they're a half Labrador, half Irish wolfhound cross isn't helping either. 'Sure now, they'll be big fellows when they're fully grown. They'll need a lot of exercise.'

I try to remain impartial as the puppies wander over to us, nibbling at shoelaces and tumbling and falling over their own paws, which seem far too big for their little bodies. But even in my heels, soon I'm down on the floor with the others, cuddling the puppies and allowing them to nibble at my ears and lick my fingers.

'I have homes for two of them,' Mary says after a while, 'and I'm going to keep one myself. 'But it's the other three I'm stuck with.'

'Which ones?' I ask casually, praying that she'll include the little brown one with the flash of white in his tail.

'That one,' she points at a multicoloured female Paddy is holding. 'Also the sandy one over there nibbling on the brush; and this little brown fellow with the white fur on his tail.'

I look at Conor, and remember what he'd said to me on the boat earlier.

A dog will never let you down …

I've always wanted a dog of my own. A couple of girls in the fashion magazine offices next to us had dogs, but they were those tiny ones that they kept in their handbags. They were one of the few fashion accessories I didn't yearn after. These puppies were going to grow up to be proper big dogs. Apart from my holidays with Molly, I'd never had the chance of keeping a dog of my own. We'd never lived in the right sort of house, or had a big enough garden for me to have a dog, or for that matter any other sort of pet when I was young. After my father left, my mother took a full-time job as a sales representative for a clothing company and that meant we were always moving around. I can hear my mother's shrill voice now as I think back: 'It will just be another thing for me to have to look after as well as you, Darcy.'

I shake my head free of that memory and think fast. 'Conor, would you like a puppy to take over to the island?'

To my surprise, Conor shakes his head. 'It's a kind offer, Darcy, but no thank you.'

I'm somewhat taken aback after his speech earlier, but at least he didn't pick the cute little brown one I've got my eye on.

'Right, well, I'd like to take the little brown one off your hands, please Mary,' and I try and call it over by patting my legs.

But both the brown and the sandy puppies come tumbling towards me, falling over themselves and each other in the process.

'Darcy, what are you going to do now?' Conor asks, grinning down at them scrabbling about on top of me. 'You can't just take one and leave the other brother behind, now can you?'

I look down at the little dogs clambering up on my lap.

'Why not take both of them?' he suggests. 'They'll have plenty of space to roam on the island. Plus, they're like the old you and the new you, aren't they? With your hair – one's got blonde hair, and the other's brown!'

I pick up both puppies from my lap and cuddle them, one

under each arm, and as they both try to lick my ears from each side I begin to experience that unconditional love Conor was talking about before.

Why on earth didn't he want to experience that with his own puppy?

Paddy cuddles the other puppy protectively to his chest. He looks reproachfully at me, and suddenly I feel guilty at just sweeping in here and buying these puppies off Mary like they're clothes on a bargain rail no one wants.

'When your hotel closes down, Mary, what will all your staff do?' I ask her.

'Most of them have already left and got jobs elsewhere. It's only really me and Paddy left now. I'll go and help my sister with her business when this place is sold . . . ' Her voice trails off, and I realise she doesn't want to say too much in front of Paddy.

I take a deep breath. 'Thing is, I don't know that much about looking after dogs,' I announce to the room in general. 'Shame there's no one coming to the island that does.'

Paddy's stroking of his puppy quickens as he watches me hopefully out of the corner of his eye.

'Paddy, I don't suppose you'd be interested in coming over to Tara, would you, and bringing the last remaining puppy with you? You'd be doing me a big favour showing me how to look after the dogs properly.'

Paddy can't pack his bags quick enough.

'Calm down, Dermot, I'll explain everything in just a moment,' I say as we return to the island and I try with difficulty to climb out of the boat at the same time as holding two wriggling dogs.

'Look, can you just take these two for a minute?' I pass Dermot my two puppies, while Conor helps me out of the boat. The puppies look even tinier against Dermot's great hulk of a body, as he holds them warily against his chest while they try and lick at his ears and nibble the buttons on his shirt.

'This is Paddy,' I explain, as Paddy climbs without aid from the boat carrying a third puppy. 'Paddy, this is Dermot, he's been in charge of all the renovations here on the island. And Niall, who's – well, he's like my right-hand man, and Roxi, who's my best friend.'

'Pleased to meet ya all,' Paddy says, doffing his baseball cap at them to reveal his mop of black hair.

While I quickly explain the whole story to them, Conor begins unpacking the boat with all the puppies' equipment that Paddy and I had gone out and bought at a local pet shop. Even if I don't have a proper bed to sleep in tonight, my puppies aren't going to go without.

And as we all head up the path towards the cottages with Dermot muttering something about Tara becoming an island for waifs and strays, the thought of such a thing only makes me smile all the more as I cuddle my new four-legged friends even closer to me and walk side by side with my slightly larger, but equally special two-legged ones.

Twelve

This isn't usually how I choose to spend my Thursday evenings, sitting on a cold floor in front of an open fire with four strange men. Even though Roxi, I'm sure, wouldn't have minded being the only female on the island, I'm glad she's here to keep me company on my first night on Tara.

We're gathered together in my site office, on the few mattresses and camp beds left behind by the workmen before they escaped to their real homes on the mainland. Everyone's rallied round and brought over their bedding so we can make the room as comfortable as possible, with a fire burning cheerfully in the grate. It's been quite cosy spending time just the six of us, chatting, with the puppies scurrying around our feet. The puppies love it here – I don't think they've ever had so much freedom in their short lives, and earlier we'd all taken it in turns to go chasing after them when they'd tried to stray a bit too far. Even Dermot, who, once we'd explained the whole story about Paddy and then the puppies, surprisingly took it all in his stride and accepted the newcomers immediately.

And I've finally come across the perfect names for my two puppies. When we'd got back, and while I'd been getting changed into something a bit warmer and more practical, Dermot and Conor had knocked up a temporary barbecue between them in an open area in front of all the cottages, so that even though one of the few things we did actually have right now was the ability to cook in our kitchens, we'd spent our first evening on the island in the great outdoors eating, drinking and chatting until it got too dark and cold for us to be out there any longer.

'What are you going to call these little fellows, Darcy?' Niall had asked when we'd been outdoors finishing off the last of the barbecued food.

I'd thought long and hard about it since I'd got them earlier today. I'd waited so long to own a dog of my own, that I didn't want to waste this opportunity by christening them something boring like Patch or Roly.

'Westwood and Louboutin,' I announce proudly.

There's a mixture of stunned silence and raucous laughter – from Dermot.

'What?' I ask them, slightly put out that my highly original choice of names hasn't been greeted with awe and adulation.

'You can't call your dogs after fashion designers, Darcy,' Niall says sensitively. 'Think about the kind of dogs they're going to grow into. It won't really suit them, will it?'

I look to Roxi for support.

'Niall's right, honey. It would be like putting Dermot over there in an Armani suit and expecting him to feel comfortable. It's just not fair, and a little cruel.'

Dermot stops laughing now.

'What shall I call them then?' I ask disappointedly. 'I liked those names.'

'What about shortening them?' Conor suggests. 'Louboutin to Louis and Westwood to ... '

'Woody!' Roxi shouts in excitement. 'Like in *Toy Story*.'

I think about this for a moment. 'Yes,' I say nodding, 'I like it, it suits the two of them. Louis and Woody it is, then. Thanks Conor, thanks Roxi.'

'Congratulations,' Dermot says, rolling his eyes. 'You've gone from naming your dogs after two international fashion designers to calling them after a Disney character and an *X-Factor* judge.'

'Well it takes one to know one, Mr Cowell,' I say, raising my eyebrows at him.

So now we're all sitting on the floor, lit only by flickering candlelight and the flames from the fire. We could use power from the generator to light the house properly, but Dermot says we should save power whenever we can. We're sipping at my Cath Kidston mugs of coffee or hot chocolate laced with tots of whiskey from a bottle that has appeared from Dermot's bag. If I could just forget that I'm going to have to sleep on one of these same mattresses on this same cold, hard floor tonight, I might even feel the tiniest bit content at what I've achieved at the end of my first day here on Tara, which is certainly not an emotion I expected to feel.

While we listen to Paddy tell us a funny story about some American tourists they had staying at the hotel once, there's a knock at the front door of the cottage.

Paddy stops talking while everyone looks wildly at each other for an explanation.

'Isn't anyone going to get that?' Conor asks, jumping to his feet.

'But who is it?' I look up at him in alarm. 'We're all sitting here inside this cottage.'

Conor grins. 'Unless this island is suddenly haunted by a headless horseman, and by the look on all your faces that's what you think is on the other side of that door right now, my guess is it's Eamon.'

Of course. I'd forgotten about Eamon.

There's a collective sigh of relief from around the room as everyone visibly relaxes.

Conor goes to the front door and quickly I follow him.

'Darcy,' Eamon nods as he sees me. He holds up a lantern with an oil-burning flame inside. The flickering light only intensifies the colour of his deep blue eyes.

'Eamon, won't you come in and join us?' I ask, as Louis wakes up and joins us in the hallway. I scoop him up in my arms.

'I won't, Darcy, no. I just wanted to make sure you'd all settled in all right today, and if there was anything I could do.'

'We've had a few hiccups, but I think everything's going to be OK now.' I glance at Conor.

He smiles reassuringly. 'Everything's going to be just grand, Darcy.'

Woody appears, joining his brother.

'Aren't you fine-lookin' wee fellows,' Eamon bends down and scoops Woody up in his empty hand. 'And you've two of them, Darcy.'

'Yes, I just got them today.'

'Would there be some Irish wolfhound in there somewhere?' Eamon asks, holding Woody up in front of his face.

'Their mother was part Irish wolfhound, according to her owner. So they're a bit of a mix.'

'I thought so,' Eamon nods knowingly as he puts Woody gently down on the ground outside. Woody quickly squats down to relieve himself, narrowly missing Eamon's boot. 'I used to have dogs myself sometime ago,' Eamon says, not seeming in the least bothered by Woody's near miss. His sharp eyes look intently into mine for a moment, as though he's searching for something.

'Did you?' I say, putting Louis down outside too, away from Eamon. He tries to chase a leaf blowing along the grass. In the patchy light a cloud-covered moon is casting over Tara tonight, he stumbles over a twig that happens to be in his path and rolls over in a ball before picking himself back up again and continuing on his way. I turn my attention back to Eamon. 'Are you sure you won't come in, Eamon?' I ask him again. 'There's a drop of whiskey doing the rounds in among the mugs of coffee.'

'No. Away and enjoy yourself. I'll be seeing you around in the next few days though, I'm sure, when the rest of your people arrive.'

'Yes, they'll be here soon.'

Hopefully after their furniture . . .

'And what will they do when they get here?' Eamon asks. 'Are they just here on a long holiday?'

'No, they're here to set up homes, to live and work here properly. You know, like farming, growing their own crops,

126

that sort of thing. They're going to be as self-sufficient as possible.'

Eamon pulls a strange face. 'Did you say grow their own crops and farm?'

I nod.

'I see.'

'What's wrong with that?' I ask, watching Conor as he lights up a torch to go after the puppies who have started to wander a bit too far away from the cottage.

'Nothing, if crops actually grew here.'

'What do you mean?' I ask, turning my attention back to Eamon.

'What I said. Why do you think this island's community died out in the past? People just couldn't, or didn't want to, survive on what the land here could provide.'

'I ... I don't understand.'

'You've seen the island, Darcy,' Eamon gestures with his hand out into the darkness. 'It's mostly hills and rocks. Yes, there's a lot of grass and greenery, but underneath that the soil is mostly peat. It's ideal for burning on your fire – you'll never get cold while you're here on Tara – but there's not many a crop that'll grow on it. Peat and rocks are hardly the perfect combination for sowing seeds and keeping animals on, are they?'

'But people must have done it in the past!' My mind is registering exactly what Eamon is saying, but my mouth is still protesting. 'How did they survive back then?'

'Potatoes and seal blubber mainly,' Eamon says, matter-of-factly. 'With the occasional fish if they were lucky.'

'But ...'

'What's up?' Conor asks as he returns, placing the puppies down firmly inside the cottage again. 'What's this about seal blubber, Eamon? One of your little beauty secrets?'

Eamon doesn't smile. 'Just telling Darcy here a few home truths about the realities of living on Tara.'

'Apparently we can't grow crops or keep animals.'

'I didn't say you couldn't keep *any* animals, just that you need certain breeds that are hardy enough to withstand the terrain and the weather conditions.'

'Why can't we grow things?' Conor asks.

'It's the soil, apparently,' I say in a dismal voice.

'And the weather conditions too,' Eamon adds. 'Believe me, I've tried. You don't think I enjoy buying all my fruit and veg from the greengrocer's in the town, do you?'

'I just assumed you weren't green-fingered, Eamon,' Conor jokes. Then he sees my face. 'I had no idea, Darcy, I'm sorry.'

'But it's what we've promised them!' I shake my head in desperation. 'Come here to Tara and live the good life – you know, like the old seventies TV show?' I look up at Eamon.

He looks blankly at me.

'Oh, never mind, it doesn't matter.' I turn to Conor. 'What are we going to do now?'

Conor shakes his head, his face for once not showing its usual convivial expression. 'I think we'd best go and discuss it with the others,' he says. 'Thanks for dropping by, Eamon.'

'Sorry if I've caused you bother,' Eamon says, his face full of concern. 'It wasn't my intention, so it wasn't.'

'No, I know, Eamon.' I try and smile at him. 'Please don't worry; I'm sure we'll sort something out.'

As Conor and I return to the others in the sitting room, we realise that the cottage is so small they've already heard a lot of what Eamon has told us.

'He's probably done you a favour,' Niall says as we ruminate over Eamon's revelations. 'Think of all the money you might have lost planting out crops that would have failed, or buying animals that might not have survived.'

'That's true, I suppose.' I look up at him from my place on the mattress, which now, after Eamon's news, suddenly doesn't seem quite so cosy.

'I've never been very green-fingered anyway,' Paddy says, tickling his puppy Brogan's furry ears. 'Mary would never even let me water the plants at the hotel.'

'You know me, Darce,' Roxi says, holding out her blue fingernails (when did she have time to repaint them? We've only just arrived today). 'The closest this body's ever got to a spade is a little incident in a garden shed in Tooting.'

I shake my head. 'Dermot?' I look over to where he's sitting quietly in the corner, nursing a mug of coffee. 'What do you think?'

Dermot looks up. His dark brown eyes blink steadily back at me as we await his verdict on the situation. 'You're buggered, basically,' he says, choosing not to beat about the bush, as always.

'Great. Thanks for the support.'

'I'm only telling it as I see it, Darcy. Look, you've managed to con a load of no-hopers into coming to live on an island with you, with the promise of some sort of Felicity Kendal-inspired utopia. And now when they arrive, not only will they be lucky if they have a bed to sleep in, but the only way they're going to see anything fresh when they're here is if they can row a boat over to a supermarket on the mainland!'

As I glare at Dermot I feel hot tears springing into the corners of my eyes, which I angrily fight back.

Great! I can't cry at a funeral, but I'm going to start now! Well, there's no way I'm giving Dermot the satisfaction of seeing me.

'I'm going out for a while to get some fresh air,' I announce in a voice that's a bit too calm. 'Perhaps we can talk about this again in the morning when we've all had a chance to think about it, and hopefully come up with some *helpful* ideas about what we're going to do.'

Then I simply turn and walk calmly out of the cottage, slamming the door behind me for Dermot's benefit.

'Great work, guys,' Roxi says as I leave. 'You handled that well.'

It's dark outside, but luckily, with the ever-changing Tara weather, the sky is now completely clear, and the almost full moon casts enough light over the island to allow me to be able to walk safely away.

I wander far enough so that I can still see the cottage, but so the others won't be able to see me, and perch myself on a large rock jutting up out of the ground. The star-filled sky above me is quite magnificent, and as I gaze up towards it, I reflect that it's definitely not a sight you see living in central London. But even that splendour is not enough to suppress my doubts as they come bubbling to the surface once more.

What on earth have I done, coming to live here? It's already been one disaster after another, and I've only been here a day.

There's some movement from my cottage as the others begin to remove their bedding, and as I watch them carry their belongings across to their own cottages I marvel at how they all cast such different silhouettes in the moonlight. There's stocky little Paddy with Brogan; slim Niall; big, broad Dermot; and then tall but lean Conor following up the rear. Roxi and I have decided that there's just not enough room in my little cottage for the two of us to share with all our things, so after a bit of rearranging, Roxi now has the cottage next to mine, so she doesn't have to go too far.

One of the figures returns from delivering their mattress back to their cottage, and heads towards me in the moonlight.

'Aren't you cold, sitting out here all alone?' Conor asks, standing in front of me with his hand in his pockets.

'Maybe a little.' I pull the zip on my hoody up a bit higher.

'Your fire's still burning merrily away to itself back there,' he nods in the direction of my cottage. 'Dermot made it up for you before he left.'

'That was good of him,' I say through gritted teeth.

'He didn't mean anything by what he said before. It's just his way.'

'I know.'

'Your boys'll wonder where you are.' Conor throws in his best shot.

The puppies ... they'll be all on their own.

'Maybe I *should* go back, now everyone's gone,' I say, climbing up from the rock.

Conor holds out his hand to help me up, and then we walk back down to my cottage together.

'Do you want to come back in?' I ask him without thinking. Then I blush. *God, have to stop that every time Conor is around!*

'I would, but I've moved my mattress now,' Conor grins.

'Plus I think you've got a lot to think about tonight. I'm sure your dogs will keep you company though, and Roxi's just next door if you should want anything. She's pretty protective of you, isn't she?'

I smile as I think about Roxi.

'Maybe another time, though.' He leans forward, and as if it's the most natural thing in the world, kisses my cheek. 'I'll see you in the morning, yes?'

'Yes ... the morning,' I mumble, surprised by his kiss.

Conor casually waves goodbye as he walks away towards his own cottage. Hastily I enter through my own front door, where I find Woody and Louis curled up asleep on my temporary bed in front of the fire. They lie next to a walkie-talkie and a note that simply reads: *Sorry about earlier. If you need me in the night, just use this. D*

Thirteen

After a restless night, which has as much to do with sleeping on a mattress on the floor with two puppies who refuse to sleep in their brand-new dog bed as it has to do with the constant worry of my latest island dilemma, I'm wandering around my kitchen trying to figure out how I boil some water in the kettle on my brand-new stove so that I can make myself a cup of tea. Someone has kindly left me some basic supplies in the fridge, so after several infuriating minutes of trying to figure out how to light the gas on the hob I've now given up, and have poured myself a glass of orange juice instead. It's just as well I never bother eating breakfast.

But my stomach gives a small grumble – must be something to do with all the sea air – and as there's no one about, I consider breaking into some of my secret chocolate stash I've snuck over and hidden well away from Roxi, in the lining of one of my larger suitcases.

So while Woody and Louis gambol around at the back of

the cottage, emptying their bladders and burning off some of their excess energy, I stand enjoying my basic breakfast of a Twix and a glass of orange juice at my kitchen door, gazing out at the view of the bay down below, which is nothing short of stunning this morning. An azure-blue sky with a few white clouds dotted across it could easily belong to the top half of a Mediterranean landscape, if the bottom half didn't so obviously belong to the craggy cliffs and pale yellow sand of Tara's Celtic past.

When I've finished my snack, I follow the dogs out onto the grass. Fresh salty sea air immediately fills my nostrils as the breeze catches my hair and billows it up around my face. Wearing only my Nike hoody, pyjama bottoms and trainers I wander out a bit further, tucking my hair up under my hood as I walk, for once not caring what I look like as I step out of my house. Who is going to see me out here, anyway? It's not like I'm stepping out into a busy London street in my night-clothes.

With the puppies racing around on the damp morning grass, and seagulls circling and crying as they ride on huge gusts of wind above me, suddenly I feel freer than I've ever felt before in my life. I almost want to join the gulls there and then as I stand as close to the cliff edge as I dare, leaping off the cliff face to soar around in the wind like they do.

Maybe when the other islanders get here they'll feel this same sense of freedom and want to stay, I think hopefully, closing my eyes for a moment to breathe in the sea air again. And maybe they won't need to do this whole self-sufficiency thing. Who really wants to grow their own vegetables and keep their own pigs, anyway? Perhaps they'll just enjoy being here for the sake of it. Who wouldn't with views like this, especially in this gorgeous weather?

As I open my eyes again, they're immediately drawn to some movement down in the water below. There it is again – something is moving about in the waves! Deciding I need to take a closer a look, I scoop Woody and Louis up and hold on to them tightly as I inch towards to the cliff edge. As the three of us gaze silently down into the sea, I don't think the puppies know what we're looking for, but I certainly know what I think I saw a few minutes ago. There ... there they are again, leaping in and out of the waves – the unmistakable curve of two dolphin backs.

Silently we watch the dolphins moving gracefully about in the sea for a few minutes, until Woody and Louis begin to get restless in my arms, probably wanting their own breakfast, and for safety I decide it's best to take them away from the cliffs and back to the cottage.

As I pour warm water onto their dry puppy food, I smile to myself. We have dolphins living around the island – surely that must be lucky? I'll look it up on the internet in a minute, and check. Damn, I almost forgot. I can't do that now. But it must mean something ... I'll ask Eamon, or even Conor when I see him; he seems to be into all that kind of thing. Maybe things are going to get better after all.

Dermot is the first person I see after I'm properly dressed and leaving my cottage. This doesn't surprise me; it is pretty early, and I bet Roxi is still asleep. Roxi can sleep anywhere; the fact that she's spent her first night on a strange island won't have affected her requirement for nine to ten hours of beauty sleep at all. But even without Roxi on hand for advice, choosing what to wear this morning has been surprisingly easy – a bit like when you're at school and you just fall into your uniform every morning. I'm determined, though, that I will not succumb to a Tara uniform of jeans, a sweatshirt and big clumpy boots. But it will do, just for today.

'Morning,' Dermot says, walking towards me. 'Sleep well?'

'Yes thanks,' I reply, feeling a bit awkward. After all, the last time I'd spoken to Dermot we hadn't exactly been on friendly terms. 'I'm sorry about last night, Dermot – for snapping at you.'

'It's already forgotten,' he says lightly. 'You had had a bit of a first day of it, what with the furniture and everything, and then the old fellow's news just to top it all off.'

'Yes, it hasn't exactly been the best of starts.'

'Any ideas what you're going to do yet?'

'Nope, not really,' I shake my head. 'I just hope that when the others get here they see how beautiful it all is and want to stay anyway.'

Dermot's eyebrows furrow. 'Hmm; that's one way to go about it, I suppose.'

'What do you mean?'

'Burying your head in the sand and hoping everything will turn out all right.'

'I'm not burying my head in the sand! I just don't see what *I'm* supposed to do, that's all. It's not my fault we can't grow crops or keep animals easily.'

'No, but it's your job to find a solution to the problems that are immediately going to arise when the – excuse my language – shit hits the fan.'

'Why, why is it?' I flap my hands around in frustration.

'Because,' Dermot continues in a voice so calm it's irritating, 'it's your island. I did warn you there was more to all this than meets the eye.'

He's right, as usual. But that doesn't make it any better.

'I'll just have to think of something before the others get here then, won't I?' I say huffily. 'Oh, by the way, my oven doesn't seem to work.'

'Did you switch the gas supply on?'

'The what?'

'The gas supply. There's a bottle in the cupboard next to the sink. You need to switch that on before any of your gas appliances will work.' Dermot pauses for a second and eyes me suspiciously. 'You do know there's no underground gas supply here, Darcy. It all comes from bottles which we have to ship over from the mainland.'

'Of course I know,' I say quickly. 'I'd just forgotten. Thanks for reminding me. Oh, and for this.' I hold out the walkie-talkie to him.

'No, you keep hold of that; it's yours. It's your only form of communication while you're on the island. We've all got one – you just need to charge it up at night like a mobile phone.'

'Right. Well, thanks again.'

'Not a problem. So, what are you going to do now?' Dermot asks, looking at the dogs' leads clutched in my other hand.

'I thought I'd take the puppies for an early-morning walk, since it's such gorgeous weather right now, and explore the island a bit at the same time. Do you know what the others are up to?'

'I think Niall and Paddy have got the same idea as you, and

have taken Brogan out for a walk, and Conor took off early this morning with his fishing rod. I haven't seen your friend Roxi yet.'

'No, you won't, Roxi will still be sleeping. She's used to working pub hours, so don't expect to see her until at least eleven o'clock.' I casually take a glance around me. 'OK, well, maybe we'll bump into some of the others when we're on our walk, eh, guys?' I pat my leg in the hope that the puppies might respond and come running to me. They look up for a moment, then carry on with what they're doing – currently investigating the entrance to a disused rabbit hole.

'I'll look out for her when she finally decides to wake up,' Dermot says, looking towards Roxi's cottage. 'But I doubt she'll sleep long once I start up my circular saw in a few minutes.'

I grin. 'I once knew Roxi to sleep through the fire brigade turning up at a building three doors down from us, with their sirens wailing full blast. She was fuming when I told her she'd missed everything.'

'Because she might have been in danger if the fire had spread?' Dermot asks with concern.

'No,' I say laughing, 'because she'd missed seeing all the hunky firemen in their uniforms!'

Dermot shakes his head. 'She needn't worry about that here, although we do have all the appropriate fire equipment in place should we need it, in the event of an emergency.'

'You've been very thorough about everything, Dermot. I feel quite safe knowing you have it all under control.'

This is obviously the type of compliment that Dermot likes, because he smiles at me approvingly.

'So,' I ask him casually, 'did you happen to see which direction everyone went earlier?'

'Conor went that way down to the beach,' Dermot says, his face taking on its usual disinterested expression again as he gestures in the direction of the coastal path that leads around the outskirts of Tara. 'But the other two went the opposite way, inland.'

I look in the direction Dermot's pointing. 'It *was* the coastal walk I was thinking of trying. The puppies would enjoy some time down on the sand.'

Dermot nods. 'Whatever you like, Darcy.'

'Right, well, I'll see you later then,' I say brightly, about to head off in the direction of the cove, then I pause and turn back. 'So what are you going to do now?'

'Don't worry about me, I've got plenty of things to be getting on with still,' Dermot glances back at the cottages.

'You'd be welcome to join us on our walk if you'd like to,' I offer politely, hoping he'll refuse.

'I think you probably need some thinking time – to consider your dilemma,' he adds when I look blank. 'Plus,' he calls as he begins to wander away, 'you know what they say about three being a crowd, and all that ...'

Inside I growl at Dermot as I watch him stroll nonchalantly across the grass. *Right, I'll show you!*

'I thought you were going on the coastal walk,' Dermot calls as I march past him in the opposite direction to the cove.

'I can change my mind, can't I?' I yell back, not bothering to turn around.

'You change your clothes often enough, so it wouldn't surprise me if you changed your mind just as often.'

But Dermot's taunts simply bounce off my departing back.

*

We continue with our walk along a narrow rocky path that climbs away from the harbour and up one of Tara's great hills. As we climb, we find ourselves approaching an old derelict building that Dermot had been talking to me about at the barbecue last night. He'd said it was massive in comparison to the other buildings on the island, and that he would be interested to know what it might have been used for in Tara's history.

When we finally make it to the top of the hill, I realise Dermot's right – the remains are vast in contrast to the rest of the tiny dwellings on the island. Woody and Louis immediately run to investigate the ruins for themselves, snuffling about for smells and leaving their own scent when they find any areas worth marking. I follow them inside what's left of the building, moving from room to room, stepping over what's left of the fallen walls and occasionally through a crumbling doorway, wondering what this building might have been used for in the past. As I come back through to what would once have been an exterior door, I stop for a moment under a large stone archway to admire the clear unobstructed view the weather is obliging me with this morning.

From the top of this hill I can see easily all the way across to the mainland, and I realise that tomorrow the boats carrying first our new furniture, and then hopefully our new islanders, will be sailing across here to Tara. I wonder how many times people before me in the past have gazed upon this very view, watching boats cross the same stretch of water.

I feel incredibly safe and secure standing underneath this archway, in among all the greenery that spreads chaotically over the surviving brickwork. In fact, looking around the rest of the building, the ivy could be the only thing holding up some of the walls, they've disintegrated so badly. I rest my hands on the abandoned building and am surprised to find it feels warm to my touch. 'What were you once?' I ask it, running my hand along the entrance I'm standing beneath. 'And what is it you would like to become?'

The puppies and I end up walking further than I'd originally intended, and find ourselves picking up the coastal path that I walked around on my first visit here in January. I'm surprised at how much I remember of the landscape I'm passing, enough to notice delicate differences in the flora and fauna that we pass on the way. Tiny white spring flowers are just beginning to bloom, tucking themselves tightly against Tara's giant craggy rocks for protection from the elements, and although we don't see any more dolphins, there are rabbits everywhere we look, their heads randomly bobbing up, then the whites of their tails disappearing immediately when they see Louis and Woody bounding over in their direction. I can tell the difference between rabbits and their bigger cousin, the hare now. There are seals basking in the warm morning sun on one of the tiny beaches that we pass, and everywhere we go seagulls swoop and soar overhead, reminding me of the police outriders I used to see clearing a path through the London traffic for VIPs.

Eventually we find a beach with a narrow path that leads down onto the sand. The puppies make a much better job of clambering down the path than me, but for the first time since I bought them, I do actually feel the benefit of the expensive walking boots I'm wearing. I can't remember ever spending so much money on shoes that are so ugly, but I have to admit that, as I scramble down the sandy path, they do stop my ankles from twisting over and my feet from sliding from beneath me, as they take me safely all the way down to the beach below.

Woody and Louis simply adore the sand. Their soft paws have never touched anything like it before, or experienced wetness like the sea. They immediately try chasing the frothy white waves as they wash in and out onto the beach. And very quickly learn to keep their long pink tongues inside their mouths during this game, when they both get mouths full of salty water.

Except for its three new visitors, the beach is completely deserted.

So this couldn't have been the one Dermot meant that Conor was fishing from, I think, feeling a little disappointed. Ah well, perhaps he's right, maybe I should spend some time mulling over my latest problem before the others get here tomorrow. As I stand gazing out to sea, with the dogs splashing about in the waves next to me, I begin to think again about what I'm going to tell everyone when they arrive.

But as hard as I try, no answers are immediately forthcoming.

I look up into the cloudless sky for inspiration.

'I need help,' I call up to it, cupping my hands. 'What do you suggest?'

A gull circles high over my head, giving nothing away.

I look at Woody and Louis galloping around on the sand. 'How about it, guys?' I call. 'Any ideas?'

They wag their tails in my direction, but continue with their game of trying to chase the waves as they roll along the sand.

'Oh, come *on*!' I call out into the vast, never-ending expanse of grey sea. 'Give me some clue … a hint, at least?' I spin around and look at the island behind me. 'What about you, Tara?' I ask. 'This is for your own good, too. Can't you help?'

But all I hear is the wind whistling over the hills and across the sea as Tara chooses to keep a dignified silence on the matter.

'Right, that's it. Woody, Louis,' I call, gathering the puppies up to head back to the cottage. 'Time to go. This is getting us nowhere. Looks like I'll just have to keep on thinking myself. Or hope one of the others has come up with something by the time we get back.' But as Woody comes running down the beach, I notice he's proudly carrying something in his mouth. 'What's that?' I ask, wrestling it from his jaw. 'Give it, there's a good boy.' In my hand I now hold a child's red plastic spade, a bit battered and chewed – probably as a result of Woody's sharp little teeth.

'Where on earth did you get that?' I ask, giving it back to him. 'There are no children playing on these beaches. Oh, it could have been washed up by the sea, I suppose.' As I stand there still thinking about the spade, I feel something tapping against my foot. I look down to see a yellow plastic bucket strewn with seaweed being drawn in and out by the tide. 'What on *earth*?' I wade into the waves a little way to pick it up as the sea pulls it away from me again. 'Anyone would think people used to holiday here, or something. What's next, a beach ball?'

Louis, jealous of Woody's find, tries to grab the bucket from me.

'No!' I tell him sternly. 'Now you *sit*, Louis.' I push his bottom down a little to encourage him. 'That's it, good boy.'

And I give him the old bucket as his reward. He runs off happily to show Woody his prize while I watch them.

Then, as I'm about to turn around to make my way back across the sand towards the cliff path, I stop suddenly in my tracks.

'Wow, that's it!' I exclaim, suddenly realising. 'That *is* it! You know, it might just work.'

'What might work?' I hear a voice next to me enquire.

I jump in fright, then relax slightly as I turn to see Conor standing grinning at me. He's got a large canvas bag slung over his shoulder and a fishing rod in his hand.

'I think I might just have come up with an idea on how we can make this island work for all the new people arriving tomorrow.'

'Grand,' Conor says, lifting his bag from his shoulder. 'Do you want to share it with me?'

Was I ready to share it with anyone? I'd only just thought of it, and I wasn't quite sure how it would work myself yet.

'I thought you were fishing this morning?' I ask him, stalling for time.

'I am,' he says, beginning to feed his rod with line. 'I wasn't getting any pulls on the other beach, so I thought I'd come down to this one, and then I saw you standing here and I knew right away my luck would be in.'

I smile at him and shake my head. Conor's certainly got the Celtic charm going on.

'What?' he asks, his blue eyes wide with innocence.

'Nothing, I'm just not used to men like you, that's all.'

'What do you mean, men like me? There's only one Conor Fitzgerald, that you can be sure of.'

'And I can well believe it!'

'You wanna go?' Conor asks, passing me the rod.

I shake my head.

'Go on,' he encourages, 'Look, I'll show you what to do.'

While Woody and Louis chase each other around the huge expanse of pale yellow sand, Conor patiently tries to explain to me the basics of fishing for salmon in the sea.

'That's it,' he says, as I manage to cast the line out into the water this time, instead of getting it tangled around the rod, myself or on one occasion, Louis. 'You're away with it now. Now reel her in.'

I'm not really that interested in learning how to fish. But when Conor had offered to show me, he'd immediately wrapped his arms either side of me to demonstrate how to cast the line out properly, so that had been an unexpected and rather pleasant bonus to the lesson, and suddenly fishing has become a lot more interesting.

In fact, I probably could have cast the line out much better quite a few attempts ago, but it seems a shame for Conor not to share his 'expertise', or his wonderfully toned arms for one last time ...

As I slowly wind the spool of fishing line back in again, I suddenly remember what I was going to ask him this morning when I'd set off from the cottage. 'What do you know about dolphins, Conor?'

'Dolphins – not a lot, why do you ask?'

'I saw two this morning down in the bay at the back of my cottage.' I lift the rod again and cast the line back out into the sea. 'Is it considered lucky to spot a dolphin?'

'That's grand, Darcy,' Conor says, looking out to sea. 'I don't know about lucky in general, but I'm sure there's an old wives' tale about dolphins and this island.'

'There is?' My eyes immediately dart from the fishing rod to Conor as I furiously wind the handle of the spool. 'What is it?'

'Darcy, your line?' Conor nods at the rod as I wind my spinner in as far as it will go, almost snapping the line in the process.

'Oh sorry, shall I throw it out again?'

'Cast it, yes,' Conor grins.

I throw my arms back and cast the line out again, while Conor watches it go sailing out to sea.

'The tale, Conor?' I remind him. 'What is it?'

'That's a great cast, Darcy, you should be proud of that. Oh, sorry, I'm not too sure; I just remember something to do with a dolphin. There are so many myths and legends associated with Tara, you wouldn't believe.'

'Are there? Like what?' I look across at him again. This is much more interesting than watching a bit of string bob about in the sea. I'd kind of lost interest in the fishing side of things when he'd taken his arms away.

'Aren't you going to wind that line in?' Conor prompts.

I turn back out to sea and begin to wind again.

'Eamon's the man to talk to about all that stuff,' Conor continues, happy now that the spinner is moving again. 'He's the expert on all Tara's Celtic connections.'

Suddenly as I'm winding I feel a sharp tug on my line.

'Conor, I think I might have caught something,' I panic, as the line starts to feel very heavy to wind in. 'Quick, help me!'

Conor looks out to sea at my taut fishing line. 'That you sure have, Darcy,' he grins. 'Come on now, let's be landing you your first fish.'

Rather than grab the fishing rod from me as I'd rather hoped he might, Conor expertly coaches me through the 'landing' process – which turns out to be much more complicated than I ever realised. I thought you just pulled in the fish and that was it – it would certainly be a lot easier. But oh, no: I have to keep slowly reeling in my line a bit at a time to make sure the fish is kept tight on the hook. I frequently offer Conor the fishing rod to see if he wants to take over, but he declines, saying I must land the fish myself. The whole process takes so long, and the fish seems so heavy, that I'm feeling quite exhausted by the end.

When eventually the fish is close to the shore Conor alarmingly pulls off his socks and boots, rolls up his trousers and wades into the sea with a landing net, where he proceeds to scoop up the fish and carry it triumphantly towards me. My natural instinct is to back away from the slimy wet creature wriggling about in the net. But Conor looks so excited that I feel obliged to stand still and look pleased at my catch.

'What do you reckon? He must be a ten-pounder at least! I had no idea he was so big. Fair play, Darcy.'

'Yes, it's, um, fantastic!' I eye the fish warily, wishing I could share in Conor's excitement.

'He'll make for a fine barbecue tonight.'

'You mean, we're going to eat it?' I ask in horror, looking at the fish squirming about in the bottom of the net.

'Sure we are! You'll never have tasted fresher salmon than this.'

Conor now produces a truncheon-like object from his bag. 'You may want to look away for a moment.'

'Why? Oh, I see.' I realise the truncheon is about to put an end to this fish's chances of ever swimming in the sea again. 'Look, I don't suppose we can just put it back, can we?'

Conor looks at me in surprise. 'Why, you're not a vegetarian, are you? No, you can't be, you ate sausages and burgers like everyone else last night.'

'No, it's not that. It just seems a shame, that's all; he's done nothing to us, and we're ruining his life just by catching him.'

Conor smiles. 'If you're here to live the island life, then I'm afraid catching and cooking fish is something you're going to have to get used to. It's really no different than the fish you buy in a supermarket back home, or eat from your local chippy – you just don't see it being caught.' His blue eyes twinkle as he looks softly at me. 'But if that's what you really want, Darcy, then of course I'll pop him back in the sea for you.'

I look down at the fish one last time, and then up at Conor.

'No, you're right,' I say bravely, holding my chin aloft. 'I've made my decision by coming here, haven't I, and I can't just bail out of it every time it suits me. Do what you need to do, Conor ... but just don't expect me to watch you doing it.' I turn my head away to watch Louis and Woody, and when I look back again the deed is done, and Conor has hidden the fish in a large canvas bag.

He smiles at me again. 'You know what you said a moment ago – about doing what I need to do?'

'Yes?'

'I was wondering ...' he says, moving closer to me, his eyes glinting mischievously. 'Since you're the boss, do you give me your permission to do what I feel I need to do in *all* respects here on this island?'

I can't help but smile at his cheek. 'I might do ... depends what it is.'

Conor is now standing only a few inches away. He looks down at me and his now familiar grin appears. 'Oh, let me assure you, boss, it's nothing bad, in fact I think it could be *very* good indeed when it happens.'

I feel Conor take hold of my hand.

'Come on,' he says, 'shall we go and find the others and tell them what an expert fisherman you've become in one morning?'

'Or about the expert teacher I had?' I gaze up into his eyes.

'Or maybe we should just keep it our little secret,' Conor whispers, leaning in towards me, his lips so close to mine I can virtually feel the vibration of his speech.

My eyes begin to close in anticipation of his kiss, but just as quickly snap open again when I realise Conor's face has pulled away and he's stood upright again.

As a wave of embarrassment washes over me and my eyes drop down towards the ground, I see Conor's bare feet still covered in sand. 'You ... you'd better put your boots back on,' I stutter, 'it's cold on the beach.'

'That I had,' Conor grins, reaching down for his boots. 'I don't want to get a chill, now do I?' He lets go of my hand and brushes the sand from his feet, then quickly slips his socks and boots back on.

'Happy now?' he asks, still smiling.

'Yes,' I reply, mortified I'd just sounded like a mother reprimanding her child. 'Much better.'

'Shall we, then?' he asks, holding out his hand again.

'Sure,' I shyly take hold of Conor's hand and, with Woody and Louis scampering about our feet, we walk back across the sand towards the cliff path together, with Conor carrying the salmon and me carrying a new yearning inside, that for once doesn't belong to a handbag or a pair of shoes.

Fourteen

Its barbecue time again on Tara, but this time, instead of sausages and burgers it's my salmon that sits proudly in the middle of the flames, roasting away wrapped in a huge tin-foil parcel.

After the glorious sunshine of the morning, the weather has miraculously held for this evening's event. But tonight we're cooking on a new barbecue that Dermot has built to accommodate the roasting of my giant fish. Dermot didn't seem to mind when we'd sprung this on him earlier; he seems to thrive on a challenge, and set to work creating this new stone-built contraption that we are using to cook with now.

The weather isn't the only miracle that's taken place this evening. Some more cans of beer and lager have appeared, just like last night. I wasn't aware when we sailed over yesterday just how many crates of alcohol we'd been ferrying back with all our other supplies. But now, as we gather around the barbecue with the sun just beginning to set, sipping on our cans and warming ourselves on the flames, I'm quite glad at least someone had the foresight to bring some. Even Eamon has joined us this evening to sample some of my salmon. Currently he's leaning on his stick next to Dermot, watching him while he tends to the fish.

Dermot has taken charge of cooking the salmon this evening, and the rest of the food to accompany the meal has already been prepared in my kitchen. It would seem that my house, being the biggest, has been temporarily chosen as the automatic meeting area for any communal gatherings.

Not only has Dermot managed to build the barbecue, but with Paddy's help he's knocked us up some new wooden benches from fallen tree trunks – which some of us are now relaxing on around the fire. Paddy had been so excited earlier when he'd told me how he'd helped Dermot scoop a quarter of the inside of each trunk out using some power tool or other, and they'd then sanded and smoothed each log into a long bench. And I have to admit, as I sit on one of them now, they really are quite comfortable.

I watch Conor standing over on the other side of the barbecue talking to Niall and Roxi, and I secretly hope he might come and sit next to me on the bench in a moment when he's finished. But it's Eamon who wanders over to fill the gap.

'How're ya, Darcy?' he asks, sitting down next to me.

'I'm OK, thanks, Eamon. How are you?'

'Oh, I'm grand, lass, just grand. You're looking very pretty this evening.'

'Thank you, I thought I'd try and make an effort.' I've changed out of my jeans and sweatshirt into a long summer maxi dress, matching cardigan and gladiator sandals. I'm just starting to get a bit chilly now as the sun gradually sets behind the island, but I'm determined to see the evening out in some sort of style.

'And a grand effort it is, young lady.' He takes a sip from his glass. 'You and your friend over there certainly brighten up the proceedings.'

I look across at Roxi. She's wearing black zebra-print leggings she bought off Wembley Market with a bright pink scoop-neck top and black patent ankle boots, and even though it's now starting to get dark, in the dusk Roxi lights up Tara like a beacon. 'Now,' Eamon continues, 'Conor is telling me you think you saw a dolphin in the bay this morning.'

'I don't *think* I saw one, Eamon, I did see one. In fact there were two.'

Eamon manoeuvres his body with the help of his stick so that he's fully facing me. 'Are you absolutely sure about that?'

'Yes, definitely. Me and the puppies stood watching them for some time.'

Eamon nods slowly as he gazes into the distance again. 'You could be right then,' he mumbles so quietly I can barely hear him.

'What do you mean, *you could be right*?' What are you talking about, Eamon? I know I'm right. What's so odd about seeing a dolphin around here?'

Eamon turns to me again. 'Do you know the last time I saw a dolphin swimming off the coast of this island?'

I shake my head.

'The last time your aunt was here. Never seen one before, never seen one since.'

This I'm not expecting. 'It could just be a coincidence.'

'That it might. But there's an old saying about dolphins and this island.'

'Yes, Conor said he thought there was.'

'The dolphins only swim around the island when there's change afoot.'

'How do you mean?'

'They come to see what's going on, to see if they're needed.'

'I'm sorry, Eamon,' I say, feeling a bit silly. 'But I still don't understand.'

'To see if they're needed to protect the ruler of the island – their king or their queen. The more dolphins you see, the more change there is about to befall either the island or the ruler. Or both.'

I stare at Eamon for a moment, wondering if he's had a few too many of our beers. But he's holding a glass with just a small tot of whiskey at the bottom.

'You needn't think it's the drink talking,' he says, seeing me looking at his glass. 'This is my first tonight. Yer man over there,' he nods at Dermot, 'gave it to me when I says I don't drink beer.'

I'm trying to get my head around all this. 'Are you saying that just because I've seen dolphins swimming off the island we're to expect some huge disaster to befall us all?'

Eamon shakes his head. 'No, that's not what I said at all. I said it meant change was afoot, either for you, for the island or both.'

'Why me?'

Eamon raises his bushy white brows. 'Because you're the owner of Tara now, Darcy. In ancient Celtic legends that would have made you the ruler – the king. Or in your case, the queen. The dolphins want to know if they can help you in any way.'

As I sit listening to Eamon I suddenly realise I'm falling for all this, hook, line and sinker – just like my salmon did. I shake my head.

'OK, stop it now,' I say, looking around me suspiciously. 'Whose idea was this to wind me up? Was it Dermot's or Conor's, hmm? Whose? Ooh, I'll get them back for this, Eamon, just you see if I don't!'

But as I turn back to Eamon again, he's not smiling. He looks at me with concern.

'This isn't a wind-up, Darcy. I'm only telling you what you asked me to – the Celtic legend associated with Tara and the dolphins.'

'Are you really serious – that's the truth?'

Eamon nods.

'But I've only seen two.'

'My bet is you'll see plenty more over the coming weeks. That's what happened to your aunt.' Eamon gazes out to sea.

'And what were they warning her about?' I ask, desperately curious now.

'Change,' he says, slowly turning his head back towards me again.

'Yes, I know you said it means change, Eamon, but in what sense?'

'Hey, what are you two guys discussing over here?' Roxi

asks, leaning her voluptuous chest over the top of the log bench. Eamon hurriedly averts his gaze from the sizeable amount of female flesh suddenly being thrust in his face.

'Roxi!' I gesture at her low-cut top.

'Oops, apologies,' Roxi says, rearranging her chest as she stands upright again. 'Didn't mean to offend.'

'No offence taken, young lady,' Eamon says, smiling at her now. 'It's been a while since I've had two such pretty young ladies to look at on Tara.'

'Well, then,' Roxi says, squeezing her plentiful behind between us on the bench, 'let me sit down here and have a little chat with you, young Mr Eamon. I always have time for a man who properly appreciates the female form.'

When finally the salmon is cooked, we all sit round the fire enjoying our meal while the sun turns the sky from azure blue to a deep crimson red, and Conor is right – it *is* the best salmon I've ever tasted, whether that's because I caught it, or whether it's more to do with Dermot's expert cooking I'm not sure, but whichever it is, it tastes extremely good.

Most of us have finished eating – Paddy seems to have an enormous appetite and can continually take in food in gargantuan proportions – and I'm just about to bring up the subject of the new islanders arriving tomorrow. We still haven't had a chance to sit down and discuss it again, what with everyone doing their own thing this morning, and me still tossing and turning my idea around in my head all day. Then Roxi stands up and announces, 'Right, I think it's time for some entertainment. What can everyone do?'

Dermot eyes her warily. 'What do you mean, *do*? I just

cooked you all supper; I don't need to *do* anything else tonight.'

Roxi rolls her eyes. 'I didn't expect you'd have much of a repertoire for entertainment, Mr Cowell. What about you, Paddy? I bet you've got a trick or two up that Adidas tracksuit sleeve of yours.'

Paddy looks up from his dinner plate. 'I can pick any type of lock you like in County Kerry,' he announces proudly, 'and there's not many I can't do over in Dublin either – cars, houses, you name it, I can get in there.'

'Um, I'll bear that in mind next time I'm trapped in the ladies'. But that's not quite what I was thinking of.' Roxi looks around the assembled group. I fire a warning glance at her when her gaze rests on me. 'Eamon, my new best bud,' she says, sitting down next to him again, 'what about you? I bet you've got some old Celtic stories or something you can tell us?'

Surprisingly, Roxi and Eamon have hit it off immediately, and have spent the entire night laughing and chatting about goodness knows what while the rest of us just marvel at the opposites sitting on the bench together; Eamon in his traditional attire of greens and browns, against Roxi's vibrant and pulsating shocking pinks and electric blues.

Eamon smiles. 'Well, young Roxi, as it happens I do know a few tales. Celtic myths and legends are one of my hobbies.'

'Let's be hearing you then, good sir. Hey, everyone,' Roxi says, holding up her hand. 'My buddy Eamon here is going to tell us a story!'

Eamon makes himself comfortable on the bench before beginning, while we all sit like schoolchildren waiting patiently for our story. 'This tale features a legend that some of you will know, but it's a story that relates to Tara. Have any of you ever heard of a character called Fionn mac Cumhaill?'

Niall and Conor nod, while the rest of us look blank. But it's Paddy, quite surprisingly, who puts down his knife and fork for a moment. 'Do you mean Finn McCool?' he asks.

'Yes,' Eamon says, turning to him, 'that would be the anglicised version of his name – the modern version many would know him by today. What do you know of him, young fellow?'

'Isn't he some Irish warrior guy that built the Giants Causeway?' Paddy says, lifting his fork and continuing with his meal.

'Legend has it – yes, and the Isle of Man, too.'

'He was some sort of prehistoric builder?' Dermot asks, suddenly pricking up his ears.

'Finn was a bit more than just a builder,' Niall joins in now. 'He's one of *the* great heroes of Irish mythology, isn't that right, Eamon?'

Eamon nods proudly. 'There are many legends surrounding the great Fionn mac Cumhaill, and storytellers throughout history have spent many an evening just like this one, seated around campfires all over our great land recounting tales of his heroic exploits.'

'But what has Finn to do with Tara?' I ask.

'Ah, young Darcy, I see patience was obviously not a virtue bestowed upon you,' Eamon nods knowingly. 'And neither did I expect it would be.'

'Why, how would you know that about me?'

'Your aunt described you to me on many an occasion.'

'Oh. Oh right, I see.' Yet again I'm left feeling ashamed that

Molly has obviously spent so much time thinking and talking about me in the last few years, and I so little about her.

'The story about Finn and Tara goes that Finn once fled to the island when he was being pursued by an enemy and was wounded in battle. The locals hid him here on the island until he was nursed back to full health again and fit enough to leave. Finn was so grateful to them for their loyalty and kind hospitality that he left in their safe keeping a precious treasure, and his word that if ever Tara was in trouble he would return to help them and collect his treasure.'

'And did he?' Niall asks, agog.

Eamon shakes his head. 'No, he never came back.'

'What happened to the treasure, Eamon?' Conor asks with interest, leaning forward.

'No one knows; Finn hid it somewhere on Tara.'

'But he must have left a clue?' Niall demands. 'Some way of tracing it?'

I smile at Niall's eagerness. I bet he loves a good puzzle. I can just imagine him doing Sudoku and crosswords in his spare time.

'All I know is that the legend says Finn left his heart as well as his treasure on Tara when he finally departed. He'd been forced into fleeing here, but when the time came for him to go he didn't want to leave.'

'Why?' I ask now. 'What happened here that was so special?'

'He fell in love, Darcy,' Eamon says, his blue eyes softening as he fondly describes this part of the tale. 'Some say he fell in love with the island, but others believe he met his one true love here on Tara.'

'Ah, that's so cute,' Roxi says, clasping her hands together,

'I'm a sucker for a soppy love story. Maybe one of us will find true love while we're here on Tara too.'

'I highly doubt that,' Dermot says, looking sceptically around the assembled group. 'You've about as much chance of falling in love with someone while you're here as finding Finn McCool's treasure.'

'I don't know,' Conor says, looking over in my direction. 'I've always enjoyed a good treasure hunt.'

Fifteen

The day our new islanders arrive dawns surprisingly bright and sunny again. But of the two types of delivery we have today, the first goes a lot more smoothly than the second.

The furniture and soft furnishings from the hotel come over in three boatloads, and are quickly offloaded and ferried into everyone's various cottages, directed by me, before anyone has a chance to notice there's anything slightly untoward about them.

As it turns out there *is* no time for questions or queries about the new interiors, for we've barely had time to unload the final set of packing cases when we notice the boat loading up again, but this time it's with human cargo.

'The new 'uns are loading up over there,' Paddy calls, looking through a large set of binoculars over to the mainland.

'What, already?' I cry, looking at my watch. 'But we're not expecting them yet.'

'Maybe the forecast is bad for later, and Liam has decided to bring them earlier.' Conor peers up at the sky.

'I'm going to nip inside and freshen up. I can't greet people looking like this, can I?' I look with horror at my scruffy jeans and sweatshirt.

Dermot tuts as he carries a final box across to his cottage. 'They're not expecting you to be in full ceremonial dress to welcome them onto the island, Darcy. You look just fine as you are.'

'I'll be the judge of that, Dermot,' I call, already hurrying over to my own cottage. 'Back in a few minutes.'

'I'm with you, Darce,' I hear Roxi call, following in my footsteps. 'There might be some talent heading over on that boat. I can't greet them when I'm not looking my hottest, now can I?'

When I get inside my cottage I wash my hands and face, brush my hair and quickly apply a bit of make-up. Then I change my clothes into the outfit I've decided to wear to greet everyone for the first time. It has been a difficult decision; after all, I don't want to go too over the top, after the nautical theme of a couple of days ago. So this time I've opted for a long black skirt with a plaited tan leather belt, long suede boots, a sheer white embroidered blouse and a long black fake-fur waistcoat. Monsoon has assured me that their Ethnic City collection will add 'a touch of sophistication with a tribal twist to any event this season', so I'm hoping it will add one to mine. It might be a bit adventurous for Tara, where it's a fashion event if someone appears in a curiously coloured raincoat, but first impressions count and I need to feel as confident as I can this afternoon.

Roxi hasn't even tried to go understated. She's wearing a brown leopard-print top, black skinny jeans and coordinating leopard-print shoes with a platform heel so high she can barely balance on them as she comes trotting down to the harbour to wait for the boat to arrive.

Suddenly we're all very quiet. We may only have been here for a few days together, but it feels odd to be welcoming strangers among us now.

As they get closer, I recognise people from their interviews and suddenly I begin to panic. These people have given up their lives to come and live here on this island with me, and now I'm just supposed to turn around and say to them, 'Thing is, hope you don't mind but the plans have changed a bit . . . '

'Are you OK, Darcy?' Niall asks with concern. 'You look a little pale.'

'What . . . Oh yes, yes, I'm fine. Just a bit nervous, that's all.'

I wish now I'd tried a bit harder to voice my idea to the others. I was going to do it at the barbecue last night, but then Eamon had started with his stories, and every time I've tried today I've been hampered by some situation that's needed attending to urgently, like last-minute adjustments to who was going to be sleeping where, or how we were going to cater for everyone tonight when we'd only been used to cooking for us. Whatever problem has arisen, it has always seemed to be up to me to find a solution. I'd thought once the boatloads of furniture arrived we might finally have a chance to have a little chat before the others came, but now they are already on their way, there's no chance.

So now I've got no choice but to wing it this afternoon, when I make my big announcement to everyone. I just have to hope the others back me up . . .

*

The boat finally arrives, this time containing a somewhat livelier cargo, and we help everyone off with their belongings.

'Can I just have everyone's attention for a moment,' I call above the noise of excited, chattering voices, as everyone begins the process of getting to know everyone else.

'Quiet!' Dermot booms.

Everyone hushes.

'Thank you, Dermot,' I nod at him, before I launch into my carefully prepared speech that I've been practising secretly in my cottage. 'First of all, welcome to Tara, everyone. I'm Darcy, as most of you already know, and in a moment if you could all proceed in an orderly fashion to see Niall over there with the clipboard, he will tell you which cottage you have been allocated.' Niall waves. 'Then when you've got settled in, I wonder if we might meet out here again – weather permitting,' I glance up at the darkening skies, 'for our first proper island meeting. In fact, looking at those skies, how long would you say before the rain comes, Conor?'

'Ten, fifteen minutes max,' Conor says, looking upwards. 'It'll pass, though.'

'How can you tell?' asks Aiden, a baker from Dublin.

'You soon get used to the changing weather on this island,' I say, sounding as if I've been here years instead of days. 'Perhaps we should meet out here again when the rain has passed, then. We have a welcome barbecue planned tonight for you all. So let's hope Conor is right. See you all later!'

The crowd swarms on Niall while I breathe a huge sigh of relief.

'Not accustomed to public speaking?' Dermot asks, wandering over towards me, an amused look on his face. 'My God, you're even shivering, too. But I'm not surprised, given what you're wearing right now. It's a lot colder than it was yesterday, even in the sun. Where's your coat?'

'It didn't go with my outfit.' I collapse down on a long flat rock while the others begin escorting people to their cottages.

Dermot tuts and shakes his head. 'I should have known. You'd best be getting one on soon before it rains though, otherwise,' he turns his head to one side and regards my waistcoat suspiciously, 'that fur thing will be looking something akin to a large drowned rat in the next few minutes.'

'Yeah, in a bit.' I just don't have the energy to respond to his taunts right now.

Dermot sits down next to me. 'OK, what's up? If I can't wind you up, Darcy, I know something must be wrong. It can't just be making that speech.'

'No, it's not that.' I look up at Dermot. 'I'm more nervous about *what* I'm going to tell them later at the barbecue, than about actually standing up and speaking in front of them again.'

'Why?' Dermot asks curiously. 'What are you going to say? You haven't told any of us yet.'

'I have tried to. But then you'll probably only think it's a bad idea anyway. You always do.'

'Maybe, maybe not. Why don't you try me?'

'Excuse me, you don't happen to know which cottage is going to be attached to the shop, do you?' a young woman dragging a heavy case behind her asks. 'So sorry for interrupting you both.'

I look up and see a pretty face with blonde hair tied loosely in a plait at the side of her head. She smiles down at us. 'I'm Caitlin, by the way,' she adds.

'Yes, I remember you from the interviews,' I return her smile. 'Hi again, Caitlin. It's that one over there,' I point to the cottage at the end of the row.

'How about we do better than that, and I carry your case over there for you?' Dermot says, jumping up. 'You can't be dragging it across this rough ground. You'll have the wheels off it in no time.'

'That's very kind of you … Dermot, isn't it?'

'Yes, that's right.' Dermot lifts up Caitlin's huge case as though it were a Tesco carrier bag. 'I built these cottages, you know.'

'Really,' I hear Caitlin say as they depart together over the grass. 'How very clever of you, Dermot.'

I sigh as I watch them depart. *Looks like operation Bucket and Spade goes ahead after all then*, I think, watching him open the door of the cottage for Caitlin. *With or without your approval, Dermot.*

'I see someone's already staking a claim on our Mr Cowell,' Roxi says, perching next to me on the rock and easing her shoes off. 'Ooh, when they say killer heels, they really mean it.'

'Then why are you wearing them?' I ask. 'Tara is hardly high-heel terrain. And Dermot's just helping Caitlin with her suitcase, that's all.'

Roxi's eyes snap open as wide as saucers. Then she shakes her head. 'Darcy, Darcy, Darcy,' she says, 'have I taught you nothing? You need to make a move as soon as you can when you have your eye on someone. And she definitely had her eye on him.' She holds up her shoes. 'And isn't it obvious why I'm wearing these little babies? Because they look fabulous!'

I glance back to the cottages. 'You really think Caitlin's interested in *Dermot*?'

'You bet your life she is. In fact, how about we have a little wager on it?' Roxi's eyes sparkle with interest, and she rubs the palms of her hands together.

'Oh, no,' I say, vehemently shaking my head, 'not one of your little bets again. The last time I agreed to one of those I spent the night in the local police station. How on earth you persuaded me to attach a life-size blow-up doll to the Eros statue in Piccadilly Circus I still don't know.'

Roxi laughs. 'Ah, that was a class night. The poor guy looked lonely, balancing up there all alone on St Valentine's Day, and him a god of love, too.'

'Hmm, it may have been a fun night for you, but it certainly wasn't for me. No, Roxi, no bets on Tara.'

'What about something more simple then?' Roxi says, ignoring me as usual. 'How about if you're proved right and Caitlin hasn't got the hots for Mr Cowell, I have to ...' she grins, '... kiss Mr Solicitor over there.'

'Niall?' I look across to where Niall is just organising the last of the new islanders into their accommodation. Conor and Paddy are assisting him by helping to carry all their belongings, and I suddenly feel quite protective of him. 'Aw, don't be mean to Niall, Roxi. He can't help that he's a bit shy with women.'

'I'm not being mean to him. I love Niall, he's wicked, you know that. OK, then, who else if not him?'

I look towards Caitlin's cottage and grin.

'No, no *way*!' Roxi insists. 'Not Mr Cowell.'

'Why not? I thought you liked Dermot when you first met him.'

'It's not that. He's quite a good-looking chap as it goes, if you like that type.' Roxi considers this for a moment. 'But he hates me, doesn't he? Have you any idea how hard it would be for even me, Roxanne Whitney Reynolds, to try to kiss him?'

'Your idea to have a bet,' I remind her. 'Plus, if you're so sure you're right, then you won't have to kiss him, will you? Anyway, Dermot doesn't hate you, it's just his way.'

Roxi's dark eyes narrow. 'Hmm, you drive a hard bargain, Miss McCall. But do you know what?' she says, fluttering her long eyelashes at me. 'I'm not as mean as you and because, obviously, I'm so going to win this bet, I'm going make this easy for you.'

'Oh, yeah?'

'Yep, so when *I'm* right, you, Darcy, well, this is hardly a forfeit, more a pleasure, you have to kiss Conor.'

I look now at Conor effortlessly carrying bags and cases just like Dermot.

I think I'm onto a winner, whether I win or lose.

'Deal,' I say, holding out my hand for Roxi to shake on it. 'But how will we know who's won?'

'Oh, we'll know all right, Darce. On an island this size you're not going to be able to keep anything secret for long.' Roxi watches me smiling shyly at Conor, as he waves casually in my direction. 'Maybe you weren't the only one that got pally with Eros that night in Piccadilly Circus.'

Sixteen

Barbecues aren't something you're invited to that often in London. It's considered a rare treat to go to someone's home that has a big enough garden to house one. But now that I've eaten barbecued food two nights running, it's becoming a bit much to stomach for a third night in succession.

Or maybe it's because I'm nervous that I've lost my appetite tonight, I wonder, watching everyone starting to tuck in to the mountains of sausages, burgers and chicken legs that were delivered along with the furniture today, and are now being expertly cooked on our two barbecues by Dermot and Conor.

Perhaps I should just get what I've got to say over and done with – at least I'll be able to relax then, once everyone knows the truth.

I climb up onto one of the wooden benches and take a deep breath.

'Ahem, if I could just have everyone's attention, please,' I call out into the throng of people milling around the fires holding plates of food, cans of beer and glasses of wine.

'Excuse me, everyone!' I try again, when no one responds to my request.

'Oi, you lot, quiet!' Dermot shouts, holding his barbecue tongs aloft. He points them in my direction. 'Darcy has something to say.'

'Thanks, Dermot.' I smile gratefully. 'Now, first, I'd like to welcome you all properly to Tara. I hope you've been able to settle into your cottages this afternoon without any trouble.'

'The decor's not quite what I was expecting,' one of the men calls. 'I've got shamrocks all over my bedroom curtains.'

'Think yourself lucky! Ours are covered in pints of Guinness,' one of the women shouts back, who I think is Kathleen, Aiden the baker's wife.

The new cottage decor has finally been outed.

When we'd gone over to the Emerald Arms Hotel, we'd discovered that Mary's idea of traditional Irish hospitality had extended far beyond the reception rooms of the hotel, and that each of her twenty bedrooms was individually designed with its own Irish theme.

There was a Guinness-themed room, a leprechaun room, a room devoted to Irish rugby and a room filled with traditional Irish musical instruments such as harps, tin whistles, fiddles and bodhráns – a traditional Irish drum. An almost life-size Molly Malone statue stood proudly in the Dublin-themed blue and white room, and there was also a room dedicated to the delights of Jameson's whiskey. The only one I'd quite liked was a room inspired by Celtic symbols. The bed in that room had a wooden bedhead with a large Claddagh symbol carved into it.

'It's a Celtic symbol of love,' Conor had informed me as I inspected the carving of two hands holding a crowned heart.

'Yes, the crown stands for loyalty, the hands for friendship and the heart for love.'

'That's right, how do you know?'

'My aunt used to have a ring with the same symbol on.' I ran my hand lightly over the wooden carving as another memory stirred within me. 'She never took it off.'

'According to tradition, the hand the owner wears their ring on, and the way the ring faces on the hand, conveys their romantic availability,' Conor explains. 'How did your aunt wear hers?'

'I can't remember,' I'd had to admit. 'Oh, that's so awful, Conor, I can't actually remember.'

'Hey, don't feel too bad. I guess it must have been a long time ago now.'

'I know, but I should still remember these things about her, I'm a poor excuse for a niece, aren't I?'

'I don't think so.' Conor had stood back and pretended to examine me. 'I think you're a pretty fine specimen, actually.'

I glance at Conor now as I stand in front of the assembled crowd; he smiles up at me encouragingly and gives me a little wink. I take a deep breath. *I can do this. I can handle these people. I'll do it for you, Aunt Molly.*

'Ah, that, yes. Perhaps I should explain. I know it's hardly what you'd call traditional decor,' I can feel my cheeks beginning to turn their usual shade of red when under pressure, but this time I desperately try to bring them under control. 'Unfortunately there was a slight mix-up in the furnishings department, and we were very lucky in finding a local hotelier that was closing down. We're extremely pleased at what we've been able to get, in the circumstances.'

One or two of the new islanders glance at each other dubiously.

'Anyway,' I continue in a bright voice. 'I'm very pleased to have you all here at last, and to begin what I hope will be an exciting adventure for us all living and working here together on Tara.' I pause to clear my throat. 'I know when we advertised for people to come and live on the island with us, we said that it would be a "grow-your-own"-type existence, with a farm and animals and so on. Unfortunately there's been a slight hitch with that side of things too.'

A murmur of discontent rumbles through the crowd, and there are more dubious looks and some raised eyebrows this time as well.

'Is this your way of telling us you're getting the animals from a zoo that's closing down now, as well?' a red-headed man shouts across the others. 'So we're looking after elephants now, instead of sheep?'

There's a ripple of laughter from the new residents of Tara.

I look closely at him. I'm pretty sure he was one of Dermot's choices.

'Oh, no, nothing like that!' I'm desperately trying to keep a confident tone to my voice as I address the new islanders. 'It seems – and I knew nothing of this until I arrived myself a couple of days ago – that the conditions here on Tara are just not suited to keeping the usual type of farm animal, or growing many of the basic crops we'd need to survive on. That, apparently, is one of the main reasons the communities here died out in the past.'

One or two of the people in front of me look a bit panicky when I use the phrase 'died out'.

'Obviously there are many more ways to get food over to us now than there were in the past,' I hurriedly remind them. 'We won't starve or anything. We'll be able to survive in a lot more comfort than our ancestors did. We have fridges and freezers to store our food. No seal blubber and raw potatoes for us! A couple of trips to Tesco and we're sorted for a week. You know what the advert says: "That's why islanders go to Iceland!" I smile at my own joke, hoping it will lighten the mood a little.

It doesn't.

'Don't believe all this blarney she's trying to fob youse off with,' the same angry man waves his hot dog in the air for added effect. 'What you're actually trying to tell us is that you've brought us all here under false pretences, is that right?'

'No,' I'm trying to remain calm, but it's becoming increasingly harder with this man's constant barrage of criticism. 'Like I said, I didn't know anything about this until a couple of days ago. It was only when one of the locals pointed it out to me that I learned the facts.'

'But you let us all arrive anyway?' he says accusingly, jabbing his hot dog in my direction like a sword delivering its final blow.

I resist countering his challenge and knocking his ketchup-covered sausage out of his hand. 'The truth of the matter is that I didn't have any choice. There aren't exactly a lot of ways to communicate with the outside world once you're here, if you haven't already noticed. And most of you were already on your way by then.'

'Is it something to do with the telly people?' a woman calls out from the crowd.

'The what?' I ask in confusion.

'The telly people,' she continues. 'Have they changed the format of the programme, is that why we're not keeping animals and stuff now?'

'Sorry,' I shake my head. 'I honestly have no idea what you're talking about.'

A few of the new residents exchange anxious looks.

'That is what we're here for, isn't it?' another man asks now. 'Look, I know you're probably not supposed to say anything, 'cos that's the format of the show 'n' all, but most of us have guessed what's going on and that's why we're here.'

'What show? What format?' I ask. 'I really don't have the faintest idea what you mean.'

'So ... we're not being secretly filmed?' the other woman chips in again now. 'This isn't a new island version of *Big Brother*?'

Oh, now I get it. They think they're part of some secret reality TV experiment.

'I'm sorry to break it to you, but no, you're not. This is not a TV show, and we're not going out live on Channel 4.'

Audible sighs of disappointment fill the air over Tara as the wannabe islanders realise they're not going to be offered a magazine deal with *OK!* or *Heat* at the end of their time here.

'But there's a bonus to us not being filmed,' I say cheerily. 'Unlike the lovely Davina, I'll allow you to swear as much as you like.'

Other than Roxi's lone squeal of laughter, my joke falls on stony ground as most of the faces look up at me with derision.

'So,' I swallow hard. 'Out of interest, how many of you thought this was being secretly filmed for TV?'

About a dozen people raise their hands. *Ouch.*

'I'm really sorry to disappoint you, but we can still make this work, can't we? Tara is a beautiful place to come and live.'

They don't look very convinced.

'All this is beside the point,' the red-haired man pipes up again. 'Just because some of this lot were gullible enough to think this was being filmed for TV, we were still brought here on false pretences, and I for one think we have good grounds to sue.'

Oh, God, this isn't going well. I look to Niall for help.

'Mr Bradley, Seamus. Please calm down,' Niall says in his Dublin solicitor's voice, walking towards the front of the crowd. 'I'm sorry some of you seem to have been under a misapprehension as to the purpose of your time here on Tara. I can assure you that it was never suggested by any of us that a television company would be involved in this project in any way. And there is certainly no need to talk about suing anyone.' Niall firmly pushes his glasses back up onto the bridge of his nose. 'And even if there was a need,' he says in an even more assured tone, glancing at Angry Seamus, 'I can assure *all* of you that you'd have no grounds whatsoever, since Miss McCall has alternative arrangements for you in hand.' Niall flashes a warning glance in my direction.

'What sort of alternative arrangements?' Angry Seamus asks, narrowing his eyes. 'I mean, if we can't keep animals and we can't farm, and there's no TV involved, what the feck are we going to do while we're here?'

'Yes,' Daniel the ex-GP asks, 'How are we to earn a living? We can't just live on fresh air.'

'Perhaps Miss McCall expects us to go on one long extended vacation?' Kathleen pipes up again.

'No, of course I don't just expect you to come here on holiday. But I can imagine a lot of people would like to spend time here getting away from it all just like you are.'

'How do you mean, Darcy?' Orla, a teacher, asks. She's looking extremely puzzled, as is everyone else who's standing around waiting expectantly for the next instalment of nonsense to spring from my mouth – including Niall, Dermot, Conor, Paddy and Roxi. (Eamon has wisely chosen to stay away from this gathering.) They're all wondering just what I'm going to say next, too.

I take a deep breath. 'You all know how keen *you* were to get away from it all and come and live here on this island. Imagine how many people might like to experience just a small part of it too? But not for a year, like you – for a short break instead.' I let this thought penetrate their minds for a moment before I continue. 'What I would like to do is to open Tara up as an exclusive holiday resort,' I say proudly, sharing my idea for the first time since it popped into my head on the beach yesterday morning. 'We'll rent out small, exclusive cottages on the island to holidaymakers who want to escape for a while, and we'll also develop a few other leisure facilities here too, so there'll be plenty for you to do.' I look around at them all, still staring up at me with a mixture of bewilderment and doubt on their faces. 'I know this idea will work: you're just going to have to trust me.'

There – I've said it.

As I look out into the crowd, waiting for some sort of reaction, there's silence before me as the enormity of what I've just said slowly sinks into everyone's head.

'Away with you!' Unsurprisingly, Angry Seamus is the first to recover his voice. 'This one doesn't know what she's rabbiting on about, so she doesn't. Who's really in charge here?'

'I can assure you, I am.' I'm beginning to take an extreme dislike to Angry Seamus now. 'But no one is *in charge*, as you put it. We all run this island equally together.'

'Who is *we*?' Seamus demands.

'Me,' Niall says, stepping forward. 'I'm with Darcy.'

'I should have known you'd be involved,' Seamus says, rolling his eyes. 'And what do you think about this *holiday* island?'

Niall stares hard at me.

I know exactly what he's thinking; *Why didn't I run this past him first?*

'In principle, I think the idea could work,' Niall says to my relief. 'But of course there would need to be a lot of discussion as to how we could proceed with the plans, so that everyone is happy with the idea and their part in it.'

Good answer.

Angry Seamus glares at Niall, while Roxi saunters forward in her latest pair of heels – purple wedges this time.

'You know I'm with you, honey,' she says, linking arms with me.

'Is that it, then?' he asks. 'You, Harry Potter and Beyoncé are all we've got to rely on to keep us safe and secure while we live here?'

'No, you've got me,' Dermot says, stepping forward and standing beside us, folding his arms. 'You got a problem with that, Rusty?'

I hear Paddy give a snort of laughter behind me as he now steps forward too. 'And me,' he says, planting his Doc Marten boots firmly down on the ground just like Dermot has done. 'Your head's up your arse if ya think people wouldn't wanna come here for their holidays,' he announces to the rest of the crowd. 'I've worked in the tourist industry all me life, and Darcy's right, they'd love it here.'

While the rest of the crowd breaks out into a heated discussion, I turn towards where Conor has been sitting a few moments ago on one of the benches. He's still there, looking completely calm and relaxed amid all the madness. He simply looks up at me and winks.

'Look, everyone,' I say, trying to calm them all down again. 'Obviously this is not how any of us quite thought it was going to be when we imagined coming to live here. I certainly didn't, I can assure you. As I said before, there's a lot we need to discuss yet, and I would very much like you all to be involved in making those decisions with us. But if you really don't want to be, then come and see me in the morning and Niall and I will arrange for transport back to the mainland again for you as soon as possible, and we will of course pay for any expenses. But for now, thank you for listening, everyone.'

I take another deep breath and jump down from the bench where I've been standing for the past few minutes, my legs almost buckling underneath me.

'Why didn't you run this past me before?' Niall hisses in my ear as a barrage of people swarm in our direction.

'Tried. Didn't have time,' I whisper back, 'Sorry, Niall, is it a rubbish idea?'

'No,' Niall grins. 'Actually it could be a very profitable one. I just wish you'd given me some notice, that's all!'

'She could have given us a bit more warning,' I hear Dermot grumble as he tries to avoid the sea of people washing towards him.

'Just keeping you on your toes, Dermot,' I call. 'I wouldn't want you to think I was conforming to type, now would I?'

Seventeen

'How much further?' Roxi pants as she trails behind Woody and Louis and me as we head off into unknown territory this morning, towards Eamon's cottage on the other side of the island.

Eamon is the only person who doesn't know about my plans as yet, and I feel it isn't fair to keep him in the dark about them too long. It isn't a conversation I'm looking forward to having; I'm never quite sure how Eamon will react to anything, let alone a big change to the island such as this is going to be. So when Roxi offered to come with us, I'd welcomed the company, even if it did mean I'd had to haul her out of bed so that we'd be guaranteed of catching Eamon when he was in a good mood. Eamon was definitely an early bird, so we were setting off on this jaunt to his cottage at a time when Roxi was usually dead to the world.

The dogs and I pause for a moment so she can catch up with us. She comes lumbering up the long, winding path that leads all the way from the other side of the island, looking most un-Roxi-like in a red polo neck sweater, white jeans and silver wellington boots with red and pink hearts scattered over them.

'Come on,' I call back down the path, 'it can't be much further, and we haven't been going *that* long.'

'I knew I shouldn't have worn these stupid things,' Roxi says as she catches up with us. 'My feet are killing me. Give me a four-inch heel any day. Who ever invented wellies wants shooting.'

'The Duke of Wellington did, actually. Although,' I shield my eyes from her boots, pretending that they're dazzling me in the early-morning sun, 'I doubt he ever imagined they'd look like the ones on your feet right now!'

'Who invented the loafer, then?' Roxi counters, shuffling her feet around uncomfortably. 'The Earl of Sandwich?'

'Ooh, nice one, Rox, I'm impressed. So why *are* you wearing the wellies then? Couldn't you have worn trainers, or something a bit less bulky to walk up to Eamon's?'

'When have you *ever* seen me in trainers, Darce?'

I think for a moment. 'What about that time you took up Boxercise for a while? You must have had trainers for that.'

'I only took that class because the instructor was fit; I sold the trainers on eBay when he left three classes into the course. Darcy, my feet just ain't happy in flat shoes! They pine for a heel when they're this close to the ground.'

'OK, OK,' I hold my hands up in submission. 'I'm afraid you're going to have to put up with them now we're halfway up this hill. Come on – we need to get moving again.'

Roxi yawns as we begin walking at a slower pace this time.

'You know, I don't think much to the talent you've assembled on this island, babe.'

I turn and look at her in astonishment. 'As much as I would have liked to set this island up solely for you to find Mr Right, we didn't have an awful lot of options to choose from. And now quite a few have gone home this morning, in case you hadn't noticed.'

'How many went in the end?'

'Twelve in total, which isn't too bad considering so many of them thought it was a TV show.'

'I don't know! People these days, anything for five minutes of fame.' Roxi tosses her raven hair back over her shoulder.

'And remind me again just *how* long did we queue last year for the *X-Factor* auditions?'

'That was different!' Roxi dramatically clasps her hand to her chest. 'I have *genuine* undiscovered singing talent.'

'Yes, *you* might do, but I haven't, and I still had to queue there with you all day.'

'But we saw little Dermot O'Leary, so that made it all worth it.'

'Correction, Roxi: we saw the back of Dermot O'Leary's head. It did not.'

Roxi shakes her head. 'You're always so negative, Darcy. Now, about these people we've got to live with, why are they nearly all coupled up? What good is that to me?'

'They're not all coupled up – are they?'

Roxi stops walking and holds her hand up in front of her to demonstrate her point as she counts on each fingernail – pillar-box red with tiny silver stars today. 'You've got the ones that run the baker's in Dublin – Aiden and Kathleen. Then the doc and the teacher, Daniel and Orla, they're married. Then there's that angry red-haired fellow . . .'

'Seamus.'

'That's the chap,' Roxi grimaces and shakes her head. 'And then of course we've got Miss Goody Two Shoes, Caitlin, and we've already talked about where her romantic objectives lie.' She gives me a meaningful look over the top of her fingers. 'Then there's Ryan – he's a bit of all right, as it goes, *if* he wasn't already paired up with Siobhan.'

'But those two aren't together.'

'They are now! They met at the interviews, apparently, and have been dating ever since. So when they both got picked to come here, they were over the moon about it!' Roxi puts her hands on her hips. 'I tell you, Darce, this island is a like a magnet for love. I felt it the moment I planted my pink suede heels on it – and they never lie in matters of the heart.'

I shake my head. 'I'm sure it won't have its effect on me. I'm off men, after the last few times – it only ends in heart-break, or it usually does for me.'

'I wouldn't be so sure. I've got a feeling Tara moves in mysterious ways, just like myself.'

'What do you mean?'

'Seen much of Mr Gorgeous since we got here?' Roxi's eyes widen as she flutters her false eyelashes.

'You mean Conor?'

'Aha!' Roxi waggles her finger in my face. 'I knew it. So you *do* fancy him!'

My face flushes the colour of Roxi's top. 'I might.'

'So what have you done about it, then?' she demands.

'Not much.'

'Why ever not? Oh, Darcy, will you never *learn*? Men need you to do all the running. They're useless, left to their own devices.'

'Maybe I don't need to do any running,' I answer. 'Maybe Conor is doing all the legwork for me.'

'Oh, he *is*, is he?' Roxi says, folding her arms and regarding me approvingly. 'Then I have been teaching you well.'

As finally we stumble upon Eamon's cottage, we find it looks much the same as all the other dwellings on Tara. But as we get closer, I realise that whereas mine and the other cottages on the island are newly whitewashed, Eamon's has suffered the extremes of Tara's ever-changing weather. There are several large patches of paint peeling from the outside walls, and his front door definitely hasn't seen a lick of anything in years. But in spite of that, it still manages to retain a homely, welcoming feel to it as we approach. In addition to the water butt that all the cottages on Tara have been provided with, Eamon also has a washing line strung up outside his home, and a homemade bird table stands a little way from his front door with kitchen scraps and a small water dish perched on top of it.

I take a deep breath as we approach the little wooden door, knocking firmly on it as soon as we get there in case my confidence suddenly deserts me and I change my mind. Having Roxi with me is all well and good, but it's me that's going to have to explain everything to Eamon.

Almost immediately we hear a shuffling behind the door as we wait for it to open, but oddly it doesn't; instead, a window to our left is suddenly thrust ajar and Eamon's head appears through it.

'What are you doing all the way over here?' he asks, not looking too pleased to see us.

'We just came over to talk to you about something,' I take a step back from the door to try to see him a bit better.

'What?'

'It might be easier to explain if we come in,' I ask, hoping he'll move around to the front door. 'It's not really something I can just tell you quickly.'

Eamon sighs. 'I'll come out,' he says, pulling the window shut. He immediately pulls the curtains closed too.

I look at Roxi uneasily; she simply shrugs.

After a minute, the front door opens a fraction. It's a gap just wide enough for Eamon to squeeze through. As I begin to wonder just what he's got hidden inside his cottage, he jerks the door closed behind him. 'Now, just what is so important it's brought you all the way around to this side of the island this morning?'

I wasn't expecting this kind of welcome – especially not since I'd brought Roxi with me. Eamon had been so friendly the other night.

While Roxi rests her feet outside Eamon's cottage, we walk along the cliff path together while I give him the speech I've been rehearsing on and off all day, about how this will be great for Tara and how it won't be like a tourist trap or anything horrific like that. The further away from his cottage we seem to get the more Eamon relaxes.

'So how many folks stayed on?' Eamon asks when I've finished explaining what happened yesterday.

I quickly work this out in my head. 'Eight, but including the rest of us that's, erm, fourteen in total.'

'Is fourteen enough folk to be here on Tara looking after all these holidaymakers you've got coming over to stay?' Eamon enquiringly raises a white eyebrow.

Wait a minute ... fourteen! I need fifteen, don't I?

'Oh, there's you, Eamon, too!' I breathe I sigh of relief. 'That makes it fifteen in total.'

'What will you do with all these folk when they get here?' he pauses to rest for a moment, and plants his stick in the ground. 'Me, I can just get by appreciating all these grand views every day, but people want more these days.'

'Conor has suggested we lay on fishing and hiking and boat trips around the island. I'm hoping to make it into an outdoor activity kind of holiday destination. We're going to be renovating some more of the cottages, too. Dermot's already said he can see to that, with some help.'

Eamon nods. 'Ah, yes, he's a hard worker, is Dermot. Stubborn mind, but there's not much'll stand in his way when he puts his mind to it.'

'Yes, you're probably right there, Eamon.'

'So what gave you the idea for this holiday island, then?'

I explain to Eamon what happened on the beach yesterday.

' ... and then this bucket and spade was washed up at my feet. And I thought it might have been a sign, Eamon, like a clue to prompt me to my idea for the island.'

'What makes you think that?'

'Well unless *you* regularly go down to the beach to make sandcastles, I'm sure no one else has ever played with a bucket and spade on these shores, have they?'

Eamon shakes his head. 'No, you'd be right there; I very much doubt anyone has ever made sandcastles on these beaches. But they have done on the beaches on the mainland. Those items could have been floating around in the sea for years, and simply been washed up here.' Eamon glances out to sea.

'Oh, yes, I suppose they could, I hadn't thought of that.'

This is not the reaction I was expecting from Eamon. I thought with him being into Celtic myths and legends and everything, he'd have appreciated what I considered my brush with something a bit mystical. Maybe he's right, though; perhaps it was just a coincidence? I'm about to question him further when I see what he's looking at. There in the waves far out to sea are the unmistakable curves of dolphin's fins dipping in and out of the water.

'They're back again,' I exclaim, staring out to sea with Eamon.

'That they are.'

'But you said that meant they were worried, or something.'

'I said they sensed change afoot, and it seems now they were right.' Eamon turns to me. 'How many did you see the other day, Darcy?'

'Two.'

We both turn to look out to sea again, and can clearly see the back of at least four dolphins diving in and out of the water.

Eamon silently turns to me.

'Oh, come on, Eamon, so you want me to believe a random bucket and spade being washed up means nothing, but an ever-growing school of dolphins does? How does that work, then? You can't have it both ways!'

Eamon sighs. Then he smiles, as his blue eyes peer intently into mine. 'You remind me so much of your aunt Molly sometimes.'

I look back into his eyes and something stirs inside me once more. A flash of something familiar.

'But you're right. As she often was,' Eamon says, pulling his stick from the ground. 'It's not fair of me to confuse you with my tales one moment, then try to find a rational explanation for things the next. But you'd be surprised at what gets washed up on these beaches; I've got quite a few bits and pieces in my cottage.'

'Like what?'

'Ah, bits and bobs. This 'n' that,' Eamon says cryptically.

'Can I see?'

'Maybe another time.' He looks up at the sky. 'You'd best be collecting up your friend and getting those dogs back before it rains, hadn't you?'

I look up into the clouds. It does look a bit dark.

'So my holiday idea, Eamon,' I prompt, gathering Woody and Louis up ready to find Roxi again. 'You don't have a problem with it, do you? You can tell me.'

'Now, why would I have a problem?' Eamon plants his stick down firmly in front of him ready to head off.

'I know you probably don't approve of the idea.'

'Did you hear me say that?' Eamon mutters, as he sets off slowly in the direction of his cottage.

'No, but I thought—'

'Don't think things about folk unless you know them to be

true,' Eamon calls, not turning around as he continues to walk back along the path. He waves his stick in the air in a gesture of farewell.

'On this island?' I say to no one but Louis, Woody and a random seagull who watches us from a nearby rock. 'I try not to think too much about any one thing for too long, or I might go insane!'

Eighteen

We don't quite make it back to our cottages in time before the heavens open and rain begins to pour down. Roxi, me and the two puppies look like we've swum over to see Eamon as we try to find our way back to our cottages through the mist and murk.

Everyone else seems to be sensibly sheltering indoors too. There are no signs of life as we hurry through the newly named O'Connell Street (we've part nicknamed, part christened the area in front of the cottages where Dermot has built his benches and his barbecues after the famous Dublin thorough-fare, and also after Dermot himself, and the name has stuck) but a few hands are waved from windows as we pass by some of the cottages – and the small gesture feels very welcome on such a miserable morning.

'Come on, guys,' I call to the puppies as we leave Roxi at her cottage and head on over to our own. 'We need to get you two dried off, and I need a hot shower, fast.'

I haven't had much success with the hot-water system in

the cottage so far. I know we're lucky even to have showers at all; we could have arrived on Tara finding we only had tin baths or something equally uncomfortable. But Dermot's somehow managed to rig up a tiny shower cubicle for each cottage – something to do with our generators and the boilers and a heating element, I think. He has explained it all to me, in great detail. But that's the thing with Dermot's explanations – although they're very thorough, they are sometimes quite long and you do tend to drift off a bit in the middle of them.

So my attempts at showers have been somewhat erratic up to now. In fact I've avoided them completely, having never been able to get the water to run at a hot enough temperature for long enough to get in properly. Instead I've bathed at my sink in the little bit of warm water I can manage to run, and I've washed my hair under the shower hose in bursts of lukewarm and cold water. But today is different; I'm soaking wet and freezing cold, and I need a hot shower to warm me up. I *have* to get this thing to work.

So after I dry off the dogs and give them some food, I go into my bedroom to collect my shower things. I claimed the Celtic-patterned room set for myself when we'd been dishing out all the hotel furnishings. I can't vouch for what the other bedrooms on Tara look like, with pints of Guinness or sheep plastered all over the duvets, but my room looks quite pretty now that it's all set up in my little cottage. As I pass by the Claddagh-carved bedhead, something makes me stop and stare at it. Like so many things here on Tara, it keeps reminding me of my aunt Molly. As I'd told Conor at the hotel, I always remember her wearing her own gold Claddagh ring. Screwing up my eyes, I try to remember again on which hand she wore it. But I can't; all I know is she never took it off.

I wonder what happened to it? It would mean so much to me to remember Molly by. Niall had given me a small wooden box of things which I'd taken a brief look through, but Molly wasn't really one for jewellery, so what few bits there were, were mostly costume. The ring definitely wasn't in there, though, or I'd have seen it. I make a mental note to ask Niall about it sometime.

I go through to the tiny bathroom and begin running my shower. It's cold, as usual. But that's what always happens; it starts off like that, then it comes through warm in a minute, and just when I've got my hopes up it might stay hot, it will go stone cold again.

'*Please*,' I wail as I hurriedly peel off my cold, damp clothes and wrap a towel around myself. 'Please, just this once can the water stay warm long enough for me to take a hot shower? I'm cold; I don't want to catch pneumonia.'

As I stand there shivering, I wonder who exactly is supposed to hear my request in the empty bathroom. Perhaps a tiny leprechaun plumber could be perched on my windowsill at this very moment, and come to my aid? On this island, it wouldn't surprise me!

Tentatively I put my hand back under the running water again, and to my surprise I find it's still running hot, and not only that, it appears to be getting hotter all the time. I glance around the bathroom suspiciously. 'Excellent work, Mr Leprechaun!' I grin, about to pull my towel off.

There's a crash from the kitchen.

'What? No, not now!' I cry, looking longingly at the steaming-hot water pouring down into the shower and running away down the plughole. 'Woody, Louis, this had better be good,' I call, pulling the curtain back around the shower and stomping out to the kitchen.

Woody has somehow managed to hoist himself up onto the sink's draining board and is growling at a large seagull perching nonchalantly on the windowsill outside, while Louis bravely eggs him on from the floor below surrounded by the remains of a broken dinner plate.

'What are you two doing?' I lift Woody down immediately and place him back on the floor. 'Woody, that's bad,' I say in my sternest voice, quickly clearing up the pieces of broken china. 'In your beds, now!' I point to their dog beds. 'I'll deal with you two later.'

I rush back to the shower, praying the water is still hot, and to my surprise it is. As I climb under the running water and allow it to pour over my body the sensation that it brings is comforting, yet at the same time quite overpowering, and I realise this is the first time I've done anything as familiar to anything I would do at home in London since I've been here.

Lathering my hair up with shampoo, I decide that these sensations must be a type of homesickness, and it's the familiar feeling of the shower and the smells of my regular bathtime products that are evoking these emotions. Rinsing off my shampoo, I apply conditioner and comb it through, then I stand in the shower allowing the product to soak into my hair, enjoying for a few minutes longer the hot water comforting me within the tiny, four-walled cubicle.

'*Aaargh*!' I scream, as the water suddenly has a change of

heart and decides instead to give me a quick slap around the face by dropping several degrees and then continuing to run at a temperature only a polar bear could love.

Pulling back the curtain, I climb out as quickly as I can and stand for a few seconds dripping water onto the floor in the hope that it will heat up again, as it usually does. But each time I put my hand under the water to test it, it's still freezing.

'No!' I cry after a couple of minutes have passed and it's still stone cold. 'I only have to rinse my conditioner out. Can't I just have enough warm water to do that?'

But when no more hot water is forthcoming, it seems the plumbing leprechaun has gone home.

'Aargh!' I shout again in frustration, leaping up and down on the spot like a Maori warrior doing a haka dance. 'Aargh! Aargh! Aargh!'

There's an urgent banging on my front door, and I hear the dogs barking.

'Great,' I say, rolling my eyes to the ceiling. 'What now?'

I pull a towel around me again and go to the door.

'What is it?' I say abruptly through the unopened door. 'I'm trying to take a shower.'

'Is that what you're doing?' I hear Dermot's voice say from the other side. 'I thought you were being murdered.'

'It felt like it when the stupid water went cold!' I say irritably, pulling my towel around me. 'I don't think the hot water in my cottage works, Dermot. This is the first time I've got it to work properly today, and even now it hasn't run for very long.'

'How long were in the shower for?'

'I don't know ... about ten minutes, maybe?'

'Are you sure it wasn't longer than that?'

'No,' I attempt a convincing voice. But now, thinking about it, I suppose it may have been a bit longer than that . . .

'Look, I can't do anything about it standing outside in the rain. Are you going to let me in? I'm probably wetter than you are, hanging about out here.'

'But I'm not dressed,' I glance at my reflection in the Celtic carved mirror that now hangs in the hallway – a part of Mary's bedroom set.

'I should hope not, if you've just got out of the shower. Look, Darcy, do you want hot water or not?'

I close my eyes for a moment and sigh. Then I pull the latch back on the door and swing it open.

Bending his head in order to do so, Dermot walks in through the low door. Pulling back the hood of his raincoat, he smirks at the puddle of water that has now gathered around my feet on the hallway floor.

'Don't say anything,' I instruct him. 'Just fix my water, please.'

'The shower, or your own personal supply down there?' he laughs.

I pull a face behind his back as he walks through to my kitchen, gripping my towel extra tightly around me as I follow him.

The boiler is housed in a little cupboard at the back of the kitchen. Dermot sticks his head in the cupboard, then just as quickly reappears again. 'How long did you say you were in the shower for?' he asks, looking me up and down in a suspicious manner.

I wish I was wearing more clothes. The towel, while it's a

bath towel, is making me feel very exposed under Dermot's intense gaze right now, and I don't feel able to defend myself in quite the way I'd like to.

'Ten … maybe fifteen minutes.'

'Was the water running long before you got in the shower?' Dermot demands, like a detective cross-examining his suspect.

'No,' I say proudly. 'I know we're not supposed to waste the water. It's one of the fundamental rules on the island.' I reinforce the words *fundamental rules* in the same way I've heard Dermot when he's instructing anyone about how to run their homes. 'I would never—'

I stop abruptly.

'What?' Dermot asks.

'I may just have had to step into the kitchen quickly before I got into the shower.'

Dermot raises an unruly eyebrow at me.

'It wasn't my fault, the puppies were causing trouble and I had to sort them out.'

'And you left the water running?'

'It was hot. It had never been that warm for so long before. I needed a hot shower, Dermot, I was freezing cold and soaking wet.'

'There's your answer then.'

'What is?'

'The answer to why you've not got any hot water now. You've used it all up from your tank. It's empty.'

I look at Dermot blankly.

He sighs. 'You've only got enough in these little tanks for a constant stream of about fifteen to twenty minutes, absolute max. By the sounds of it, you must have been running the water much longer than that.'

I look towards the cupboard, then back towards Dermot.

'You mean, my water is kept in *there*?' I ask, feeling stupid.

'Your hot water is stored in there while it's heated, yes. I thought I explained all this to you the other day.'

You probably did . . .

'But when I was in London I just had hot water all the time. I didn't have a tank with it all in, I'm sure.' I think quickly; maybe we did have a tank in our flat and I'd never noticed it. No: the flat was barely big enough for us to fit all our clothes in. I couldn't have missed something like that. Could I?

'You probably had a combi boiler,' Demot says matter-of-factly. 'They just heat your water all the time over elements. They don't store it in a tank like these systems we've got here.'

'Oh,' I say quietly, 'I see.' Then another thought occurs to me. 'So how long before I can get hot water again?'

'Twenty minutes to half an hour, if you've drained it completely.'

'What!' I'm starting to feel very cold again now, as the warmth of the shower begins to drain from my body as quickly as the water had done earlier down the plughole.

'That's what happens when you don't listen to what people tell you.' Dermot shrugs, reaches down and begins stroking Louis behind the ears, who immediately rolls over on his back for his tummy to be tickled.

Standing in my kitchen wrapped in only my towel and with conditioner plastered through my hair, I feel angry, awkward and cold all at the same time.

Dermot turns his head back up to look at me. 'You could

come over to my cottage and finish your shower, if you like?' he suggests, standing up again.

I narrow my eyes at him, not quite sure how I feel about this suggestion. 'And just how will I get over there? I'm already soaking wet!'

Dermot shrugs again. 'Dry yourself? Put on some clothes?'

I think this through. Roxi would be unlikely to have any hot water left – she would have used all hers up when she had her own shower.

'That could work, I suppose.'

'Thank you, Dermot. What a wonderful suggestion,' Dermot says, grinning at me. 'And how wonderfully generous of you to let me use your very precious hot water, when I've so carelessly used my own up in such a carefree manner.'

'All right, don't go over the top,' I smile ruefully at him. 'Yes, thank you then, I would like to use your shower if I may, please, Dermot.'

'You may indeed, Darcy. Now get dressed, for goodness' sake before you leave more puddles. The puppies will think they need to house-train *you* in a minute!'

The shower in Dermot's bathroom works a treat, and I manage to have another lovely wash, rinsing my now very well-conditioned hair out in a constant stream of hot running water.

When I've finished, I towel myself dry and dress again. But before I leave, I can't help having a little nose around Dermot's bathroom. Not that there's much to see; Dermot obviously isn't the sort of man who's heavily into aftershave balms and cleansing lotions. In fact, once I've gathered my own beauty products up there's hardly anything left to see at all. There's a toothbrush and some toothpaste sitting in a glass, a bar of soap in a dish, a can of deodorant, a cut-throat razor and some shaving foam – very disappointing.

I return to find Dermot making breakfast in his kitchen.

'Better?' he enquires.

'Yes, thanks. Much.'

'Tea?' he asks, holding out a mug.

'Why not?'

'Milk and sugar?'

'Just one, please,' I nod.

I watch Dermot make the tea. He does it in the way he seems to do everything – practically and with little wasted effort.

'Now, can I get you some breakfast?' Dermot enquires, adding some rashers of bacon to the sausages that are already sizzling away in a frying pan on his stove.

I shake my head. 'No, thanks. I don't really do breakfast.'

Dermot raises his eyebrows. 'Why not?' he demands.

'I don't know. I never really had time when I was in London.'

'You've got time now. Let me cook you some. You look like you could do with some decent grub inside you.'

I peer over the top of his frying pan, wrinkling up my nose when I see the fat sizzling and spitting up around the meat.

'What's up, not used to a good fry-up in the morning?' Dermot enquires, grinning. 'It'll put hairs on your chest.'

'Thanks,' I say, screwing up my face, 'but that is something I can well do without.' I eye Dermot's chest through the opening of his shirt. 'Looks like you've had a few over the years, though.'

Dermot smiles wryly. 'Come on, Darcy, you can't live on crispbreads all your life. What about eggs on toast, then?'

I haven't had a fried egg for years. I suppose one wouldn't do me any harm ... 'Go on, then. Just the one, though.'

Dermot swirls some fresh oil around the bottom of a second small frying pan, then expertly cracks two eggs into the oil once it's heated.

The rain beats down on the window outside. 'I hope that soon clears up,' I say, to make conversation while we wait for the eggs to cook.

'It will,' Dermot tilts his head to look out of the window. 'I can see patches of blue sky out there already.' He takes four slices of bread and lays them under the grill.

'What do *you* think of my idea?' I ask, while I watch Dermot cook. 'I know you stood by me yesterday. Thanks for that, by the way.' I smile at him. 'I appreciated your support.'

'Couldn't have old Rusty thinking he'd got one over on you, could we?' Dermot winks, moving his bacon around with a spatula. 'So how *are* you going to run this island as a holiday resort, then? That was all a bit sudden yesterday.'

I think it's probably best I don't share the bucket-and-spade story with Dermot, since I'm still not too sure of what happened on the beach myself.

'I just had to think of something quickly, and it came to me in a flash. Don't you think it will work?'

Dermot considers this for a moment while he jiggles the eggs in the frying pan. 'It could do, if you handled it right.'

'Right, being...?'

'That they all know who's in charge from the start. None of this cooperative sharing, namby-pamby nonsense. You tell them who's doing what and where, and they get on with it, no questions asked.'

'I can't do that!' It had been bad enough just standing up in front of everyone yesterday, let alone the thought of bossing them all around. 'We do need *some* people to stay on the island with us. I want people to be happy while they're here on Tara; this is their home, too, not just their place of work.'

Dermot smiles at me and shakes his head.

'What's wrong with that?'

'You can't be in charge *and* be everyone's friend, Darcy, it just doesn't work.'

I think about Jemima back at *Goddess* magazine. There is no way I want to throw my weight around like she does, and have everyone afraid to say a word to me. And if Dermot thinks he's turning me into a carbon copy of Jemima, he's got another think coming.

'No, I won't be like that with people. It *will* work if we all take the time to discuss, listen, then agree on what everyone's going to do here on the island. Tara is the sort of place that works with a bit of give and take, not with a tyrannical ruler lording it from a castle somewhere high up on the hillside.'

'They'll take all right, if you let them,' Dermot says, slurping a quick gulp from his mug of tea. 'You just wait and see. And I never meant that you should be a tyrannical ruler, Darcy, far from it. I've never seen many of them painting their nails in preparation for an important battle, have you?'

Like a wounded soldier, I sip at my own tea now while I prepare my defence. 'So what's made you so cynical about life and the human race, then?'

'I'm not cynical; I'm just realistic about people and how they're likely to behave in certain situations.'

'But not everyone's like you.'

'Be a damn sight better world if they were, though,' Dermot smiles into his frying pan of bacon and sausages before lifting them off the stove and tipping them onto a plate.

I shake my head in disbelief.

'I'm just warning you, Darcy, that's all. Be careful, not everyone's as naive as you are.'

'I'm not naive.'

'All right, maybe naive is the wrong word. Innocent, then. Easily led.'

'I prefer to call myself open-minded. Prepared to give people a fair chance to prove themselves. Which, it seems, you're not.'

'And how have you come to this conclusion?' Dermot says, flipping the toast under the grill.

I think for a moment.

'OK, apart from your statement just now about the islanders messing me about, and your insistence when we first met that I was "of a type", what about Conor? You didn't want to give him a chance when we interviewed him, did you?'

'No, that's true. I didn't.' Dermot makes no attempt to defend himself.

'There you go, my point exactly.'

'What do you mean, *your point exactly*? My opinion about Conor still stands. I don't trust him.'

'But why? What's he done to you?'

Dermot shrugs, sprinkling salt and then pepper on the top of each egg while they're still frying in the pan. He carefully flips each one over with a spatula. 'Nothing,' he says, looking at me now. 'Doesn't mean I have to trust him, though. But it proves my earlier point about *you* being easily led. He just flashes his blue eyes in your direction, uses some of his Celtic charm on you and you're putty in his hands.'

I'm slightly distracted by what Dermot's just done to the eggs. I've only ever seen one other person cook eggs that way before: my aunt. She used to cook them for me for breakfast, usually before we'd take the dogs out on a long walk together. She'd never let me go out without a good breakfast inside me, either. I try and gather my thoughts back to the present once more. 'I am *not* putty in Conor's hands! Don't be silly.'

Dermot attempts a high-pitched voice: 'It *was* the coastal walk I was thinking of trying, Dermot. I think the puppies would enjoy some time down on the sand . . . Hmm,' he holds his finger to his lips and pretends to think. 'Now let me see, who did you *accidentally* end up fishing with all morning on that walk?'

I narrow my eyes at Dermot. 'Conor and I are just friends. He was simply teaching me how to cast out. Although why I should have to explain what I get up to to you, I don't know.'

'Where's your friend now, then, to help you out of your hot water emergency?' Dermot just as carefully flips the eggs back over again and places them gently on the toast he's just lifted from the grill.

'Conor is over on the mainland collecting supplies for Caitlin's shop. I expect he's just got caught up in the bad weather.'

Dermot seems unconvinced by this excuse. 'It's possible

he's not returned yet,' he says grudgingly. 'I haven't been down to the harbour to see if the boat's back.'

'And if Conor and I are supposed to be having some passionate affair like you think we already are,' I continue, 'then I can assure you I'd definitely have been showering in his cottage and not yours, this morning.'

Dermot stares at me for a moment, but it's difficult to read what's going on behind those dark eyes of his as they dart across my face. It's not anger I can see reflected back at me, but it's not upset either.

Maybe I went a bit far with my last comment. I'm about to apologise when Dermot shoves a plate in my hand. 'Breakfast is served,' he says, walking past me to sit at his kitchen table.

I look down at the plate to find a beautifully cooked egg perching on a piece of toast browned to perfection. 'Don't eat it all at once,' he says, pulling out a chair to sit on.

I follow Dermot to the table.

'This looks lovely,' I say to him by way of apology for my earlier comment. 'I've only ever had eggs cooked like that once before – with the salt and pepper added to them during cooking.'

Dermot looks up at me with interest while he tucks into his own breakfast.

'By my aunt Molly,' I say smiling at him. 'So I'm sure these will be just as good hers used to be.'

We eat our breakfast in relative harmony for Dermot and me, and I'm just about to suggest I help him with the washing-up when there's a knock at his door.

'Won't be a moment,' Dermot says, jumping up to go and answer it.

I recognise Caitlin's voice.

'I'm ever so sorry to bother you, Dermot,' she says. 'It's just my roof seems to be leaking in all this rain, and I wondered if you'd come and take a look before the puddle in my kitchen turns into a flood of biblical proportions.'

'Leaking!' Dermot exclaims in horror. 'Surely not, that can't be possible. I'll come at once, Caitlin.'

He immediately rushes back through to me in the kitchen. 'I've got to go,' he says 'Caitlin's got—'

'Yes, I heard. Go and tend to the emergency, Dermot. I can clear up here and let myself out, don't worry.'

'Right,' Dermot pulls on his jacket. 'I'll see you later, then. Are you sure you don't mind?'

'No, of course not. And thanks again for the shower, and for breakfast.' But I hardly think Dermot hears me as he dashes out. I follow him through to the hall and wave to a surprised-looking Caitlin as Dermot bundles her out of the front door.

I catch a glimpse of my reflection in the glass of a picture as I return to the kitchen. It's no wonder Caitlin looked surprised; not only has she found me here early in the morning with Dermot having breakfast, but I've forgotten I've still got my damp hair wrapped up in a towel turban. I quickly remove the towel, rub my hair dry and put it back in Dermot's bathroom. Damn, I've not brought a comb with me. I wonder if Dermot has one in his bedroom?

I feel a bit awkward as I venture inside the room. It's not like I'm snooping or anything, but this is Dermot's private space and I'm not sure what I might find. I see he's managed to wangle himself the rugby-themed room, although I'm sure I'd earmarked another of the room sets for him when we were planning what would go where. But knowing Dermot, I shouldn't really be surprised by this. He always seems to be able to get what he wants without creating too much fuss. Now I'm in here, I really don't want to spend long looking at the decor; I just want to find a comb or a brush or something to run through my hair before I walk back across to my cottage. It was bad enough Caitlin seeing me in here, looking like this; the last thing I need is anyone else seeing me coming out of Dermot's cottage with dishevelled hair at this hour of the morning. It will be all around the island in minutes, and I don't want Conor getting the wrong idea.

I spy a comb sitting on the chest of drawers, so I pick it up and begin to run it through my long hair. As I'm doing so, something else catches my eye. It's a picture frame, and in the frame is a photo of Dermot with a young girl sitting next to him on a swing. I stop combing my hair for a moment to look more closely at the photo. Yes, there's no denying the resemblance. The young girl, who must be about five, is the spitting image of Dermot.

Nineteen

Staring out of my window at the sea crashing against the rocks down on the coast, I wonder just how Tara has managed to survive for so long with this constant bashing and buffeting from Mother Nature.

If it's not the sea attacking her from below, it's the weather assaulting her from above, and just at this very moment I can feel her plight as Niall and Dermot discuss – well, argue over – the plans, timetables and itineraries for the island while I play piggy in the middle.

'Darcy, will you tell him, please?' Dermot sighs impatiently, folding his arms. He stands up. We've been sat around a desk in my front room for the last hour discussing everything since our first island meeting was called to a close late this morning. The other islanders had quickly disappeared, leaving us with the incredibly difficult task of organising things and keeping them all happy. I'd made Niall, Dermot and myself a sort of brunch, even though Dermot and I had already had breakfast earlier (what is it about food here on this island? Everyone always seems to be hungry!), but even that isn't keeping things calm as Niall and Dermot continually come to blows about how the island is going to be run. Now I almost wish I had taken up Roxi's offer of a leg-waxing session.

'It's no good you appealing to Darcy. I'm in charge of the finances here, and I'm telling you, that's far too much capital to be spending on machinery.' Niall pushes his glasses firmly onto the bridge of his nose and sits back in his chair, looking at me determinedly.

'What?' I ask in exasperation, my eyes moving between the two of them. 'What am I supposed to do?'

'Make a decision,' Dermot says bluntly. 'It's your island.'

'Oh, not this again.'

'Yes, this again. You have to.'

'He's right, Darcy,' Niall says softly. 'If we can't agree then you will have to make the decision for us. Anyway, I thought you did very well out there, dealing with the meeting.'

'I suppose it didn't go too badly,' I admit. I'd actually been quite proud of myself. When, as Dermot had correctly predicted, things did start to get a little out of hand, I'd remained firm but fair. I'd listened to all the different views being aired about island life, and then I'd noted them all down in a big black notebook that Niall had lent me. Then I'd returned here determined to keep everyone happy.

'In fact I was going to say the same thing,' Dermot remarks, to my astonishment. 'You did very well when they started kicking up a fuss about who was going to do what and when.'

I'm stunned into silence. Was Dermot complimenting me, for once? I stare at him.

'What?' he asks. 'You did. But then I did warn you they'd mess you about unless you played a firm hand. So technically it was me that was right.'

That sounds more like it.

I smile wryly at him, while Dermot grins at me in amusement.

There's a knock at the door. 'Anyone home?'

It's Conor.

'We're in here,' I call, subconsciously running my hand over my hair to check it's tidy.

Dermot rolls his eyes.

'Howdy, folks,' Conor says, dipping his head to enter the room.

Didn't people ever grow above six foot tall on this island, I wonder?

'How's it going?' he asks, looking between the three of us. 'Are we all rota'ed up and ready to go?'

Dermot makes a sort of *hmph* noise, and strides over to one of Niall's whiteboards to examine his workings-out.

'Don't you be messing with that now, Dermot,' Niall calls, hurrying over to him to make sure Dermot doesn't *accidentally* smudge any of the figures.

'It's not going all that well just now, no,' I whisper, taking Conor to one side. 'We've got a bit of a problem with the financial side of things.'

'So what are you going to do about it?'

'Not you as well,' I sigh.

'What do you mean, not me as well?' he asks, folding his arms and tilting his head to one side. 'It's simple, Darcy: it's your island, what do *you* want to do?'

'At this very moment?

'Yes.'

'Get out of here. I've had enough of names, numbers and charts for one morning.'

Conor grins. 'Well, why didn't you say so before?' he clears his throat. 'Darcy,' he says in a stern voice, 'those poor puppies, when were they last out? They look like they're bursting, so they do.'

'No, they can't be, they were only out—' I suddenly get where Conor is heading with this. 'It must be a while now, yes. Maybe they could do with a walk.'

Even Woody's and Louis's young ears know the word 'walk' by now. Immediately they come bounding over with their long tongues hanging out and their tails wagging in excitement.

'Just as I thought,' Conor says, matter-of-factly. 'Darcy and I will be back in a while,' he announces. 'When we've taken these poor creatures out to do whatever they must all over Tara's sacred soil.'

Dermot looks down at the puppies and then up at me. 'They look all right to me,' he shrugs, choosing deliberately not to look at Conor. 'But it's your life, Darcy.' He gives me a meaningful look.

Conor cheerfully ignores him. 'I'll just be away and fetch the puppies' leads, Darcy, just in case we head anywhere near the cliffs.'

'Thanks, Conor,' I reply, breaking eye contact with Dermot.

'But what about all of this?' Niall asks, gesturing at the papers and plans strewn over the desk. 'We need to finalise everything. So we know what we're doing.'

I take a deep breath and close my eyes for a moment.

'Just give him the money, Niall,' I say decisively, as I open them again. 'Give Dermot whatever he wants to get the cottages renovated as soon as possible.'

I know Dermot's grinning without even looking at him.

'The way I see it, the quicker it's done and the quicker we get people over here, paying for the privilege, the quicker we recoup some of the initial outlay.'

'That's one way of looking at it,' Niall grudgingly admits.

'Come on, Niall,' Dermot encourages, looking a bit too pleased with himself as I correctly predicted he would. 'Admit it, Darcy's right. Her mind works quite well when she puts it to good use. On certain subjects, anyway,' he adds as Conor returns, clutching a red and a blue dog lead in his hand.

'Ready?' he asks me.

'Yep, I just need to pick up my jacket. Right – I'll leave you two to it, then.' I try to soften the impact of my impending departure, as tiny waves of guilt begin to lick at my conscience. I put on my sweetest smile. 'You know I trust the pair of you to make a great job of anything you do.'

Niall returns my smile. Dermot doesn't.

'Nice try, Darcy,' he says. 'But the fact remains you're still leaving us to do all the donkey work while you go gadding about with Golden Balls here.'

Conor just grins 'I'll take that as a compliment, Dermot, since Mr Beckham is not only considered one of England's greatest footballers, but a bit of a handsome fellow to boot.'

Dermot allows his eyes to flick momentarily towards Conor, where they narrow for a moment, before they return to me.

But I'm not going to let him see he's getting to me.

'Perhaps I am "gadding about", Dermot. But everyone

keeps telling me I need to make all the decisions, so I'm going to make an executive one of my own and take my dogs for a long walk in some very pleasant company. Come on ...' I'm about to say Conor, but I see an opportunity of striking the winning goal in this match of words with Dermot: '... *David*,' I say, firmly knotting my raincoat around the waist of my jumper. 'Shall we go?'

A grinning Conor follows me out of the cottage, quickly pulling his own sweater on, as I stride away across the grass with Woody and Louis.

'Whoah there,' he says, eventually catching me up, 'slow down a minute, will you? My legs may well be a lot longer than yours, but they won't motor at the speed you're going right now!'

I cease marching up the path for a moment. 'Sorry. It's just that he makes me so mad sometimes.'

'Who, Dermot?'

'Yes, Dermot.' I look back towards the cottage in frustration. 'They go on about me being in charge of everything and making all these important decisions, and then when I do, they don't like it.'

'You call taking your dogs for a walk making an important decision?' Conor asks, quizzically raising an eyebrow.

'No, not really, I suppose,' I sigh. 'Oh, but you know what I mean.'

'Come on,' Conor turns to face me as he begins to back away along the path with Woody and Louis. 'Let's see if Tara will blow away some of the frustration from that pretty brow of yours.' He grins. 'You'll get wrinkles if you keep pulling those sorts of faces.'

'Oi,' I shout, chasing after him as he turns around and begins to run up the path. 'I will not. I'll have you know I use the same face cream as Jennifer Lopez.'

'It's not doing much of a job on her,' Conor calls, still rushing on ahead of me. 'I bet she still has to have everything airbrushed out.'

After a few minutes of this cat-and-mouse game along the path that leads around the edge of Tara's craggy coastline, with Conor slowing down then deliberately speeding up again when I've nearly caught him, he stops at the top of a fairly steep climb so I can catch up with him.

'That's better,' he says, smiling, as I finally reach his side. 'Now you've got some proper colour in those cheeks. You were looking a bit pale back there.'

'That's why I've just been chasing you up this path?' I pant, still trying to catch my breath. 'To add some natural blusher to my cheeks? I could have done that using a lot less energy and with much less pain using my make-up bag.'

'But you wouldn't have looked half as pretty as you do right now.' Conor takes my hand and pulls me towards him. 'A lovely colour glowing on this delicate white skin of yours.' In the gentlest of movements I feel his thumb caress my cheek, 'With your hair all billowing in the wind like it is just now? That is quite something to behold.' He catches hold of one of the wisps of hair that constantly seem to float around my face whenever I'm outdoors and carefully he tucks it behind my ear. 'And then there's your lips,' he continues, while I swallow hard and hope my legs don't suddenly buckle underneath me, knowing that if they do it won't be from the exertion of running up that hill. 'They're just so full and

213

beautiful right now, from your heart pumping hard. It makes me want to—'

Woof, woof!

What? Did I make Conor want to bark like a dog?

Oh, the puppies!

We both turn our heads to see Woody precariously close to the edge of the cliff face. He's seen a seagull and he's not happy. *What* is *it with him and seagulls?* He barks at it again while he balances on a piece of rock jutting out from the land.

'Woody!' I shout. 'No! Get back here now!'

Woody turns his head to look at me for a moment, then immediately turns his fearsome gaze back to the seagull and begins barking again. The gull doesn't seem very impressed with the little dog's attempts at ferocity; he simply flaps his wings at him in response to the yapping and lets out a fighting cry of his own. I'm about to shout again when Woody appears to decide that perhaps I'm the lesser of the two evils on this occasion. Scrambling back down from where he's been trying to get his footing on the rock, he bounds over to join his brother on the grass. Louis, as usual, is behaving himself and is doing something much more innocuous – sniffing at some fresh rabbit droppings.

I breathe a huge sigh of relief and clasp my hand to my chest where my heart is still racing – from Woody's little incident, or from what was about to happen before it I'm not too sure.

'Oh, my God, I can't bear to think what might have happened then if he hadn't barked! I should have kept a better eye on them while we were up here.'

'No,' Conor says, shaking his head while still watching the puppies. 'It was my fault. I was distracting you.'

'Yes, but in a good way,' I smile up at him.

'You think?'

'I certainly do.'

Conor grins. 'Then perhaps we should continue this walk a bit further. But maybe inland, away from these dangerous cliffs.' He looks around him. 'Have you been up to visit the ruins yet?'

'Up on the hill?' I ask, shyly taking hold of his outstretched hand. 'Just the once.' It feels good to be holding Conor's hand again. I'd enjoyed it the first time down on the beach, but this time it feels more permanent.

'Want a tour guide this time?' he winks, squeezing my hand.

'Only if he knows his stuff.'

'Oh, I know my stuff all right,' Conor says, patting his leg to call the puppies. We begin to walk in the direction of the steep hill that leads up to the ruined building. '*And* I might know quite a lot about that old building, too.'

He raises his eyebrows at me, and I grin at his cheek. If anyone else had said that to me it might have sounded leery, but with Conor it just seems to add to his appeal.

Walking hand in hand to the top of the hill, we take a few minutes to enjoy the sun's rays that have managed to penetrate the deep bank of cloud enveloping Tara today. While Woody and Louis snuffle about in the grass and the bushes, we sit on my unzipped raincoat with our backs against one of the crumbling walls, looking down over the view.

Conor closes his eyes as he leans his face back in the sun. 'Nothing better,' he sighs.

'It is lovely up here,' I agree, looking out over the sea to the mainland in the distance.

Conor tips his head forward again and opens his eyes. 'No, I meant being with such gorgeous company, out in the fresh air in this glorious weather.'

I laugh.

'What?' he asks.

'You certainly have the gift of the gab, Mr Conor Fitzgerald. Did your parents take you to kiss the Blarney stone when you were young, by any chance?'

Conor pretends to look shocked. 'What are you saying, Miss McCall, that you're immune to my Irish charm?'

'I didn't say that. It's just that you don't have to lay it on quite as thick with me, that's all.'

'Like the more subtle approach, do you?' Conor sits up properly again. 'Perhaps Mr Did You Know I Built this Cottage with My Own Hairy Hands O'Connell down there is more to your liking? Actually I don't think Dermot is that subtle. His idea of chatting up a woman is probably hitting her over the head with his all-in-one power tool and dragging her back to see his recently refurbished cave,' Conor grimaces.

I burst out laughing, and immediately put my hand to my mouth. 'Oh, Conor, stop, that's not fair, Dermot's very clever with his tools and you know it. He's done such a lot on this island already.'

'Yes, like annoy the hell out of you.'

'That's just his way. He can't help it.' *And just why am I defending Dermot?*

'Perhaps.' Conor considers this. 'He certainly seems to push your buttons.'

'Dermot and I don't exactly see eye to eye, it's true.' *In fact, come to think of it, I've probably had more cross words with him in the short time we've known each other than with anyone in my whole life.* 'But I think there might be more to Dermot than what we first see.' I think again about the photo in his cottage. I haven't told anyone about it, not even Roxi. I wonder if I should mention it to Conor now?

'Oh, yeah?' Conor asks, raising an eyebrow.

I decide against it. 'We'll find a way of getting along, though; there aren't many people I ever come to blows with.'

'You don't like confrontation, do you, Darcy?' Conor asks as his blue eyes penetrate mine in search of an answer.

'What do you mean?'

'I mean, you don't like disagreements or problems. You like everyone to just swim along happily together all the time.'

'Maybe, but why *would* I like people arguing? It would be an odd person that did. I just want people to be happy.'

Conor's eyes narrow as he considers this. 'But what about you, what do *you* really want out of life?'

'Don't know,' I shrug. 'Same as everyone else, I guess. Good health, more money, the usual.'

'I notice you didn't mention love in that list?'

It's my turn to stare hard at Conor now. Has he been talking to Roxi about my love life? 'No, that's true, I didn't,' I reply, without enlightening him further about my failings in the relationship department.

Conor grins. 'Ooh, you're as deep as that sea out there, aren't you, and just as mysterious. I bet there's a man or two that have wrecked their boat in your treacherous waves.'

I drag my eyes away from Conor's. I don't know what it is about his eyes, but they're hypnotic. If this line of conversation continues, heaven knows what he'll have me telling him.

'Anyway,' I say, keen to steer the subject away from my love life – or severe lack of one – 'why are we talking about this? Why don't you try out some more of your Blarney on me and see if it works this time?'

'I might just do that,' Conor says, relaxing back against the wall and crossing his legs again. 'You'll just have to wait and see, Miss Darcy.' He thinks for a moment. 'You know what we were saying before about kissing the Blarney stone? Even though it's an old yarn put on for the tourists, they make a lot of money out of it, enough to keep Blarney Castle running as a result. Perhaps you should try something like that here?'

'How do you mean?'

'I don't know. Maybe you need something more than just the island and a few cottages to attract people. Perhaps you need a *thing*, too.'

'A thing?'

'Like a theme, something for people to hook into.' Conor closes his eyes and settle downs in the sun again. 'Might be worth thinking about.'

'But I wouldn't want to commercialise Tara.' I look down at him lying in the sun's golden glow. 'It's too unspoiled.'

'No, I don't mean theme as in theme park,' Conor holds his hand above his eyes, shielding them from the bright sun. 'I mean theme as in something different, that no one else can offer.'

'Like what? We're stuck in the middle of the Atlantic Ocean, it's not exactly Las Vegas.'

'And thank the Lord for that small mercy. Been there, done that. No, you're thinking inside the box, Darcy, stuck in the little world you're used to inhabiting. Think outside of it for a while.'

Conor closes his eyes again and returns to basking in the sun's warm rays while I sit quietly next to him, mulling over what he's just said.

'You've gone awfully quiet,' Conor says after a while.

'I'm just thinking.'

Conor opens his eyes and sits up properly again. 'Don't stress yourself over what I said. It was only a suggestion.'

'But I think you could be right. Why *will* people want to come here? Yes, it's quiet and peaceful – if you like that sort of thing. And the scenery is stunning. But it's so remote, and you know how dodgy the weather can be, it's hardly a tropical island we're asking them to take their holiday on. It's a cold, windswept Irish island.'

Conor looks at me for a moment, then reaches forward and runs his thumb gently between my eyebrows. 'There,' he says, rhythmically stroking my forehead. 'That's ironed out that furrowed brow again. Stop fretting, Darcy. Relax, it will all sort itself out in the end.' He removes his hand and this time, with no puppies in mortal peril to prevent him from carrying out his will, he leans forward and places the gentlest kiss upon my lips.

'Feeling any better now?' he enquires, a lopsided grin appearing on his handsome face.

'Just a bit,' I whisper back. 'But perhaps you should try it once more, to make sure I don't start stressing out all over again.'

Conor leans in towards me. 'Anything to oblige.'

And unsurprisingly, for the next few minutes I not only forget what I was worrying about before, but any worries I have full stop about Tara, and even the fact that I'm actually on an island at all, as Conor works his own very individual magic upon me.

Twenty

It's amazing what can change in a few weeks.

We've been on Tara nearly a month now, and in that time we've almost finished renovating five new cottages. These, added to the seven empty ones vacated by our departing TV wannabes, has left us with a dozen holiday homes waiting to be filled. We've been blessed with some of the mildest spring weather I can remember for a long time in the UK, let alone on a remote Irish island in the Atlantic Ocean. And most importantly of all, everyone is now beginning to pull together like a team, instead of fighting about who is doing what job.

The only thing that hasn't changed in a month is my puppies' ability to listen to anything I tell them, and Dermot's annoying attitude.

I'm on my way over to Caitlin's small shop right now – small only in size, that is. Caitlin has managed to turn her tiny extra cottage into an Aladdin's Cave of treasures. She stocks things that we just can't manage without until Conor takes the boat over to the mainland for our regular orders of supplies – treasures like milk, toilet rolls and chocolate.

As I enter, a tiny bell rings above my head. 'Morning, Darcy,' Caitlin says, appearing from the back room. Dermot has cleverly knocked a doorway through from her adjoining cottage. 'How are you today?'

I adore Caitlin's dress sense. She insists she doesn't buy anything from the high street, and that everything she wears – incredibly – comes from charity shops or jumble sales. But somehow she always manages to look fabulously stylish in a boho-chic Sienna Miller meets Kate Moss way. Today she's wearing jeans, as all of us seem to wear most days on the island now (except Roxi, who still insists on her tight skirts, skinny jeans or leggings – always with heels, of course), but as usual Caitlin's teamed it inventively with a long colourful denim waistcoat, a white cotton smock top and a large pendant with a purple gemstone in the centre.

'I'm good thanks, Caitlin! I was wondering if you had any chocolate left?'

Caitlin looks at me in surprise. 'Again, Darcy?' she asks. 'That must be the third bar this week. And they were the large size.'

I blush awkwardly. 'I'm just a bit stressed, that's all. Chocolate's my thing, helps me cope.'

Caitlin smiles. 'I'll just check out back for you. I think there might still be an odd bar in one of the boxes, if you're lucky.'

While Caitlin disappears back through the door again I glance around the little shop. It really is amazing what she manages to pack in here. Dermot has completely lined three walls of the largest front room of the cottage from ceiling to floor with shelves, and on these shelves is packed everything, from tins of beans to deodorants, and jars of honey to boxes of matches. As I stare at the brightly coloured packaging, a brief memory comes flitting back to me of watching TV with my aunt Molly in her sitting room in the house in Kerry. It then begins to pad itself out with more detail, until it's a full-blown image in my mind.

It's Sunday night, and we're watching *Open All Hours*. That's exactly what Caitlin's shop reminds me of – Arkwright's shop from the show. The island's shop is a bit smaller than the TV one, but it's stocked in just the same jam-packed, bursting-at-the-seams way.

I think about my aunt again, and remember how we often used to sit together during the winter evenings when I was staying with her and watch lots of comedy shows, and how she used to laugh. Molly had a wonderful laugh – so animated and vibrant – and a wonderful sense of humour, too. I'd forgotten that about her . . .

The bell rings behind me again, and Roxi bursts in through the door wearing a denim jumpsuit and red high heels. 'Look!' she instructs me, thrusting her hand under my face.

'Just what am I supposed to be *look*ing at?' I ask, examining her outstretched hand.

'The state of my nails, Darce, they're *ruined*! I was trying to be helpful by sanding some wood down for Dermot in one of the cottages, and look what I get for my efforts! So I told him it was an emergency, went back to my cottage to get my nail varnish remover and guess what?'

'What?' I ask, shaking my head in disbelief.

'It's completely empty. I used the last of it the other day, I wasn't expecting to repaint them again so soon, you see, so I was going to ask Conor to pick some up when he went over to the mainland to get our next order.'

'You're in luck, Darcy,' Caitlin says, reappearing waving a 500g bar of Cadburys Dairy Milk. 'One left. Oh, hello Roxi,' she says, smiling at her, 'What can I do for you?'

'Nail crisis, Caitlin,' Roxi says, waving her hand under Caitlin's nose now. 'Do you have any remover?'

'Sorry Roxi, I only keep the basic supplies here. You know, day-to-day necessities.'

Roxi eyes Caitlin suspiciously, simply not understanding why Caitlin doesn't class repainting your nails as a basic necessity in life.

'Don't worry, Rox,' I assure her. 'I've got some back in my cottage you can borrow; I've hardly used it since I got here.' I glance down at my nails. Eck, they're a sight, I really must give myself a manicure sometime soon.

'You're a lifesaver, Darce. So, what are you in here for?' Roxi asks, looking round the shop.

'Chocolate,' Caitlin says, just as I say, 'Tea.'

Roxi's eyes open wide. 'Oh yeah, which is it then?'

'I came in for some tea originally, and then thought I'd treat myself to a small bar of chocolate while I was here. But unfortunately it seems this is all Caitlin has.' I turn my back on Roxi and try to mouth 'Please don't say anything' to Caitlin across the counter without Roxi noticing, but I should have known better.

'Are you on the chocolate again, Darcy?' It's as though Roxi's asking a reformed alcoholic if they've opened a bottle of whiskey.

Slowly I turn back around to face her with a fixed smile planted firmly on my face. 'I might just have had the occasional *small* bar.'

'*Caitlin?*' Roxi challenges, hands on hips.

I swing back around and look pleadingly at Caitlin.

'Well, this is the only bar I have in the shop right now,' Caitlin says, holding up the chocolate with an innocent smile.

'Hmm,' Roxi looks between the two of us suspiciously.

'Why can't you have too much chocolate, Darcy?' Caitlin asks. 'Are you diabetic?'

'No, nothing like that. I'm prone to getting a little bit addicted to it, that's all. Roxi's just worrying over nothing.'

'Pah,' Roxi puffs. 'Have you ever seen that episode of *The Vicar of Dibley* when Dawn French wallows in chocolate bars on her settee when the chap she fancies leaves her?'

Caitlin grins. 'Yes, I loved that show.'

'Well, that was Darcy one Christmas when she broke up with her boyfriend. She eats it when she's worried, upset or stressed – and when I say eat, I mean *eat*! She makes Paddy's portions look like Cheryl Cole's.'

'OK, OK! I'm not *that* bad!' I plead, holding up my hand. 'So I *might* have had the odd bar lately. But it's not a crime; I've got a few things on my mind.'

'Like what, Darcy?' Caitlin asks with concern. 'Aren't things going well with the new cottages?'

'They are, but if we don't get anyone to fill them when they're complete, then what's the point?' I look from one to the other of them. 'Just between the three of us, I'm not having much luck getting any bookings so far. The only way I've been able to advertise them is with an agency that does holiday lets, which would be fine if I was able to keep in touch with them easily by phone or email, but I had to make a special trip over to the mainland just to sort it all out with them. How am I supposed to know if we've got any bookings until we get some mail? You know how long that can take to get here.' I sigh. 'What I could really do with is a website and some proper online advertising of my own. But it's impossible from here, and I can't keep jumping in the boat every five minutes and asking Conor to sail me over to an internet café.'

Caitlin exchanges a knowing look with Roxi. 'But I'm sure he would if you asked him to.'

I smile coyly as I think about Conor. We've been spending quite a bit of time together since our walk that day up to the ruins, and the more I'm with him, the more I want to be. Conor's laid-back attitude means one moment he'll be smoothing on his Irish charm like thick honey on soda bread, and the next he's disappeared, and I'll eventually find him all alone on a beach or perching on a rock with his fishing rod, like one of the island's cormorants ready at any moment to soar off into the sky. But his unpredictability is one of the things I like about him; it keeps our relationship fresh and exciting, and his other attributes that are more immediately visible to the eye are quite a bonus too.

'You two *are* an item, then?' Caitlin asks, seeing the look on my face. 'We thought as much.'

'Depends what you mean by an *item*,' I reply, feeling my cheeks beginning to flush. 'And who's *we*, anyway?' I glance at Roxi, who hurriedly turns her face away.

'Darcy, this is a small community. Two people going for

225

walks together and sneaking about in and out of each other's cottages. It's hardly going to go unnoticed, is it?'

'I suppose not.' Especially when certain *other* people begin gossiping about it too. I look towards Roxi again; she's examining with great concentration the label on a tin of peas. Roxi detests peas.

'Good luck to you both, that's what I say,' Caitlin continues. 'He's a rare-lookin' fellow, if you like that type.'

'So I've nothing to worry about from you then, Caitlin,' I say lightly. 'Conor's not *your* type?'

Roxi thrusts the can of peas down with such force she almost knocks the display over.

Caitlin smiles. 'No, you're quite safe, Darcy. He's a bit too smooth for me, is Conor with all his blarney.' And she begins to load some unpacked boxes up onto the desk.

'So who *would* be more your type, then?' Roxi asks, sidling over to join the conversation again.

'Oh, I don't know,' Caitlin replies coyly. 'I don't really have a type, as such.'

'Come on, you must have a preference?' Roxi raises her eyebrows at me while Caitlin reaches for another box. 'Dark, fair, tall, short?'

Caitlin shakes her head and turns around for a Stanley knife to undo her boxes.

Roxi gives me a gentle nudge.

'If you know what you don't like, you must have some idea about what you do?' I ask hurriedly.

'Erm ...' Caitlin struggles. 'Someone more ... rugged, perhaps?'

'Like? Give us an example.' Roxi demands.

'Look, I really don't know,' Caitlin says quickly, stabbing the knife through the tape on the box in front of her and slitting it open. 'Just not someone like Conor, all right?'

We watch her blushing profusely as she pulls tins of tuna from the box and begins stacking them up on a shelf behind her.

Roxi purposefully nods her head in a *told ya so* fashion.

'Right, well, I can't stand around here all day chatting,' I say, struggling to slide my big chocolate bar into my raincoat pocket and heading towards the door. 'I've got to pop over and see how Dermot's getting on.'

Our eyes shoot back to Caitlin for a reaction. But there's no flicker as she turns around.

'Before you both go,' she says, 'take one of these.' She reaches under the counter and pulls out a basket filled with little coloured pebbles.

'What for?' I ask.

'Please, just do it. I'll explain in a moment.'

Roxi and I examine the stones. 'Which one do I pick?' Roxi asks.

'Whichever one you feel drawn to,' Caitlin says mysteriously.

I cast my eyes over the pretty coloured stones. There are purple ones, brown, green, blue – every colour you can think of. But I'm particularly drawn to a pale pink one.

'Is this one OK?' I ask, picking it up to inspect it.

'I thought that's what you'd choose,' Caitlin says knowingly. 'That's a rose quartz. It's a very calming stone. It will help to heal your heart and inner emotions, and to find love.'

I look again at the pale pink pebble in my hand, and then

I look up at Caitlin. 'What do you mean?' I ask, not following her.

She smiles. 'The stones in my basket are all healing crystals. They each have individual energies that promote healing in different ways. Most people subconsciously know what they need, and will choose a crystal to suit their purpose without even knowing they're doing it.'

'Ooh, ooh, my turn!' Roxi says excitedly. 'I choose . . .' she hovers her hand over the basket, closes her eyes and picks a clear pebble with no colour.

'Oh pants, that's boring, I didn't mean to pick that one. Let me choose again.'

'Actually, Roxi, a clear quartz contains every colour inside, and is *the* most powerful crystal there is. It's a very wise choice.'

Roxi's chin juts out. 'I guess that makes it perfect for me, then.'

'What are we supposed to do with them?' I ask, looking at the little pink stone in my hand again.

'Nothing in particular. Just keep them about your person; occasionally hold them in your hand. For instance, your rose quartz should help you deal with your stress a lot better and with a lot fewer calories than your chocolate habit.'

'No stress *and* fewer calories than chocolate?' I toss the little pink stone up and down in my hand. 'Wow, sounds good. I'll certainly give it a try!' I stick the pebble in my pocket. 'Right, I'd better get back to the grindstone. I'll catch you guys later.'

'Wait, I'm coming too,' Roxi says, examining her stone very closely with one eye, like it's a diamond.

'Remember, Darcy, if you start feeling stressed, just hold onto the rose quartz for a while, it will help, I promise,' Caitlin says, nodding.

'Sure, Caitlin,' I reply, humouring her. 'I'll do that.' *Or maybe, just in case, I'll just make sure I order myself a bit more chocolate next time.*

'Well, what did you make to all that?' I ask Roxi as we step outside into the fresh air again and walk into the centre of O'Connell Street.

'Oh my God, she *so* has the hots for our Mr Cowell.'

'What?'

'What she was saying in there,' Roxi says, blinking at me in amazement, 'about liking someone more rugged, and all the blushing and stuff when we pushed her for more info.'

'Oh, that.'

'Why? What were you talking about, then?'

'The stone basket and all the things she was saying,' I take my pink pebble from my pocket again. 'Do you think she was serious?'

'Yeah, probably. Lots of people are into all that kind of stuff, aren't they? And Caitlin looks the sort.'

'What sort?'

'The "let's heal you from within" type. I've met them down the pub a few times. They really believe in all this holistic healing stuff. I went out with a guy once who was just the same, except with him it was daily meditation and a strict vegan diet.'

'What happened?'

'It all fell apart when he caught me listening to my iPod and sneaking a packet of pork scratchings when we were supposed to be in a session of deep meditation. He didn't quite get that

229

my way of reaching deep relaxation is getting on down with a bit of Luther Vandross.'

I laugh. 'If Caitlin likes Dermot, looks like you win the bet then, Rox.'

'Ah,' she says, waving her hand at me. 'All bets were off ages ago when you started cavorting about with Lover Boy behind my back. Maybe we should set up a new one.'

'No,' I insist. 'No more bets!'

'Aw, come on, Darce, it's so boring here. There's nothing to do. I tried helping out with the cottages, and look where that got me.' She flutters her chipped fingernails at me again.

'I'll think of something for you to do.' I begin to walk away in the direction of the second bank of cottages that are being refurbished. 'If it means no more bets, trust me, I will.'

'Bet you can't think of something I'll like doing!' Roxi calls. 'After all, you ruined the last deal we had by double-dealing behind my back with the stakes.'

I march right back over to her. 'Ooh, you drive a hard bargain, Miss Roxanne Reynolds. Go on then, but only because I'm so confident I'll come up with something.'

Roxi grins. 'If you do, let's keep my forfeit the same – to kiss Mr Cowell.' She screws up her nose. 'You've no chance of finding me something I like doing here – not unless Will Smith pops by for a holiday and he needs a daily masseuse to visit him for an hour or two.'

'No way! Dermot's not going to be the stakes this time. If we're going to do this let's make it more interesting . . .'

Roxi's eyes light up. 'Now that's what I like to hear! You've clearly been spending time in some more . . . *daring* company of late. What do you have in mind?'

I think for a moment. 'If I win, and find you something to do here on Tara you enjoy doing, you have to give me your secret stash of Hotel Chocolat you keep hidden under your bed.'

Roxi's eyes open almost as wide as her mouth. 'You know about *that*! What are you, some sort of chocolate sniffer dog, trained to track down the scent of cocoa beans at thirty paces?'

'You don't deny it, then?'

Roxi tosses her hair back over her shoulders. 'No, but I was only hiding it for your own good.'

'Ha, yeah *right*.'

'If I'm to give you all my chocolate, it seems only fair that you should have to give up something too.' Roxi looks challengingly back at me.

'Like?'

'Chocolate.'

'But I only have this bar,' I say, tapping the slab of Dairy Milk in my jacket pocket.

'No, I mean permanently.'

Now it's my turn for my jaw to drop open.

'Fair's fair,' Roxi sings. 'If you're so confident about finding me something ...'

'No problem,' I say, grabbing hold of her hand and pumping it up and down. 'You've got yourself a deal!'

'You're kidding me – *you* are willing to risk never having chocolate again?'

'Yep, you'll see,' I say, leaving a shocked Roxi standing in the middle of the square while I stride confidently away. 'Everyone has a place here on Tara. And I'm going to find one for you!'

*

231

I happily munch on some squares of chocolate as I head over towards one of the cottages that are being renovated. It's such a lovely morning that I pull off my raincoat and wrap it around my waist, walking along in just my jeans and a red Gap sweater and white t-shirt, enjoying feeling the sun's rays on me on this beautiful May morning. Dermot and the others really have done a sterling job over the last month. I can't really take any credit for the work; I've been busy organising other elements of island life, and planning what's going to happen when *and if* we ever get more visitors. But I have tried to be of assistance when I can, and I've watched the cottages turn one by one from derelict wrecks into comfortable, cosy dwellings.

'How's it going?' I ask, popping my head around the door of Cottage Seven.

'Hi, Darcy,' Siobhan calls, roller in hand, as she and Ryan busily coat a wall in white emulsion. 'What do you think?'

I have a lot of time for Siobhan and Ryan; they're a lovely young couple, always keen to pitch in and help – nothing's ever too much trouble for them, and they never seem to moan about anything. I think they're just happy to be here on Tara together, now they've fallen in love and in the most unexpected of places.

I smile warmly at them. 'It's looking fantastic, guys! As always, everyone's doing a great job. Is Dermot around, do you know?'

'He was going on about roofing tiles the last time I saw him,' Ryan says, lifting the peak of his cap so he can see me properly. 'Something about them being loose.'

'Oh, right. I didn't notice him outside. I'll go and take another look.'

Conor wanders through, carrying two tins of paint. 'Hey, you,' he says with that cute lopsided smile of his.

'Hey,' I reply, smiling coyly back at him.

Siobhan nudges Ryan, and they swiftly return to their painting.

Conor puts the paint down next to them. 'That should be enough for this room; give me a shout if you need any more.'

'Cheers, Conor,' Ryan says. 'You off now?' he enquires innocently.

Siobhan fires him a warning look.

'Yep, think I'll take a break and get some fresh air in my lungs.' Conor stretches. 'You guys have pretty much got this one covered now.'

Conor nods in the direction of the door, and we both head towards it.

'See you later,' I call to them. 'Thanks for all your hard work.'

'No problem, Darcy,' Siobhan smiles at me. 'Have fun, you two.'

As soon as we get outside, Conor pins me gently up against one of the exterior walls of the cottage. 'Did you come over here just to find me?' he asks. 'I've missed you,' he leans forward to kiss me.

'Conor, I only saw you a couple of hours ago,' I tease, delaying his kiss for a moment. 'And as much as I miss being with you, too, I actually came to find Dermot. You being here is a wonderful bonus, though,' I add when he pouts.

'A couple of minutes is way too long to be away from you, Darcy,' Conor says, making sure I can't delay his kiss any longer by planting his soft lips firmly on mine.

'You do realise everyone knows about us,' I tell him after I've enjoyed his lips for a few minutes.

'Yeah, I'd kind of guessed that,' Conor says with his arms around me, while he strokes my loose hair back into place. As usual, the wind has been playing havoc with my locks.

'Had you? I didn't know they knew.'

Conor smiles. 'So innocent,' he says, kissing the tip of my nose. 'You never know quite what's going on underneath this pretty nose of yours, do you?'

'I wouldn't say that,' I begin to protest. 'I think I—'

'Oi, you two!' I hear suddenly from above. 'Don't you know voices carry? Me and Paddy up here are having to listen to all your loved-up nonsense. You're like a Mills and Boon audio-book!'

Conor and I move away from the wall and look up to see Dermot peering over the edge of the roof, wearing a yellow hard hat.

'Let me assure you, Dermot, if I'd had any idea you were within earshot I'd have kept my thoughts well and truly to myself.' I turn back to Conor and shake my head in annoyance.

'Just letting you know we're up here,' Dermot continues from the roof. 'To what do we owe the honour, Darcy? Did you get bored doing your desk job?'

'I'm going to take off,' Conor says, kissing me on the cheek. 'I can see where this is heading; you and Dermot obviously have things you need to *discuss*.'

'But—' I protest, as I watch him bound off down the hill. I look up at Dermot.

Right.

I march away from the cottage so I can see fully up on top

of the roof. Paddy is balanced on the tiles wearing jeans ripped at the knee, his DM boots, a Gorillaz t-shirt and, like Dermot, a yellow hard hat. Dermot is wearing his usual attire of jeans, heavy boots and a heavy cotton shirt – today it's checked.

'Yo, Darcy, it's a great view from up here,' Paddy calls. Seeing me for the first time, he precariously tries to stand up on the roof. 'I'm king of the world, so I am. From up here I can see for miles.'

'You'll be king of your own coffin in a minute if you fall off this roof,' Dermot grumbles, turning around to look at him. 'Now sit back down and try and replace that tile like I showed you. I'm going down to see Darcy for a minute. The ladder's over the other side,' Dermot says for my benefit, gesturing across the roof.

I walk around to the other side of the cottage to find Dermot swinging his leg over the top of a ladder that is propped up against the wall, and beginning to climb down. 'Loose tiles,' he states matter-of-factly as he jumps down the final couple of rungs. 'Least he'll know how to replace them in future.'

As irritated as Dermot makes me much of the time, this is one aspect of his character I like. 'I've noticed you've been teaching Paddy quite a lot since he arrived.'

Dermot shrugs as he brushes some dirt from his hands. 'The lad's keen to learn, when he stops messing about. I don't mind showing him.'

I wonder if Dermot secretly yearns to have someone to pass all his knowledge on to, and I'm reminded of the photo of the young girl in Dermot's cottage again. Who is she? I still haven't found out. He never mentions any family, and I wonder if he ever sees this little girl any more. 'You're very good with Paddy.' I smile at Dermot. 'You seem to have a way with him. In fact, you've got everyone working really well together.' I try and swallow my pride and my annoyance for a moment. 'It's a brilliant team we've got here on Tara, now. I don't think I could have brought everyone together like you have.'

'Like I've said before, Darcy, you've got to make it clear from the start how things are going to be. People will respect you for that in the long run.'

I nod in agreement, but I can't quite admit out loud that he's been right. That would just bring on one of those self-satisfied looks from Dermot that I just can't bear.

'So,' Dermot asks, 'did you want me for something in particular?'

'I was just coming to see how you were getting on.'

Dermot nods approvingly 'Extremely well. As with all my projects, it will be completed on schedule and you'll have five more cottages ready to receive visitors, just as you requested.'

Pity you're not in charge of getting the visitors here too, I think to myself. Maybe I'd have more of a success rate then.

'You've all done a brilliant job, Dermot, thank you.'

Dermot glances at me in surprise. 'Have you got many bookings through yet?' he asks, beginning to gather up a few tools that are lying around on the grass.

'That depends what you mean by bookings. There have been a few enquiries.'

'How many, exactly?' Dermot sticks a hammer in his tool belt and some loose nails in his pocket.

'Two.'

'What, two actual bookings?'

'No, two enquiries.'

Dermot swivels around to face me. With the sun lighting him from behind, he looks a bit like a big tough cowboy with guns hanging either side of his hips in a holster, except with Dermot it's his tools hanging off his belt, and instead of a Stetson it's the yellow plastic hard hat he's wearing. 'You have no actual bookings yet?'

'No, but it's virtually impossible from here to do anything more than list the cottages with a holiday lettings agency. If I had internet access, this would all be so much easier,' I sigh.

'Why?'

'Because then I could set up my own website for the island, and receive email enquiries. I could have a Facebook page and Tweet about it and, oh, Dermot, the possibilities are endless with the internet.'

'Are they indeed?' Dermot sounds unconvinced. 'Unfortunately, the internet is something you don't have the luxury of here, so you're going to have to think of something else.'

I stare at him. Couldn't he at least sound sympathetic for once?

'What's that look for?' Dermot demands. 'Do you expect me to try and dream up marketing ideas for you as well as do all this?'

'But ... ' I begin.

'And it's not like we've exactly seen much of you over here, have we?' Dermot continues before I can even try and tell him how much I've appreciated what he's done. 'How many brushes have you lifted over the last few weeks, Darcy, that haven't been for your hair?'

My eyes narrow as my patience thins. That's below the belt, even for someone wearing such a boring one as Dermot. 'That's not fair, and you know it. I've been busy doing other stuff.'

'Other stuff that doesn't risk chipping your nail polish?'

'For your information, Dermot, I haven't actually painted my nails since I got here, see?' I thrust my hand in Dermot's face.

Dermot pretends to examine my nails, then screws up his nose disdainfully. 'Bit of a mess, aren't they?'

I snatch my hand away. 'I can't win with you, can I? I'm going to go now, before I disturb your busy work schedule any further. I'm so sorry to have bothered you with my very minor issues.' I march furiously away before he can wind me up any further. *That man, he's insufferable!*

But as I descend back along the path, I begin to feel myself grow calm much more quickly than I usually do after I've had 'words' with Dermot. Maybe it's because I'm breathing so heavily and taking great big gulps of fresh sea air down into my lungs as I walk back to my cottage. But I also begin to wonder if it's anything to do with the fact that my fist is gripped very tightly around not the giant bar of chocolate in my coat pocket, but what's sitting in the pocket of my jeans. The little pink stone.

Twenty-one

Later that afternoon, I'm sitting at my desk gazing out of the front window of my cottage still wondering how on earth I'm going to get people to visit this island when I can't advertise it properly. What's the point in even putting ads in papers or magazines, if people can't get an immediate response to their enquiry by phone or email? No one has the patience for 'snail mail' any more. Factoring in the boat trips, the whole process will probably take about a fortnight, if I'm lucky. We should probably rename our postal service 'whale mail', instead.

There's a knock at the door.

'It's open, come on in.'

I swivel my chair around to see Paddy appear at my office door.

'Hey, Paddy, did you get the roof fixed?'

'Yeah, had to, or I don't reckon Dermot would have let me off till I finished the job proper.'

I smile. That sounds about right.

'But he's OK. He's teaching me plenty.'

'I know, and you'll learn a lot from him, he's very clever. So, what can I do for you?'

'I couldn't help hearin' what you two were talkin' about when I was on the roof back there, earlier. About the cottages and advertising and stuff, and I heard you say you could do with the internet.'

'Yes, that right.' I look wistfully at my trusty laptop sitting on the desk behind me. Since I've been here it's only really been used by Niall, for timetables and financial spreadsheets. I almost feel like I'm letting it down by not allowing it to be put to its full use.

'Only Eamon's got a computer, see, and I wondered if he could get the internet on it.'

I open my eyes wide and stare at Paddy. *What did he just say?*

'Paddy, did you just say Eamon's got a computer?'

'Yeah, I clocked it the other day when I was walking Brogan up near Eamon's place. She got caught in some brambles growing up the side of his cottage, and when I untangled her I just happened to take a gander in one of Eamon's windows, and that's when I saw it.'

'A computer?' I ask doubtfully. 'At Eamon's? Are you sure?'

Paddy raises his dark eyebrows and looks reproachfully at me. 'I may not know how to fix tiles on a roof, Darcy, but sure I know what a computer looks like.'

'Yes, of course you do. But why would Eamon of all people have a computer?'

'I don't know,' Paddy shrugs. 'Why don't you just ask him?'

Paddy's answers, although sometimes simple, are always refreshingly straightforward. I smile at him. 'I might just do that. It's about time I took the dogs for a walk, anyway.'

'Can I come too, and bring Brogan? Much as I love learning the tricks of the trade from Dermot, he was mentioning something about us putting ballcocks into the cisterns this afternoon, and I'm sorry but,' Paddy pulls a face, 'that just sounds wrong to me, Darcy.'

I laugh. 'Sure, you can come. It would be good for us to have some company, and while we're out maybe Brogan can teach my two terrors how to behave.'

We head over to Eamon's cottage together. As our three dogs bound about in front of us as we walk, I'm pleasantly surprised that Paddy and I find lots to chat about along the way – Tara, Dermot, Paddy's life back at the hotel with Mary, and I'm also surprised at the frequency with which Niall's name crops up among all these subjects. For two such opposites, they seem to have hit it off extremely well and become great friends already. When we finally arrive in front of Eamon's cottage, we find the curtains are drawn and there's no sign of life.

Paddy walks over to one of the windows. 'This is where the computer was.' He presses his face to the window to see if he can see through the curtains.

'Anything?' I ask.

'Nope,' Paddy peels his face away from the window. 'Nothing's getting through there.'

We wander around the cottage to see if there are any other visible ways to see inside, but all the windows are barricaded shut.

What has Eamon got stored in there, and why doesn't he want us to see it?

'Nothing left for it, then,' Paddy says.

'Go back?' I say, beginning to turn around.

'No.' Paddy shakes his head as though I'm being really dumb. 'Break in!' he announces, his eyes lighting up.

'We can't just break in to Eamon's cottage!'

'Why ever not?' Paddy asks in amazement. 'It's not like we're going to steal anything. We just want to have a look.'

'It's Eamon's private property. It's not right.'

'Ah-ha.' Paddy knowingly holds up his finger. 'But who owns the island now?'

'I do, but—'

'And therefore, in theory, who owns all the property that is built on Tara?'

'Me, I suppose . . . No, Paddy,' I say, sternly holding up my own finger now, 'that still doesn't make it all right to break into someone else's home.'

'All right, it's your choice. But I could have you in and out of there in five minutes flat, and no one would ever know we'd been here.'

For a split second I'm tempted. But I shake my head. 'I'm in no doubt you could have, Paddy. But no; I'll wait and ask Eamon when I see him.'

'Ask me what?'

We both spin around to find Eamon standing a few metres away from us. 'Well?' he asks as he walks towards us, his walking stick gripped tightly in his right hand. 'What's your question, Darcy?'

'Er . . . ' I stare wildly at Paddy.

242

Paddy turns away and starts whistling.

I turn back to Eamon. 'You see, the thing is, Eamon, I … I was just wondering if you had a computer in your cottage, that's all.'

Eamon is startled for a moment, but recovers his composure quickly.

'Now what would I be needing one of those contraptions for?'

'I don't really know. So are you saying you don't have one, then?'

'Now did I actually say that, Darcy?'

Did he? Now I was getting confused. I turn to Paddy again.

Paddy rolls his eyes and shakes his head. 'I saw you the other day, Eamon, when I was up here with Brogan. Sitting in that window you was, clear as day.'

Eamon nods.

'So you *do* have a computer?' I ask, my eyes wide.

Eamon nods again. 'I cannot tell a lie.'

'But why?'

Eamon smiles. 'And why ever shouldn't I have one, Darcy? Just because you might think of me as some old codger doesn't mean I can't work a few buttons on an oversized calculator.'

'Can we see it?' If Eamon's computer is able to hook up to the internet, I might have half a chance at some form of contact with the outside world. Visions of emails, Facebook and Twitter flash through my head, and then the Holy Grail … internet shopping.

'Sure,' Eamon says, heading towards his cottage. I make a move to follow him but he turns back. 'You'll be fine here. I'll be right back.'

I turn and frown at Paddy. How can we see the computer if we wait outside?

Eamon emerges a few moments later with a very modern-looking, state-of-the-art laptop. I don't know why, but when Paddy had said he'd seen Eamon at a computer I'd imagined him at a huge old desktop PC, with a box-screen monitor and a big old grinding hard drive.

'There now,' Eamon opens up the lid and shows me the inside. 'What's so special about that?'

'Nothing, I . . . I mean, it's a nice laptop, Eamon. Does it do much?'

Paddy sighs impatiently. 'What Darcy is trying to say is, do you use it for the internet?'

Eamon narrows his eyes. 'Why?' he asks suspiciously. 'Who wants to know?'

'Er, we do?' Paddy says, turning away from Eamon. He pulls a *well, duh* face at me.

Eamon pulls his computer protectively towards him. He looks between the two of us. 'Why?' he asks again.

'Because I could really do with being able to advertise the cottages properly over the internet. We haven't got any bookings so far.'

And without any bookings, I can't guarantee enough people constantly on the island, and without enough people on the island not only will there not be any work for anyone, or enough money coming in, but I won't be allowed to inherit any money at the end of my year here . . .

Eamon looks at me, and for one awful moment I think he's going to snap the laptop lid shut in my face. But he doesn't, and his eyes dart to and fro across my face as through he's considering something. Then his expression softens as he speaks.

244

'Yes, you can get the internet here, and the phone too, if you want to.'

'What? How?' I ask in astonishment.

'Let me just put this away first,' he says, closing the lid of the laptop, 'and then I'll show you.'

Eamon re-emerges from his front door a few moments later and beckons for Paddy and me to follow him around to the back of his cottage. He pauses at a tall, fenced-off structure that I had wrongly assumed was a small shed when we had hurriedly made our way around here before. But while we'd been trying to take a peek through the windows, I hadn't really been taking much notice of anything else – let alone a garden shed where Eamon probably kept his fishing rods and tools.

But now as I look at it properly, while Eamon unlocks the padlock holding the door bolted shut, I realise the structure doesn't actually have a roof; it's simply four walls bolted together like a large square fence.

Eamon pulls the door open and Paddy and I peer inside.

'It's a satellite dish,' Paddy states unnecessarily, as hidden behind the fencing we find a large round dish about two feet by three feet sitting on the ground, pointing up at the sky.

'That's right,' Eamon says.

'But that's what you use for Sky TV and stuff, isn't it?' I look at Eamon in confusion. 'How do you pick up the internet from it?'

'Is there a satellite near here?' Paddy looks up into the sky. 'Is that how you're managing it?'

Eamon nods.

'And I bet you've got your coaxial cables running under the ground to your modems in the cottage, right?'

Eamon looks impressed.

'You must need two, though, for satellite internet,' Paddy says. 'One for uploading stuff and one for downloading. It's more complicated than your bog-standard dial-up, or even your broadband.'

'You certainly know your stuff, young Paddy,' Eamon nods at him in approval.

Paddy grins. 'Bit of a techno dude, me. Did all the computer stuff at the hotel. Got a bit of a taste for it, so I set up some more advanced systems while I was there. Mary had no idea how to work any of it, bless her.'

'Just hold on a minute,' I say, holding my hand up. 'I'm not following this. Are you saying that this satellite dish picks up the internet, here on the island? Like some sort of WiFi signal?'

'No, Darcy,' Paddy grins. 'If only it were that simple. The dish can pick up the internet for any computer plugged into it, that's all. I'm right, aren't I, Eamon?'

Eamon nods.

'So if I wanted to use the internet ...?' I look hopefully at Eamon.

'You'd need to get your own dish,' he helpfully suggests.

I sigh. *Great*.

'Couldn't I just have a go on your computer, Eamon? Just temporarily, until I can get my own system set up?'

Eamon shakes his head. 'No, I don't think that's a good idea.'

'But why not? I wouldn't be long, I promise. I just need to set up a proper website for the island, and maybe get on Facebook and Twitter, and ...' *So maybe I* would *be a little while*.

'I'm not comfortable with people in my cottage, Darcy. I just like to keep myself to myself.'

'Please, Eamon?'

Eamon looks at me, and for a moment I think he's going to crack. But then he quickly closes up the gate on the satellite dish, padlocks it and begins to walk back to his cottage. 'I'm sorry, Darcy, my answer is still no,' he calls behind him. 'Now, if you'll just go and leave me in peace, please.'

We watch in silence as he disappears around to the front of his cottage.

I turn to Paddy.

'We made a right hames of that,' Paddy says, removing his baseball hat and ruffling his black curls up from their flattened state.

'Hames, Paddy?'

'Hames. You know, er . . . a right balls-up.'

'Oh, I see, yes. It was hardly our fault, though. I just don't see why Eamon won't let anyone inside his cottage. Do you think he's got something hidden in there?'

Paddy shrugs. 'Don't know,' he says, whistling Brogan over to his side. 'Hey, maybe he's got old Finn McCool's treasure hauled up in there, and doesn't want anyone to find it.' Annoyingly, Woody and Louis come running over to Paddy too. I can barely get them to respond to their names, let alone come on a whistle.

I think about this for a moment. 'You don't really think that, do you, Paddy?'

Paddy grins. 'Na. If I was you, Darcy, I'd just forget about him,' he says, beginning to walk away. 'Put a Santa hat on it and call it Randal.'

I shake my head. *What did Paddy just say?*

I run to catch up with him. 'Say that again, Paddy?'

'What?'

'What you just said – something about a Santa hat?'

'I said put a Santa hat on it and call it Randal. It's something one of my pals from up north used to say. It means the thing is crazy, messed-up, beyond your understanding.'

'Just like this whole island, then.'

'You wouldn't be far wrong there, Darcy,' Paddy says, as we descend back down the hill towards the rest of the cottages and O'Connell Street again. 'You wouldn't be far wrong there.'

Twenty-two

'Niall,' I shout, banging on the door of Niall's cottage early one June morning. 'Niall, wake up!'

A bleary-eyed Niall eventually opens the front door, standing in a burgundy dressing gown and navy-blue slippers. 'You'd better have a good excuse for waking me up at ...' he pulls back the sleeve of his dressing gown and squints at his watch, 'six thirty-five in the morning, Darcy!' Niall unfolds his glasses, places them on his nose and runs his hand through his unkempt hair.

'I have, Niall, I have,' I say excitedly. 'Can I come in?'

'Er ...' Niall looks back into his cottage. 'It's just, it's not very tidy at the moment, and—'

'Don't be daft, that doesn't matter. Come on, I need to tell you something.'

'Well, all right, I suppose so then.'

Niall lets me in through the cottage door and leads me into his front room.

'What are you talking about, it looks fine in here,' I say, looking around at Niall's immaculate living area.

'I didn't mean in here, I ... I meant in the kitchen,' he says hurriedly.

'Oh, right. Well, that doesn't matter now, 'cos guess what? We've only gone and got a booking.'

Niall stares at me. 'Darcy, have you run all the way over here and got me up at this ungodly hour just to tell me that another person has rented a cottage? I know since you persuaded me to let you have all that satellite equipment, you've felt the need to inform me every time you've felt it's "paid its way", but this is getting ridiculous now.'

'No, Niall,' I'm barely able to contain my excitement. 'It's not just any old booking, it's a *massive* one! All the cottages are being booked out by the same company at once, for one of these team-bonding sessions that companies do. They're going to want to do everything while they're here – fishing, walking, nature trails, the lot.'

Niall removes his glasses again and massages the bridge of his nose. 'When?'

'In a few weeks. Apparently they had somewhere else booked, but they've been let down – a flood or something at the venue. They need somewhere last-minute, and we're it.'

Niall nods, and I can see him thinking this all through in his usual meticulous way. 'Can we cope with this, do you think? I know we've already had *some* visitors, but that was just a few at a time. This is big stuff, Darcy; we're not used to it yet.'

'We can do it, Niall, I know we can. We'll just have to rally everyone around. Get people organised. And now Dermot's almost finished the pub, that's going to be an added bonus.

Plus,' I add, knowing just how to push his buttons, 'think of all the revenue it will pull in.'

Niall's eyes light up. 'Hmm, perhaps spending all that money on getting internet access installed wasn't such a bad thing after all.'

Of course, after our little trip up to see Eamon, there was no way I wasn't going to have internet access on the island, however much it cost. And as I had suspected, it didn't come cheap. After I found out just how much it cost to set up, I did wonder how on earth Eamon could afford it. Basically you had to pay a monthly cost to the satellite company providing the internet signal, depending on how much of their signal you used every month – much like you would your usual internet provider. But it was more the initial cost of all the equipment that made Niall's glasses steam up, and almost caused him to self-combust when he had to write out a cheque to cover the cost. But when all the equipment eventually arrived, and Dermot had set it all up and I was finally allowed to use it, it was like heaven to be back online again and definitely worth every penny and all my hours of gentle persuasion with Niall. I still let him deal with the financial side of things; now that I had the internet, I didn't trust myself when it came to some of my favourite shopping sites. Although I hadn't actually had a chance to browse any of them yet, I'd been so busy with the cottages, which was a surprise to me; usually they would have been my first port of call when logging on.

My first priority had been to set about blogging, Facebooking and Tweeting all about the island, and then I'd spent a very happy day designing my own website for Tara, after I'd spent another taking photos and videos of all her scenic places and all the cottages we had to let. I'd had to wait for the weather to change so I could show Tara at her very best, but when it had, it had taken me just a day to take the photos.

And then I'd sat back and waited.

But for once, luck had been with me and I hadn't had to wait too long before we had our first cottage booking, and then there'd been another, and soon a steady flow of them had come in to take us right through the summer months. It wasn't enough to support a community of fifteen people permanently with work, but it was a start.

With the cottages now complete, Dermot is at a bit of a loose end. I've discovered that Dermot is the type of person that always needs to keep himself busy. He's not like Conor who, once his daily tasks are done around the island, and he's made any boat trips needed, is quite happy just to take himself off fishing for the rest of the day. Dermot always needs a new project to tackle, and it worries me that if I run out of things for him to do he'll get bored and want to move on. As much as Dermot and I don't see eye to eye most of the time, I wouldn't want him to leave. Tara just wouldn't be the same without him.

So with my bet to find Roxi something interesting to do still in mind, I've come up with what I think is a rather fantastic plan to keep both Roxi and Dermot busy – Tara's first pub! It will be a place for the islanders to meet when the weather is too wet to gather outside in O'Connell Street, and another way to keep Niall and his account book a little happier, although he wasn't that overjoyed when he'd had to pay out yet more money from his ever-thinning chequebook for Dermot to begin the alterations to one of the cottages.

*

I'm heading back now towards my own cottage, full of the joys of spring – well, technically now that its mid-June, it's officially summer – and for once I'm smiling.

'Come on, you guys,' I call to the puppies, who are hardly puppies after four months. 'Let's have an early-morning walk while everyone's still in bed.'

But I'm wrong. As we follow one of the paths around Tara's rocky west coast, we stumble across Orla doing what looks like yoga out in the sunshine. She turns to face us as we approach.

'Good morning, Darcy,' she says, still continuing with her postures. 'You're up early today.'

'Morning, Orla. I had some good news that I went to tell Niall. We've had a large booking come through overnight for a few weeks' time.'

'Excellent,' Orla says, still moving gracefully around on the grass. 'I can see that's brightened your day.'

'Is that t'ai chi you're doing?' I'm sure I've seen Orla's graceful, flowing moves being demonstrated before at a health and beauty exhibition I'd attended for work.

'It is. Would you like to have a go?'

'No, not me, I'm not coordinated enough.'

'You'd do just fine, Darcy. It would help with your stress, too.'

'But I'm not stressed!' I let out a nervous laugh.

Orla ceases what she's doing and bows before she turns to face me properly. 'Darcy, even if I didn't know you, I can tell you're emotionally wrung out just by looking at you.'

'You could?'

Orla nods, 'You really should try and find a way of easing your worries.'

253

'Caitlin gave me this a few weeks ago.' I feel around in my pocket and pull out the little pink stone I always carry around with me.

'Oh yes, a rose quartz,' Orla says knowingly. 'That will help with any emotional stress.'

'You *know* about these stones?' I ask her in surprise.

'Uh-huh, I use crystals in healing too.'

'You do? What sort of healing?'

'Oh, just to help myself along sometimes, when I've got the old ailment or I need a boost. I don't do anything more complicated on the healing front, though, so if it's something like reiki you're after then you'd be better talking to Siobhan, she's been attuned.'

'Siobhan does reiki?' I exclaim. I know a little about reiki; one of the girls in my office had several sessions after she'd slipped a disc in her back, and she'd sworn by it. Said it was the best thing she'd ever had done. It was non-invasive and incredibly relaxing at the same time. It was also one of the things that Jemima, my ex-editor, had been on about me experiencing and writing up in my column before I left the magazine. One of the more pleasant ones, along with turning me into a human pin cushion.

Orla nods. 'I thought you knew.'

Considering this is such a small community, there seems to be an awful lot going on I'm unaware of.

I shake my head. 'No, I had no idea; she looks so normal.'

Orla throws back her head and laughs. 'Darcy, do you think because we take part in a bit of holistic therapy we should all be going round wearing open-toed sandals and chanting mantras?'

'No, not at all,' I reply, feeling my cheeks begin to burn. 'But it just seems odd that I didn't know you were into all this stuff. I mean, there's only a few of us here, and yet here's you with your t'ai chi, Caitlin and her crystals and now Siobhan and her reiki. It's as if Tara is some sort of magnet to a more spiritual way of life.'

Orla nods. 'Maybe she is,' she says, gazing around her at Tara's landscape. 'There are many powerful vibes coming from this ancient soil and these rocks. That's why I come up here to do my t'ai chi.'

Then before I've got time to question her, another thought occurs to me. 'Orla, you don't happen to *teach* t'ai chi, do you?'

'I did have a couple of classes at Daniel's practice when we were back in Waterford.' She smiles. 'My husband thought I was mad at the time, offering t'ai chi at a doctor's surgery. But it was so popular we had a waiting list for the class.'

I smile now, too. 'Then I might just have the perfect job for you and Siobhan here on Tara – and I think you'll find it a bit more enjoyable than changing a few beds.'

Twenty-three

'Come on, Darcy, get up there and give us a song!'

'No way!' I call, picking up some empty glasses and returning them to Roxi at the bar. 'The only time you'll hear me singing might be at closing time, when Roxi needs to empty the pub.'

'Who's going to, then?' Seamus calls. 'What sort of an opening night is this for an Irish pub, if we haven't had any music, or even a sing-song?'

It's our opening night at our new pub on Tara: The Temple Bar. We've stuck with the Dublin theme and named our pub after the famous area of Dublin that contains many pubs and drinking taverns. So far, tonight has been a great success; the drinks are flowing freely and everyone is enjoying themselves. Even Eamon has made a rare appearance at one of our gatherings to investigate the new hostelry, or more likely what it's serving up.

The pub, although small, has a proper wooden bar with two

pumps and some optics mounted behind it on the wall. Alongside those, hang shelves filled with glasses and bottles containing beers and spirits. There are a few tall bar stools and some tables and chairs in the area in front of the bar for our customers, and we've borrowed some of the Guinness memorabilia from Kathleen and Aiden's house to complete the pub effect.

We've got eight guests staying on the island with us just now, who I'm relieved aren't on Tara solely for the peace and quiet, because tonight the atmosphere in the pub is more akin to the real Temple Bar in central Dublin on a Friday night.

Roxi, as I suspected she would be, is in her element as The Temple Bar's new landlady, and she's being ably assisted in her bar duties in busier times by Ryan and Paddy. Apparently Ryan worked as a barman in the real Temple Bar when he was at university in Dublin, and Paddy says he's seen the inside of more Irish bars than a Guinness delivery man, so between the three of them we should be more than capable of handling my slightly boisterous crowd this evening.

Standing back, looking at everyone enjoying themselves I feel a great sense of achievement. I didn't for one moment expect to feel like this while I was here. I just expected to spend the year trying to get through each day one by one, crossing them off on my *Vogue* calendar. I realise now that I haven't even got around to hanging that calendar up. There have been more important things on my mind.

'Seems to be going OK,' Dermot says, standing next to me with a pint of Guinness in his hand and surveying the room in front of him, as I am.

'It's going more than OK, Dermot, and you know it.

Another success to add to your ever-growing list of achievements.'

Dermot turns towards me. 'It's not only down to me, Darcy.'

'No, Roxi is doing a fantastic job of running the bar, too, as I knew she would.'

Dermot smiles. 'I'm actually talking about you. You've got to take some credit for all this.'

'Have I?'

'Darcy,' Dermot says, shaking his head. 'It's *you* that's pulling all these people together, can't you see that? You've taken a bunch of complete strangers and slowly turned them into a tight-knit little community. Just look at them all gathered here tonight.'

I look again at everyone mixing together; young and old, male and female, all from very different backgrounds, yet all happy in each other's company.

Dermot carries on: 'If I'd had my way, we'd have had a very different set of people here on Tara, and you know it. Yes, they might have got the jobs done a lot quicker and with less aggro, but they'd have been a hell of a lot more boring to live with after the work was done.'

I smile at Dermot. Was this his way of saying I was right about something, for once? If this was what a few pints did to him, I'd have to make sure Roxi set up a tab for him and gave him his own stool and silver tankard to hang over the bar. I'm about to thank him when I feel an arm drape around my shoulder.

'*With or with or without you … Oh, oh …* ' Conor croons into my ear. '*… I can't live, with or without you!* There, will that do for some Irish music?' He grins lopsidedly at me.

'Conor, that's U2,' I look at him wryly. 'I don't think that's quite what Seamus has in mind, do you?'

Conor sways a little from side to side.

Blimey, how much alcohol has everyone put away in this bar tonight? I have some serious catching up to do!

'I'll leave you to it,' Dermot says, starting to edge away. 'I can see you've got your hands full.'

'Dermot, you really don't have to—' I begin.

'Yes, Darcy, I really *do*.' Dermot states clearly, walking over to where Caitlin is sitting at a table with Orla and Daniel.

'What's up with him?' Conor asks, beginning to nuzzle my neck. 'Has he been inhaling his glue gun again?'

'Stop it, Conor,' I say, turning my attention away from Dermot and back to him. 'Not here, OK?' I manage to push him away from my neck and drape his arm back around my shoulders again.

Conor, happy with this arrangement, relaxes. 'So, my beautiful island princess, what can this handsome Irish prince do for *you*, tonight?'

'Apparently we need music for this party to be successful,' I tell him matter-of-factly. 'So you can start by telling me how we're to provide that without us all taking a turn with my iPod.'

'Hmm ... that's not *quite* what I had in mind,' Conor says, his brow furrowed like one of those mimes who exaggerate their gestures. Then in the same vein he lifts one finger in the air and then kisses the end of my nose. 'Leave it with me, my princess in peril,' he says, tapping the side his nose with his finger now. Your knight in shining armour has a plan.'

I knew Mary's room sets would come in handy one day. But I would never have guessed it would be Angry Seamus that would benefit from them this time. Conor, with help from Aiden and Daniel, go over to Daniel's house and collect all the musical instruments they have in Daniel and Orla's cottage. Arriving back at the pub with them, it's none other than Seamus (no longer angry once he starts producing music) who pounces on them and begins to play a series of traditional Irish tunes first on the tin whistle, and then on the fiddle.

'Who would have thought it?' I remark to Eamon as I sit next to him, clapping along to Seamus's tunes. There are even a few people trying to have a dance in the tiny bar, while Paddy struggles to keep time with Seamus on the bodhrán drum. 'All along that Angry Seamus was capable of bringing so much joy to the human race. I'll have to stop calling him "Angry" if he carries on like this.'

Eamon smiles into his glass of whiskey before draining the last few drops of it dry. 'Nothing surprises me any more, Darcy,' he says, putting his empty glass back down on the table. 'And especially not when people come here to Tara.'

'How do you mean?'

'You'll realise soon enough,' he says mysteriously. 'It's already happening.'

'What is?'

Eamon yawns now, and stretches. 'Now it really is way past my bedtime. So I'm going to leave you young wans to it and say goodnight.'

'Eamon, you can't go yet, the party's just getting started. Can't I persuade you to stay with another tot of whiskey?' I ask, holding up his glass. 'It's on the house.'

Eamon smiles again. 'Ah, it's a kind offer. But you'll never make a profit like that, Darcy. No, you go and attend to your other island folk. I think there are others that need your guiding light right now.'

Eamon glances in the direction of the bar, and I see a forlorn Caitlin gazing in Dermot's direction.

'Oh, I see.' I wink at Eamon. 'I'm on it.'

What can I do to help that situation along?

'Kathleen,' I ask, interrupting her vigorous jig to Seamus's latest tune. I gently steer her away from the impromptu dance floor for a moment. 'I don't suppose you know any more formal Irish dances, do you? Ones that involve couples?'

Kathleen happily spends the next hour teaching us all some traditional Irish dances. Most of us, that is; I haven't counted on Dermot's absolute stubbornness when it comes to placing his size twelve boots on a dance floor.

'No,' he says firmly, when I try to persuade him to partner Caitlin.

'But why not?' I ask, realising I haven't figured on this slight technical hitch in my plan.

'Because I don't do dancing.'

'But Caitlin needs a partner.'

'Then let one of the other men partner her.'

I sigh. 'Oh, Dermot, just for once stop being so damned awkward.'

'Why?'

'Just *because*, that's why.'

But as hard as I try, Dermot will simply not set foot on the dance floor.

Stepping away from the dancing for a while, I stand at the side of the bar, thoughtfully sipping at my drink.

Roxi comes whizzing over to me from the dancing. 'I

thought Irish dancing was just that Michael Parkinson bloke, but this is *wicked*!' she pants, thirstily grabbing hold of her drink.

'Rox, you mean Michael *Flatley* not Michael *Parkinson*! And aren't you supposed to be serving behind the bar, not dancing the night away with the punters?'

'It's called customer relations, Darce, don't you know anything?' Roxi grins at me, 'This is the best fun I've had in ages, and I don't just mean the dancing. The pub was a brilliant idea. I love it – thank you!' She leans forward and gives me a big hug.

'And?' I ask, raising my eyebrows as she releases me from her embrace.

'What?' She looks back at me innocently blinking her bright blue eyelashes. 'Oh *that*.'

'Yes, that. So when are you bringing my winnings over?'

'Are you really sure you want to start that habit up again, Darce? Think of your figure.' She looks me up and down teasingly. 'A moment on the lips ...'

'Just bring the chocolate over to my cottage, Roxi,' I say in desperation. I really don't need winding up any more tonight, after Dermot. A nice smooth block of chocolate would go down just perfectly right now.

'Ooh, Mrs Snappy, who's been swimming in your lagoon that shouldn't? You see, this is what happens when you try and wheel and deal in banned substances. You can't take the consequences.'

'Roxi,' I say, placing my hands on my hips, 'I'm talking about a few bars of chocolate. It's hardly an illegal drugs ring.'

'You'd think it was, from the look of desperation on your face right now.'

'It's not just the chocolate.' I glance over at Dermot, sitting sullenly sipping at his pint of Guinness in the corner.

'Why, what's up, honey?'

I tell her about Dermot, Caitlin and the dancing.

'That's because you're going about it the wrong way,' Roxi says knowingly. 'Blokes like our Mr Cowell there don't like being pushed into something head on; they need to be gently cajoled into it so they don't know what they're actually doing until they're already doing it.'

'Like what, for instance?' I ask, my brow furrowed in concentration. How did Roxi always know so much about men?

'Giving a nice gentle dinner party.'

'But you know I can't cook! We tried to have that breakfast meeting at mine the other morning, and I burnt all the sausages. Conor had to scramble a load of eggs to save the day.'

'Or even save your bacon!' Roxi jokes with a flourish of her hands.

'Roxi!'

Roxi shushes me with her hand. 'All right, keep your pony-tail in. Actually, Darce, I've been meaning to have words with you about that hair of yours, you've been wearing it in that same style every day since you got here.'

I reach protectively for my hair. 'I have not! I do vary it a bit. Besides, it's always windy here, I have to keep it tied back.'

Roxi purses her lips. 'What, indoors as well? You don't see my hair tied up with a bit of elastic, do you?'

I look at Roxi's mane of black hair clipped up on one side with a bright orange flower. 'No, but ... Look, we're not supposed to be talking hairdressing now, we're supposed to be talking dinner parties. Just how do you propose me of all people is going to cook an appetising and glamorous meal here, on a remote island in the middle of the sea?'

'Hmm, toughie,' Roxi says, looking around the room. Then she grins. 'You, Darcy, are not going to need to cook at all. Leave that minor detail with me. You've got a much more difficult problem to deal with than your lack of cookery skills.'

'Such as?'

'Getting Mr Cowell over there to come to the dinner party at all.'

Twenty-four

'But you *have* to come, Dermot,' I insist, when yet again Dermot is proving elusive on the subject of whether he will turn up later or not.

'Why do I? So I can watch you and Casanova drooling over each other at the table all evening?'

'No.' I must remain calm if I'm to get Dermot to come. My hand reaches for the rose quartz that I now carry around with me always in my pocket. 'Because otherwise my numbers will be out. You always have a dinner party with an even number of people.'

'Is that the best you can come up with?' he asks, while he adjusts some loose guttering on one of the holiday cottages. He sighs heavily. 'Go on then, I'll come. But I'm not dressing up.'

'I wouldn't expect you to, Dermot,' I reply, calmly trying to contain my joy. 'Just make sure you turn up at my cottage at seven o'clock tonight wearing some clean, decent clothes, and I'll be happy.'

'I am capable of dressing myself, Darcy,' he mumbles through the nails he holds in his mouth. 'I'm not a child.'

I'm about to leave him to his repairs, happy I've at least got him to agree to attend, when I turn back. 'Just out of interest, Dermot, what *are* you thinking of wearing?'

Dermot pulls the nails from his mouth and looks down at me from the ladder he's balancing on. 'Why?'

'I was just wondering, that's all. I mean, you are going to make an effort, aren't you?'

Dermot narrows his eyes. 'Depends what you mean by making an effort. I'll be having a wash and putting a clean shirt on, what more do you want?'

'Is that it? There's nothing wrong with a man trying to look his best, you know, especially when he's going out to dinner with a lady.'

'I'm not going out to dinner with a lady, though, am I? I'm going round to your cottage for supper.'

'Thanks,' I say, rolling my eyes.

'You know what I mean. And I've never been one of these metrosexual types that put creams and potions all over themselves.'

'No, I know, I saw inside your bathroom, remember. I couldn't help but notice your lack of equipment.'

Dermot gives me a wry smile. 'Can I ask you to rephrase that statement if you repeat it to anyone else, for both our sakes?'

Blushing, I think quickly. 'How about I come over to your cottage this afternoon and give you a bit of a makeover before tonight?'

'Uh-uh,' Dermot shakes his head. 'No way are you bringing

that tool kit full of make-up you have in your cottage and using it on me.'

'No, I don't mean make-*up*. I mean a make*over*, like they do on television. If you like you could think of it more in terms of home improvements, only on yourself instead.' I smile at Dermot, hoping he'll like this analogy.

Dermot grimaces. 'Nice try, Darcy, but DIY's answer to Gok Wan you are not. Just forget it and pass me up that hammer, will you? I am not having, and nor do I need, a make-over.'

Hmm, I don't give up that easily, Dermot. You're not the only one that likes a challenge ...

I reach into his tool box and pass him the hammer, and as I do I have an idea. 'How about if I can pass you the next three tools you name out of your tool box, you have to let me give you a makeover later?'

Dermot's eyes sparkle with interest. I knew he wouldn't be able to resist.

'Deal,' he climbs down from his ladder so we can shake on it. 'You've no chance.'

'Right, so what's the first one?' I ask, folding my arms and casually standing back so he can choose.

'A plumb-bob,' Dermot says, without thinking too hard.

'Easy,' I reach down, and after moving a couple of things about in the metal box I find a small brass pendulum-like weight, hanging on a piece of string.

'This what you're looking for?' I ask, holding it up and swinging it in front of his nose.

'That'd be it.' Dermot snatches the weight from me. 'Good guess. Bet you don't know that it's for, though.'

'Measuring vertical lines, isn't it?' I say calmly. 'That's what I'd use it for, anyway.'

'Hmm,' Dermot eyes me suspiciously. 'Right, well, I'll take a spokeshave next, then.'

After a few seconds of rummaging in the box, I lift up something similar to a plane for smoothing wood. 'Would this be it?' I ask, handing over the tool.

'Yes . . .' Dermot examines it warily. 'I should have thought that one through a bit better. The word *shave* must have given it away.'

'Perhaps.' I shrug. 'But if I get this next one right, I'll have you doing a lot more than just shaving before you go to dinner tonight.' I wiggle my fingers like a magician about to perform an illusion. 'The tools in my beauty box don't have such fancy names as yours, but they still do just as good a job where they're required.'

Dermot winces. He takes his time before laying down his final challenge. 'How about you find me a grubbing mattock, Darcy?' he announces, trying to keep the satisfaction from his voice.

I look him steadily in the eye for a moment before pretending to bend down towards the tool box again. 'Nice try, Dermot,' I say, standing up again to face him, my hands on my hips. 'But I'm not going to find a grubbing mattock in there now, am I? Looking a bit like a pick axe, it's far too big to fit inside your tool box!'

'How do you know all this?' Dermot demands. 'The only tools you know about are nail files and hair straighteners.'

'My first job in journalism was on a building trade magazine. I had to write about this kind of stuff all the time. Pretty boring, but the information stuck.'

Dermot shakes his head. 'You conned me.'

'No, I didn't. I didn't say I knew nothing about building tools; you just assumed. I told you once before, Dermot, don't assume you know me when quite clearly you don't.'

Dermot's deep brown eyes scan my face. 'I disagree, Darcy. Every day we spend on this island I think I'm getting to know you just that little bit better.'

I'm not really sure how to take this. 'So, then . . .' I glance at my watch. 'Shall we say your cottage, four o'clock?'

'For?'

'For your makeover, Dermot,' I flamboyantly spin around on the grass with my hands held out. 'Move over, Mr Gok Wan, Miss Darcy McCall's coming to town!'

At four on the dot I turn up at Dermot's cottage with my beauty box clutched tightly in my hand. It had seemed like a good idea earlier, taking on this challenge – I wanted Dermot to look good tonight for Caitlin's sake. But now, as I knock on the front door of his cottage, I feel quite apprehensive.

Back at my cottage, preparations are in full swing for the dinner party tonight. Roxi has suggested to Kathleen and Aiden that they help out by cooking food to serve at the pub, Aiden being a baker. Tonight is a trial run, to see if their culinary skills reach beyond baking bread and cakes. Roxi's managed to find a way around my complete lack of cooking skills and arrived at a new way to generate revenue on the island – sometimes I temporarily forget how amazing she is.

When I'd gone over to see them in their cottage earlier, they'd been happily discussing suitable menus for the evening and told me that they'd always dreamed of starting up their own restaurant but had never had the finances to do so. They were thrilled to be given the chance to have a go here on Tara.

So now I've left them cooking away in my little kitchen, while Roxi bosses Conor as he moves furniture about in the front room so that we can fit in the table and chairs borrowed from the pub. Roxi insists she's going to decorate the front room to a theme for our dinner guests – in addition to myself and Roxi, we'll have Conor, Dermot, Caitlin and Niall around the table.

I've been surprised how enthusiastic Conor has been about the dinner party. He hadn't seemed too keen at first, but once we'd explained it was to try and get Caitlin and Dermot together he'd sprung into action, offering help and assistance wherever it was required.

But it's got so stressful at the cottage over the last hour with all the plans and preparations that I'm quite glad to get away for a while and head over to see Dermot.

'All right?' Dermot enquires, eyeing up my box as he opens the door to his cottage.

'Yes, fine thanks. You?'

'I'll let you know that in a while.'

I follow Dermot through into his cottage. 'Right, shall we start in the bedroom then?' I ask, walking past him and heading in that direction.

Dermot grins. 'I've met some forward women in my time, Darcy, but that takes the biscuit.'

I stop at the bedroom door as I feel my cheeks begin to flush. I turn back to face him. 'In your dreams, Dermot,' I say, deliberately keeping my face poker straight. 'Since it's a bedroom, I assume you keep your very limited wardrobe some-where in here.'

Dermot nods, still smiling. 'Yes, my clothes are in there. In you go.'

As I head purposefully across the bedroom I pause for a moment to place my beauty box on the chest of drawers, and I notice that the photo of the little girl has been put away. Dermot obviously doesn't want me delving into anything deeper than his wardrobe today, so I go over to it and pull open the wooden doors.

'Is this it?' I enquire, looking at the pitiful array of clothing hanging up in front of me. 'I've seen more clothes hanging on a scarecrow.'

'Very funny,' Dermot says, leaning up against the door frame. 'I've got a few things in the chest of drawers, too.'

'Like?'

'T-shirts, underwear, socks ... That kind of thing.'

'I suppose if this is all you've got, then this is what we'll have to work with.'

'Why does all this matter so much to you anyway?' Dermot asks, watching me as I begin to pull from the wardrobe various shirts, jeans and jumpers, hoping magically to put together a good-looking outfit for the dinner party later.

'What do you mean?'

'Appearance. What people look like seems to be very high on your list of priorities.'

'Not really.' I'm holding up a blue-and red-checked shirt against a pair of blue jeans, hoping to gain some inspiration. Why are so many of Dermot's shirts checked? Does he have a secret longing to become a lumberjack? 'That makes me sound very shallow.'

Dermot watches me silently from the door.

I turn towards him. 'Are you saying I am shallow?'

'No, it's just that when I first met you, you seemed to put a lot of importance on what you and other people look like. But since you've been on Tara, I think you've realised that having the latest designer handbag over your shoulder and straightening your hair every five minutes isn't the be-all and end-all. That there is more to life.'

'I never thought those things were that important before, actually!' I feel my cheeks begin to burn with frustration. How does Dermot always manage to push my buttons like this? 'But what's wrong with trying to look your best? When people look good, they feel good.'

Dermot sits down on the end of his bed. 'I take your point. But you can go over the top. Your appearance should reflect your personality, not be a mask to what's underneath. Why try and hide what's really going on with a lot of unnecessary gift-wrapping? Let your hair down for once, Darcy, as well as your guard.'

I stare at Dermot as he blinks unwaveringly back into my eyes; it feels right now like he's the one digging around in the things I want to keep locked away, not the other way around.

This is all getting a bit too intense, so I decided to lighten the mood.

'Can't do that here, can I?' I turn back towards the wardrobe and begin pulling a few more items off the rail.

'Why on earth not?'

'I've tried letting my hair down on Tara, but it's just too windy. It gets in a complete mess and takes far too long to sort out, it's just not worth the hassle.'

I hear Dermot sigh.

'So,' I say lightly, 'I'm thinking this shirt,' I hold up a plain mid-blue cotton shirt, 'and these jeans. But what we really need is a nice white t-shirt to go underneath it. Have you got one in here?' I head over towards the chest of drawers.

'No, that's OK, I'll get it!' Dermot leaps off the bed, intercepting me before I can get there.

'Ooh, what have you got hidden in there?' I laugh, before immediately realising that's probably where he's put the photo.

Dermot hurriedly pulls a plain white t-shirt from the middle drawer and snaps it shut again. 'Will this do you?' he says, passing me the shirt.

'Yep, that's perfect.' I look at the drawer for a moment, wondering if this would be a good time to mention the photo. But Dermot doesn't look like he'd willingly share his secrets, even though he's just been doing his best to convince me to open up and share mine.

'So, I've tried to keep the outfit plain,' I say, gesturing to the clothes I'm now arranging into an outfit out on the bed. 'Just like your decor in here. You seem to like keeping things plain and uncomplicated.'

'Can't be doing with a lot of fuss,' Dermot says, suspiciously regarding the clothes on the bed as if they're going to jump up and force themselves on his body at any moment.

'You don't seem to have brought many knick-knacks from home or anything,' I continue. 'You only have the furniture from the hotel. Didn't you bring any personal mementos with you, like photos, for instance?'

Dermot looks at me suspiciously now. 'Tell me, Darcy, how many photos do you have in your cottage?'

Damn. 'None, but—'

'There you go; maybe we don't want our friends and family on display for others to see.'

It was no good. Dermot is as inflexible as one of Tara's huge mountainous rocks when he digs his heels in. There's no way I'm getting anything out of him if he doesn't want to be moved on the subject. I decided to give up – for now.

'What do you think?' I ask him, nodding to the outfit on the bed.

Dermot stares at my carefully selected ensemble. 'They're clothes,' he replies in a flat voice.

'Yes, I know that, but what do you think about the combination of them together?'

Dermot shrugs. 'It's OK, I suppose.'

I sigh. 'They'll look better when you put them on.'

'Let's get this over with, then.' Before I can stop him, Dermot pulls the shirt he's wearing up over his head without unbuttoning it and reaches down towards the clothes on the bed. 'You want me to wear this white t-shirt first?' he asks.

I know I'm opening my mouth to speak, but for some reason there's nothing coming out. Dermot just stripping his shirt off in front of me like this has shocked me for two reasons: first, I hadn't actually meant him to try the clothes on right at this very moment. And second, the sight of him standing there bare-chested in just his jeans and boots is a lot more pleasant than it should be, because Dermot does particularly well in the torso department. He's exceptionally muscular, but not in that 'I've pumped a bit too much iron' bodybuilder way. There's a fine layer of dark hair covering his extremely well-developed chest, but not so much that we're talking grizzly bear alert.

'Er . . . yes, that's right, the t-shirt underneath the shirt,' the words manage to find a way out at last. I sit down on the bed and watch as Dermot pulls the white t-shirt on, and as his torso disappears order is immediately restored to my brain once more.

'You don't need to put those on,' I hurriedly instruct him as he reaches for the jeans, 'they're not that different from the ones you're wearing.'

Dermot shrugs. 'OK,' and he begins to tuck the white t-shirt into his jeans.

'No – no tucking in!'

'Why not? It's neat and tidy.'

'It's neat and tidy if you're over seventy, maybe! I don't suppose there's any chance of a decent belt hidden in those drawers, is there?'

Dermot rolls his eyes and goes to his chest of drawers again. He opens the bottom one and pulls out a brown leather belt with an ornate silver buckle. 'What about this, will it do?'

'That's perfect, Dermot,' I say, examining the belt. 'Where did you get it from? It looks like it's quality leather, maybe a designer label.'

'It was a gift.'

That figured.

I hand him back the belt and he feeds it through his jeans. He pulls on the blue shirt and begins to button it up.

'Don't button the shirt.' I instruct from the bed.

'Why on earth not?'

'It will just look better if you leave it undone. Look,' I get up from the bed and begin to undo the buttons Dermot's already done up. His chest begins to move in and out a little bit faster as I do, and suddenly it begins to feel very warm in the bedroom. I'm aware of the heat radiating from Dermot's body as we stand this close to each other. I can feel his warm breath on the top of my head as I quickly pull the shirt loose and arrange it so it hangs around his hips and the t-shirt sits just above his belt. Then I stand back and pretend to admire my handiwork while I steady my own breathing.

'Yep,' I say, not daring to look him in the eye. 'Not bad, even if I do say so myself. What do you think?'

'What I can see looks pretty good to me.'

I stop admiring Dermot's clothes and look directly up at him. His brown eyes gaze unblinkingly back into mine. 'But you don't have a mirror in here, how do you know until you've seen yourself in a mirror?'

Dermot suddenly jolts into action like he's just woken from a daydream. 'No, you're right. I need to see it properly. I'll go into the bathroom – back in a minute.'

Still in a daze myself, I begin hanging Dermot's other clothes back in his wardrobe.

'I have to hand it to you, Darcy,' he says on his return, 'it's pretty good. I like it.'

'Great. I'm glad you do.' We stare at each other again for a moment.

'Right, I'd better get these shirts off in case I get them messed up before tonight.' Dermot begins stripping off again.

'And I'd better head back,' I say, grabbing my beauty box and hurrying towards the door.

'Is that it? Torture over?' Dermot asks, already shirtless again. 'I thought Mrs Gok would have had a lot more in store for me than just a few wardrobe adjustments. You didn't even break into *the box*. Not that I'm complaining, mind.'

'No, I think Mrs Gok's seen . . . *done* plenty for one session.' I'm trying so hard to keep my eyes on Dermot's face and not let them roam to his bare chest again.

'Well, I think she's done a grand job,' Dermot says, following me as I scuttle towards his front door, now desperate to escape. 'Oh, you've forgotten something.'

'Have I?' I turn back, my hand already on the door handle. *Oh, I wish Dermot would cover himself up!*

'Yep, aren't you supposed to ask me that all-important question before we finish?'

I look at Dermot in confusion. My brain is scuppered enough at the moment, without any guessing games. What on earth is he going on about?

Dermot rolls his eyes. 'From that TV show. Do I look good naked?'

Twenty-five

Tonight is turning out to be one of the loveliest nights I've spent here on Tara. The dinner party has been a very elegant affair so far; Roxi has adorned my front room, the table and our chairs with trailing greenery and wild flowers to make it feel like we're in a magical fairy glen. The conversation throughout the evening has been fun and flowing at a constant pace, with no awkward breaks, and the food that Kathleen and Aiden have served us has been exquisite. Conor and Dermot have been civil to one another for once, and most importantly, Caitlin and Dermot seem to be hitting it off.

Dermot has turned up in his outfit newly styled by me, looking altogether quite un-Dermot-like. I wonder, as I look at him, if it's just the way he's wearing his clothes that's making him appear different. But he seems to have made a bit more effort with his whole appearance tonight, too. He's styled his hair and has taken more care with shaving, and he's smiling more than he usually does, mostly in Caitlin's direction.

Something doesn't feel quite right seeing Dermot like this, but I have no idea why it's bothering me.

Us girls have all made a big effort tonight too, and are wearing dresses for the occasion. Caitlin's is a long, flowing, flowery gown that if I attempted to wear would look like I was going to a 1970s fancy-dress party, but which on Caitlin simply accentuates her willowy figure. She's wearing minimal make-up, and this, with her blonde hair cascading down over her slim shoulders, makes her look like an old, glamorous advert for Cadbury's Flake. I feel very formal, sitting opposite her wearing that dinner-party staple, the little black dress. It's a simple, long black gown from French Connection, with tiny diamantés around the neckline and a deep slit up one side. I'm not too sure why I brought it with me – it had seemed a bit over the top at the time, when I'd been packing – but I always like to be prepared just in case, and now I'm really glad I did bring it. This dinner party deserves a bit of glamour with all the effort everybody's put in, and jeans and a jumper, although they've become my day-to-day Tara uniform, just wouldn't have done at all.

Tonight Roxi has put my hair up for me in a style we've seen Cheryl Cole wear on *The X-Factor* a few times, and Roxi has even persuaded me to wear a tiny silver tiara in my hair.

'No,' I insisted when she produced it from her jewellery box.

'But Darce, you look so elegant in that black dress, and with your hair up like that, you remind me of Audrey Hepburn in *Breakfast at Tiffany's*.'

'I hardly think so, Roxi,' I'd replied, craning to view myself in the tiny mirror in Roxi's bathroom. But the tiara went so beautifully with the diamanté in the dress that I decided to let it stay. How often do you get the chance to wear a tiara to dinner, after all?

But now, seeing Caitlin's understated style and Dermot's reaction to it, I do feel a bit overdressed. Maybe I have overdone it? Conor has told me I look gorgeous tonight, though, so what does it matter what anyone else thinks?

Roxi, as ever, has gone for full-on glitz and glamour. She's wearing a scarlet red-sequinned minidress with matching platform shoes, and has accessorised her look with a red rose-and-diamanté headpiece, which is pinning up her long black locks.

Niall has produced a plain grey suit and white shirt from his cottage (I knew he'd have to bring one suit with him!), so it's only Conor, although clean and tidy, who doesn't look much different to usual in his blue jeans and white t-shirt. But he still looks gorgeous as he sits next to me now, tucking into his dessert. He winks as he sees me watching him.

'So, Conor, you seem to have travelled the world,' Dermot says, scraping the last of his sticky toffee pudding up with his spoon. 'Don't you ever feel like settling down in one place?

'Nope,' Conor lifts the bottle of wine from the table to refill everyone's glasses.

'But you must want a base, somewhere to call home?' Dermot persists.

Conor shakes his head. 'You've heard of the song "Wherever I Lay my Hat (That's my Home)?" Well, this is my home for now, here on Tara. More wine, Dermot?' he hovers with the bottle over Dermot's glass.

Dermot shakes his head and holds his hand over his half-empty glass.

'It must be wonderful to have been to so many places,' Caitlin says. 'I'd love to travel more.'

'You should do, Caitlin. Travel broadens the mind so much I can't begin to tell you. I've learned more in my years of travelling than I ever learned when I was home. But there's still so much more of the world I've yet to see.'

'So why are you here, then?' Dermot asks. 'Why stop on Tara?'

Conor finishes filling his own glass and places the bottle carefully back down on the table. 'Maybe I've found something here on Tara I like,' he smiles at me.

'But you couldn't have known what would happen between the two of you when you applied to come here. So, no offence, Darcy,' Dermot continues, glancing across at me, 'but something else must have brought you to Tara.'

I roll my eyes. 'No offence taken, Dermot.' Picking up my glass, I sigh. I don't like where this is heading: everything has been lovely and dinner-partyish up until now. Why does Dermot have to start being awkward?

Conor eyes Dermot over the dinner table. And for a moment, the two men lock into each other's stare.

'I just wanted a break from travelling for a while,' Conor says eventually. 'After my mam died. So what better way than to spend it here, near to where I grew up, reliving old memories?' He picks up his wineglass and takes a large gulp.

I glare at Dermot. *After all I've done for you this afternoon.*

'Now then,' Roxi says anxiously, looking between Dermot and me, 'since we've finished dessert, how about we all have a game?'

I'd tried to encourage Aiden and Kathleen to stay and join

281

us once all their lovely food had been served up, but they insisted on going to join the others at The Temple Bar and leaving us to enjoy ourselves. In fact, I'd felt guilty that I hadn't been able to invite everyone to our dinner party – I didn't like excluding anyone – but as Ryan had quite rightly pointed out, someone had to look after our island guests and the pub that night, so he and the others had encouraged Roxi and me to take a night off.

We really are such a close community now. Everyone on Tara is always so lovely to each other.

Everyone except Dermot and Conor, that is.

'What sort of a game?' Dermot asks suspiciously.

Roxi's dark eyes dart between the five of us. Knowing Roxi like I do, I dread to think what she's got in mind. I see her eyes rest on the wine bottle in the middle of the table, and I fire a warning glance at her.

'Spoilsport,' Roxi says, giving me a mock pout.

'How so, Roxi?' Caitlin asks, looking between the two of us. 'What do you want to play?'

'Roxi's thinking of playing spin the bottle,' I answer for her, while she tries to suppress a cheeky smile.

'No way,' Dermot says, resolutely placing his empty wineglass back down on the table and lifting the bottle to fill it again. 'This is all this bottle is going to be used for tonight.'

Caitlin looks faintly disappointed.

'Come on, Roxi, you must know some other party games?' Niall suggests helpfully.

'Kiss chase,' Roxi says, winking at me.

I shake my head.

'OK, OK. How about I Never?'

'What's I Never?' Caitlin asks. 'I don't think I've ever played that before.'

'It's easy,' Roxi explains. 'We all take it in turns to make a statement, like "I never ate six Cadbury's Creme eggs in one sitting", for example. If you haven't ever done that you remain sitting. If you have, then you stand up. For instance,' she says, pointing at me, 'Miss Chocoholic over there should be standing up right now.'

'Ha, I'm not that bad,' I stick out my tongue at Roxi.

'It sounds fun!' Caitlin says, clapping her hands together.

'It sounds about as much fun as putting my hand in a vice and turning the handle,' Dermot grumbles.

'Stop your moaning, Mr Cowell,' Roxi admonishes him, 'and lighten up for once! Right, I'll go first then.' She thinks for a moment. 'Hmm, I've never . . . been arrested,' she says, her eyes lighting up.

Myself and Roxi immediately spring to our feet, followed by Niall, who is dragging himself up also. The others remain seated, and look with interest at each other and with surprise at Niall.

'What?' he asks. 'I was young once, you know. At university, there was a minor incident with a fountain and some bubble bath.'

'Well, that's certainly got the party started,' Roxi laughs as we finish telling our own stories of minor misdemeanours with the police. Roxi's and mine obviously relating to the Eros incident. 'Now, whose turn is it next?'

'I'll go,' Conor says, raising his hand. A sudden flash of something flickers in his eyes, and then he smiles at us all, waiting. 'I've never … wondered what Eamon has hidden in that cottage of his.'

We all stand.

'So, what *do* you think he has hidden in there?' he asks, looking around the table as we take our seats again.

Niall shrugs. 'I don't know, but he keeps it well hidden. Paddy says when he goes up there to help him with his satellite equipment now, it's always well locked up.'

'Hmm, Paddy spends far too much time with Eamon when he should be helping me,' Dermot grumbles. 'I know he's doing Eamon a favour, but there are jobs to be done around the island. All right, all right,' he says reproachfully when we all simply stare at him across the table. 'What do you lot reckon, then – he's hiding a secret lady friend up there?'

'What, and he never lets her out?' I exclaim. 'I hardly think so, and Eamon must be well into his seventies now. I think secret dating might be a bit past him.'

'What about you, Roxi?' Conor asks, looking intently at Roxi. 'You're always up there with Eamon, haven't you seen anything?'

'Nah,' Roxi shrugs, lifting her wineglass. 'We always sit outside the cottage, or if the weather's bad Eamon comes down to my house for our little chats.' As Roxi takes a sip of her wine, her eyes glint mischievously. 'It could be Finn McCool's treasure he has stashed in there.'

We all stare at her.

'Eamon knows loads about all these myths and legends, he tells me the stories behind them all the time. It's really interesting. Can't get my daily dose of the soaps over here very easily, can I, unless I steal Darcy's computer away from her, so Eamon's tales fill the *Corrie* and Albert Square-sized gap in my life right now.'

We all laugh and go back to our wine and last spoonfuls of dessert, but Conor still seems keen to know more.

'Do you really think that might be the case, Roxi?' he asks, leaning across the table. His blues eyes watch her intently while he waits for her answer.

Roxi rests her elbows on the tablecloth and meets Conor's gaze face on. She wrinkles up her nose, 'No!' she says grinning. 'Not really. Goodness knows what he's really got hidden in there. But he's happy, and not doing anyone any harm, so what does it matter? Someone else's turn now.'

Niall suggests: 'I've never got so drunk I can't remember getting home', another one I have to stand for – this game is not exactly showing me in my best light. But luckily Roxi, Conor and, surprisingly, Dermot stand up too. Dermot is then forced in to taking the next turn. Hilariously, he comes up with 'I've never wanted a game to end as much as I do right now'. He's the only one that stands, thankfully, so the game moves on and I take my turn.

Right, I think, trying not to catch Dermot's eye, *now we'll see if you're truly being honest tonight*. I take a chance. 'I've never . . . been married.'

Roxi's eyes open wide as she remains in her seat. I look around the table as everyone else remains seated too. My eyes rest on Dermot. He takes a long sip of his red wine while he regards me over the top of his glass. Then, very slowly, he pushes back his chair and stands up.

A tiny gasp escapes from Caitlin's mouth.

'So you're married, Dermot?' she asks, trying to keep her voice as steady as she can.

'Divorced. Three years ago.' Dermot's dark eyes continue to watch me while he stands towering above us, awaiting my next move.

'Oh, I see,' Caitlin visibly relaxes.

'Any children?' I ask bluntly, my eyes not leaving his.

Roxi kicks me under the table.

But Dermot just continues to look intently down at me. 'Yes, one. A daughter, Megan.'

That explains the photo then ... I know I probably should stop there and keep this for another time. But now the truth is out, I can't help but dig a bit deeper. I just have to know why he won't tell me about something as important as a daughter.

'Does she live with her mother?' I ask, still watching him for some sort of reaction to all this, a flicker of emotion.

'Yes.' Dermot says curtly, pulling up his chair to sit down again.

'Do you get to see her often?'

Dermot stares hard at me across the table, and finally it's there, the merest trace of something. But it's not anger I see reflected back at me in Dermot's eyes. It's sadness. 'No, I don't. She lives in the States with my ex, Eileen, and her latest toy boy. I haven't seen Megan since she was seven.'

I know instantly I shouldn't have pushed him so far, as I feel a huge wave of guilt wash over me. Suddenly my dinner feels too heavy, and the wine feels too strong. I've said too much.

'And how old is she now, Dermot?' Caitlin asks gently, looking at Dermot with such compassion I feel even worse for questioning him so fiercely.

'Eleven.' Dermot picks up his glass and, realising it's now empty, grabs the bottle from the table and hastily refills it.

We all sit silently around the table, not knowing what to say. I *really* wish I hadn't said anything now. I should have asked Dermot about the photo privately when no one else was about. When I get the chance, I'll apologise to him properly.

'Look, do you mind if we don't talk about this any more?' Dermot asks, still taking large sips from his wineglass. 'It's something I prefer not to talk about.'

'No, of course not,' I say hurriedly. I look desperately around at the others. 'So, who's going next? Caitlin, you've not had a turn.'

'Oh … oh, right. Erm, yes, now what was I going to say?' Caitlin looks flustered for a moment, then blushes profusely. 'Oh, yes, that's it.' She glances nervously around the table. 'I've never found anyone on this island attractive.'

Conor and I immediately stand up and exchange knowing smiles over the table. Then, cheeks burning bright red, Caitlin joins us, followed by Roxi. 'I suppose I'd better stand,' she says grudgingly. 'Darce won't mind me admitting that I think you're gorgeous, Conor, even if you are already taken.'

Conor winks at her.

To my surprise, Dermot suddenly springs to his feet. He glances at Caitlin, who immediately turns away and blushes even more. Lastly, Niall stands to join the six of us.

'Yes, even me,' he says, looking apprehensive as we begin to sit back down again.

'What's wrong, Niall?' I ask, suddenly feeling uneasy as Niall still stands in front of us. He's fiddling with the corner of the tablecloth, twisting it round and round in his hands.

'It's just that, after we've all shared so much tonight, it seems like the right moment to tell you something important.' He nervously glances around the table again, lifts up a glass and takes a quick sip of the wine. Even Dermot senses this is not the time to point out it's his glass Niall's picked up. 'The thing is, I've not only found someone attractive since I've been here on Tara, but it's turned into more than that. It's blossomed into love between the two of us. And that someone is . . .' he swallows hard and looks around the table one last time, as if he's searching for our approval before he speaks. 'That special someone is . . . Paddy.'

Twenty-six

Now I know about Paddy and Niall, I realise the signs have been there for ages. The fact they always spend so much time together; the morning I'd gone over to Niall's cottage early and he'd been very shifty about letting me in; the way Niall always brings Paddy up in conversation at every opportunity.

After Niall's revelation at the dinner party, we'd all immediately been very supportive in our own way. Roxi had thrown her arms around him and hugged him to within an inch of his life. Caitlin had gently sat and talked to him about how he felt and if he wanted help telling anyone else. Conor and Dermot had found the whole thing a bit more difficult to handle, and had stood for a few minutes trying to look as manly as possible with their arms folded across their bodies and their legs planted firmly apart. I'd encouraged Dermot to go and get Niall some of the Irish whiskey I had in my kitchen, given to me by a grateful holidaymaker. Niall had thrown back the tot of whiskey in one and immediately asked for a refill, which

Dermot obliged him with, but Niall was still shaking when I put my hand on his and spoke to him.

'Is this the first time you've told anyone?' I ask gently.

Niall nods. 'Paddy wanted me to tell you all earlier. He never wanted us to keep it a secret. It's not Paddy's style, keeping things hidden. But the thing is, it was all new to me.' Niall looks at me, his pale blue eyes shining brightly through his glasses. 'Not just this type of relationship, but *any* type of relationship.' He looks at everyone sitting and standing around the table. 'I didn't know I was gay when I came to Tara. Until I met Paddy, I didn't know who I really was. I'd never felt that I belonged anywhere, not at university, not in the solicitor's office. And now that I'm here, for the first time in my life I do belong. I belong here on this island, with all of you, and most importantly with Paddy. It's like I needed Tara to show me who I really was.'

I hear the wind suddenly gust up around the outside of the cottage, tapping against the window panes, as if Tara wants to come into our little gathering and give Niall her own seal of approval. Sitting here watching him talk, it's as if he's growing in stature as we speak. The slight, nervous solicitor I first met in my aunt's back garden has disappeared, and here in his place now sits a confident and happy young man.

I reach out my arms and wrap them tightly around him. 'Niall, I'm so happy for you.'

'This is all thanks to you, Darcy. Thank you for letting me come here and find myself.'

'Don't be daft, Niall.' I look around at the others in the room as I release myself from his embrace. 'We're all in this together. Living here isn't just about one individual; it's about all of us pulling together and making a community. So it's Tara you should thank. She's the one that brings about change for people.'

As I stand and watch my guests depart that night, I begin to understand what Eamon was hinting at, that night in the pub. Change is what happens when people come to Tara: some of the changes are there for all to see and comment on, and others are more subtle, but much more significant.

Roxi walks arm in arm with Niall back to her cottage. Niall then waves confidently to Roxi and back to me, before he happily departs in the direction of Paddy's cottage, to share the good news with him.

Being chivalrous for once, Dermot offers to walk Caitlin back to her cottage too. With only a half-moon to light their way, Caitlin stumbles on the rocky ground, but quickly Dermot reaches out his hand for support. Caitlin willingly takes hold of it, and they walk slowly back towards her cottage together.

Considering this had been the whole aim of the evening – to get Caitlin and Dermot together – the sight of this second new couple on Tara doesn't fill me with anywhere near as much joy as the news of Paddy and Niall had earlier, but I can't quite figure out why.

Roxi had said she thought Tara was a magnet for love, and now she's proving herself to be right, as usual. First there was Ryan and Siobhan, then Conor and me, Niall and Paddy, and now it seems Dermot and Caitlin are the newest targets for Tara's cupid.

I look up into Tara's faintly moonlit sky. There's still a funny feeling inside me since I asked Dermot those questions at the table earlier, and it doesn't disappear as I watch his back disappear into the night. It's an aching feeling; it begins around my heart and runs right down to my stomach. But it could just be all that rich food and wine we've indulged in.

Yes – that would be it. After all, I've got Conor waiting for me as I turn back into my cottage, and what else would make me happier on Tara right now than the thought of spending the rest of the night with him?

Twenty-seven

After three and a half months, Tara has become like one of the smooth, flat pebbles that I find when I walk the puppies along the beach, and not like the sharp and jagged rocky cliffs that line her shores. Island life is polished and easygoing: there's nothing awkward or out of place. Even the weather is calm and tranquil right now, as we're treated to a gloriously dry and sunny July to add to the feelings of peace and serenity that are currently a feature of the island. In fact, everything is running so smoothly here on Tara that I'm starting to feel suspicious! Finally, things are going right.

We've got a constant stream of holidaymakers staying in the cottages, and the visit from the company employees on their bonding trip was enormously successful. The managing director is even going to recommend us to the other departments in his large corporation.

And love still continues to blossom here on Tara, too. Niall and Paddy's relationship is now completely out in the open, and the two of them look much happier in themselves, both together and as individuals. Dermot and Caitlin seem to be going from strength to strength, too. Both being private, modest types, they keep themselves very much to themselves, and we are rarely treated to overt shows of affection from either of them. But they've been spotted around the island going for long walks together, visiting each other's cottages and, on one occasion, it was excitedly reported on the island telegraph that they were seen holding hands in O'Connell Street.

Conor and I are still together, but as blissfully happy as I feel when I'm with him, and as content as I am with the way everything else is going on the island right now, I still have this niggling little doubt that something isn't right. And that niggle isn't helped by the return of the dolphins to the bay once more. As they happily dive in and out of the waves outside my kitchen window, I know they're there to warn me of something, but the question is, what? And when will it happen?

'There's a boat coming over to the island,' Ryan shouts, knocking on my door one afternoon. 'Paddy just spotted it with his binoculars and said I should come and tell you,' he pants as I fling open my front door to let him in.

'What sort of a boat?' I ask, rushing over to the front window that looks out onto the mainland.

'You can't see it from here, it's too far away at the moment. You'll have to come out.' Ryan runs back to the door. 'It's a motorboat by all accounts, and a flashy one too, Paddy says.'

I take a quick glance at the sky before I leave the cottage, something I've become accustomed to doing now having been caught out too many times without a raincoat. But the skies above continue to look clear, so I take a chance and leave the house without one. As I hurry down the hill and towards the harbour, there's already quite a crowd gathering to welcome the oncoming boat.

'Who is it?' I ask Daniel and Orla as I arrive next to them. 'Do we know?'

Daniel shakes his head. 'No, apparently Paddy can't see clearly enough yet.'

I push my way through the crowd towards Paddy, who's standing on top of a used oil drum, peering though his binoculars.

'Paddy, who's on the boat?' I ask, trying to see across the sea into the distance myself.

'I'm not too sure at the moment,' Paddy says, squinting into his binoculars. He tries adjusting the focus on them by twisting the ends. 'Think these things are bust; they don't seem to be working properly.'

I sigh.

'What's going on?' Conor asks, appearing next to me.

'Apparently we've got some uninvited guests arriving.' I point to the boat that's getting ever closer to the island.

'But *I* do all the trips back and forth to the island.' Conor sounds affronted. 'Who's that?'

'I don't know,' Paddy calls from up above. 'But they've got a mighty fast boat on them, Conor. She's fair whizzing across the sea, so she is.'

We all stand and watch as the little motorboat approaches. Word has quickly spread across the island, and now everyone has stopped whatever they're doing and joined us to await the visitors.

All except Dermot.

'Where's Dermot?' I ask, looking around me as the boat gets closer.

'He told me he'd be over in a minute,' Siobhan says. 'He's just finishing off fixing some taps in our kitchen. He didn't want to leave until the job was done.'

Typical Dermot – ever the perfectionist.

Paddy is still balanced precariously on the oil drum. 'It looks to me like a man driving the boat with a woman passenger. I think there might be a second passenger too, but it's difficult to say yet.'

Who on earth is coming across to Tara? We aren't due any new visitors today. It's unheard of for someone to just rent a boat like this and sail over unannounced.

As we all stand silently, watching the little white speedboat get closer, Paddy excitedly calls out, 'There's a chiseller on the boat!'

'A what, Paddy? What's a chiseller?' I ask, thinking Dermot might have ordered a new carpentry tool.

'A kiddie – a child,' Paddy explains.

'Let me have those binoculars, Paddy!' I try and grab them from his hand, and in my haste almost pull him off the oil drum when I forget they're still looped round his neck. 'How can you see that?' While Paddy untangles himself from the strap, I try to focus the binoculars so that I can see the people on the motorboat. 'These things are so out of focus I can barely see the boat, let alone the people.'

'Try these,' I hear a calm voice call from a few metres away, as Dermot holds out another set of binoculars. 'They're more powerful than Paddy's. You can see exactly who's on that boat with them.'

I hurry over to Dermot and take the binoculars from him, then I point them out to sea at the little white motorboat that is jumping and bobbing over the waves.

'But there's no need,' Dermot continues, as I finally get them to focus in on the three figures. 'Because I know who two of them are already.'

'Who?' I ask, as the binoculars pick out a woman and a young girl sitting in the back of the motorboat trying to shelter from the sea wind.

'It's my ex-wife, Eileen and my daughter, Megan.'

I almost drop the binoculars in shock. 'Your what?' I ask, staring at Dermot, who is calmly looking out to sea at the oncoming boat.

'I said . . . ' he begins again.

'I know what you said, but why? How? I thought they were in America.'

'They were. But Eileen has split up with her partner and has come back to live in Ireland again, Dublin to be precise.'

I still stare at Dermot. 'But that doesn't explain why they're here now, coming over to the island.'

Dermot turns his head away from the boat to face me. 'Eileen's been sending me letters . . . '

I open my eyes wide, suggesting perhaps *a tiny bit* more information than that would be good right now. And fast.

'Letters asking if I'll see Megan again.'

'And this is a bad thing because . . .?'

It's Dermot's turn to stare blankly at me now.

'Dermot, please, tell me what's going on. They'll be here on the island in a couple of minutes. I need to know, so I can help.'

Dermot sighs and stares at his boots. 'The thing is, I haven't replied to all of the letters. Eileen knew where I was because I've always let her know my whereabouts – you know, just in case.' He looks up at me. 'A bit like you, I don't have many close relatives. I guess that's something else we have in common.'

I nod at Dermot, but I'm too eager for him to continue to think any further about his odd comment.

'But when Eileen's letters started mentioning me looking after Megan, I couldn't reply.'

'Why?'

Dermot shrugs. He plunges his hands deep into his pockets and repeatedly kicks at a tuft of grass. 'I don't know. I'm not sure I want to get involved in Megan's life after all this time. I don't know if I can let her back in just to have her taken away from me again. It hurt too much the last time.'

As Dermot looks up at me from his turf inspection, I see something in his big brown eyes I've never seen before – fear. And in the same way as I'd seen Niall's strength and stature growing in front of me in my cottage that night, suddenly I see all Dermot's crumbling away.

I can hardly bear to tear my eyes away from him to look at the fast approaching boat again. It's getting very close now.

I think quickly about the best way to handle this.

'It doesn't look like you're going to have much choice,' I say in a practical voice that belies how I'm really feeling inside. I'm hoping Dermot will respond well to this type of 'pull yourself together' treatment, when actually all I want to do is hold him close to me right now and give him all the reassurance he needs. But a public show of affection like this is probably not the best of ideas, not when the entire population of Tara are standing just a few metres away from us, and Dermot's ex-wife and daughter are about to land on the island at any minute. The 'tough love' approach is my only option. 'So you had no idea they were coming over here today?'

Dermot stares back at me like a scolded puppy. After a few seconds he shakes himself and immediately regains some of his usual bravado. 'No, I damn well didn't,' he says, gazing out to sea. 'This is typical of Eileen, though, just charging in with all guns blazing when she doesn't get what she wants. She's obviously decided to bring Megan anyway, and to hell with the consequences.'

I'm suddenly aware that the assembled islanders are spending as much time looking in our direction as they are watching the speedboat.

'You'd better go and explain to the others what's going on,' I tell Dermot while I smile back at them. 'They're beginning to wonder why we're over here whispering to each other.'

'Sure, I'll do that,' Dermot says, looking over towards the crowd. 'Thanks, Darcy, for ... well, you know. I needed that.'

I nod at Dermot.

'You won't say anything, will you?' He looks at me now, his hand on my shoulder. 'About what I just said.'

I shake my head. 'Don't worry about me.' I look out again at the boat, which is nearly at the little jetty now. 'You've got much bigger problems to deal with, arriving down at that harbour right now.'

Twenty-eight

Dermot quickly explains to the others who it is on the boat, and that it's a complete surprise that his daughter is coming over to visit him.

Conor, Daniel, Dermot and I go down to the jetty to help moor the motorboat, while the rest of the islanders, including Roxi and Caitlin, remain up on the hill, watching. When Dermot announces his news, I watch Caitlin carefully for her reaction. But after initial shock flickers across her face, she appears to take the news calmly, which is her attitude to everything in life. Roxi is keen to come with us down to the harbour to greet our new visitors. All right, she wants to have a good nose at Dermot's ex, I know that. But I ask her to stay and keep an eye on Caitlin; this can't be easy for her.

Now the boat is safely moored up, I wait in anticipation to find out what our new visitors to Tara are going to be like, and just what sort of woman Dermot would choose to marry. Or, more accurately, what sort of a woman would choose to put up with him long enough to become his wife.

Alighting from the motorboat first is a man; he wears cream trousers, a navy blazer and a navy and white peaked captain's hat. A slim, elegant-looking blonde-haired woman wearing a crisp white linen trouser suit follows him; she wears red high-heeled sandals on her beautifully pedicured feet, and carries a Chanel clutch bag which matches the pillar-box red of her immaculately painted nails. A young, dark-haired girl wearing jeans, purple Converse trainers and a Kermit the frog sweatshirt printed with the slogan *It's not Easy being Green* hangs back behind them as they walk forward to greet us.

'So this is where you're living now, Dermot,' the woman says, kissing Dermot on both cheeks as he moves forward to greet her. 'It's certainly ... *rural*, isn't it?'

'Eileen,' Dermot unceremoniously wipes away the red lipstick kisses still left on his cheeks. 'This is an unexpected surprise.'

'Well, when you stopped answering my letters I had to take matters into my own hands,' Eileen says with a bright smile. 'I couldn't have you missing out just because some of your mail might have gone astray, now could I?' She looks with interest at her welcoming committee. 'Dermot never was all that good at social etiquette. Too many hours spent with Neanderthal building types, I expect.' She smiles at us. 'Now, we haven't been introduced properly. I'm Eileen Drury.' She offers a perfectly manicured hand to each of us in turn.

'Darcy McCall,' I say when it's my turn, hurriedly thrusting my hand back in my pocket in an attempt to hide my own inferior nails. I've long since given up trying to keep my nails long and manicured. It was becoming too time-consuming to keep filing and repainting them when all they kept doing was breaking and chipping, and to be honest I haven't missed it one bit until a few moments ago when I'd seen Eileen's fabulous talons glinting at me in the bright afternoon sun.

'Darcy!' she gushes, 'Finally I get to meet the *owner* of this wonderful island. How fantastic for you to be in charge of all this. I do like to see a woman in charge of all the men, don't you?'

I smile politely at her.

'Let me introduce you to my own little crew,' she says, turning back to the man and the girl. 'This is Geoffrey, my own ship's captain.'

'Stop it, bunnykins,' Geoffrey says. 'You know I only put on the outfit as a joke. I don't usually dress like this when I take a boat out for a spin.'

Again, I smile politely, and I see Dermot raise an eyebrow.

'And this,' Eileen says, turning around to propel the young girl forward in front of her, 'is, of course, Megan.'

Megan looks as embarrassed at being the centre of attention as Geoffrey should have been by his outfit. She looks down at her Converses.

'Megan, don't look at your feet,' Eileen snaps. 'People want to see your face at least, when they're introduced to you – especially your father, who hasn't seen you for years.'

Megan looks up sulkily at us. 'So which one of you is he, then? It can't be you,' she says looking at Conor, 'you're much too young and, besides, you're too good-looking to fall for my mother.'

Conor grins while Eileen purses her lips.

'Megan, you know perfectly well which one is your father. Dermot,' Eileen grabs hold of Dermot and pulls him forward, 'be reunited with your daughter.'

Megan and Dermot stand eyeing each other warily for a few seconds in silence. Then Megan simply blows a large pink bubble of gum out of her mouth, pops it and then begins chewing on it again.

'So Dad,' she says, looking up at him, 'how's it going?'

Dermot blinks slowly back at his daughter.

'Megan,' he says, screwing up his face in disdain, 'please do not burst that vile stuff in my face again. If you must chew on it, at least have the decency to keep it to yourself.' Dermot's face softens. 'And it's going very well just now, thank you. How about you?'

Megan grins before removing the gum from her mouth and folding it up carefully in a wrapper from her pocket. 'Deal,' she says, and she and Dermot shake on it. She takes a look around her. 'Now I want to take a look around the island. Will you be my tour guide?'

Our guests have been introduced to the islanders. Eileen's introduction to Roxi produced looks so scathing from both of them that they could have sliced through Tara's rock face. Dermot spends the next hour or so showing them around. Megan and Geoffrey, that is; Eileen decides that perhaps, in her current footwear, she's better off staying on more stable ground, so I offer to make her a cup of tea back at my cottage.

It takes longer than normal for Conor and me to walk to my

cottage, with Eileen tottering behind us across Tara's undulating ground in her red heels, trying to smoke a cigarette as she balances. But when we eventually get there she drops the cigarette butt on the ground outside my door and stubs it out with the sole of her sandal.

'Oh, how very quaint,' she exclaims as we all go inside. 'It's like a little doll's house in here.'

'So,' I ask, as I begin gathering the tea things, 'what are your plans now you're here, Eileen?' I couldn't fail to notice the lack of luggage on the boat as it pulled up in the harbour. There had been a few bags, but not in the sort of quantities that a woman like Eileen would travel with – and I should know.

'Oh, just to enjoy this beautiful weather, darling,' Eileen peers out of my kitchen window at the bay down below. 'What lovely views you have from here.'

'Yes, they are quite special,' I agree. 'Sometimes you can see dolphins down in the bay, too.'

'Oh, do they do any tricks?' Eileen turns back to face me. 'We once went to this fantastic sea-life show when we were staying at our villa in Portugal. The chap had the dolphins jumping through hoops and balancing balls on their noses, it was quite a sight.'

'Yes, I can imagine,' I nod. 'But no, these aren't performing dolphins, they're wild ones.'

'Oh,' Eileen looks disappointed. 'Oh well, never mind. You can't have everything.'

Conor grimaces behind Eileen's back and pretends to balance a ball on the end of his nose. To stop myself laughing, I turn away and busy myself for a moment, making the tea.

'So, Eileen, Megan seems like a lovely young girl.' Conor makes polite conversation.

'Yes, she is.' Eileen inspects the sofa before sitting down, and then only perches on the very edge. 'When she wants to be.'

'Knows her own mind, does she?' Conor sits down next to her. 'She seems spirited.'

'Spirited,' Eileen rolls her eyes. 'You might call it that. Megan thinks she knows her own mind all right, but she doesn't seem to accept that occasionally I might know what's best for her.'

Conor and I exchange glances.

'Milk, Eileen?' I ask politely, hovering a milk carton over the top of her mug.

Eileen eyes the carton disdainfully, and suddenly I find myself wishing I owned a china tea service. 'Is it skimmed?' she enquires. 'Oh, good,' she says with great relief when I nod. 'No, no sugar!' she waves frantically at me when I reach for the packet on the counter. 'I always carry my own sweeteners in case of emergencies.' She reaches for her bag and produces a pack of Canderel.

I carry Eileen's tea across to her and she takes the mug from me as though I've passed her a dumbbell. 'Well, this will certainly last me a good while,' she says, peering into the mug.

'You were saying, Eileen, about Megan?' I prompt, keen to hear more about Dermot's daughter. So far I only feel sorry for poor Megan, having to live with a mother like Eileen.

'Oh, yes,' Eileen is keen to continue with her moaning. 'For instance, when I said we were moving back to Ireland for a while, she made such a fuss and bother over it. She said it wasn't fair, and that I wasn't thinking of her moving again. Of course I was thinking of her – I'm always thinking of her. I've spent the last eleven years of my life doing it, and what thanks do I get?'

I feel a pull in my stomach, somewhere near where I keep my own locked box of memories. 'Perhaps she doesn't like change,' I suggest. 'Most children of that age don't.'

'But we all have to change, Darcy. Move on in life. We can't keep being held back all the time by situations and people that are ... past their sell-by date, so to speak.' Eileen's smile is as artificially sweet as her tea.

Politely I return her smile, but I sense there's something else. 'So how long are you thinking of staying here with us, Eileen? We've got plenty of room at the moment. There's a lovely cottage free that would be perfect for—'

'Oh, we're not staying,' Eileen looks horrified at the thought. 'Geoffrey and I aren't, anyway. We couldn't possibly stay here. I have to get back to my job. I work for a very successful cosmetics company. I'm overseeing a new concession opening in Dublin just now, but then it'll be back over to London. And then next month, New York ...' She sighs. 'It's a very busy lifestyle.'

I just stare at her.

'I could leave you some free samples, if you like?' she says, giving my face a quick once-over. 'You can't get too many opportunities to buy make-up.'

A few months ago you'd have had no reason even to suggest that I needed free samples of make-up. *But I've got more important things to discuss with you right now than lipstick*, I think, biting my tongue.

'You said you and Geoffrey aren't staying – so what about Megan?'

Eileen smiles her sickly-sweet smile again. 'My dear Darcy, that is, of course, why we're here today. Oh, does that ex-husband of mine still not tell anybody anything?' She sighs dramatically. 'We're here today to drop Megan off so that she can spend the six-week summer holiday getting to know her father again, here on this quaint little island of yours.'

Twenty-nine

When Dermot and Megan finally return from their exploration of the island, Geoffrey is nowhere to be seen.

'We dumped him up on some old building,' Megan laughs.

'We didn't *dump* him,' Dermot corrects her. 'We simply stopped for a rest for a while, and when Geoffrey nodded off in the sunshine it seemed a shame to wake him.'

They both smile at each other, and Dermot winks at Megan.

'Will he be able to find his way back again?' Eileen says, beginning to fret. 'Geoffrey's never had much of a sense of direction.'

'Don't worry, Eileen, Tara isn't that big,' Dermot says. 'I'm sure Geoffrey is quite capable of navigating his way back towards you – an experienced sailor such as he is. He was telling me all about his very large yacht in the south of France, and how the two of you met at a party in Cannes this year – and there was me, wondering just what you saw in him.'

Eileen still looks agitatedly towards the window, but giving a quick shake of her head she turns her attention back to Dermot and Megan. 'So,' she says, choosing to ignore Dermot's jibe. 'I see the two of you have been having a fine time together.'

'Yeah, Dad's cool,' Megan says matter-of-factly.

I stifle a snort of laughter. I can't imagine Dermot's ever been described as cool in his life. Not unless he's mending a fridge-freezer at the time.

'Megan has turned into a fine young lady,' Dermot looks proudly at his daughter. 'She's done well.' The unsaid words *considering what she's had to deal with* hang silently in the air, and I can imagine how much Dermot must be having to restrain himself not to say them.

'Good! I'm glad you think so.' Eileen smiles a smile that's as genuine as her nails. 'Then you'll be more than happy to look after her for the rest of the summer holidays, won't you?'

'What?' Dermot's jaw drops wide open.

'If you don't want me here, then that's fine,' Megan says, folding her arms.

'No, it's not that, Megan,' Dermot says softly, squatting down so he's more at her level. 'It's just come as a surprise, that's all. Your mother never mentioned it.' This time there's a harder edge to Dermot's voice as he glares up at Eileen.

'Oh, come now, that simply isn't true.' Eileen's eyes narrow, and coupled with her long, skinny body she looks remarkably snake-like. 'You know I mentioned the possibility of Megan staying with you in my letters.'

'You mentioned the possibility of a few days, not six whole weeks!'

'Just because you choose to interpret it like that, Dermot,

doesn't mean that's what I meant. This is just typical of you,'
Eileen waves five red talons in Dermot's direction. 'You have
to have everything spelled out to you in black and white. You
wouldn't understand subtlety if it jumped up and bit you. But
then, why should you? There never was anything subtle about
you, full stop.'

'Nothing subtle about me?' Dermot draws himself up again
to match the increasing volume of his voice. 'I'm not the one
standing there looking like Paris Hilton's waxwork.'

I have to bite my lip to stop myself laughing at that one. But
I'm quite impressed Dermot knows who Paris Hilton is.

Eileen thrusts her chin in the air. 'This is exactly why we
split up. You've no appreciation for anything other than what's
in that tool box of yours.'

'At least I appreciate the things that matter in life.'

'Such as?'

'People, not just possessions.'

Eileen's eyes narrow even further. She's about to step up for
the next round, but I stop her before she can say any more. In
their anger, the warring parents haven't noticed that Megan has
begun to look upset at the verbal boxing match that's being
fought right in front of her.

'Look, I'm sure you two have plenty you need to say to each
other and much you need to discuss,' I find myself standing
between the pair of them, holding out my hands in an attempt
both to calm them and to try and shield their words from harm-
ing Megan further. 'But I don't think Megan really needs to
hear this, do you?' I turn towards her. 'How about we go and
take my dogs out for a while? They could do with a little walk,
and we could go and see if the dolphins are in the bay and then

call in on my friend Caitlin's shop. She might have some choco-late in there, if we're lucky.'

'Dad and I already got sweets at the shop,' Megan says, 'but I'd like to take your dogs for a walk – they're cool.'

'Good,' I smile, 'Shall we go, then?'

Conor, Megan and I gather up Woody and Louis and head out of the door, leaving Dermot and Eileen to sort out their dif-ferences.

What on earth did Dermot ever see in Eileen? She didn't seem his type at all, with her designer labels, fake tan and bright red nails. But then what *was* Dermot's type? I suppose Caitlin, with her vintage clothes and hippy chic.

'Do you think I should go and hunt for this Geoffrey fellow?' Conor asks Megan when we get outside. 'Is he likely to get lost, do you think?'

'Geoffrey could get lost in a cardboard box,' Megan says, rolling her eyes. 'He's not the sharpest tool. Mum's only in it for his money, and if he can't see that then he deserves her.'

Conor pulls a face at me over Megan's head. 'Better go see if I can find him, then. Catch you again later, Megan.' *Good luck*, he mouths at me.

'Yeah, later,' she says, with a wave of her hand as Conor wanders away in the direction of the hill with the derelict build-ing on top.

'He's hot,' she says, grinning at me.

'Megan!' I say blushing.

'He *is* hot. You must think that, or you wouldn't be with him.'

'How do you know I am?' I ask her, as we begin walking in the opposite direction towards the bay along the cliff path.

'Dad told me.'

'Oh.' I wonder what else Dermot has told Megan about me?

'Dad doesn't like him much, though.'

'How can you tell?'

'I just can,' Megan says knowingly. 'Grown-ups think kids don't know anything, but we do. They also think they can just pass us about, do what they like with us and we won't understand what's really going on.'

'I'm sure that's not true.'

Megan stops walking. 'What do you think's going on here, then?' A pair of deep brown eyes that remind me very much of Dermot's stare piercingly up into mine. 'Why is my mum trying to dump me here now, with my dad?'

'I . . . I don't know. Maybe she just wants you to get to know him a bit better, that's all.'

Megan turns her face out to sea and laughs. 'Yeah, that'd be about right – after all these years? Why so suddenly now? More like I don't fit into her plans this summer, with Geoffrey, and it suits her to get rid of me for a while.'

'I'm sure that's not true, Megan,' I try to say in a reassuring voice. 'I'm sure she has your best interests at heart.'

Megan turns back to look at me again. 'If you believe that, you'll believe anything.' She sighs. 'You obviously have no idea what I'm talking about. Come on, guys,' she calls to the dogs.

As I stand watching Megan descend effortlessly down the path onto the sand below with Woody and Louis in hot pursuit, I experience another pull around my heart again.

Actually, Megan, I understand just *what it's like . . .*

Thirty

After much negotiation between Dermot and Eileen, it's agreed that Megan will stay and that Eileen will collect her at the end of the summer holidays. Megan seems happy to remain on Tara with her father. In fact, she settles into island life remarkably quickly, much faster than any of us had done when we first arrived here a few months ago.

A few months ago.

I can hardly believe we've been on Tara for nearly four months now. It almost seems like the norm, so having Megan here is just the tonic we need to spice things up a bit. Life has started to become a bit dull, doing the same things day in and day out, even with new visitors arriving all the time. Megan's bright, breezy attitude and straight-to-the-point views on life are just what's needed to stir things up. Everyone loves having her around – especially Paddy, who adores her. Dermot's attitude has completely changed: he's been almost pleasant since she arrived, and for Dermot, that's a huge step forward.

This afternoon, Conor and I are down on the beach with Megan while Dermot does some repairs to one of the holiday cottages.

'Can you remember being eleven years old?' I ask Conor, as we sit on the sand watching Megan splash energetically about in the sea with Woody and Louis. 'That great sense of freedom, and not knowing what was to come in your life? No ties or worries? How wonderful would it be to go back to that way of living!'

Conor sighs and lies back with his hands behind his head. 'Who says you need to be eleven to live like that?' he says, stretching himself out on the sand.

I look down at him. 'Are you suggesting you live like that now, Conor Fitzgerald?'

'I try my best.'

'It's not possible, as an adult. There are too many commitments to be made, things that tie you down all the time – like jobs and family.'

'Not necessarily,' Conor opens one eye and squints up at me in the bright afternoon sunshine.

'You're telling me that you have absolutely no commitments, nothing that ties you to any one place or any one person?'

'Nope,' Conor says firmly, with his eyes shut this time. 'And I like it that way.'

I watch him silently for a moment. Conor's last statement should upset me; after all, he's virtually saying our relationship means nothing to him. But have I really ever expected anything more from Conor than what we have now?

Conor opens his eyes. 'You've gone awfully quiet. You OK?'

'Yeah, sure.' I force a smile. 'See, maybe you feel that way now, but one day you might change your mind when you want to settle down and have a family of your own.'

'I doubt it.' Conor props himself up on his elbows. 'Look, don't get me wrong, Darcy, I think kids like Megan are great, and I've had fun getting to know her – in fact, I can't quite believe that one as smart as she is was fathered by a Neanderthal like Dermot.'

I give Conor a reproachful look. Why does he keep calling Dermot names like that? He isn't that bad ... he's quite kind when he puts his mind to it, especially where Megan's concerned.

'But,' Conor continues, 'a little house surrounded by a white picket fence with two kids running around in the yard and a wife inside cooking my dinner, that's not how I see my future.'

I laugh at him, but in a way I'm kind of relieved. As much as I adore being with Conor, he does remind me of the gulls that temporarily perch on Tara's rocks – there's always the sense that he might just soar off into the sky at any moment until another, better resting place comes along. I've never met anyone quite like him before; he seems to live completely for the moment, and although it's exhilarating in the short term, in the long term I'm not so sure.

'What?' he asks.

'That isn't exactly want I want either, at this very moment, but that doesn't mean I'll never have children or settle down in a relationship.'

Conor sits up fully now. 'How *do* you see your future, Darcy?' he asks, stroking a stray hair away from the side of my face. 'You don't see yourself living here on Tara for ever, then?'

'No way!' I say, a bit too hastily.

Conor grins. 'I thought you liked it here.'

'I do. I just can't see myself living here for ever, that's all. It's not me, living on an island.'

'I thought you were fitting in like a real local these days.'

I look hard at Conor. Is he trying to wind me up?

'What?' he asks innocently. 'I happen to think you are. So what would you do with the island, then, if you didn't live here – sell it, and live on the proceeds?'

I look around at Tara – the beach in front of me, the rocks that protect her and the waves that crash up against them in a constant attack. Could I really sell them all on to someone else?

'I thought not,' Conor says, gently turning my face back around to meet his. 'It means too much to you.' He leans forward to kiss me, which as always throws my thoughts off track for a moment. 'You're nothing like me at all.'

'Get a room!' Megan calls from across the sand as she sees the two of us huddling close together. 'Either that, or at least wait until you're alone.'

I close my eyes for a moment. *How do kids know so much these days? I'm sure when I was eleven I was just moving on from Barbie dolls and the latest* Sweet Valley High *book.*

'We were only talking!' I call, turning my face towards Megan.

'Yeah, talking, is that what you call it?' She hurls a stick out into the sea for the dogs to chase. 'I'm not a kid, you know, I'll be twelve in October.'

Conor stands up and holds his hand out for me to take. 'Come on you, let's go join the party-pooper. Maybe she can teach us old 'uns a thing or two about life.'

'Knowing Megan, it wouldn't surprise me one little bit.'

'Conor?' Megan asks when we've been running around on the beach for while, and all three of us, including the dogs, are sitting down on the sand again having a rest.

'Yes, Megan.'

'Have we met before?'

'I very much doubt it.'

'It's just, you seem awfully familiar to me.'

Conor sits up crossed-legged on the sand and looks at Megan.

'Megan, sweetheart, I'm flattered you think you've met me before, but I can honestly say I've never met you – I'd have definitely remembered if I had.'

'Ah, maybe we knew each other in a past life, then,' Megan says matter-of-factly, reaching out to rub Woody on his tummy.

Conor and I exchange a look of surprise.

'What do you mean, Megan?' I ask.

'Past lives,' she says, looking at both of us. 'You know the theory that when you die you're reincarnated as someone or something else. It could be another human or an animal. Just think, Woody and Louis might have been your sister or your husband in a previous life.'

'Er ... yes.' I try to shake that thought from my mind. 'I know what reincarnation is. But what has this got to do with Conor?'

'It's just that from the moment I saw him I thought I knew him.' Megan looks at Conor with a puzzled expression. 'Apparently that's what happens. You meet someone you don't know and you've never even met before, but they're instantly familiar to you. It can happen when you take an instant dislike

317

to someone too; you've probably had issues with them in a past life as well.'

My mind flickers to Eileen for a moment, but I quickly remove the thought.

'Megan,' I say gently, 'I don't think you knew Conor in a past life. Conor is just one of those likeable people who you can take a shine to easily. I even thought I recognised him the first time we met. He probably has one of those faces.' I look at Conor to back me up.

'She might have done,' Conor says, as if he's considering the matter. 'It is possible.'

I shake my head.

'See,' Megan says knowingly. 'Have you ever done a past-life regression, Conor?'

What do they teach these kids in America?

Conor is about to answer, but I stop him.

'How about when you worked in the States, Conor?' I prompt, hoping he'll take the hint. 'Maybe you bumped into Megan somewhere then.'

Conor shakes his head, and I feel like shaking the rest of him.

'Wait a minute,' Megan says, her eyes narrowing. 'Holy moly, I think I've got something coming.' She buries her head in her hands in deep concentration.

'Megan, what are you doing?' I ask in concern. 'Conor, what's she doing?'

Conor shrugs.

'I'm thinking,' Megan replies in a muffled voice. 'This helps me to remember.'

We watch helplessly while Megan sits with her face buried

in her hands for a minute. I'm just glad Dermot can't see any of this.

'Got it!' she exclaims suddenly, her heading jerking up from her lap. She grins at Conor. 'Now I know where I've seen you before.'

Conor looks ever so slightly worried. But that's not surprising; so do I after what Megan's been talking about over the last few minutes.

'*Patterson Place*, right?' she says, her eyes sparkling as she looks at Conor.

Conor shakes his head. 'I . . . I don't know what you mean.'

'You were in *Patterson Place*. You played the lover of the owner of the pet-grooming salon. You were only in it for about six weeks, but I remember you because I watched every one of those episodes when I was stuck at home after I'd ruined yet another of my mother's holidays by breaking my arm and leg in a skiing accident.'

I look at Conor. His face tells me everything I need to know.

'*You* were in a soap opera?' I try to say without laughing.

Conor nods in embarrassment. 'In my defence, it was one of those very bad ones on one of the more obscure cable channels. I never thought anyone I knew would see it. I only did it for the money when I was desperate, and I met the casting director in a bar one night. It's amazing who you can meet in a bar.'

'No wonder there was a gap on your CV when you applied to come here,' I grin, 'and there was me, thinking you were rather mysterious and had been up to all sorts of mischief you couldn't tell us about, and all the time you were playing at being a toy boy in a big glossy soap!'

'He was actually quite good,' Megan says. 'Especially that scene in the jacuzzi with the bubble bath.'

Conor rolls his eyes. 'Oh my God, you saw *that*?'

'Yup!' Megan grins. 'Now what was your character's name in it, Conor? I can't seem to remember.'

'Neither can I,' Conor says a bit too quickly.

'Oh, come on, Conor,' I tease. 'Surely you wouldn't forget something like that?'

'Didn't it begin with R?' Megan suggests, her face screwed up in concentration again. 'I know it was Randy something.'

Conor sighs in defeat. 'Randy Colossus.'

'Randy Colossus!' I repeat, falling back on the sand with laughter. 'Oh, that is priceless, Conor! That's the best thing I've heard in ages, it so suits you, too!'

Megan squeals with laughter, and the two of us are paralysed with mirth. We lie back in the sand, laughing at the white clouds above us.

'OK, OK, enough,' Conor insists, standing up. 'I cannot sit here and be ridiculed any longer.'

'Got enough of that for your acting, did you?' I say, setting off another fit of the giggles.

'Ladies, ladies, enough!' Conor holds up his hands as he looks down at us on the sand. 'That was all in my past, I'm a changed man now. Do I look like a bit-part soap star to you these days?' he gestures to himself.

Megan and I lean together in a huddle for a moment, as if considering this. Then we screw up our noses as we give our verdict.

'Nope, you're right,' I say, looking up at him. 'You've no chance of making it as a rich lady's toy boy these days.'

'Right, you pair!' Conor grabs the bucket Megan's been playing with. 'Just for that, you're going to get a soaking!' He runs down to the edge of the waves to fill the bucket while Megan, the dogs and I make a dash for it across the sand. Megan holds tightly onto my hand while we run, and I feel a strange sensation around my heart again. But this time it's not a feeling of discomfort, but a warm glow of happiness.

Thirty-one

'Have you got those figures done yet?' I ask Niall, placing a mug of coffee down in front of him on the desk.

'Almost.' Niall shuffles a few pieces of paper around and writes a few more figures down in his big red accounts book, like he's just spent the last hour and a half doing.

'So, how's it looking?' I ask, sitting down opposite him with my own mug of tea.

Niall pulls a face. Much like the type I imagine Dermot pulls when he's quoting for a building job. 'It could be better,' he says. 'But then, it could be worse.'

'What does that mean?'

'You're not in the red as far as the business side of things is going. If anything, you're turning over a nice little profit with the amount of bookings you've got coming in.'

'But that's good, isn't it?'

'Yes, it is.' Niall taps his pen on the cover of the accounts book. 'But for how long, Darcy? We're in the last few days of

August, when the summer comes to an end, and you've no guests booked in beyond that. How are you going to make the island pay for itself off-season? People aren't going to want to come and stay here in the cold of the winter. Plus,' he adds before I've got a chance to reply. 'When I say Tara is making a profit at the moment, that's not allowing for all the outgoings that have come from your own pocket, or should I say the fund that was allowed to you to set everything up here. Let me warn you: that's dwindling quicker than I'd like, a lot quicker. Tara *has* to keep making a profit, or she won't be able to survive.'

I take a gulp of my hot tea, hoping it will soothe my troubles. 'I'll think of something,' I say with reassurance. I'm suddenly feeling much happier with my island responsibilities and, for the first time, I'm even quite enjoying them. This is my island, my business – I want this to work for all of us here on Tara.

'You always say you'll think of something,' Niall says, sliding his glasses back up his nose.

'And you always keep doing that – pushing your glasses back up your nose, knowing they're just going to slide right back down again. But you still keep doing it, in the hope that one day they might just stay there.'

Niall smiles. 'I get your point.'

'And anyway, I always *do* think of something, don't I?

'You always seem to. How do you keep managing that?'

'I've no idea, Niall, but as long as it keeps happening I'm just going to go with the flow – just like Tara has all these years.'

*

'Have you seen Megan?' Dermot asks me later, as I'm about to take the dogs on their daily jaunt around the island. I'm just crossing O'Connell Street, and Dermot is standing by one of the benches in the centre looking most un-Dermot like – he looks anxious.

'Why, is something wrong?'

'It's just that I haven't seen her for a while,' Dermot says, looking all around him again, 'and no one seems to know where she is. I just wondered if she was with you.'

'No, sorry, I haven't seen her today; I've been with Niall for most of the morning doing the accounts. Why would you think she'd be with me, anyway?'

Dermot shrugs. 'No reason; she just seems to get on well with you.'

'Paddy's the one you should be asking; they're always off doing things together.'

'No, Paddy's been with me all morning, working on cottage repairs.' Dermot looks worriedly out across Tara's landscape again.

'Dermot,' I say, resting my hand on his arm, 'she'll be fine. Megan's a tough cookie, she knows her own mind.'

Dermot looks down at my hand. 'Yeah, don't I know it.' He manages a half-smile. 'I have no idea where she gets it from, though – she's so direct about everything when you talk to her, and she knows exactly where she stands on so many subjects. There's only black and white with Megan – she's straight down the line, that's for sure.'

I smile now, too. That sounded like a very good description of someone standing not too far away from me right now. 'She'll be fine,' I say again, reassuringly rubbing my hand up and down his arm. 'We're just going for a walk up the hill, so we'll keep an eye out for her on our travels. Don't you worry, we'll find her for you. Won't we, boys?'

Woody and Louis look up at me eagerly, but apparently they're not the only ones watching Dermot and I as Caitlin suddenly appears from her shop and hurries across the square in our direction. Her eyes don't miss my hand still resting on Dermot's bicep. Quickly I draw it back.

'Any luck yet, Dermot?' she asks, slipping her hand into his.

'No,' Dermot says, immediately looking worried again. 'No one's seen her. But Darcy's going to keep a lookout when she takes the dogs for their walk.'

'Ah, that's good. Are you off now, then, Darcy?'

'Yes ... yes, I am.'

'Have you got a walkie-talkie so you can keep in contact?' Dermot asks, looking me up and down.

'Er...' None of us has been that good at the whole walkie-talkie thing, now that the initial fascination has worn off.

Dermot rolls his eyes. 'Look, take mine.' He pulls his walkie-talkie out of his pocket and holds it out to me. 'I'll get yours from your cottage. Is it open?'

'Niall is still in there with the accounts, so it should be.'

'You'll let me know straight away if you find her, won't you?'

'Of course I will. I still think she might be hanging around here somewhere, though.'

'Maybe, but if she doesn't turn up soon I think I'll take a walk around the other side of the island and check there.'

'Right then, we'll be off. I'll see you guys later.'

'Bye, Darcy,' Caitlin says abruptly, still gripping Dermot's hand. She turns her back to me. 'Don't worry, Dermot, I'm sure Megan will be just fine.'

Dermot nods at her, then smiles at me over the top of her head. 'Yes, I feel happier now that Darcy is going to look out for her.'

The dogs and I take one of our usual routes up towards the hill where the old ruined building sits looking proudly out to sea. As we approach the remains, I can see immediately we're not alone. There are two figures up near the ruins already – the smaller figure wears brightly coloured clothing and sits swinging her legs back and forth as she perches on top of a wall. And the other figure is taller, older and wears clothes that blend in with the colours of the landscape. A walking stick leans against the wall next to where he rests.

They look up at me as I draw near.

'Darcy!' Megan calls, beaming at me. She jumps down off the wall to greet the dogs, who as usual have rushed on ahead of me. They fuss around her, wagging their tails.

'Hi Megan,' I wave, following the dogs up the path. I arrive beside them both at the wall. 'Your dad's really worried about you, Megan; he was about to send out the search party.'

'I was just taking my daily stroll around the island and found the young girl up here all alone,' Eamon replies calmly. 'I was simply keeping her company until someone came.'

'Eamon's been telling me all sorts of interesting stories,' Megan says excitedly.

Great, that's all we need, Megan's head being filled with even more mysteries.

'Has he?' I smile. 'About what?'

'About Tara and her history, and your aunt Molly and what you used to do here when you were a child, Darcy.'

I stare at Eamon. *I don't remember you being here when I used to come and visit.*

'Did my aunt tell you about my visits here to Tara?' I ask him.

'Aye, something like that,' Eamon says, looking out to sea.

'Only, I don't remember anyone else being here back then, only her.'

'The mind can be a funny thing when it wants to be,' Eamon says mysteriously. 'It can bury all sorts of things deep within that it doesn't want uncovered.'

I'm about to question Eamon further, but he pulls himself up with his stick and stretches. 'It's passed a fine few minutes, so it has, spending time with you, my girl,' he says to Megan. 'Make sure you don't go a-wandering too far on your own next time, though. Them down there, they worry if you stray a bit too far away from the usual, if you know what I mean.' He winks at Megan.

Megan grins at him. 'I will, Eamon, and thanks for all the stories.'

'Any time, young miss,' he says as he begins to make his way down the hill again. 'Any time.'

'So then,' I say, pulling myself up on to the wall next to Megan. 'What are all these stories that Eamon has been filling your head with?'

'Oh, just stories.' Megan jumps off the wall and goes in search of Woody and Louis.

'Yes,' I call, determined not to move now I've got a seat for a few minutes. As used to walking around the island as I am now, the climb up that hill still gets to me. 'But stories about what?'

'About your holidays here when you were little.' Megan bends down and begins picking daisies that are growing in the grass.

'Eamon seemed to know quite a lot about that. What sort of things did he tell you?'

'Just what you and your aunt used to get up to.' Megan gathers her daisies up in her cupped hands and comes back over to the wall. She places them in between us and pulls herself up next to me.

'Will you help me?' she asks. 'Make a chain, I mean.'

'I'll try.' I pick up two daisies and find to my surprise that I can quite easily join them together. Then I pick up another and another, until I'm very quickly making quite a long chain.

'You're good,' Megan says admiringly as she struggles with her own meagre string. 'How'd you do that?'

I show Megan how I've been joining the two stems together so they hold tightly.

'Oh, *that's* how you do it,' she says, trying it for herself. 'Great! I've never been able to do this.'

'I didn't know I could until just now,' I admit.

'I knew you could,' Megan says, working away on her own ring of flowers.

'How?'

'Eamon told me.'

How would Eamon know? I wonder, looking in the direction he's just walked. Then, as I glance down at the cottages, I suddenly remember Dermot.

'I haven't told your dad you're safe. Hold on a moment,' and I pull the walkie-talkie from my pocket.

After I've radioed down to Dermot that Megan is safe, we continue to sit happily in the afternoon sunshine making daisy chains together for quite some time. It feels quite comforting to be sitting up here with Megan, and I find I'm in no hurry to leave.

'So how have you found it here on Tara?' I ask her. 'Not too dull, being stuck with a load of boring adults?'

Megan shakes her head. 'Nope, I like it here. It feels much more settled than back home.'

'Does it? Why's that?'

Megan thinks for a moment. 'Back home, I never knew whether Mum was going to be in, or whether she'd be working or going out entertaining business clients. I never knew where I'd be, or who would be looking after me. At least here you know where everyone's going to be, and what they're going to be doing each day. I feel at home here. I feel safe.'

'Good.' I smile down at the top of Megan's bent head as she concentrates hard on her ever-lengthening chain of daisies. 'I'm pleased.'

'Do you feel like that about living on Tara?' she asks.

'It's not quite the same for me, is it?'

'Why not?'

'Because I'm responsible for the island, there are more pressures and worries involved.'

'But you like living here, don't you?' Megan asks, looking up at me now.

'Yes, of course I do.'

'And you like the people?'

'Yes, very much so.'

'Especially Conor,' Megan grins, wrinkling up her nose in delight.

'Yes, especially Conor.' I grin back at her.

'He's funny though, Conor,' Megan states matter-of-factly.

'How do you mean?'

'He's good looking, anyone can see that.' As she looks up at me, her dark eyes dart to and fro across my face. 'But there's just something about him.'

I wait for her to continue.

'What do you mean, Megan?' I ask when she doesn't.

'It's his eyes, Darcy. Try looking into them. I mean *really* looking into them. You might be surprised what you see.'

What does she mean? I fiddle with my daisy chain for a few seconds while I silently consider her words.

Megan continues to watch me. 'Don't worry about what I just said. It's probably just me. I read this thing once on the internet about eyes, so I've become a bit obsessed with them.' She continues happily feeding daisies onto her chain again. 'What about the others here on Tara, how do you feel about them?'

I know children can ask lots of questions, but are they supposed to be this probing?

'I like the others, of course. Some of them are my best friends.' I think about Roxi and Niall.

'Do you like my dad?'

I hesitate for a moment. Dermot has been a lot more bearable since Megan arrived, and I've definitely seen a softer side to him I never thought could possibly exist.

'Yes, I like your dad,' I admit.

'He likes you – a lot.'

I nearly fall backwards over the wall. 'He does?'

'Yep.'

'How do you know this?'

'I can tell.'

Megan appears to like asking questions, but getting straight answers from her is damn hard work. No wonder Megan and Eamon were getting on so well.

'Well, I'm happy your dad likes me,' I say lightly. 'It wouldn't be good to have enemies on an island as small as this, would it?'

'No, I mean *really* likes you.'

I stare hard at Megan. 'What makes you think that?'

'Just the way he talks about you.' She holds up her chain of daisies. 'Look.'

'Very pretty,' I say, admiring her handiwork. 'What kind of things does he say?'

'Erm, I can't really remember. I just know that when we're together he talks about you a lot more than he talks about Caitlin.'

'He's probably moaning about me, in that case.' A nervous laugh escapes my mouth. 'Just because my name's mentioned a lot doesn't mean it's always good.'

'No, it's always nice things actually, and he hardly speaks about Caitlin at all unless she's there. Caitlin doesn't like me, anyway.'

'Of course Caitlin likes you, why wouldn't she?'

Megan shrugs. 'Don't know. Like I said before, past life issues maybe – who knows?'

I shake my head. *I haven't had much experience of children, but are all eleven-year-olds like this?*

'Thing is,' Megan continues, 'I've consulted my angel about it and he says I should just let it go – nothing I can do if our auras aren't compatible. I've just got to ride it out.'

Whoah, hold on just one minute.

'Megan, did you just say you'd consulted with an angel?' I ask slowly.

'Not just any angel,' Megan looks up from her flowers. 'My guardian angel.'

'*OK*,' I say in the same slow voice again.

'It's all right, Darcy, you don't need to be scared by it, we all have them. It's just that some people choose to use them and some don't. But the angels are cool with it; they just stand back and let you get on with your life. They're there if you need them, though. Most people are using them every day and don't even know it.'

'Are they?'

'Uh-huh.'

'How?'

Megan thinks about this for a moment. 'Take, for instance, the amount of times that an idea suddenly springs into your head out of nowhere. That's your angel helping you.'

'Is it?' I ask dubiously.

'Yep,' she says, nodding. 'You just don't realise it if you don't connect with them. It's up to you whether you choose to believe or not, but this place is full of it.'

'Full of what?'

'Spiritual energy. I felt it as soon as I arrived here. Once you're open to this sort of stuff, you just know when it's around you.'

'How do you mean?'

'There's all the stuff you've got going on here already,' she says, jumping off the wall. 'The t'ai chi classes and the reiki, that's very spiritual.'

'But you can do those things anywhere, Megan, it doesn't mean there's anything special about Tara.'

'Oh, there is something special, Darcy,' Megan insists, looking me straight in the eye. 'You just haven't opened your mind up wide enough to see it yet. You're still all shut off at the moment, like an ancient fortress.' Megan is talking to me as though she's the adult and I'm the child. 'Take some time to think about what I've said, and then you'll see what I mean.' She lifts up a perfect chain of daisies and places them around my neck.

I watch open-mouthed while Megan begins to skip away down the path. 'Where are you going now?' I call after her.

'Back down to see Dad,' she calls back. 'You stay there and have a think. Open your mind up, Darcy, as well as your eyes. You'll be surprised what happens when you do!'

Dermot, you've got your work cut out with that one, I think as I watch her run down the path and back towards our little village. That's one very old head on those young shoulders. It's like she's lived for hundreds of years on this earth instead of nearly twelve. I jump down off the wall and turn around, taking in the derelict building again. I never did get to the bottom of what it had once been. It seems such a shame for it to stand up here all alone.

I wander over to the doorway I've stood beneath many times when I've come up here with the dogs, either to shelter from some of Tara's inclement weather, or just to take in the magnificent view that this building offers. I stand beneath it this time wondering just how many people have stood here before me on this very same spot. Perhaps even Finn McCool himself, when he was recuperating here. What had Eamon said? The islanders looked after him so well that when the time finally came for him to leave, he hadn't wanted to go, and he'd left his heart here along with his treasure. It's quite a sweet tale really; I wonder if any of it's true? I've always felt especially calm and comforted when I've been up here in this old ruin. Perhaps others before me have, too. And now, as I look out over the view into the distance, I can quite understand why Finn fell in love with Tara, or fell in love with *someone* while he was here; or maybe it was a bit of both.

And it's then that it hits me, an idea that could change Tara's future for ever.

I put my hand on the daisy chain that Megan has placed around my neck. 'Perhaps you might be right about all this stuff, Megan. This is certainly an idea I would never have thought of before on my own.' I leave the safe cocoon of the building and step outside to view my idea from a different angle. Could it really work?

It's then that I notice it for the first time. Immediately I rush forward towards the doorway and try and scrape back some of the greenery that has been entwining itself around the ancient brickwork for so many years, in an attempt to disguise the form that lies hidden beneath. And as the branches loosen their hold on the stone, I find it: my final stamp of approval – from my aunt Molly.

Thirty-two

'Roxi,' I hiss over the top of the bar that night, 'I need your help.'

'What's up, honey?' she asks, sauntering over in her blue neon satin shoes. Roxi still insists on wearing her heels even now, after all this time on the island. I don't know how she manages it. But Roxi is adamant she just can't get comfortable in flats, and since she doesn't venture much further around the island than her cottage, O'Connell Street and the pub, she seems to get away with it. The only time she relents is on her regular visits up to see Eamon, when she borrows a pair of Niall's trainers to 'travel' in.

'I need you to distract Caitlin for a few minutes tonight,' I whisper, glancing over at her sitting with Dermot across the other side of the pub.

'Why?' Roxi asks suspiciously, narrowing her eyes.

'Because I need to get Dermot on his own.'

Roxi's eyes shoot open as wide as saucers. 'Oh, do you,

now?' she says, putting her hands on her hips. 'And does Conor know about this?'

'Not like that! I need to talk to him about something, and Caitlin won't leave his side just lately,' I look down at the bar for a moment, 'especially when I'm around,' I mumble.

'What was that?' Roxi says, leaning in towards me across the bar.

'I said, especially when I'm around. I don't know what's up with her recently, she's gone all funny on me.'

Roxi stands upright again for a moment to look over at Caitlin, then leans back down again on the bar, her lips formed into a bright pink 'O' shape. 'I see,' she says knowingly.

'What do you mean, you see? You see what?'

'I thought I saw this coming,' she tilts her head to one side and then to the other. 'But I didn't want to admit it. I think Caitlin's a teeny bit jealous.'

'Of?'

'You, you daft Mars Bar. Of your relationship with Dermot.'

'But Dermot and I don't have a relationship, not *that* sort of relationship, anyway.'

'I know that, and you know that, Darce. But she doesn't.'

I glance over at their table again and, as if by magic, Caitlin notices me at that very moment and immediately reaches for Dermot's hand.

I thrust my head into my own hands and rest my elbows on the bar. 'Argh! All I want to do is talk to him without Caitlin being there.'

'Why?'

'I just do, Rox.' I look up at her. 'I can't tell you at the moment. Please just trust me on this.'

'Babe, I'd trust you with my life.' She takes hold of my hand. 'How long do you need?'

I smile up at her. 'As long as possible.'

Roxi winks. 'Right, you leave it to me. Come back in an hour and he's all yours.'

When I return to The Temple Bar after an hour, like Roxi has instructed, I find the pub absolutely jam-packed with customers. Not only is Roxi rushing to and fro behind the bar with pints of beer and glasses of spirits in her hand, but so is Caitlin.

'What did you do?' I ask her quickly, as she stands still for a few seconds pulling a pint of beer.

'Put the word about the island that drinks are all half price for the next few hours, then made sure Ryan had the night off with Siobhan. Paddy's already babysitting Megan tonight – so I'm *oh so desperate* for staff. That's where Caitlin comes in. She told me the other night she'd done some bar work in a hotel once.'

I shake my head at her ingenuity and guile, and give thanks for about the hundredth time since I've known her that she's my friend.

'Go!' she says, nodding her head in Dermot's direction, 'while you've got the chance.'

Thank you, I mouth to her as I fight my way over to Dermot, who is still sitting at a table in the corner of the bar. He's quietly drinking a pint of Guinness amid the chaos that surrounds him.

'Can I join you?' I ask, standing next to him.

'It's a free island.' Dermot pulls out the chair next to him where Caitlin was sitting earlier.

Caitlin immediately appears in front of us at the table.

'Darcy, I didn't see you come back into the pub, I'm just helping Roxi out for a bit.' She looks between Dermot and me. 'Can I get you something to drink?'

'You're busy, Caitlin, there's no need to wait on us at the table, but thanks.'

'No, it's no trouble, really.' Caitlin insists. 'Anything for my man!' She puts her hand protectively on Dermot's shoulder.

'I'll have whatever he's having then, please,' I gesture to Dermot's almost half-empty pint glass. 'Can I get you a drink, Dermot? Same again, is it?'

'If I wasn't a gentleman I'd ask for a double whiskey,' Dermot says, looking at me with a straight face, then he smiles. 'Yeah, another pint of Guinness would be great please, Caitlin.'

Caitlin picks up his glass. 'Back in a minute, then,' she says, scuttling off to the bar.

'So, what do you want?' Dermot asks, turning to me.

'How do you know I want something?' I reply with an innocent face.

'You regularly come up to men in pubs and buy them drinks, do you?' Dermot raises an eyebrow.

'All right, all right, yes, I do want something from you.' As I launch into my carefully prepared speech, I keep an eye on the bar as Caitlin begins to fill two glasses with Guinness. 'How are you finding living here, Dermot?'

'Fine, Darcy, why?' There's a hint of amusement in Dermot's eyes as he enjoys watching me squirm.

'You're not finding it boring in any way?'

'No,' Dermot folds his arms and sits back in his chair.

'I just wondered, that's all. Now that the cottage renovations are complete, and all you're really doing is a bit of maintenance work, I thought you might find it a bit beneath your capabilities.'

Dermot looks at me suspiciously now. 'And?'

'And, I wondered if you might be in need of something a bit more challenging to get your teeth into – or even your power tools.'

There's not even a hint of a smile from Dermot: he simply waits. Then he lifts his half-empty glass. 'Do you want some of this, Darcy? You sound like you could do with some balls before you ask me whatever it is you're going to Timbuktu and back to pluck up the courage to ask.'

I pull a face at Dermot and take the glass from him. Then I take a few long gulps before passing it back.

'I want to build a holistic healing centre,' I say, coming right out with it.

Dermot stares at me for a few seconds before taking several long gulps from the glass himself. 'Where?' he asks, not mincing his words, as always.

'Here, on Tara, up the hill, on the site of the old ruins.'

'Why?'

'Because it makes perfect sense, that's why. We need to attract visitors to Tara all year round, not just through the spring and summer, and with this we could cater for people throughout the year, whatever the weather. I'm thinking along the lines of a holistic health resort, Dermot, with all the activities we've already been providing and more. Things like yoga and alternative therapies – I think there'd be a real market for it. These days, people are crying out to get away from it all and find relaxation in the peace and quiet, and we could provide them with that without having to fly thousands of miles.'

Dermot considers this for moment. 'Be a bit of an eyesore, wouldn't it; a great big building sitting up on top of that hill?'

'Not if we designed it right. I'm not talking about some huge five-storey monstrosity of a building, but something that would blend in with the history and landscape of Tara. Working with what was once there many years ago.' As I'm talking, I notice Dermot's eyes glaze over as he thinks this all through himself. 'Think of it, Dermot,' I say, sweeping my hand across in front of our faces, 'you'd be starting from scratch, designing a building of your very own.'

'It wouldn't come cheap,' he says, looking at me. 'If you wanted to do it right, that is.'

This is the only slight drawback to my plan – finances. After my conversation with Niall today, I know funding this project is going to be difficult. But that little setback isn't going to stop me. I'll think of something ...

'I know,' I say excitedly, pleased to have sparked his interest. 'I'd want it to be in keeping with whatever building was there before; even rebuild it if we could, to look like the original. We'd need to do some research to find out.'

'I don't even know if you can get bricks like that any more,' Dermot says, his own mind beginning to tick over the many problems he might encounter if he took on this project.

'I'm sure you could find something similar.' I smile enthusiastically at him. 'So, do you think you could do it?'

'Darcy, that question was never in doubt,' Dermot says firmly. 'The question that does remain, though, is what is everyone else going to think about it?'

'I think it's best we don't mention it to anyone else yet,' I lean in towards him in a conspiratorial fashion. 'Not until we've got everything sorted in our own minds what we want to do. Then I'll bring in everyone else who needs to be involved individually, one at a time. Eventually I'll make a general announcement to everyone when we know exactly what our plans are.'

'What about Conor?' Dermot asks, turning away from me and picking up his glass again. 'Will you tell him?'

I think about this. Do I want to tell Conor my plans? He was the one who originally suggested I find a 'thing' for Tara, so that we can continue attracting visitors to the island, so I suppose I ought to. But lately I've felt less and less like sharing things with Conor, plus I really want to keep Dermot on side. 'Not to begin with, no.'

Dermot nods. 'Good.' He puts down his glass again.

'So we've got a deal then?' I ask, smiling at him.

'Yes, Darcy,' Dermot turns to me reaches out his hand under the table and we have a tiny, inconspicuous shake on it. 'We've definitely got a deal.'

'Two pints of Guinness,' Caitlin says suddenly, plonking two glasses down in front of us on the table.

'Thanks, Caitlin.' Quickly I release Dermot's hand and reach for my glass.

'So what have you two been talking about?' she asks, hovering. 'I would have brought your drinks over sooner, but I've been caught up at the bar.'

'Oh, not much,' I say, lifting my glass for a much-needed drink.

'The weather mostly,' Dermot suggests, draining the last of his first glass and picking up his new one.

'I see,' Caitlin says, biting on her bottom lip.

'Really, Caitlin, we've been chatting about boring building stuff,' I say, telling the truth.

Caitlin nods, but she doesn't look very convinced.

'Caitlin!' Roxi calls from the bar, 'I *really* need your help over here.'

'Just coming,' Caitlin calls back. 'I've got to go. I'll be just over there if you need me, though.'

What she actually means is *I'll be just over there watching.*

'Sure, Caitlin, we'll shout if we want anything, thanks.'

'Shall we get out of here?' Dermot asks as soon as Caitlin's gone. 'It's going to be difficult to keep this quiet in here with so many people about, and if we went over to yours we could check out some information on the internet.'

I look at my watch. 'Thing is, I said I'd meet Conor in here at nine. He's taken himself off fishing tonight while he's got some time off from the visitors.'

'Oh right, well, not to worry then.' Dermot picks up his glass and takes a long drink. 'We can do this some other time.'

Damn it, I don't want Dermot to lose interest. Not while he's so enthusiastic about the project. 'No, its OK, Conor seems to forget all about time when he's fishing; he might not come off that beach until midnight. Let's go now.'

As I get ready to leave the pub, I lean across the bar while Dermot is still at the table trying to waste as little of his Guinness as he can. 'Rox,' I call, but Roxi's busy serving, so Caitlin comes over.

'Yes?' she asks. 'Can I help?'

'Could you tell Conor that I've gone back to my cottage, if he comes in here to meet me later?'

'Sure,' Caitlin says, smiling brightly. 'That's grand, Darcy, I'll tell him. Are you going now, then?'

'Yes, I am,' I look back for Dermot. 'Are you ready, Dermot?'

'Yep,' Dermot walks over, drains the last of his pint glass and bangs it down on the bar. 'Cheers for that, Caitlin, you pull a fantastic pint. I'll see you later.'

I can almost feel the daggers hitting my neck and back as I leave the pub with Dermot while Woody and Louis run about our feet, happy to be outside in the fresh air once again.

On our way we drop in to check on Megan, who's over playing at Paddy and Niall's cottage tonight – and I mean playing. When we arrive, Paddy has got two tents erected in their front room that he's made by draping bed sheets across the lounge furniture. He and Megan are playing cowboys and Indians in full headdresses that they've made earlier today, while Niall sits quietly trying to read a book in the kitchen. And I marvel yet again at how Megan can at one minute be so grown-up, and the next so childlike. Leaving Niall and Paddy's, we continue on across O'Connell Street towards my cottage.

We've spent a good couple of hours perched in front of my computer, scribbling down ideas and pricing up materials. So far we've discovered that not only is this project going to cost an awful lot of money, but the building we're going to renovate appears to have been used in the past as a place of worship – the islanders' own little church. While we stop to have a break for a few minutes, Dermot picks up the bottle of Irish whiskey we'd decided to break into about an hour ago. It's another gift sent over from a contented visitor after his holiday. They seem to like sending me whiskey – I have quite a stash now. He proceeds to top up our glasses once more.

'How on earth did you come up with this idea?' he asks, pouring whiskey into my glass.

'It was your daughter that prompted it, actually.'

'Who, Megan?'

'Just how many daughters do you have, Dermot? Are there more hidden away you're not telling me about?'

'I think one is more than enough, don't you?' he says, topping up his own glass now.

'She's certainly special.'

Dermot grimaces. 'You could call it that.'

'Aw, Megan's a good girl. She's incredibly bright and knowledgeable for one so young – on many subjects.'

Dermot screws the lid back on the bottle. 'She'll be telling me how to build this centre of yours if I don't watch out, just you wait and see.'

Dermot moves some papers on the desk to find a space for the bottle of whiskey. 'What's this?' he asks, holding up a sheet printed from the internet.

'It's nothing,' I try to grab it from him.

'Rings, Darcy?' Dermot holds the paper out of my reach and looks with interest at it. 'Are you thinking of getting married? Does Golden Balls know about this?'

'No!' I manage to snatch the paper from his hand now. 'Actually they're Claddagh rings. A Claddagh is an Irish token of love, if you must know.'

'Meaning love, friendship and loyalty, yes I do know. My father was Irish, in case you forgot. And if I remember rightly, it makes a difference how you wear the ring, too. If you wear it on your right hand with the heart facing away from you, it means you're not romantically linked to anyone. When it's turned the other way it shows that you're in a relationship, or your heart has been captured. If you wear the ring on your left hand with the heart facing away from you, it means you're engaged; turned the other way, you're married. Am I right?' he finishes, a pleased expression on his face.

He's right. I'd looked them up ages ago, meaning to ask Niall about my aunt's ring, but as usual here on Tara I'd been distracted by other things. But this afternoon I'd searched for the page again, and now we had a printer I'd printed all the details out for another reason.

'If you know so much about the Claddagh symbol, you must have noticed the one on the old ruined building, then.'

'What, the one up on the hill?'

I nod. 'There's a Claddagh symbol engraved in the brick-work over the doorway that looks out over the sea. It's got a bit covered up with all the greenery over the years, but it's definitely there. I saw it this morning.'

Dermot nods. 'Looks like the old building was used for a bit more than a few religious meetings, then.'

'How do you mean?'

'To have that carved above such a prominent doorway, it must have been used for weddings, too.'

I consider this. 'Yes, I suppose it must. It's such a big building, I bet they did everything up there. It would have been a real focal point for the community, just like it's going to be for our island.' I look at Dermot nursing his glass of whiskey, and I debate for a moment whether to share with him what I'm going to say next. 'It's very special up there, you know; it's like nothing I've ever felt before. When I'm up there it feels like someone's comforting me, holding me, even. I feel safe. In fact, that's how this whole island makes me feel.'

I smile as I remember something.

'Roxi said to me when we held the dinner party that I looked like Audrey Hepburn that night. I clearly didn't. But in *Breakfast at Tiffany's*, that's how the Tiffany's store makes Holly Golightly feel – safe.'

Dermot looks at me, and for a moment I actually think he might say something supportive. 'You feel like that about an island and a building?' he asks sceptically.

I should have known.

'Yes, I do. Not that I'd expect you to understand. To you, all buildings are bricks and mortar; they couldn't possibly hold any history, memories or feelings inside them.' I take a swig of my drink, then continue to study the inside of the glass, swirling my ice cubes around in the bottom.

Dermot sighs. 'You couldn't be further from the truth, Darcy. I may erect brand-new buildings now for a living, but when I was at college I studied history and architecture. I wanted to restore old buildings for a career, not produce new ones.'

I look up at Dermot in surprise. 'You went to college?'

He grins. 'Yes, I haven't always been a builder.'

'But what happened? Why didn't you carry on with what you studied?'

'Eileen happened, just after I left university, and very shortly after that Megan, so Eileen and I decided to get married before she was born. I had to start earning some decent money, and fast, so that's where my architectural and building skills came in, but Eileen and I were never compatible. We should never have got married, but that's what you do, don't you, when there's a baby on the way.' He looks up at me and smiles. 'Where do you think I got these grey hairs from at my age?' He gestures to the side of his head. 'It's a wonder I'm not snowy white all over!'

I think about my own parents, and the lid on my internal box is lifted slightly. 'My parents divorced when I was young,' I say, looking into Dermot's eyes, still reflecting on his own past. 'My dad disappeared from our lives shortly after the divorce, and my mum passed away a few years ago. That's how come I got this island. I'm Molly's closest living relative.'

'I know about your parents,' Dermot says, understanding now reflected in his eyes. 'Roxi told me.'

'Did she?' I'm surprised at Roxi mentioning this; I barely ever talk about my parents with her, so it seems odd for her to talk about it to someone else.

'Only because I asked her. I kind of guessed you might have some unresolved issues.'

'What do you mean, *unresolved issues?*' I demand, feeling myself beginning to bristle.

'Hey, calm down,' Dermot says, holding up his hand. 'I only meant the person I met when you first came to Tara isn't the same person I'm sitting in front of now.' He thinks for a moment. 'It's like you've been hiding behind a mask, and now the true you has been unveiled. It's like finding Audrey Hepburn underneath a Marilyn Monroe costume.'

I'm still not sure how to take this.

'OK, I'll try and explain it another way,' Dermot says, thinking again. 'When you first came to Tara, you were standing there behind this thick layer of make-up, with your silly nails, your dyed hair and your designer clothing. That's the Darcy you wanted people to see – your version of Darcy. The one no one could hurt. But since you've been here I've got to know the real you, the Darcy behind the mask, and she's a lot more beautiful without the disguise.'

I stare at Dermot. Was I really hearing all these lovely words flow from his mouth?

'Anyway,' he says, swinging himself up from the chair and grabbing the bottle of whiskey again even though his glass isn't empty yet. 'These plans won't make themselves. More whiskey?'

I shake my head. 'I'm not the only one who's been wearing a mask since I've been here.'

Dermot tops up his own glass. 'What do you mean?'

'The mask *you* put on all the time – the "I don't care. It's all black and white. It's no skin off my nose" one. The truth of the matter is, Dermot, you *do* care, and you care very much about a lot of things. I've seen you put in more hours on this island than anyone else, including me. I've seen you with the others, especially Paddy, patiently teaching them over and over again how to make, build and fix things. And most importantly I've seen you with Megan, become the solid, dependable parent she's never had in her life, and that is probably one of the most important things you'll ever do. So when you try and pretend that you don't care about situations or people, as you so often feel you need to, that's just you putting on your own mask to hide your real emotions.'

I've watched Dermot throughout my little speech simply stand and listen to what I'm saying without expression. Now he takes a long gulp from his glass. 'Seems like Tara's really stripping us back to our true selves tonight, eh? No one usually sees below my outer shell, Darcy.'

'And no one usually sees beneath mine, either.'

Looking up into Dermot's eyes, I feel the bond between us strengthen, as the uneasy feeling that's been troubling me of late is replaced by something much more pleasant.

'There's definitely something about Tara, isn't there?' Dermot says, still watching me.

'Yes,' I nod in agreement. 'Even Roxi believes it's a magnet for love.'

Dermot smiles. 'A magnet for love – I like that. Next you'll be wanting to perform wedding ceremonies on the island in our new building.'

I stare at him. 'Dermot, that isn't such a bad idea.'

'You *are* joking,' he says, his eyes wide.

'No! It could be another string to our bow. We could hold Celtic-themed weddings, and the guests could stay in the cottages and we could serve local foods, and—'

'Whoah, just one minute,' Dermot says, holding up his hand in my direction. 'You'd need a licence to do something like that, and a minister on hand to perform the ceremonies.'

'Yes, minor details, we can sort all that out, I'm sure. Oh, Dermot, it's just perfect,' I say, happily clapping my hands together. 'It's what Tara was made for, to bring new loves together and join them as one for ever.'

Dermot smiles softly at me. 'I didn't think you were the romantic type.'

'I'm not, normally. After my parents, and relationships of my own that haven't gone too smoothly, I was a bit anti-love before

I came here. But this island does have an effect on you. Like you said before, it seems Tara's managed to change me, not just on the outside, but on the inside as well.'

'It will take me a while to be convinced that marriage is a good thing, after the last time.'

'Whatever *did* you see in Eileen?' I blurt out, and immediately regret this. The last thing I want to hear is all the finer details of Eileen and Dermot's relationship.

Dermot looks across at me with a grave expression. 'Do you know something, Darcy?'

'What?' I ask, nervous of what he's about to reveal.

'I really have no idea whatsoever,' he says, his dark eyes sparkling with mischief.

'*Dermot*!' I hit him playfully on the shoulder. 'That's not fair. I wondered what you were going to say then.'

'Well, what did you expect from me, secret revelations about my inner thoughts and emotions?' Dermot grins at me. 'I think you got enough of those from me earlier. I felt like I was in an episode of *Jeremy Kyle*.'

'No, you couldn't ever be on *Jeremy Kyle*,' I reply in all seriousness.

'Why?'

'You're just too darn dull, Dermot O'Connell!'

'Ooh, touché, Miss McCall,' Dermot calls in a fake French accent, reaching over to the chair next to him and grabbing a cushion. 'But now I have ze weapon to defend myself against your barbed comments!'

'And what are you going to do with that, smother me to death?'

'No,' Dermot tosses me a second cushion, 'We're going to

have a pillow fight to settle this. My daughter informs me it's *the* thing to do, and has been teaching me all the latest moves.'

Dermot leaps to his feet while I sit still in my chair holding the cushion.

'Come on, Darcy,' he encourages, 'get into the spirit of it.'

'Why?'

'Why what?' Dermot stands in the middle of the room with a cushion poised in front of him like a shield.

'Why do we need to do this?'

'Because it's fun, that's why.' Dermot lowers his defences for a moment. 'Come on, didn't you ever have pillow fights when you were young?'

'No.'

'What, never?'

'No, I was an only child. I never had anyone to play *with*.'

'Oh,' Dermot dejectedly comes back to sit down in his chair. 'I'm sorry, I didn't think.'

'Didn't think I was clever enough to outsmart you, you mean?' and I give him a huge whack with my cushion as I leap out of my chair.

'You little minx,' Dermot shouts, jumping up out of his own seat now. 'Right, that's it.'

I run into the kitchen squealing, followed by Dermot and the dogs, now woken up by my noise. But the problem with playing this sort of game in such a small house is there's nowhere to run, and Dermot quickly has me cornered.

'So now I've caught you,' he says as he pins me up against the sink, 'what *am* I going to do with you?'

I look up at Dermot leaning menacingly over the top of me with a cushion poised in the air above my head. But the thing is, he isn't that menacing close up, he's actually very attractive in a ruggedly handsome sort of way. When I'm this close to him I can see that this late in the evening his square jaw is now covered in a fine layer of dark stubble, and that his soft brown eyes, usually hidden under a pair of dark, unruly eyebrows, contain tiny flecks of bright green. And standing this close to me, feeling his warm, rhythmical breath on my face, I can also feel the warmth of his body radiating through his shirt, and I'm reminded of the time in his cottage when he removed a similar shirt and stood in front of me in just his jeans.

Dermot slowly lowers the cushion from above his head. But he doesn't move away from me as I expect him to, he simply stands there, looking into my eyes in the same way I'm looking up into his. And at once I feel that same bond tighten all over again.

Just as Dermot leans forward I hear a voice, but surprisingly it's not Dermot's deep, slightly gravelly tone that speaks my name, but Conor's Irish lilt.

'Darcy, what's going on?'

As Dermot spins around we both suddenly realise we're not alone in the cottage as we see Conor and Caitlin standing at the door of the kitchen.

'Conor, Caitlin,' I say brightly, smiling at them. 'Dermot and I were just having a bit of fun. I ... I mean, playing a game. We were just having a pillow fight.'

Whatever I say will sound wrong.

Caitlin glares at me, while Conor simply shakes his head.

'Darcy and I have had a few too many whiskies, that's all,' Dermot states matter-of-factly. He turns to me. 'I think I should probably go now, anyway, and collect Megan. Perhaps we can finish our discussions tomorrow?'

'Sure. Thanks for all your help tonight.'

'Any time,' Dermot walks towards the door. 'Are you coming?' he asks a stony-faced Caitlin. He passes the cushion to Conor on the way out. 'Perhaps you can teach her how to have a good pillow fight, Conor,' he says as he leaves. 'I didn't get very far tonight, I can assure you. We'll see ourselves out.'

Conor takes the pillow and coldly watches Dermot escort Caitlin through the door before he turns towards me. 'Darcy, I think you've got some explaining to do.'

Thirty-three

I spend a lot of my time over the next few weeks explaining.

I try to explain to Conor just why Dermot was chasing me round my kitchen with a cushion, eventually having to tell him all about the holistic resort idea. Eventually Conor accepts my explanation without too much fuss.

In fact, I think I might have preferred it if he *had* shown a bit more hostility towards the situation. He could have seemed at least a *bit* bothered that another man was chasing his girlfriend, and then had her pinned up against the sink apparently about to kiss her. But not Conor: he takes his usual relaxed attitude to the situation once he's got over his initial flash of jealousy, and immediately moves on, and I begin to wonder once again about Conor, and our relationship.

And what *was* Dermot going to do in my kitchen that night before we were interrupted – *was* he going to kiss me? I spend a great deal of time trying to explain this one to myself.

Dermot's changed since coming to Tara. It's like he's peeled away some of his rough, spiky outer layers to reveal an inner Dermot he's always kept hidden. He's just the opposite of the ruin up on the hill. The building had its engraved heart on the outside for all to see, though it's walls were crumbling. Dermot's always been a solid, dependable person, but he's kept his heart hidden. Now I can see what's going on inside Dermot, and I'm noticing that what's on the outside is in pretty good shape, too.

But over the next few weeks, my changing feelings towards Dermot and Conor are just one of many worries. I have to explain to everyone else my plans for the building and the island, and they are met with mixed reactions. But most of the islanders turn from sceptical to enthusiastic once I've taken them aside individually and spoken to them about how I see their own role in this new project. It's only Niall who looks like the proverbial rabbit in headlights – only this rabbit is wearing glasses.

'Darcy, where are you going to get all the money for this?' he asks. 'I told you the other day – you're nearly broke.'

'And I told you I'd think of something.'

'Yes, something that doesn't involve shelling out loads more cash first.'

'It'll be fine, Niall,' I reassure him. 'By the time Dermot's finished all the plans, and we need to start buying building stuff, I'll have a plan of my very own to find the money.'

Niall doesn't look too convinced, and at this moment I feel pretty much the same.

Eamon is surprisingly quite relaxed about the project.

'If that's what you want to do with Tara, Darcy,' he says, 'then I'm sure you'll do it well.'

'You mean, you're not going to kick up a fuss, Eamon?' I ask in surprise. 'I really thought you'd hate the idea.'

Eamon holds his walking stick out in front of him and balances himself on it with two hands. 'My time to have any say in what goes on here has long gone. The future is in your hands now, Darcy. *The King is dead; long live the King.*'

I watch Eamon walk away up the hill and back to his cottage. He really is getting stranger by the day.

But if my explanations to everyone else go reasonably smoothly, my explanations to Caitlin surprisingly do not fall on such willing ears, and it's not for the reasons I expect.

'I'm leaving, Darcy,' Caitlin tells me one Saturday morning when I've popped across to the shop for some milk.

'What? Why, Caitlin?'

'I just don't think it's working out.' She straightens some boxes of matches that are stacked up on the counter.

'Of course it's working out! You've done a wonderful job in the shop here, what would we have done without you?'

'You'd have managed,' she says, avoiding eye contact with me.

'But why now? I just don't understand.'

'I've decided to go travelling.' Caitlin begins unloading packets of biscuits from a cardboard box. 'I need to go and see what's out there in the world, and if I don't do something with my life now then I'll end up forever stacking shelves just like this one.' She slams a packet down on the counter and looks at me for the first time.

'Have you been talking to Conor?' I ask, thinking this sounds like his handiwork.

'I might have.'

356

'Has he persuaded you to do this?'

'No, I've been thinking about it for a while now. I've just never had the guts or the reason to do it before. I thought that coming here to live on this island was going to be an adventure, but I'm falling into just the same traps I fall into back home. I'm virtually doing the same job, and my personal life is beginning to repeat itself too.' She drops her head again and turns away.

'Are you talking about you and Dermot?'

'If there is such a thing as me and Dermot.'

'Of course there is. You've been together for, what?' I think quickly. *It's mid-September now* … 'It must be about three months.'

Has it been that long? It doesn't seem five minutes since the dinner party.

'You'd think after that long we'd be a proper couple. But I'm not so sure Dermot sees us that way.' Caitlin now begins rearranging some cereal boxes stacked up behind her.

'Caitlin!' I snap, losing patience. 'Talk to me, I'm your friend.'

'Are you?' Caitlin suddenly spins around. 'Are you really, Darcy?'

I'm shocked by Caitlin's sudden change of tone, and her quite aggressive stance with her hands on the counter, glaring at me.

'I … I don't know what you mean.'

Caitlin relaxes slightly, but she still looks upset. 'I never stood a chance with you here.' She hangs her head and looks at the counter. 'Not with Dermot. And then when Megan came to stay with us for those few weeks in the summer, it just made it even worse.'

She looks up at me now, waiting for my defence.

But I'm not sure what I'm supposed to be defending myself for. I haven't actually done anything, have I?

'I'm sorry, Caitlin, but I really don't know what you're talking about.'

Caitlin takes her hands off the counter and stands up straight. 'You see, that just makes it all the worse, Darcy,' she says with a sigh. 'You really don't know, do you?'

I shake my head.

'Dermot is in love with you.'

Whoah, I wasn't expecting that. Looking around for something to steady me, I rest my hand on the shop counter.

'Don't be daft,' I say lightly, trying to think where she could have got such a notion from. There was the kitchen sink incident a few weeks ago, but that was just a one-off, and we'd explained that – it was just a few too many whiskies – hadn't we? 'Dermot's not in love with me. Whatever gave you that idea?'

'His daughter.'

'But why would Megan say that?'

'I don't know, you tell me.'

Helplessly I shake my head; this is all getting too much. I can't think about Dermot like that right now; this situation is just becoming way too confusing. I don't need someone else making things even worse with the announcement that he's in love with me. Then there's Conor to think of. I've been having my doubts about our relationship for a while, but that's to do with him and me; Dermot's not a factor in that.

Caitlin sighs. 'But it wouldn't matter what Megan said, the writing was on the wall before she even got here. I can never match up to you, no matter what I try to do. You're like a Greek goddess on this island, Darcy, everyone thinks you're wonderful, no one can come close to you.'

Now she's just being ridiculous. Greek goddess? I was more like the court jester when I first arrived on Tara.

'You shouldn't take it to heart, Caitlin. Megan's only eleven, she doesn't know—'

'Stop right there,' Caitlin says, cutting me off. 'Megan knows everything she needs to, don't let her fool you, Darcy. She's smart, that one.'

'I know that. But you can't just give up on a relationship because your partner's daughter has made a mistake. She's probably just a bit protective of Dermot. She wouldn't be the first daughter to be looking out for her dad in matters of the heart.'

Caitlin shakes her head. 'It's not just Megan. It's you. It's Dermot. It's the way he is around you, the way he looks at you. You must have noticed it.'

'No,' I say, slapping my hand down on the counter. 'No, you're wrong. Dermot doesn't feel like that about me, we're just friends and we've been spending a bit more time together lately because of planning the renovations, that's all. Anyway, I'm with Conor.'

Caitlin raises her eyebrows. 'And that, Darcy, is precisely why you don't notice any of this going on, and why Dermot would never tell you. He's too much of a gentleman.'

I've heard enough.

'I'm sorry if you feel you want to leave Tara. And I'm sorry you feel that your relationship with Dermot is not working out. But I will not take the blame for it happening, and neither should you blame Megan.' I let go of the shop counter for the first time since Caitlin's revelation and fold my arms. 'When would you like to go?'

Caitlin sighs. 'As soon as I possibly can.'

'Then I'll arrange for Conor to take you across in the boat sometime tomorrow. I'm really sorry this didn't work out for you,' my voice becomes softer as I relax my arms again. 'You'll be greatly missed by many of us here, including me.'

Caitlin doesn't speak, so I go to leave the shop.

'Darcy,' she calls, as I'm about to go out through the door. I turn back.

'One day you'll know the truth,' she says. 'This island seems to have a habit of making people realise what they truly want in life. It certainly has me.'

I nod at Caitlin as I leave the shop, the tinkling of the doorbell still ringing in my ears as I walk away across O'Connell Street.

If that's the case, then please, Tara, when are you going to cast that particular spell over me?

Thirty-four

Caitlin departs after a riotous leaving party that sees much merriment in The Temple Bar pub, with dancing both on the floor and on the tables by some of the more intoxicated members of the island. Dermot has decided not to attend, and instead spends the night at his cottage working on the plans for the new building.

I don't know what was said between the two of them that night, or if Caitlin ever told Dermot all the reasons she was leaving Tara. But Dermot has chosen not to talk about it to anyone, and the last time I see the two of them together is when we are all seeing Caitlin off from the harbour.

'Good luck, Caitlin,' I say, hugging her as she goes to get on the boat.

'And you, Darcy,' she says, smiling at me. 'I've a feeling you'll need it, keeping this lot in line.' She leans in towards me. 'I've left you a present,' she whispers in my ear, 'under the counter in the shop. Just to show there's no ill will between us. I know you'll find a use for them.'

After we've watched her sail away with Conor, and everyone begins to wander back to their cottages and jobs, I go back to the shop to take a look. And there, as promised, is a blue box with a label on it. *To Darcy, one day you'll understand. Caitlin x*

I open up the lid of the box and inside find a multitude of coloured stones. They're the crystals Caitlin used to keep in the basket.

'I hope so, Caitlin,' I whisper, as I run my hands through the contents of the box, letting the crystals slide through my fingers. 'I really do.'

With Caitlin gone, things change on Tara, so that when Megan arrives for the half-term holiday Orla has taken over the running of the shop, but is being assisted by Siobhan. This allows them both time away to teach their t'ai chi classes and perform their reiki and massage sessions. Dermot, with extra encouragement from me, has asked his daughter if she'd like to return to Tara for another holiday, and both Megan and Eileen jump at the chance for her to come to the island again.

'Why did Caitlin leave?' Megan asks me one morning, when we've gone up to the ruins with Dermot to look over some of the plans. Dermot is inside, double-checking some measurements, while Megan and I sit on the wall outside and wait for him. 'It all seemed a bit sudden.'

'She just decided she wanted to go travelling and see more of the world,' I explain while I take my sweatshirt off. It may be the end of October, but it's still a warm day. 'It wasn't really all that sudden.'

'Hmm,' Megan says thoughtfully. 'Just seemed odd, that's all, when Dad told me.'

'So,' I say to change the subject, 'how are we going to celebrate your birthday this week? What would you like to do – have a party?'

Megan shrugs. 'I don't know. What do you usually do to celebrate people's birthdays here?'

Not an awful lot. My birthday was in January, so I'd not celebrated one since I'd been here. But there have been a few others, and they usually just consist of a few drinks in The Temple Bar and a few toasts to the birthday boy or girl. At Paddy's insistence we've done a bit more for Niall at the end of September when we'd all had a meal together, but other than Conor and I celebrating his birthday together in June when we'd had a moonlit picnic down on the beach, birthdays are a pretty uneventful affair for the islanders here on Tara.

'Not that much, really,' I say carefully, not wanting to disappoint Megan. 'But with you it will be different. We could have a party.'

'Like a themed party?' she says excitedly. 'With fancy dress and costumes?'

'I'm not sure about costumes. We don't really have the resources here for that.'

'It wouldn't have to be anything exciting, we could just make costumes out of things we find lying around in our cottages, or we could borrow things from others. I know, we could call it a scavenger party!'

'Yes, that's a good idea . . . ' I glance across at Dermot. 'But I'm still not sure everyone will want to dress up.'

'*Please*, Darcy,' she blinks up at me with a pleading expression. 'I never get a proper birthday party. Not unless it's something Mum organises at some fancy restaurant.'

'Oh, all right then,' I sigh, giving in. 'I guess everyone should be able to find something to pull together.'

'Wicked!' Megan says, clapping her hands together. 'Dad, Dad!' she calls, jumping off the wall and rushing over to him. 'Guess what? Darcy says I can have a fancy-dress party for my birthday.'

'That's great, darling,' Dermot wraps his arms around Megan and hugs her. He gives me a wry smile over the top of Megan's head, and rolls his eyes.

'All done?' I ask Dermot as they walk back over towards me.

'Yep,' Dermot says, rolling up his plans. 'It's looking good, Darcy. Even if I do say so myself. This is going to be some building when I've finished with it.'

'I never doubted it for a second.'

Dermot smiles at me, and we hold each other's gaze for a moment. I so want this building to go ahead for him, as much as anything else; he's put so much time and effort into getting the renovation plans exactly right. Everything's been chosen so that the new building will be an almost exact replica of the old one on the outside, from the bricks to the wrought-iron fixtures and fittings. It's only the inside that will differ; it will be more luxurious and comfortable than the building would have been in its heyday, with hints of its original style.

'What did you do for Dad's birthday?' Megan asks, keen to bring the subject back to birthdays again as we begin to walk back down towards the village.

364

'You haven't had one since we've been here have you, Dermot?'

Dermot remains silent.

'Dad's birthday is May first,' Megan informs us. 'He's a Taurus.'

'Dermot,' I say in frustration. 'You never said it was your birthday. Why didn't you tell us?'

'I didn't want a fuss, and we'd not been here that long then.'

'But you still should have said.' I'm sad to think of Dermot celebrating his special day alone.

'You can share my birthday, Dad,' Megan says, slipping her hand into his. 'We can't have you missing out.'

'That's very kind, Megan. But a fancy-dress party to celebrate my birthday is my worst nightmare. It was bad enough when I was young, and I had people dancing around maypoles.'

I laugh. Somehow Dermot being born on a festival renowned for its joy and the coming of spring doesn't quite ring true.

'Actually, May Day *was* originally a Celtic festival,' Megan says. 'It marks exactly halfway through the year. And my birthday's on Samain, another festival that marks the beginning of the Celtic year. It starts on October thirty-first and ends November first, marking the end of harvest time.'

Dermot and I stare at Megan for a moment.

'Where on earth do you get all this stuff from, Megan?' Dermot asks in a mixture of bewilderment and awe.

'The internet mostly,' Megan says. 'And books.'

'You'll notice the books come second,' Dermot says to me, shaking his head.

'Is Samain like Halloween, then?' I ask Megan, suddenly interested in this.

'Yeah, I think it's related in some way. I don't like Halloween though; it's always ruined my birthday.'

'It can't have been easy living in America with a birthday on that day. They really go to town on it, don't they?'

Megan nods. 'Stupid trick or treat. What about "Happy Birthday, Megan"?'

'Don't worry, Megan,' I say, smiling at her. 'We'll make sure that this thirty-first of October is all about you, and there's not a witch or a pumpkin anywhere to be seen.'

'That might be a bit difficult,' Dermot says, looking doubtful.

'Why?' Megan and I both ask at the same time.

'The holidaymakers in Cottage Five at the moment look decidedly spooky.'

'I understand you're going to have a party on Samain,' Eamon says to me a couple of days later when I meet him outside the shop.

'Yes, for Megan's birthday. It's also her last day here for a while. Eileen is coming to pick her up again the next day.'

'You'd be knowing that Samain is a very important festival in the Celtic calendar, would you?' Eamon says, planting his stick in the ground and leaning on it.

Oh dear, that means Eamon is going to be talking for a while.

'Megan mentioned it was something to do with Halloween, yes.'

Eamon opens his eyes wide. 'Oh, Darcy, it's far more than that. Samain is believed to be the beginning of the Celtic year; the end to the lighter half and the start of the darker side.'

'That's just great,' I say, thinking of the winter weather

366

coming to Tara. It has been bearable living here through the spring and summer months, but what's it going to be like through the cold and wet of winter? Storms and freezing temperatures definitely won't bring the holidaymakers in and pay the bills. I had to find a way of financing this new building, and fast.

'Its associations with Halloween are echoes of the festival of the dead. Folk would wear costumes or masks to replicate the spirits, or some say to placate them.'

'Just as well it's a fancy-dress party, then, isn't it? We can all wear masks,' I say quickly. 'So, are you going to come?'

'Darcy, I wouldn't miss it for the world,' Eamon says, surprisingly. 'I've a feeling this Samain celebration could be a very important one.'

Thirty-five

'What is she doing here?' I ask, watching a boat powering over towards the island. 'I didn't think she was coming to get Megan until tomorrow.'

'Neither did I.' Conor looks out to sea with me. 'That's all poor Megan wants today, her mam here on her birthday stirring up trouble.'

Eileen – without Geoffrey – arrives in a hire boat from the mainland. The skipper helps Eileen and her luggage onto the island, and then roars away again.

Eileen is slightly more practical today in a camel-coloured jumpsuit, but she's still wearing ridiculously high-heeled tan leather boots.

'Darling,' Eileen cries, throwing her arms around Megan. 'You didn't think I'd miss your birthday, did you?'

'Wouldn't be the first time,' Megan grumbles, not hugging her mother in return.

Eileen smiles brightly. 'You know that was just the once. I was stuck in the Maldives,' she explains to the rest of us who have come down to the harbour to greet her arrival. 'There was a mini-tornado and my plane couldn't take off.'

'Whatever,' Megan says.

'I've brought you a present, it's in my bag,' Eileen turns towards the designer suitcase that sits propped up against some tyres. 'If someone would be so kind as to take it up to one of your quaint little cottages for me, I can get unpacked and give it to you.'

'The thing is, Eileen,' I explain, 'we didn't think you were coming until tomorrow to collect Megan. We're full up this week, what with it being the half-term holidays.'

'Oh,' Eileen looks back to where her boat is now a mere speck in the distance. 'If you've nowhere for me to stay . . .'

'She can take my bed for the night,' Dermot says, folding his arms and sighing.

'But where will you go, Dermot?' I ask.

'I'll just bunk down in Paddy's cottage. He spends most of his time at Niall's now, anyway. I'm sure he won't mind for one night.'

'That's very gallant of you, Dermot,' Eileen flashes her dazzling white teeth at him. 'I don't remember you being this chivalrous when we were together.'

'Don't push it, Eileen,' I hear Dermot mutter as he picks up Eileen's bag and we all begin to traipse up the slope towards the village. 'Or you'll be sleeping under the stars tonight.'

'This is the best birthday ever!' Megan says to me as she tucks into yet another iced cupcake courtesy of Aiden and Kathleen.

'It's all wicked – the food, the decorations, everyone's costumes, even the weather has stayed dry for me tonight.'

'Wicked' is the perfect word to describe the party.

All the islanders and some of the visitors have really pulled together and produced tables of delicious party food, homemade decorations that cover the whole of O'Connell Street and some wonderfully innovative costumes, considering the limited resources we have on Tara.

Megan is dressed as a sort of twenty-first-century angel. She's partly wearing her own clothes – a long-sleeved pink top with the word *Angel* written across it in sequins, white denim shorts, pink Converse trainers and thick red tights. She's also managed to create a pair of angel wings from some wire and feathers she's collected from around the island. And I wonder if any of the birds on Tara have any feathers left to fly with when I see that Niall and Paddy have had the same idea, and are dressed as red Indians in real feather headdresses. Roxi, donning silver high heels, a blue satin dress and carrying a tennis ball glued to an empty toilet-roll tube covered in tin foil announces she's Beyoncé for the evening. Conor, surprisingly, appears dressed from top to toe in black; he wears a black mask and carries a sword.

'Who are you? I ask him. 'And where on earth did you get the sword from?'

'I am Zorro!' he says in a dodgy accent, wielding the sword through the air in a Z shape. 'Eamon loaned it to me for the party.'

'Where on earth did Eamon get it from, then?'

Conor shrugs. 'Who cares, but it's great, isn't it?' He brandishes the sword around a bit more, and then goes off to torment Roxi with it.

I shake my head: boys and their toys.

For my own outfit I've taken inspiration from my bedroom, and I've fashioned a long robe from my Celtic-patterned quilt cover, and with some of my jewellery and some wire I've managed to make quite an elegant-looking crown. I hope Dermot doesn't need any wire to mend anything any time soon, because the amount people have 'borrowed' for their costumes I doubt there's any left anywhere on the island. I team this with my smartest black trousers from Hobbs, black high-heeled suede boots and a black cashmere jumper with silver and black sparkly detailing.

But although the boots are already starting to make my feet ache – *I'm so out of practice with heels these days* – the overall effect is quite regal, I feel, and even though this *is* only a fancy-dress birthday party, it feels good to make an effort and dress up once again.

'Hey girls,' Dermot says, as he rolls up next to Megan and me looking very Dermot-like wearing jeans, a checked shirt and a tool belt slung around his waist. He carries a yellow hard hat in his hand as though he's just been off fixing something around the island.

'*Dermot*, its fancy dress,' I say, sounding disappointed. 'You could have made an effort.'

'I have,' Dermot makes a show of placing the hard hat on his head. 'I'm Bob the Builder.'

Megan pulls an embarrassed expression.

'That didn't take much effort.' I say. 'At least *I* tried.'

'And a very fine queen you make too.' Dermot takes his hard hat off again to bow.

'I'm meant to be a king,' I say, looking down at my legs. 'You don't see many queens in trousers.'

Dermot glances in the direction of the two red Indians, helping themselves to sandwiches at one of the tables, then grins at me.

I shake my head at him. 'I thought I'd come as a king since Tara is my island, and the Tara in County Meath is supposedly the hill where all the kings of Ireland were crowned in days gone by.'

'Is it?' Dermot asks. 'I didn't know that. How did you?'

'I think Roxi told me. I guess Eamon must have told her, in one of their story sessions.'

'She's right,' Eamon says, wandering over to stand next to us. He holds a glass of whiskey in one hand (everyone else has bottles of beer or soft drinks, but we've allowed Eamon his usual tipple) and his trusty stick in the other, but unusually for Eamon, instead of his ever-present greens and browns, tonight he wears a black bow tie, an ill-fitting evening suit with trousers that are slightly too long for him and a jacket that's a size too big, as his nod to the dress code for the evening. 'The hill of Tara *was* the ancient crowning site of the kings of Ireland. They also held a great assembly there on Samain, where a bonfire would be set alight on the great hill. It served as a beacon to the people all over the rest of Ireland to light their own ritual bonfires, to banish the evil spirits and to aid their own spiritual purification.'

'Maybe *we* should have a bonfire,' Megan suggests. 'I don't want any evil spirits at my birthday party.'

Great! Someone else is filling Megan's head with more nonsense.

'There are no evil spirits here, Megan,' I try to reassure her. 'Are there, Dermot?'

Dermot glances towards Eileen, who tonight is dressed in a black and red cocktail dress.

'No, Darcy,' he says quickly. 'No, of course not.'

'But couldn't we just have a bonfire in case, Dad? *Please,*' Megan asks, looking up at Dermot with her big brown eyes, which I notice for the first time have got those same little green flecks in as Dermot's.

Dermot sighs. 'There *is* all that wood from that rotting tree I chopped down the other day. We could use that.' He looks down at Megan again. 'Oh, go on then, if that's what you really want, but only because it's your birthday.'

'Yey!' Megan claps.

'Come on, if we're going to do this you can at least help me with carrying the wood. We'll be back in a bit, Darcy.'

'Good luck,' I smile, watching them go.

'She's a grand young one,' Eamon says. 'She reminds me of you when you were that age.'

'You were here, then, when I used to come and visit the island?' I turn to Eamon. 'It's just that I don't remember you.'

'What about yer man that used to bring you and your aunt across in the boat?' Eamon looks at me with interest.

'You mean, the chap that used to give me sweets if I felt seasick on a rough crossing?' I say, as a sweet taste begins to form in my mouth.

Eamon nods.

'He was such a lively fellow. I remember he used to do this thing where he'd leap off the boat with a rope when we got to the island. Sometimes I didn't think he was going to make it across the water, he'd try and jump from so far out.'

'And would he sometimes carry your picnic basket up the hill and down to the beach for you, if you were carrying a lot of other stuff? Do you remember him doing that, Darcy?'

I nod slowly. 'And my aunt would ask him to stay and join us, but he never would.' I look into Eamon's eyes. 'That was you?'

'It was.'

'When I first arrived here with Conor he leaped off the boat in a similar way – I thought it seemed familiar.' I think back to that time. 'But why didn't you mention this before?'

'It wasn't the right time,' he says slowly, leaning on his stick.

'So why is it now?'

'Let's sit down,' Eamon gestures to one of the benches; 'my old legs don't like standing too long these days.'

We sit on one of the benches that Dermot carved for us at the beginning of our time here on Tara.

'You've done a grand job here on the island, Darcy, so you have,' Eamon says, looking around at everyone enjoying themselves. 'When you first came here I wondered just what you were going to do with Tara, with all your fancy ideas, but you've come up against some situations since you've been here that have tested you, and you've passed those tests with flying colours.'

I'm touched by such high praise from Eamon.

'Thank you. But you don't know the half of it, stuck all the way over there on the other side of the island. You miss most of the dramas that go on over here, and the things I get wrong.'

'Oh, I hear about it all,' Eamon says, nodding slowly. 'Be in no doubt of that. Young Conor keeps me informed of a lot when he brings my post and supplies.'

Of course, I'd forgotten Conor still popped over with all Eamon's bits and pieces when they arrive from the mainland, just like he had before we'd all arrived.

'You must have known Conor a long time now, Eamon,' I say, smiling at him. 'Do you remember when Conor was a boy and he used to visit Tara?'

Eamon looks oddly at me. 'No, Conor wasn't here when he was a boy. I only met him a couple of months before all of you got here and he took over the job of sailing the boat from young Liam. I always wondered why Liam gave up that job, he seemed happy enough in it.'

That's odd. I distinctly remember Conor saying he grew up with a view of Tara. Perhaps Eamon's mind is starting to go a little, as well as his body. He has been looking quite frail of late.

'But then my memory isn't quite what it used to be,' Eamon says, backing up my own thoughts. 'I might be mistaken.' Eamon considers this for a moment. 'But we must return to your aunt, Darcy. It wasn't until young Megan turned up that I truly understood just why Molly wanted you to come to Tara so badly.'

I was keen to know the answer to this one myself. 'Why *was* that, Eamon? Everyone keeps saying that Tara's special, and that she can help you know what you want in life. But if it was Molly who wanted me to come here so badly, what was it she want me to find out?'

'Darcy, quick, while Megan is out of the way, let's get her cake ready!' Paddy calls, running across the grass towards us. 'It's a deadly birthday cake Aiden has knocked out, like. Have you seen it?'

I look anxiously at Eamon.

'Go,' Eamon says, nodding. 'They need you. They all need you, Darcy. And Tara, that's what all this has been about.'

'What do you mean, Eamon?' I ask, half standing up. I'm desperate to know what Eamon is about to reveal.

'Darcy, come on!' Paddy calls again.

'You'll know when the time is right,' Eamon says. He reaches out his hand to me. 'You have my blessing, though, Darcy,' he says, and I feel his bony yet firm grip on my arm, just like I had that first day we'd met on the cliff edge. 'Look inside yourself and always do what feels right, and you'll never go far wrong in life, just remember that.'

'Sure, Eamon, I will,' I smile at him, my eyes looking deep down into his bright blue ones. 'Can we talk again later? I'd really like to remember more about my time here as a child, and for you to tell me more about my aunt.'

'Trust me, Darcy; you'll know the truth very soon now. About many things here on this island. Now go.'

I take a couple of steps away when I have a thought. 'Eamon, my aunt, she wore a Claddagh ring, didn't she?'

Eamon nods, 'Yes she did, on her right hand.'

'What happened to it, do you know?'

'Soon, Darcy,' he says mysteriously. 'Soon.'

I rush over to the pub kitchen with Paddy, and help him light the twelve candles on Megan's birthday cake. I'm still thinking about Eamon's words, and as I do I suddenly remember which way round the ring faced . . .

Thirty-six

The rest of Megan's birthday party is a great success. We do indeed have a bonfire, and after much of the wonderful food has been demolished by everyone, a sing-song and then some party games. Some of these are traditional, like blind man's buff and musical chairs – which ends up being hotly contested by Conor and Ryan for the last chair, with Ryan narrowly being crowned champion.

We then move on to some less well-known games, but according to Eamon traditional to Samain. One of these involves peeling an apple and throwing the peel over your shoulder, the shape the peel forms apparently determining the initial of the person you'll marry.

This sounds like a recipe for disaster to me, with the amount of couples already on Tara. But Niall and Paddy are ecstatic when they both form what roughly look like each other's initials during the game. Most of the others who join in get on well with their predictions, even the ones that are already married. Conor throws a shape illegible as any initial, and Dermot as usual refuses to join in. Roxi is in raptures when her apple peel forms a shape resembling a W.

'I'm going to marry Will *Smith*, I'm going to marry Will *Smith*!' she calls, dancing around and throwing her arms up to the clear night sky above. 'I knew it was written in the stars all along!'

'I don't want to put a spanner in the works,' Dermot says, inspecting the apple peel, 'but isn't he already married?'

'Listen here, Mr Cowell,' Roxi says, eyeing Dermot fiercely, 'you can't mess with true love.'

'Roxi, why do you insist on calling me Mr Cowell?' Dermot asks, matching Roxi's dark brown stare with his own equally forceful one. 'I clearly don't look anything like Simon Cowell.'

Roxi stares hard at Dermot, then she screws up her nose and shrugs. 'Don't know, really, it just kind of stuck. If anything, you've more of the George Clooney about you than Simon Cowell.'

I can't help but grin at the expression of shock and pride that sweeps over Dermot's face.

'Just don't go telling anyone I told you that, though,' she threatens him.

Roxi's right, though, now I consider this statement; Dermot does look a bit like George, only broader and with more muscles.

'Come on, Darcy,' Megan encourages me. 'It's your go now.'

'I'm not sure I want to know,' I say, twisting my apple peel up in my hand.

'It's only a game, and you're the last one. Then I think we're going to have some dancing! Apparently Seamus has written me my own song as my birthday present.'

'Oh, all right then,' I sigh, standing up. I quickly toss the apple peel over my shoulder and turn around to look. 'There, you can't really tell what it is,' I say, glancing down at the apple peel in relief. 'It's very round, most probably an O.'

'Could be a C?' Roxi says, her eyes twinkling. 'With the two ends almost joined up. See, they're not actually touching each other on that side.'

I daren't look at Conor.

'No, it's definitely not a C, Rox,' I say quickly.

'I think it's a D,' Megan says, with her head tilted to one side. 'See, that left side is much straighter than the other curved one.'

'Maybe the D is for Darcy, and it means I'm just going to stay single all my life then,' I conclude, swiftly gathering up the peel. 'Now, let's get that music started. Where's Seamus when you need him?'

We have great fun for the next hour, dancing to Irish jigs and reels with music provided by our now resident musician Seamus. I'm just taking a breather and sitting this one out with a well-earned drink, when Eileen comes over and sits down next to me. As always, it's not many minutes before she lights up a cigarette, and I'm glad we're outside as her smoke begins to swirl around our faces.

'You've put on some party for my daughter here tonight,' she says as she watches the dancers spinning around. She takes a long drag on her cigarette, then exhales the smoke through her mouth in long, toxic spiral.

'Megan seems to have enjoyed it.'

'She's done more than that,' Eileen says, still facing

forwards. 'She's just informed me she doesn't want to come back with me tomorrow, and wants to stay here with you and Dermot permanently.'

'What?' I swivel around to face her. 'Eileen, I had no idea. Megan has never mentioned this before.'

Eileen turns to face me now. Like a dragon breathing fire on its victim, she empties a plume of smoke in my face before speaking. 'Don't think I don't know what your game is, Darcy, with your holier-than-thou attitude and this perfect little set-up you've got going on here.'

I open my eyes wide, and then have to blink hard to try and get rid of the stinging sensation from the smoke. 'What do you mean?'

'You're after him.'

'Who?' I need to take a sip of drink to try and get rid of the taste of smoke from my mouth as well now.

'Dermot.'

I nearly spit my drink all over Eileen, which considering what she's just emptied all over me, wouldn't be such a bad idea.

'Why on earth would I want Dermot?'

'That's just what I've been trying to figure out. Mind you,' Eileen looks across to where Dermot stands, keeping well away from the dancing by talking to Daniel and Orla. 'I suppose he is still quite handsome, if you like the more rough-and-ready type. And he can't be that bad; after all, I once saw something in him myself.'

I rub at my forehead, knocking my crown back slightly in the process. Why does everyone think that Dermot and I are desperately in love with each other? Are we the only two that haven't been told?

'You are completely wrong about this, Eileen. I don't want Dermot. Anyway, I'm in a relationship with Conor.'

'*This* is where my little theory goes slightly off track,' Eileen gazes across at Conor now. 'Why on earth would you want Dermot when you've already got that rather handsome specimen over there?' Eileen looks Conor up and down admiringly.

'Eileen,' I'm beginning to get impatient now, 'have you got anything more concrete to add to this conversation other than some ridiculous fantasy you seem to have dreamed up for yourself?'

'Yes.' Eileen manages to turn her attention away from Conor for a moment. 'Stop making my daughter's time here so enjoyable. That's all I heard when she came back after the summer, Tara this and Darcy that. It got so bad that I nearly didn't let her come back again this holiday.'

I stare at Eileen in disbelief. 'But you must let her come and visit Dermot. He loves having her back in his life again after all this time, and Megan loves being with him, too.'

'Well, they're going to have to get used to going back to the way things were before,' Eileen flicks grey ash onto Tara's grass. 'Because *I've* decided to move back to the States again.'

'But why?' I ask, completely stunned by her latest declaration. 'You've only just moved back to Ireland. You said you had business to attend to here.'

'My business is with an ever-changing, multinational company. Sometimes we need to change our plans.' She takes another long drag on her cigarette, before slowly blowing the smoke out into the atmosphere to pollute it even more than her words have.

I shake my head in frustration. 'But you can't just drop

Megan into Dermot's life like this, and then simply pull her right back out of it again. Like ... like a tea bag dunked in and out of a mug! It's not fair on either of them.'

'I'm her mother, Darcy, I can do whatever I like.'

Now I've heard the phrase 'seeing red' before. But right now I actually *feel* like my whole body is burning a very intense shade of bright fiery red from my head right down to my toes. I try to calm myself by holding onto my little rose quartz crystal, but even that is powerless against the force that's rising up within me, as an emotion I've never felt before explodes inside.

'But that's exactly what a mother *isn't* supposed to do,' I turn around so my body is fully facing her, and my mind is perfectly prepared for a head-on battle. 'A mother is supposed to do what's best for her child, not what's best for herself. You should be putting Megan's happiness first, not your own. When you gave birth to her, you gave up the right to do whatever you liked, whenever you wanted to. You gave that right to your daughter, to look after until she was old enough to make her own decisions in life.'

Eileen's face looks as shocked as her Botox will allow at my outburst. She opens her mouth to speak, but I've not finished with her yet. More fireworks are exploding inside me.

'And do you know what? If you'd been a proper mum, Megan wouldn't even want to make her own decisions about where she wants to live. She's twelve years old, for goodness' sake, but you'd think she's thirty the way she speaks sometimes. What sort of mother can't even manage to buy her own daughter something she actually *wants* for her birthday?'

'But ... but I thought she'd like a voucher to have a fun day at the spa with her friends!' Eileen manages to get a word in at last.

'No, *you'd* like a fun day at the spa with *your* friends, Eileen, but that's not what Megan wants. You don't know her at all. If she was my daughter I'd know what she wanted, I'd know how to be a proper mother to her, and do you know why?' I demand, pointing my finger accusingly at her.

Eileen recoils against the bench. 'No,' she says in a small voice.

'It's because you treat Megan just like my own mother treated me,' I say, each word shooting from my mouth, extinguishing my internal fire a little bit more. 'And if Megan wants to come and live here with her father, away from you, just like I used to escape my own mother when I came to Ireland to stay with my aunt Molly, then I'll do everything I can in my power to help her!'

I turn away from Eileen now, and realise something else. My voice has been so loud and so forceful, as I've finally let loose the repressed emotions I've kept boxed up inside me for so many years, that it's carried way above the sound of music and merriment, and everyone has stopped dancing and is standing like statues witnessing my verbal attack on Eileen.

As they stand silently watching me, waiting to see what I'll do next, I can do nothing else but leap up from the bench and run in the opposite direction away from them, glad for once when I don't even have to call Woody and Louis. For the first time ever they just come running after me of their own accord.

It's a clear night with a full moon sitting high in the night sky, lighting my path like a beacon as I run past my cottage and along towards the beach. I stop at the top of the cliff and pull off my high-heeled boots before I descend the path onto the sand below. Then, tucking myself underneath the rock face so no one else will see me, I curl myself into a tight ball, and with Woody and Louis sitting either side of me, I begin to cry like I've never cried before. For once, tears that should have been allowed to fall years ago stream from my eyes, dropping down onto the beach in a seemingly never-ending flow that, after a while, begins to mingle with the salt water that rolls rhythmically back and forth in front of me across the sand.

Thirty-seven

I sit on the beach for a long time, just watching the sea crash against the rocks and the waves roll in and out along the sand, and all the time Woody and Louis keep me company. They don't go off foraging for whatever it is they usually go in search of, they simply sit either side of me occasionally giving me a lick or a nuzzle, depending on whether I'm dropping tears on them at the time.

And if I'd seen and felt red when I was up at the party, now I feel very much surrounded in a cloud of blue as I sit on the beach drowning in my own sorrowful thoughts. In fact, the only thing that prevents me from falling asleep there and then once my tears cease falling, and a wave of extreme exhaustion comes crashing in, is a strange feeling inside me that something isn't right.

Woody and Louis's ears suddenly prick up, and their heads turn towards the end of the beach. I look in the direction they're wagging their tails in to see Dermot walking along the beach towards me.

'This is where you're hiding,' he says, bending down to fuss the dogs as he arrives next to us. 'We've been looking for you.'

'Have you?'

'Of course,' he sits down on the sand next to me and pulls a walkie-talkie from his pocket. 'Niall, this is Dermot, over.'

A crackly voice feeds back over the speaker. 'Niall here, Dermot, any sign yet? Over.'

'I've got her, Niall. She's quite safe. I'll take it from here. You can tell the others the hunt's over, and they can go to bed now. Over.'

'Righty-ho, Dermot, will do. Over and out.'

Dermot puts the walkie-talkie back in his pocket and looks at me. He raises his eyebrows. 'I thought you said you weren't a queen, earlier? That little charade at Megan's party looked pretty drama-queenish to me.'

My head falls into my hands in shame. 'How is Megan?' I ask in a muffled voice.

'She's fine, Darcy. I think she quite enjoyed seeing you stand up to Eileen like that.' He nudges me. '*I* enjoyed seeing you stand up to Eileen like that. I was never brave enough.'

I look up at Dermot now, and find he's smiling at me. 'Really?' I ask. 'Megan's not cross at me for ruining her party?'

'Megan, cross at you?' Dermot laughs. 'Are you kidding? Megan adores you. Everyone adores you on this island, Darcy.' Dermot swiftly turns his head away and appears to concentrate on the waves that ebb and flow along the beach.

'I shouldn't have said those things to Eileen, though, it wasn't my place to.'

'It was about time someone did. There was no point me saying anything, she wouldn't have listened.' Dermot still gazes out to sea. 'And it certainly helped open up *negotiations* between Eileen and myself after you ran off. She told me what she's thinking of doing.'

'You talked?'

Dermot turns his head back now and nods. 'Yes, and we've agreed to sit down and discuss Megan's future between the three of us properly, tomorrow, and decide what's best. It seems I owe you thanks again, Darcy, not only for helping me bring my daughter back into my life, but for helping me to keep her there.' Dermot's eyes roam over my face as though he's trying to take in every inch of it in the pale moonlight, and for a moment neither of us speaks.

'Did Conor come looking for me too?' I suddenly ask, wondering where he is. Shouldn't it be Conor sitting here with me on this beach, looking at me like this, not Dermot?

Dermot sits bolt upright at the mention of Conor's name, as though hit by an icy-cold wave. 'I'm not going to lie to you, Darcy,' he says, looking me straight in the eye again, but this time it's concern I see reflected back at me, not – well, what did I see before in Dermot's gaze? 'I haven't seen Conor since you ran off.'

I look with disbelief at Dermot. 'But where would he go?' *And why didn't he come looking for me like Dermot and the others did?*

Dermot shrugs, 'Fishing, maybe? You said he liked to go out at night.' But he doesn't look very sure of himself.

'It's possible, I suppose.' But even I'm having a hard time convincing myself now.

'I wouldn't worry; I doubt he's too far away. He always seems to turn up.' I just know Dermot wants to say *like the proverbial bad penny*, but he stops himself just in time. 'So,' he says, standing up and holding out his hand, 'Shall we get you into bed then?'

I can't help blushing as I reach for Dermot's hand.

'Like the others, I mean,' he says, a pink glow spreading across his own cheekbones as I take his hand and he pulls me effortlessly up from the sand.

'Sure,' I smile, as we begin to walk back down the beach together. 'I know what you meant.'

But as we reach the little path that climbs up the side of the cliff, I realise that we've walked the entire length of the beach still holding on tightly to each other's hand.

I don't sleep at all well in what little is left of the night. In fact, by the time Dermot has walked me back to my cottage and I've settled Woody and Louis down, I only doze for a couple of hours before I'm awakened again by the dogs barking. I roll over in my bed and put my pillow over my head in the hope that they'll settle down again. But they don't, they keep on going. So I roll out of bed to see what the problem is.

Dawn is just starting to break outside my window as I go through to the hall to find the two dogs pawing and scratching at my front door.

'What on earth is wrong with the pair of you?' I ask, rubbing my eyes. 'We barely came back from the beach a couple of hours ago; you can't need to go out again already.'

But still they press their noses to the bottom of the door, sniffing and clawing at it in turn.

'All right, all right, just give me a minute,' I say, grabbing a sweatshirt and my UGG boots to pull on over my pyjamas.

Just about suitably dressed, I open the door expecting them

just to wander out onto the grass in front of the cottage and do their business out there. But they don't, they go bounding down the hill towards O'Connell Street.

'Hey, wait!' I call out as I hurry after them. 'Where are you going?'

I follow the dogs past all the other sleeping cottages down through the deserted square where, just a few hours ago, it had been alight with music and merriment, as they head towards the harbour. As our little jetty comes into view, I see that we're not the only ones up at this hour of the morning.

'Conor, Dermot, what are you doing up so early?' I call, running down to the harbour after the dogs.

Both men spin around at the sound of my voice. But neither look particularly pleased to see me.

Conor is standing on the deck of the little red boat surrounded by wooden packing cases.

Dermot has one foot on the side of the boat and one foot on the jetty. He looks as if he's about to climb aboard.

'Darcy, just go back to your cottage,' Dermot calls. 'I'll deal with this.'

'You'll deal with what?' I ask, coming closer to them. 'What's going on?'

Conor doesn't speak. He just stares at me.

Woody and Louis sit down either side of me as I stand on the side of the harbour wall waiting for an explanation from one of them.

'Do you want to tell her or shall I, Conor?' Dermot asks, swinging his leg back onto the jetty.

Conor's head drops as he stares at the deck of the boat. 'You had to ruin it, didn't you?' he says, shaking his head. He lifts his

389

head again and glares at Dermot with such venom I'm quite shocked. 'You couldn't just keep those great boots of yours out of it.'

Dermot just folds his arms and waits.

'Please, you two, stop messing about and just tell me what's going on.' I'm starting to feel nervous. There's a really strange atmosphere between them.

Dermot sighs. 'Since Golden Balls here obviously doesn't seem to have *any* balls, it looks like I'll have to explain.' Dermot looks across at Conor, who just scowls back at him. 'Conor here is trying to abscond from Tara with stolen goods.'

I look at Conor, still standing in the boat and shooting daggers at Dermot. 'What stolen goods? What's he talking about, Conor?'

Conor looks at me apologetically, but he still doesn't try to explain.

'Still nothing?' Dermot enquires, looking at Conor with disdain. 'You're even less of a man than I thought you were.' He turns back to me. 'Stolen goods from our Eamon's cottage, apparently.'

'From Eamon? But what's Eamon got that's worth taking? And more to the point, why would you even think of taking anything from him, Conor?' I look desperately at him, standing bobbing up and down in the moored boat. I can't believe this is happening. Surely this is some weird dream I'm going to wake up from, in a minute. In a moment I'll be back in my bed, remembering that I have to apologise to Eileen for my harsh words and to Megan for messing up her party. It *must* be a dream; this can't be happening.

'Artefacts,' Conor says now, addressing me properly for the

first time. 'Eamon collects old Irish antiquities – mainly weaponry, swords, shields, things of that nature. But there was also jewellery and amulets up in that cottage of his. It was a complete treasure trove for a buyer of that sort of thing.'

'But you're . . . *stealing* them?' I can hardly bear to say the word, let alone ask him the question. 'And from Eamon, too, a friend. He's an old man. What's he ever done to you?' I can feel tears beginning to form in the corners of my eyes. And there was me, thinking I'd cried myself completely dry last night. 'What have *any* of us done to you to deserve this?'

'Darcy, I never meant to hurt *you*,' Conor makes a move towards the edge of the boat. Louis and Woody both growl as they immediately stand up either side of me.

'It's OK, guys,' I say, patting their backs. I turn to Dermot. 'Dermot, can you give us a moment alone, please?'

Dermot looks like he might start growling in a minute too. 'Sure, whatever,' he nods. 'But I'm watching you,' he assures Conor as he moves a little way up the hill to give us some privacy.

Conor climbs out of the boat and stands facing me on the jetty. I can hardly bear to be this close to him, knowing what he's done, and yet I have to hear it from him.

'Why?' I simply ask, looking up into his big blue eyes. I feel I should be angry with him, shouting or doing something more dramatic. But my heart is beating so hard against my chest it feels like it's going to break right through and burst out into the harbour. I feel completely empty, as if it's not really happening. 'Why are you doing this?'

'Because that's what I do, Darcy,' he says, at least having the grace to look shamefaced. 'I'm . . . not what you think I am. I'm a con man. I take advantage of situations. I meet women and convince them to part with their money in my favour. I thought, what with you inheriting this island . . . '

'You thought you could get money out of me?' I can only stare at him.

'Yes, that's the truth of it. But with you I'd taken on a bit more than I could handle. You're stronger up here than most, Darcy,' he taps his forehead with his finger. 'And I realised you were falling in love with this island; there was no way you were ever going to leave it. I knew that any money you inherited at the end of your time here you'd just plough right back into Tara, so . . . '

'So there was nothing here for you,' I finish for him, feeling the words hit the bottom of my stomach like cold stones. He'd been using me this whole time.

'I need cash, there are . . . people I need to pay back. So that's where Eamon came in. I'd suspected for a while he might have something valuable hidden up in that cottage of his. When I found out exactly what it was I came up with a plan. I just had to wait for a suitable time to get in there. You running off like you did tonight, with the whole island distracted looking for you, was just the chance I needed.'

I stare at Conor, unable to believe what I'm hearing.

'B . . . but you couldn't possibly have removed all this stuff,' I wave my hands at the wooden boxes, 'without anyone seeing you. And what about Eamon? How come he didn't wake up?'

'I actually waited until everyone was tucked up in their beds. At least, I thought everyone was.' He glares over at Dermot again.

'But what about Eamon?' I repeat. 'I know he's elderly, but he's not deaf.'

'That's the thing,' Conor says, a puzzled look crossing his face. 'Eamon wasn't there when I broke into his cottage.'

'So where was he?'

Conor shrugs. 'I don't know. Maybe out for a walk?'

'In the middle of the night?' I exclaim.

'Funnily enough, Darcy, it wasn't the first thing on my mind at the time.'

'No,' I say sarcastically, 'I suppose it wouldn't be.' I still can't believe I am actually having this conversation with Conor. The man I'd just spent the last six months of my life with. *Conor*, even his name should have warned me of what was to come. 'But wait a minute,' I exclaim as something suddenly occurs to me. 'You said you were going to con me out of my inheritance at the end of my year here, but you couldn't have known when you came to Tara that I was going to inherit any money. No one knew Molly's plan, only Niall and Dermot.'

'And a certain bartender you told your life story to in London one evening, when you'd been chucked out of your friend's party. They're a great place to meet wealthy, good-looking women – bars.'

I think about what he's saying. 'Oh, my God, that was *you*!' I exclaim, remembering Samantha's party in the wine bar. 'But I was so drunk that night.'

'I know,' Conor smiles, 'but you were very talkative.'

My mind is racing almost as fast as my heart now. 'I told Megan I thought I knew you from somewhere when I first met you, just like she did.'

Conor nods. 'I suppose I must be a better actor than they

ever realised on that Yankee soap opera. It's part of what I do. But here, I was virtually playing myself.' He shrugs and looks out at the landscape. I search the sea-blue eyes that I once described as clear and inviting. They now seem nothing but treacherous. Megan had been right. 'But there was one drawback to my whole plan, Darcy, apart from you falling in love with this damn island.'

I look up at him in bewilderment.

'Me falling in love with you.'

My bewilderment turns to astonishment.

'It's true,' he says, gazing at me with those big blue eyes. 'You, Darcy McCall, are something a bit special, so you are.' He glances up at Dermot still standing on the hill a little way away from us. 'Come away with me, Darcy,' he whispers, running his hand gently down my cheek. 'We can still make away with the boat before Bob the Builder gets to us. The stuff on board is worth a fortune; we can live like kings for years on this. Forget about Tara; you can have designer clothes and shopping sprees every day, if you like. What's that in comparison to a draughty old island and some faded memories?'

I look back at the deck of the boat covered in the boxes full of Eamon's things, and then I look at Conor's expectant face, waiting for my reply. Finally I turn to Dermot, waiting patiently on the hillside.

'Dermot, I think you'd better get back down here,' I call. 'Golden Balls is being shown the red card. Please escort him from the island.'

Dermot immediately jumps down into the boat and begins unloading the boxes that contain Eamon's things, while Conor simply watches stony-faced, occasionally trying to catch my eye. But I'm having none of it, and stand resolutely on the harbour with Woody and Louis by my side.

The last I see of the two of them is the boat finally departing from the harbour, unusually with Dermot at the helm. While I'd been waiting I'd wondered whether I should contact the Garda across on the mainland; after all, Conor was stealing from Eamon. But I didn't want to make this any worse or upsetting than it already was. Eamon and the others would be devastated when they found out than Conor had been fooling us all with his act; they didn't need police officers asking them hundreds of questions.

His act. I could hardly believe I'd fallen for it. He'd seemed so convincing, so genuine. How could I have been so gullible? The final straw had been all that waffle he'd tried to fob me off with just now, about falling in love with me. Even to the very end he'd been trying to spin me his blarney.

Maybe I had been right about love, before I'd come here to Tara. You *were* better off without relationships. They were nothing but trouble, and they always finished badly in the end.

I look down at the boxes on the harbour. It's already daylight, and it won't be long before Eamon wakes up and notices his things are missing. But Conor had said Eamon hadn't been in his cottage when he'd taken all this stuff. Where on earth could he be at this time of the morning? I decide to take Woody and Louis to investigate, and to explain to Eamon just what has been going on.

But as the dogs and I head up the path towards Eamon's cottage, I stop and pause for a moment to look out over the bay at all the dolphins swimming about in the sea below. 'Guys, just look at them all!' I exclaim to the dogs, as they sniff about on the grass next to me. 'I've never seen so many down there before.'

But these dolphins look different. When I've seen them down in the bay before they've always been diving and playing in the water. These ones just swim mutedly round and round in circles. They seem very calm. Too calm, almost...

We carry on along the path, and when we finally arrive at Eamon's cottage we find no signs of life. The front door is left banging open in the wind. *Damn you, Conor*, I think as a feeling of revulsion spreads right through me. *How* could *you do that to Eamon?*

I gently pull the door closed and wonder which way Eamon might have headed off in. He's obviously gone on one of his early-morning walks. But even for Eamon, this is particularly early. 'Let's go this way,' I instruct the dogs, heading towards the coastal path I know is one of Eamon's favourites.

As we approach the edge of the cliff I can see a large cluster of rocks facing out to sea, and leaning up against one of the rocks is Eamon's walking stick.

Two legs protrude from in front of one of the big rocks, as though someone's sitting with their back against it, soaking up the sunshine and enjoying the view out to sea.

At last, I think, heading around to the other side of the rock. And there he is; Eamon, sitting, looking as relaxed and happy as I think I've ever seen him, with the early-morning sun pouring down on his face. He has his eyes closed, so I assume maybe he's nodded off in the sun.

'Eamon,' I whisper, crouching down next to him. 'Eamon, it's me, Darcy.'

He doesn't appear to hear me, so I speak a bit louder.

'Eamon, wake up, you've nodded off in the sun.'

I reach out to touch his arm, but I snatch my hand back immediately when I find his skin isn't warm to the touch like it should be but cold, very, very cold.

'No!' I cry, leaping to my feet. *This can't be happening, it can't. Not after everything.* I shake my head. *No, this still must be that awful dream from before.* I even pinch myself hard on the arm in the hope I'll wake up. But I don't.

'Eamon,' I say again in a small voice, looking down at him. 'Please, you can't leave us now. We need you here on Tara. I need you.'

But Eamon doesn't respond.

Woody and Louis wander around the other side of the rock. They take one look at Eamon and immediately lie down next to him, their tails drooping and their heads bowed.

I kneel down next to Eamon myself and take hold of his hand, holding it in between my own. 'Oh, Eamon,' I sob, tears beginning to run down my face and onto his tweed jacket. 'You were my only link with Molly. My last bit of family. And now you're gone.'

Thirty-eight

'Am I really the right person to be doing this?' Dermot asks as we're about to let ourselves into Eamon's cottage. 'I feel really uncomfortable about it.'

'I'm hardly over the moon to be going through Eamon's belongings either, but we need to find out if he had any relatives before the funeral next week, and this is the only way.'

After the traumatic events of that fateful morning, Eamon's body had been carried back from the cliff edge and laid out to rest in a plain coffin that Dermot and Paddy had immediately built after hearing the news. The next day we then had to witness the sad sight of watching the coffin being sailed away from Tara in a boat back to the mainland, where it was to remain in a funeral home until Eamon's service next week at a church in the town.

Everyone is devastated.

'For someone who lived apart from the rest of us, Eamon

really seems to have had a profound effect on everyone,' Niall comments to me.

'He didn't say much,' I say, thinking about him. 'But what he did say really meant something.'

We debate whether the best thing for Megan is to return with Eileen for the time being. But Megan insists she wants to stay. In the middle of everyone's grief and sorrow comes the complicated task of explaining Conor's sudden absence from the island. I end up telling everyone that his wanderlust has kicked in again, and that he has needed to move on. Most of the islanders seem to accept this.

But not Roxi.

'Something isn't adding up, Darce,' she says when I try and fob her off with the usual reasoning behind his disappearance. 'The guy was nuts about you.'

'No, he wasn't,' I sigh, knowing I should have just come clean with her to begin with. 'He was nuts about my money – or at least, the thought of it.'

I explain the whole sorry tale to Roxi.

'And you let him get away with it!' she explodes as I finish. 'I'd have taken his golden balls and raised them up above Tara on a flagpole if he'd done that to me ... and to poor Eamon.' She crosses herself and wipes away a tear; Roxi has taken Eamon's death very badly. Then she takes a deep breath. 'What a sleazebag.'

I nod sadly. 'Yep, a sleazebag indeed. But I didn't want to cause more upset by making a fuss. We'd have had all that to cope with as well as a funeral to organise.'

'I suppose.' Roxi shrugs. 'Oh, *Darce*.' She throws her arms around my neck and almost strangles me with the ferocity of her hug. 'I'm sorry it went so wrong. Even I thought this was a good 'un.'

'Thanks,' I say, loosening myself from her grip slightly. 'I think I'm giving up on men altogether from now on.'

'No!' Roxi admonishes, waggling her finger in my face. 'Don't you ever say that. I swear to you, Darcy, you *will* find your Mr Right one day.'

'You've been saying that for years, Roxi. I really think I'm past caring now.'

Roxi narrows her eyes in a determined fashion. 'Hmm, we'll see about *that*.'

With everyone up to speed on Conor, and the task of organising the funeral under way, it's left up to Dermot and me to find out whether Eamon has any other family we need to contact about his death. I've never known Eamon mention anyone, but that doesn't mean he doesn't have any. We decide the only way to find out is to visit his cottage. We've also left it until now to return all the boxes of things Conor tried to steal from Eamon. No one has quite felt like returning to his house in the last couple of days, so as we stand outside the little cottage now, we're surrounded by wooden packing cases and crates of antiques.

'Perhaps you should have asked Niall to accompany you,' Dermot suggests as I turn the handle and open up the door to Eamon's cottage.

'Niall is busy organising some paperwork for the funeral.'

'What paperwork? I thought you were doing most of it.'

I wasn't too sure either what Niall was doing, but he's said he's got things to organise, so I've left him to it.

'I'm not sure, and anyway, you make a better removals man.'

'Thanks,' Dermot says with a lopsided smile, lifting one of the larger crates off the ground as though it's a beach ball.

'Wow! Just *look* at all this stuff!' I exclaim as I walk though into one of the little rooms.

'What is it?' Dermot asks, following me. 'Blimey, if Conor had tried to take all this he'd have sunk the boat.'

The tiny room is lined from ceiling to floor on two walls with shelves containing vases, pots, goblets, plates and many other ancient-looking objects, and on the other wall are swords and shields. There are empty places where Conor has removed some of the items, and a shiver runs through me.

'What's up?' Dermot asks, seeing me. 'Are you cold?

'No,' I hug myself. 'I just can't bear the thought of him in here stealing from Eamon while Eamon ...' I turn my face away and go over to the window. I stare out of it and try not to think about Eamon all alone by that rock.

Dermot joins me, and I feel his arm around my shoulders.

'It's OK, I feel just the same. It was pretty hard for me not to deck him that night at the harbour. Or when I took him back across to the mainland. And that was before I even knew about Eamon.'

I look up at him. 'I can imagine. So why didn't you, then?'

'Because I knew that's not what *you* wanted.'

Why does everything always feel like it's going to be all right when Dermot's this close? Why do I always feel so safe when his arms are around me ...?

'So anyway,' Dermot says suddenly, pulling his arm from

around my shoulders. 'We'd better get the rest of these boxes in.'

He leaves me standing alone by the window, and immediately the little room feels cold and unwelcoming again.

Dermot begins systematically loading the boxes back into the room, while one by one I begin unpacking them. I'm not sure why, it just seems important to put things back in their rightful place. For Eamon.

'So this explains why Eamon had the internet,' I say to Dermot as we're loading things back on to the shelves and many empty hooks on the wall. 'He must have used it for buying and researching some of his bits and pieces.'

'Probably,' Dermot says, lifting a large iron shield back onto the wall. 'This stuff must be worth a fair bit if Conor was trying to steal it, or he wouldn't have gone to all the bother. Whoever inherits it is going to get a pretty valuable collection.'

I clutch the brass goblet I'm holding protectively to my chest. 'You don't think they'd try to sell it, do you? It's part of Eamon; it should remain here on Tara as a sort of shrine to his memory.'

Dermot shrugs. 'Let's just put it back as it was, for now, hey? That's the least we can do for him.'

We finish replacing all the antiques, and begin exploring the rest of Eamon's cottage to see if we can find evidence of any relatives.

In the room where he keeps his laptop we find more shelves, this time containing files and boxes. Dermot picks up a random file and begins thumbing through it while I switch on Eamon's computer.

'What are you doing?' he asks. 'This is no time to be surfing the net.'

'I'm going to check and see if he has anyone in his email contacts. If Eamon was smart enough to set up the internet on the island, it's likely he used email to contact people.'

'Oh, clever,' Dermot says, raising an eyebrow.

'Damn,' I say, as I realise I need a password to get into the computer. I think for a moment, then type the word *Molly*.

Bingo.

'What's up?' Dermot asks, looking up from his file.

'Oh, it's nothing. I just needed a password, that's all. But I'm in now.'

'And you've worked it out already? Remind me not to try and hide anything from you.'

I spend the next few minutes looking though Eamon's files and contacts to see if I can find anything, while Dermot starts to make his way through some boxes. But it seems that Eamon only used the internet for browsing, not for contact with the outside world.

'Darcy, I think you'd better come and see this,' Dermot suddenly says, holding up an old black and white photo.

'What have you got?' I ask, going over and kneeling down next to him on the floor where he's sorting his way through a large brown box containing photos and papers.

He holds out a photo to me. 'Recognise anyone on there?' he asks.

I look down at the old faded photo of a young couple from the fifties. 'It's my aunt Molly!' I exclaim in surprise. 'And that looks like a young Eamon.'

'I thought so,' Dermot says, looking at the photo again. 'So they knew each other a long time ago?'

'Yes, and long before I came to the island, by the looks of it.' I stare at the photo.

'There're quite a lot of them in this box.' Dermot says, digging a bit further down. He lifts out a pile of photos and I begin to thumb through them.

'Oh,' I say as I lift up another photo. This time it's a colour one. It's of an older lady and a young girl standing together on a beach.

'Is that you?' Dermot asks, seeing the look on my face.

I nod.

'With Molly?'

I nod again.

'Do you remember it being taken?'

'Yes, and I remember now who was taking the photo, too.'

'Who?'

'Eamon.'

'How *could* I have forgotten him?' I fret as I pace about the room. 'All this time I was here on the island with him. How could I have forgotten I knew him before? Poor Eamon, now I'll never be able to tell him, to apologise.'

'But it was a long time ago,' Dermot sits on the floor watching me. 'Our memories fade. I'm sure he understood.'

'But why didn't he tell me? I mean, he did tell me, the night before he died. He told me he'd been here when I came over to the island, but he made out he was just the man that ferried us over in the boat, like Conor had that time. I even told him that when Conor leaped off the boat onto the little jetty it reminded me of when he'd done it!' I hit my head with the heel of my hand. 'But even then I didn't remember him properly. Now I do.' I flop down next to Dermot again and pick up the photos once more. 'Eamon was my aunt's special friend – that's how she described him when we came here. And he *was* special, Dermot, he was lovely. That's how I remember him back then, as a really lovely, kind man.'

'So Molly knew him for a good while?' Dermot asks. 'If that photo was taken in the fifties and this one in the, what—'

'Late eighties, early nineties,' I add for him. 'Yes, they did know each other for a very long time.'

'And were they together all this time?'

'No, my aunt was married for a short while in the late sixties, but my uncle died.'

'But Eamon was obviously the love of her life,' Dermot says, taking the photo from me again and gazing down at it. 'No wonder this island meant so much to her. It was the one place she could be with him.'

I look across at Dermot. Was this a soft romantic side breaking through his tough exterior?

'Either that, or Eamon was just after her money,' he says quickly, seeing me smiling at him.

'I don't really think that, and I don't believe you do, either.'

'Why did your aunt move to Dublin, then, before she died, if Eamon meant so much to her?'

'She needed specialist medical treatment at the time. She mustn't have been able to get it near here.'

Dermot and I think for a moment what this parting must have been like for Molly and Eamon.

'And I remembered something else the other day about

Molly. Her ring – the Claddagh one, Eamon confirmed for me not only that she wore one on her right hand, but I remembered which way around it faced.'

'Heart inwards, crown out?' Dermot asks, already knowing the answer.

I nod. 'Her heart had been captured – by Eamon.'

'What happened to the ring? Do you have it now?'

I shake my head. 'No, I inherited a lot of Molly's jewellery but I don't know what happened to the ring. I keep meaning to ask Niall about it.'

Dermot shuffles through the box again 'What's this?' he says, pulling out a brown envelope from under the photos. 'It doesn't look that old. Do you want to open it?' he asks, offering it to me.

'No, you go ahead,' I say, picking up more photos of Molly and Eamon in their youth.

Dermot opens the envelope and begins to read the contents.

'Oh,' he says, screwing up his face. 'Oh dear, this is *not* good.'

'What?' I ask looking up. 'What is it?'

Dermot hesitates; his eyes scan my face protectively.

'Just tell me, Dermot.'

'First, it's a document stating exactly what Eamon wants to happen at his funeral. Who the executor of his will is, and who we should contact regarding guests and things.'

'That's helpful. It's saved us searching through the whole cottage.'

'And this piece of paper,' Dermot continues, holding up a second sheet and looking at me with a worried expression, 'is the title deeds to Tara.'

'How can Eamon have the title deeds to Tara?' My brow furrows as I try to figure this out. 'Surely Niall has them until I complete my year here?'

'It would seem, Darcy, looking at these, that perhaps your aunt may not have been the legal owner of Tara after all.'

'Not the legal owner, what are you talking about, Dermot?' I grab the paper from him. 'But if my aunt Molly wasn't the legal owner, then who was?'

'According to this document – Eamon.'

Thirty-nine

I've never liked funerals.

It's a time when we should be celebrating the life that someone's had, not sitting here feeling despondent and miserable. But that's how most of us are feeling today, as we sit in the little church just over the sea from Tara.

Most of our misery comes from the fact we're about to say goodbye to our dear friend Eamon. But a certain amount of my own despondency comes from the fact that I may have to say goodbye to Tara soon, as well.

On finding the title deeds, Dermot and I had spent a few silly minutes debating whether we should just pretend we'd never found them.

'After all,' Dermot says, 'who's ever going to know about them other than the two of us?'

'But we can't just hush it all up. This island doesn't belong to me now. If it never belonged to Molly in the first place, she had no right leaving it to me.'

'But how did that happen?' Dermot asks, his forehead scrunched up in confusion. 'She must have known.'

'I have no idea. I'll have to speak to Niall about it. But all I know is if it belonged to Eamon, it will be up to his family what they want to do with Tara when they find out.'

Dermot sighs. 'You can't just give up on everything, Darcy. What about all your plans for Tara?'

'They'll be someone else's plans now, Dermot,' I shrug. 'It obviously wasn't meant to be.'

Dermot shakes his head in frustration. 'But what about everyone that lives on the island? You can't just give up on them. What about Niall, for instance, and Paddy, and even Megan? You've changed all their lives. And now you're just going to walk away from us all like you don't even care.'

Dermot stares at me defiantly, very much aware of his Freudian slip in using the word *us* and not *them*.

'Of course I don't want to leave you all,' I stare back at him, equally defiant. 'If I could do anything about it, then I would. But Tara doesn't belong to me now. So if I have to go, I'll go quietly without making a fuss.'

'Make a bloody fuss!' Roxi demands, stamping her heel on the floor when I tell her, which is unfortunate as we're outside and she then has to balance on me while she retrieves her shoe from the damp grass. 'You can't go down without a fight! Finn McCool would have fought for Tara, and so should you.'

'What has Finn McCool got to do with any of this?' I ask, looking at her quizzically while she replaces her shoe.

Roxi, looking embarrassed, screws her face up.

'Roxi?'

'Well, you know when I used to go and see Eamon and he used to tell me all these tales about Irish myths and legends? I asked him to tell me about this Finn guy after he mentioned the Tara connection, and then I did some of my own research on the internet when you weren't about.'

'*You* were researching Irish myths and legends on the internet? I thought you were only capable of accessing Will Smith's fan site!' I'm laughing but, seriously, Roxi reading about anything other than what's hot in the shops this season and celebrity gossip was pretty amazing stuff.

It was Tara working her magic yet again.

Roxi rolls her eyes. 'Ha, ha, very funny. Actually I quite enjoyed it; I've started reading some other historical stuff now, too. Who'd have thought it, Darce, me interested in all that ancient history malarkey? But *anyway*,' she says, pointing her finger at me. 'Back to you, missy. This Finn chap has so much in common with you, you wouldn't believe, so I think you should take a leaf out of his book and fight for Tara.'

'What do you mean, *so much in common*?'

Roxi holds up her hand and begins to count on her pink neon fingernails. 'One – Finn had two big dogs like Woody and Louis, only his were likely to have been pure Irish wolfhounds, not crossbreeds like yours. Two – he caught this fish, the Salmon of Knowledge Eamon said it was called, like you did when you first came here, and then afterwards he could do loads of stuff that he couldn't do before.'

I look blankly at Roxi, not following this.

'Sweetie, look how much more confident you are now than when you first came to Tara! *You*,' she says poking my shoulder, 'kick ass now when something isn't right. You never did that

410

back in London. Three,' she continues holding up her counting hand, 'he saved the people of Tara on Samain from an evil fire-breathing fairy called Aileen.' She stares at me, waiting for the penny to drop. 'Megan's party ... chain-smoking Eileen?' she prompts.

'It was more like a con man called Conor that night, actually. This theory of yours is all a bit vague, Rox.'

Roxi, refusing to be beaten, stamps her foot again. 'Obviously it's a bit vague, Darce, it's meant to be, it's a *legend*.'

I think about this for a moment. 'I can find one slight issue with your comparisons, Rox.'

'What's that?'

'Finn was supposed to find the love of his life on Tara. I haven't done that.'

'You leave that to me,' Roxi winks, tapping the side of her nose. 'Me and Finn are working on it.'

I shake my head in defeat. You just can't argue with Roxi sometimes.

If Roxi had been angry, Niall had seemed remarkably calm when I'd explained everything and handed the deeds and Eamon's letter over to him.

'Don't worry, Darcy,' he said, pushing his glasses up his nose as he finished reading through first the letter and then the deeds. 'We'll sort something out. I'm a genius solicitor, remember?'

'Did you know anything about all this, Niall?' I ask him, wondering how he can be so calm when it's such major news. 'Wouldn't Eamon have had to ask you to make you executor of his will? And what about all those documents you had in the pub that night? What were those?'

Niall nodded. 'Eamon did ask me to be his executor, not that long ago actually. But please try not to worry too much about everything else, Darcy. It will all be fine. I promise you.'

Each and every walk Woody, Louis and I took from that moment on felt like our last on Tara. I'd spent so much of my time to begin with thinking about leaving, that now I'd been given the opportunity to, I realised how much I was going to miss this island when I was no longer here.

Standing on top of the cliffs one day, I allowed the cold wind to blow across my face. I reached behind my head and pulled out the band that had been an almost permanent fixture in my hair in some form or other since I arrived. My hair fell loose against my shoulders. Almost immediately the wind picked it up and billowed it about my face, but I didn't care. I felt so free standing there, surrounded by the sea and the sky, with the sound of the waves crashing against the rocks below, and the smell of the crisp salty air filling my lungs.

As I looked out into the bay I no longer saw the dolphins jumping and playing in the waves, either. They'd disappeared the day Eamon had left on the boat. It was him they were here to help all that time, not me. He was the one they were warning of change. Eamon was the rightful owner of Tara, and once he was gone, so were they.

I thought again about everything that had happened since we'd arrived here. About everyone else's lives changing for the better. I'd thought mine had, too, for a while, and now it was being snatched back away from me again.

'So, Tara,' I called out into the wind, 'between the two of us we seem to have sorted out everyone else. And I've even helped you by bringing people here again, so you're not lonely any more. Why don't you prove to me you really are magical, and do one thing for me in return? Then I can believe in you too.'

I closed my eyes and waited for Tara's wind of change to blow its magic through me.

Eamon's funeral is a simple but emotional service. The tiny church's pews are filled with his fellow islanders and the few local townsfolk who knew him from his occasional visits. As Eamon's body leaves the church to be taken to a local crematorium, I'm moved to shed even more tears when I hear the strains of 'Forty Shades of Green' floating up into the rafters of the church – it was one of Eamon's final requests that it be played today. And now I know why my aunt loved it so much. It had been one of their favourite songs.

After the service, we hold Eamon's wake in one of the town's hotels. Eamon has requested that his wake is to be a lively affair with no mourning. So I've made sure there's plenty of alcohol, food and a band playing traditional Irish music. The band is very good, but no one feels particularly like dancing tonight.

I'm in the ladies' loos, composing myself yet again under the guise of washing my hands, when there's a knock on the door.

'Darcy,' Paddy says apologetically, opening the door just wide enough to poke his head through the gap. 'Sorry to disturb you, like, but Niall wants to begin reading Eamon's will in a minute.'

413

'Now?' I ask in astonishment. 'But there's only us from the island here: everyone else has gone.'

'I don't know,' Paddy shrugs, 'them's my instructions, that you're to come through for the reading. I've gathered everyone else now.'

I finish drying my hands and Paddy leads me through to another room in the hotel where Niall has set up some chairs in a large circle. At the head of the circle is a table and another chair where Niall is already sitting. Most of the chairs are already filled with the islanders with just one left empty, so I sit down in the last remaining seat. I glance around; everyone looks as confused as I feel right now.

Niall shuffles some important-looking papers on the table in front of him and clears his throat. 'Thank you, everyone, for breaking away from your food and drink to attend this official reading of Eamon Patrick John Murphy's last will and testament.' Niall is talking in his best solicitor's voice. 'I have attended many will readings in my time as a solicitor, but it was recently brought to my attention that not everyone either understands, or enjoys hearing, our lawyer-talk at these occasions,' he looks affectionately at me. 'So from here on in, if acceptable to everyone, and seeing as we all know each other so well, I shall convey Eamon's will to you in layman's terms.'

'Great,' Paddy mutters. 'I don't know that language either.'

Niall picks up an envelope in front of him on the table and opens it.

'Eamon came to me while we were living on the island and asked for my advice on legal matters several times,' Niall informs us. 'But he asked that I act on his behalf anonymously. So I'm afraid that I had to keep everything that is about to be revealed over the next few minutes a secret from you all. And for that, I hope you will forgive me.'

Niall looks around nervously at us. He pushes his glasses up his nose, even though they haven't actually slipped down.

I watch him and wonder what he's going to say next. I glance at Dermot sitting across from me; he looks as mystified as me, and shakes his head.

'Eamon was a straightforward man, of simple pleasures and usually few words, and he has asked that I read his will in the form of a letter to you all.'

Niall looks around at us again; his eyes rest on me for a moment. Then he takes a deep breath before beginning to read from Eamon's letter.

'"If you are all sitting here now, listening to this, then I must be gone, so I hope you've had a good few drinks to celebrate that fact. Especially you, Niall; you need to loosen up a bit."' Niall blushes as he reads. '"You'd better have had a damn good party somewhere, with lots of music and dancing. Seamus, if you don't play my favourite song tonight then I'll come back and haunt you with that damn tin whistle of yours."'

Seamus salutes the sky.

'"Aiden and Kathleen, you make a grand Irish stew, one of the best I've ever tasted. So keep up the good work cooking for all those folk on Tara."' Aiden and Kathleen look on proudly. '"And Daniel, hurry up and make an honest woman out of Orla, she's your soulmate for God's sake, man. Stop messing about."' Orla blushes profusely, while Daniel just shakes his head and smiles.

'I thought you two were married?' I ask them in surprise.

'We just said that in case it went against our application,'

Orla says. 'Once we were there, it seemed easier to keep up the pretence.'

Is *anything* ever what it seems on Tara?

One by one, Eamon has words of encouragement and advice for each and every person that has lived with him on Tara. Considering I'd felt Eamon didn't interact with any of us that much, he certainly seems to know us all pretty well.

'"And now I come to those I wish to leave a personal possession to,"' Niall continues, still reading from the letter.

'"Paddy, I leave you all my computer equipment and satellite dish. Use it wisely, my young friend, to further the cause of Tara, and you won't go far wrong."'

'Bleedin' deadly.' Paddy beams from ear to ear. 'Fair play to you, Eamon!' he lifts his bottle of beer.

'"Niall, my font of all things legal, and executor of this will, I leave to you my walking stick, or my staff of knowledge, as I like to call it. May it bring you even more wisdom than you already have, good sir."'

Niall looks up proudly, before continuing.

'"Roxi, my vibrant and wonderfully colourful companion on many an occasion. Thank you for listening to all my tales with such patience. It was a joy to share them all with such a beautiful young woman. I leave to you my library of history books. Enjoy them, my young student, and you shall go far with your studies."'

Roxi smiles with tears in her eyes.

Niall breaks off from reading the letter for a moment. 'And he particularly wanted me to mention you should immediately go to his cottage and find a book on Finn McCool when we get back to the island today. He says,' Niall looks at the letter again,

'"You will find something in there I trust you to use wisely in the future."'

'I will, Eamon. I will!' Roxi blows a kiss up to the sky.

'"Dermot,"' Niall continues, '"I know we didn't always see eye to eye to begin with, but you've proved you're a hard worker, a talented craftsman and a good, genuine and honourable man. So I leave to you all my tools. They may not be some of your newfangled nonsense. But there are some fine, trustworthy pieces there that I know you'll make good use of. Dermot, I trust you will look after all that I hold precious to me in the future."'

Dermot nods. 'Don't you worry, Eamon, I'll take the greatest care of them.' He makes a small fist. 'Good man.'

'"Megan, the jewel in Tara's new crown, to you I leave my star." Do you know what he means by that, Megan?' Niall asks, looking over the top of his glasses at Megan.

Megan nods enthusiastically. 'There's a really bright star that comes up over Tara every night in exactly the same place. You can see it if you stand on one of the cliffs, Eamon took me up there to see it one night. You can even make wishes on it. And now it's all mine,' she says pulling her legs up on the chair and hugging her knees tightly to her chest.

We all smile.

'"And finally, Darcy."'

I look at Niall. I've been waiting for this. What is Eamon going to say to me that is going to make up for all that has happened?

'"Darcy, I imagine you're probably sitting there thinking that I deceived you when I let you think you owned Tara. Or perhaps I deceived your aunt in letting her think *she* owned it."'

417

The thought has crossed my mind.

'"But the truth is we both deceived you, and for that I'm truly sorry."'

What?

'"I was always the rightful owner of Tara from the beginning. My family owned the island, when there were small communities of people living on it in the past. That's how I met Molly when she lived on Tara as a child. But her family moved from the island when Molly was just a teenager in the early fifties. Sadly we didn't see each other again until Molly moved back, alone, in 1985. By that time she'd been married to your uncle. Molly loved Tara just as much as I did, and would come across to the island to visit me regularly. Later she would bring you with her when you were staying for your holidays. I never had children, as you now know, and neither did Molly, but she had you, Darcy, and I know she thought of you as her own."'

Niall pauses for a moment to see how I'm coping with all this.

Not well, is the answer. I'm trying to hold back my tears, but they're already beginning to spill down my face and into the lap of my black dress as I let my head hang down.

A clean white handkerchief is thrust under my nose. I look up to see Dermot standing in front of me. Gratefully I take the hanky from him and pat at my tears while Dermot returns to his seat.

'Are you all right, Darcy?' Niall asks gently.

'Yes, I'm fine, please continue.'

'"Time passed too quickly,"' Niall says, reading from Eamon's letter again. '"We were both growing old, and it came

418

time for us to start thinking about the future of the island, so that when we were gone Tara would remain in the hands of someone who would love it as much as we did. Molly was convinced that you would fall in love with Tara if she could just get you back here somehow. I wasn't so sure; it had been so long since you'd even been to see your aunt, let alone visited the island. So we came up with quite an intricate plan. The plan involved drawing up some fake documents to make it look like Tara belonged to your aunt. And we have Niall's father, a long-time friend of Molly's, to thank for helping us make them look as legal as we could without actually breaking any laws. This meant that when Molly died the island would look as if it automatically went to you, Darcy. By this time Molly was already living in Dublin for her treatment, and her visits to Tara and to me were very rare. Whatever the medics said, we both knew she hadn't got that long to live, so time was of the essence."'

'But why go to all that trouble? Why didn't Eamon just transfer Tara to my aunt there and then?' I ask, my tears turning to astonishment at what I'm hearing. This is all too much to comprehend. 'Surely that would have been much easier than creating fake documents?'

'It's all coming, Darcy,' Niall says, nodding at the letter. 'Just be patient. Believe me, I was as surprised at this as you when I found out. I thought my father was straight down the line.'

'"I'm so sorry I wasn't able to trust you, Darcy, back then,"' Niall continues, reading Eamon's words. '"But if we had transferred the island to Molly legally, and then you'd passed up her offer to come and live here, who knows what might have happened. But Molly was right, as she often was: you didn't pass up the challenge, and you did come to Tara, and you've changed not only your own future by doing so, but the future of the island for many years to come."'

I think about this as Niall turns over to the next page of the letter.

'"When you first arrived, I did wonder just what sort of hands my island was being put into, with your modern ways and peculiar ideas. But a wind of change has blown across Tara, and it's left in its wake a trail of positivity and success. Tara has a future, in which many others can not only come and appreciate her beauty, but also experience just a little of what makes her so magical. Your aunt would have been very proud of what you've achieved here. She wanted nothing more than to let others benefit from the magic of Tara, and now they can. Darcy, you have proved yourself to be a capable leader, and a fine young woman, and I'm so proud to have known you. Tara and I will be happy for you to go on looking after her for as long as you choose to. So this is what I leave to you, Miss Darcy Fiona McCall – all my other worldly possessions, including my island, my Tara."'

Everyone, including me, is stunned into silence.

Then a round of spontaneous applause breaks out around the room, and one by one I find myself surrounded by the people I've spent the last seven months living with, and who now, suddenly, I can't imagine living without.

Epilogue

'Ashes to ashes, dust to dust,' Dermot says, looking out over the cliff.

'Dermot, what are you saying?' I ask. 'That's what they say when they bury someone, not when you're sprinkling someone's ashes.'

'Well, I don't know,' Dermot replies huffily. 'I've never done it before. What should you say, then?'

'You should say something profound and lovely about the person,' Megan says, pushing her beanie hat up out of her eyes so she can see me. 'Isn't that right, Darcy?'

'Yes,' I nod at her. 'Yes, that's exactly right, Megan.'

'Come on then,' Dermot says, wrapping his arms around his body and patting his gloved hands against his arms to try and keep warm. 'Hurry up and say something profound, Darcy. It's bloody freezing standing out here at this time of night in the middle of winter.'

Eamon's final instructions in his will had been for us to scatter his ashes over the same cliff that I'd scattered Molly's ashes when I'd first visited Tara. The only difference being he wanted it doing on a clear moonlit night.

So myself, Dermot, Megan and the two dogs have climbed to the top of the cliff on a freezing-cold December evening on the first clear night we've had on Tara in ages.

As I stand thinking about what I'm going to say, I suddenly remember.

'I know, I've got just the thing.'

'Hurry up then,' Dermot says, his breath forming an impatient haze in the cold night air.

'Megan, have you got the casket ready?' I ask her.

'Yes, it's here,' she says, a pair of red mittens holding out a plain black urn.

'Right then, here goes,' I pull my scarf away from my neck a little and clear my throat.

May the Irish hills caress you.
May her lakes and rivers bless you.
May the luck of the Irish enfold you.
May the blessings of Saint Patrick behold you.

It's the same blessing that Eamon had spoken when we'd released Molly's ashes free into the wind almost a year ago. But this time as I nod at Megan to empty the casket, it's Eamon that is picked up by the wind and goes soaring into the sky to meet her.

'Look,' Megan shouts pointing to the sky, 'Eamon's star is out.'

'It's your star now,' I remind her. 'Eamon gave it to you, remember?'

'I'm going to make a wish,' Megan says, screwing her eyes tightly shut.

As I look up at the bright white star in the sky, I feel a hand reach out behind Megan and gently pull off my glove. Then as the warm hand wraps itself tightly around mine, I feel that same sense of comfort and reassurance spread through me once more.

I smile at Dermot in the moonlight, and he gives my hand a gentle squeeze.

'What did you wish for, Megan?' Dermot asks, dragging his eyes away from mine for a moment to look down at his daughter.

'She can't tell you that or it won't come true,' I say, still smiling at him.

Megan looks up at the two of us holding hands in the moonlight, and she grins. 'You know something? I think it's already starting to.'

There's a sudden crackling in Dermot's pocket and I hear Roxi's voice. 'How do you work this stupid thing . . . Oh right, I get it . . . Mr Cowell, are you there? Over.'

Dermot rolls his eyes. 'Can't we even have a moment?' he says, reaching into his jacket pocket to retrieve the walkie-talkie. 'Yeah, Roxi, I'm here. What's the problem?'

'There's a problem over here I really think you need to deal with. Er, over.'

'What sort of a problem?'

'Um . . . I don't know,' Roxi's voice goes a bit muffled for a moment, as though she's consulting with someone. 'But I really think you should come at once.'

'All right, where are you?'

'Up at the old ruin, see you in a minute. Over and out, good buddy!'

'Roxi, it's not CB radio,' Dermot mutters, but she's gone.

'Why on earth is Roxi up at the old ruin at this time of night?' I ask, as Dermot grabs mine and Megan's hands and we're suddenly making our way towards the hill. We're still refurbishing the building and it's coming along very nicely, but there's not usually anyone there after dark.

'Maybe there's some problem with the scaffolding,' Dermot says as we hurry along.

It had been a very difficult decision to make, but I'd decided to sell some of Eamon's artefacts to fund the restorations to the building. We'd had the collection valued, and the entire amount was worth over five times what the renovations were going to cost. So after great thought, and remembering Eamon's advice about always doing what my heart felt was the right thing to do, we'd put a few things up for a sale in an auction house in Dublin and they'd sold for far more than their reserve price. So in addition to the renovations on the building, we'd decided to turn Eamon's cottage into a proper little visitor centre dedicated to both his collection and his memory, so that all future visitors to Tara would be able to appreciate them too.

As we approach the entrance to the building, Megan runs on ahead.

'Where are you going?' I call. 'It's dark, be careful.'

But she vanishes into the black of the night.

'Aren't you worried?' I ask Dermot, looking up at him in the moonlight as we continue walking.

But Dermot is strangely silent.

'Right,' I ask, stopping in my tracks. 'What's going on?'

'This is what's going on,' Roxi calls from the building as suddenly hundreds of tiny fairy lights are switched on and the Celtic stonework is lit up like a fairy-tale castle.

'What are you doing, Rox?' I ask in astonishment as she appears in the archway looking like a Russian princess dressed all in white, with a matching fur hat and muff. 'I thought there was a problem up here.'

Roxi shakes her head. 'No, no problem. We just had to get you up here. Isn't that right, Dermot?'

'You knew about this?' I ask, swivelling back around to face him.

Dermot nods.

'We all did!' Megan cries excitedly as Niall and Paddy wrapped up like Eskimos now appear to join the gang. 'Dad's got something he wants to give you.'

'All right, Megan,' Dermot warns, throwing her a look of caution. Dermot takes my hand again and leads me so I'm standing right beneath the archway, while Roxi takes Megan's hand and leads her over to join Niall and Paddy. 'First, I want to thank Roxi for making this setting look so magical tonight,' he says, smiling at her. 'It's perfect, Roxi.'

'Just call me Roxi Llewelyn-Bowen,' she says with a grin.

'And for organising the next part of this ceremony too.'

'No, you've got to thank Eamon for that,' Roxi says, looking up into the clear night sky, 'it was all his idea. And there was me thinking I was the only matchmaker around these parts.'

'Eamon,' I ask, looking around at everyone. 'But I don't understand.'

'Darcy,' Dermot says, taking my hand. 'When Roxi went to read up on Finn McCool in Eamon's history books she found a little bit more than some faded old text. She found *this* hidden inside the pages of the book, with a note.' Dermot holds up a gold ring. 'It's your aunt's Claddagh ring. It seems your aunt returned it to Eamon for safe keeping, to be passed on to you at an appropriate time.'

I stare at the ring in Dermot's hand. I can hardly believe I'm seeing it again after all this time.

'Apparently the ring is not just valuable because it was your aunt's, but it holds a significance to others in both rarity and value.'

'It does? How's that?'

Dermot looks to Roxi. She eagerly nods her encouragement.

'It seems there is a legend that goes with the ring, that it has been passed down from generation to generation of islander for many hundreds of years.' Dermot hesitates again. 'Some say it may even go as far back as Finn McCool's time on Tara.'

'His treasure!' I exclaim. 'The ring could be the treasure Finn left on Tara for safe keeping. So Eamon might have had Finn's treasure in his cottage after all.'

Dermot nods. He still seems uneasy, though, and his cheeks flush a little redder in the cold now. 'Perhaps, if the legend is to be believed. But Eamon also had one further request.' He clears his throat. 'Eamon has asked ... Well, he thought in his wisdom that I should be the one to return the ring to you.'

My heart races inside my chest while I wait for what Dermot is going to say next.

'Would you like to wear the ring, Darcy?' he asks, looking down at me.

I nod silently and pull off my right glove. I can't believe Eamon has had Molly's ring all along. And for him to suggest that Dermot be the one to give it to me ...

Dermot shakes his head. 'No, Darcy, if I'm going to give you this ring, then the only way I'm doing it is if you'll wear it on your left hand.'

I stare up at him. 'Are you serious?'

'Can you put up with me?' he whispers, his big dark eyes looking questioningly down into mine.

I put my hand up to his face, run the tips of my fingers gently along his furrowed brow, then down along his cheek, smoothing any worry he has about my answer away. 'I've managed to pretty well over the last year, haven't I?' I answer, smiling up at him.

As we stand under the archway gazing helplessly into each other's eyes, we suddenly realise what everyone else seems to have known all along.

'Is that a yes?' Megan asks impatiently.

We both turn towards her. 'It's a yes,' I smile, as Dermot pulls the glove off my hand and slips the ring onto my finger.

'Yey!' she shouts in glee as a round of applause breaks out.

'Tara's magic has struck again,' Roxi grins. 'With a little help from me, of course.'

'And me!' Megan insists.

'And Molly and Eamon,' I say, as above our heads two bright stars shoot across the night sky together.

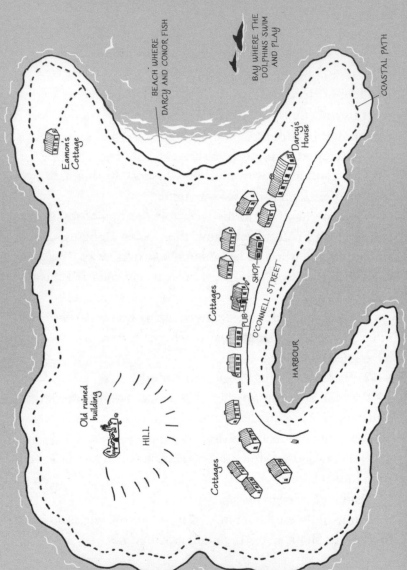

TARA

BEACH WHERE DARCY AND CONOR FISH

BAY WHERE THE DOLPHINS SWIM AND PLAY

COASTAL PATH

Eamon's Cottage

Darcy's House

Cottages

O'CONNELL STREET

PUB SHOP

HARBOUR

Old ruined building

HILL

Cottages

Turn the page to find out more about Ireland and exactly why Ali McNamara loves the Emerald Isle so much.

Why I Love Ireland

I love to visit Ireland; it's been one of my top holiday destinations over the last ten years. I've had family holidays there, romantic weekends away and even walked the length of it for charity with a famous pop star on a couple of occasions! But why do I love it so much and what are my favourite things to do when I'm there?

Ireland's capital city, Dublin, is a great place to start if you've only got a weekend. My top tips are the Guinness Storehouse, you'll never taste a fresher pint of Guinness than at the top of their visitor centre; a visit to Trinity College Library to see the ancient illuminated manuscripts of the Book Of Kells; a spot of shopping in Grafton Street and Henry Street; and a walk along the quays, stopping to view the many bridges that line the River Liffey. And if a single pint of Guinness isn't enough for you, a trip to the infamous Temple Bar one evening to sample some of Ireland's famous craic is an absolute must.

While in the Dublin area you must stop off at a little harbour town called Malahide. It has a beautiful coastal walk that stretches for several miles to the next town of Portmarnock, which is gorgeous on a lovely sunny day, but equally bracing on a cool one, and if Dublin's Temple Bar was a bit too raucous and full of tourists, Gibney's pub in Malahide will show you some traditional Irish hospitality along with some fantastic local food.

Over on the west coast, the ring of Kerry is well worth a drive around for its stunning scenery. Just be prepared to stop off every few miles in one of the handy lay-bys to snap 'just another quick photo.' Just above Kerry, there's the Dingle Peninsula with the pretty town of Dingle, famous for Fungie, a bottle-nosed wild dolphin who has lived and played in the mouth of the harbour since 1984. A boat trip out to see Fungie is an experience you will not forget.

Head as far west as you can on the Dingle Peninsula and you will be able to see Great Blasket Island itself (find out more about Great Blasket's history on the following pages), the island that *Breakfast at Darcy's* was inspired by. I highly recommend taking a boat trip out to the island and seeing for yourself the striking unspoilt landscape, and crumbling remains of some of the original islander's homes.

There's so much to see in Ireland that I can't recommend it enough as a holiday destination. I can't guarantee you'll bask in a hot, sunny climate while you're there, but what I can promise is you'll receive a warm Celtic welcome that will remain long after you've left the Emerald Isle and leave you longing to return in the future.

Ali McNamara

The Reality Behind the Myth: the Fact Behind the Fiction of Breakfast at Darcy's

Great Blasket Island

I had my idea for a story about a fictional island called Tara after I had visited the island of Great Blasket, off the south-west coast of Ireland.

Great Blasket is the largest of a small cluster of islands called the Blaskets and has a literary history of its very own. In the 1920s and 1930s, the Blasket Island writers (Peig Sayers, Tomás Ó Criomhthain and Maurice O'Sullivan among others) wrote about the landscape and way of life on their island. They wrote their stories in the Irish language and their books are still considered classics in the world of literature today.

The Blasket Island community began to decline as a result of the continual emigration of its young people, until the 1950s when it became almost uninhabited.

Today, it's only the many visitors that venture over to visit the island by boat that provide its inhabitants, even if only temporary. Great Blasket is a wild, rugged, yet extremely beautiful place and you can spend several hours or all day enjoying its natural beauty.

The Real Tara

The Hill of Tara in County Meath, Ireland, is said to be the ancient crowning place of the Kings of Ireland, so it is a particularly appropriate name for my fictional island, whose ownership is passed on from one great leader to another during the story.

Finn McCool

Roxy and Eamon both tell Darcy tales of Finn McCool, a mythical warrior of Irish mythology or, to give him his 'proper' name, Fionn mac Cumhaill. One of his most famous tales involved a young Finn meeting a leprechaun-like druid near a river. The druid had spent seven years trying to catch the salmon of knowledge; the myth said that whoever ate the salmon would gain all the knowledge in the world. The druid suddenly became successful at catching the salmon, and he asked Finn to cook it for him. While doing so, Finn burned his thumb and instinctively put it to his mouth, swallowing a piece of the salmon's skin. This gave him all the salmon's wisdom and in further stories he was able to call upon the knowledge of the salmon by simply sucking his thumb.

Holistic Healing

Caitlin, Orla and Megan talk a lot about alternative forms of healing and about Tara having a unique energy about her. Reiki, t'ai chi and crystal therapy are all forms of holistic healing. Taking a holistic approach when seeking treatment for a physical or emotional condition means you treat your whole self instead of just treating the problematic symptom.

All the characters that come to the island benefit from Tara's healing properties in some way. Some are inspired, some gain new knowledge, others simply fall in love. But everyone who comes to Tara changes . . . and it's always for the better.

Ali McNamara

Out now

FROM NOTTING HILL WITH LOVE . . . ACTUALLY

Ali McNamara

Scarlett loves the movies. But does she love sensible fiancé David just as much? With a big white wedding on the horizon, Scarlett really should have decided by now . . .

When she has the chance to house-sit in Notting Hill – the setting of one of her favourite movies – Scarlett jumps at the chance. But living life like a movie is trickier than it seems, especially when her new neighbour Sean is so irritating. And so irritatingly handsome, too.

Scarlett soon finds herself starring in a romantic comedy of her very own: but who will end up as the leading man?

'Perfectly plotted, gorgeously romantic, has some great gags and leaves you with that lovely gooey feeling you get at the end of a good Hollywood rom com'
Lucy-Anne Holmes, author of *The (Im)Perfect Girlfriend*

978-0-7515-4495-4